Archibald Clavering Gunter

Miss Nobody of Nowhere

A Novel

Archibald Clavering Gunter

Miss Nobody of Nowhere
A Novel

ISBN/EAN: 9783337033910

Printed in Europe, USA, Canada, Australia, Japan

Cover: Foto ©Andreas Hilbeck / pixelio.de

More available books at **www.hansebooks.com**

Miss Nobody
of Nowhere

Archibald C. Gunter

MISS NOBODY OF NOWHERE

A Novel

BY

ARCHIBALD CLAVERING GUNTER

AUTHOR OF

"MR. POTTER OF TEXAS," "THAT FRENCHMAN," "MR. BARNES OF NEW YORK," "SMALL BOYS IN BIG BOOTS," "A FLORIDA ENCHANTMENT," "MISS DIVIDENDS," "BARON MONTEZ OF PANAMA AND PARIS," ETC.

———

NEW YORK
HURST & COMPANY
PUBLISHERS

CONTENTS.

BOOK III.

MISS SOMEBODY OF SOMEWHERE.

MISS NOBODY OF NOWHERE.

BOOK I.

A College Cowboy.

CHAPTER I.

THE LAST KICK OF THE HARVARD-YALE FOOT-BALL MATCH.

THE game is drawing to a close !

It is the contest of the season, the foot-ball match between Yale and Harvard.

The shivering spectators are trying to keep themselves warm with enthusiasm. There are only some seven hundred of them, for the day is a miserable one, and every undergraduate of Harvard who looks on this game and sports the crimson does so despite the frowns of his faculty; and every student from Yale who has come to Boston to wear his cherished blue and cry his college cry has hanging over his head the promise of suspension from the authorities of the old Connecticut seat of learning.

Besides, in 1878, college foot-ball had not reached the popularity that has come to it with advancing years. The dons of the universities frowned upon the sport, the public gazed on it with partial indifference ; and there were no crowded ovals and but little of the attendant beauty and fashion that give to great college games the brilliancy and excitement that have come upon them in the last few years.

But every man-jack of these foot-ball pioneers, spec-tators or players, are devotees of the sport and their colleges.

They have come from Harvard to the Boston base-ball grounds in omnibuses, street-cars, and private turn-outs, singing their time-worn ditties, in spite of their faculty, who have prevented their playing this match on their own college field, because one of their team is sus-pended and cannot step on university soil.

They have come from Yale by train, singing that old-time glee with which the Sophs used to taunt the Freshes into the annual class foot-ball scrimmages that called the beauties of New Haven to the State House steps, Chapel Street, and the hotel balcony to see the great class con-tests that have now degenerated into class rushes.

This ditty half the undergraduates now suppose ap-plies to their professors, and consequently sing this year with additional fervor:

> " Let them come on, the base-born crew,
>   Each soil-stained churl, alack !
> What gain they but a splitten skull,
>   A sod for their base back ! "

Only the distance from New Haven to the Boston base-ball grounds being much greater than the distance from Cambridge to that point, the Harvard partisans greatly exceed in numbers the Yale delegation. So it is with the girls, who, being Boston ones, wear crimson in some aggressive form and shout Harvard Rahs !—all save one, a little maiden of about twelve, who has a blue ribbon in her hat, and enthusiastically swings a blue parasol over her pretty head whenever Yale makes a tell-ing play.

All through the long game that is even now drawing to a close she has kept her eyes on one of the blue half-backs ; in every scrimmage and every rush her gaze has followed him, as if upon his prowess alone depended the fate of the contest.

Were she older, one might suppose her his sweetheart, for her blue eyes have love in them of some kind, and the figure she is gazing on might well inspire admiration, even passion ; for its physical development is superb both as regards its graceful activity and direct strength,

and it is surmounted by a head and face which are not
only beautiful but intellectual. While playing, though
his great muscles work his lithe limbs like those of an
animated giant, his bright eyes also flash with excited
idea—he fights his college battle not alone with his body
but with his head ; and head is the only thing that will
settle this contest now, for both sides have tried brute
strength time and again without avail.

The little lady's relationship to the Yale half-back is
not long undetermined. Whenever Harvard makes a
telling play and Cambridge cries fill the air, and the
crimson color is flaunted on high, she gives a Yale yell
with all the power of youthful lungs, and waving her
blue parasol in the faces of the lovers of magenta, shouts
out : "Just you wait and see my brother kick !"

This aggressiveness angers a Harvard girl, who whispers to her next neighbor: "Who is that little blue
fiend ?"

"*Fiend !*" answers the other. "She's worse, she's a
TRAITOR ! She's Bessie Everett, and lives on Beacon
Street."

"A *Boston* girl a YALE girl ?" whispers the first, overcome by this awful thought.

"Yes, and her brother's that nasty Yale creature who
scrimmages so fearfully—the one who's just downed
Blanchard. Ain't he horrid ?"

"Yes, and he's downed another one !" cries Bessie,
whose pretty ears have caught this conversation. "And
he'll down some more—Y ! A ! L ! E !—YALE !"

But here her voice is drowned by the tumult of the
grand stand. Aided by the wind that is blowing with
them, the blues have got the ball well into the crimson
territory, and are now fighting like giants for goal or
touch-down, while their opponents are struggling with
equal will and vigor to get the ball out of bounds and so
gain time, for in two short minutes the second three-
quarters of an hour will have passed and the game will
be over.

So far neither college has gained a point, though by a
wedge rush Yale had made a touch-down in the first half,
which had not been allowed, as it had been gained twenty
seconds or so after the forty-five minutes for play had
expired.

That half the wind had been against them. This half it is in their favor; and now, thinking themselves robbed by the umpire's watch, and remembering that the blue this year has been beaten both at base-ball and regatta by the crimson, they are desperately fighting to make the slight advantage they have productive of a football victory;—with only two short minutes in which to do it.

But now a mighty though discordant noise comes from the upholders of the blue.

Some cry: "Kick it! kick it *quick!*"

Others yell: "Run, Everett, RUN!" for the little girl's brother has caught the ball from a fair kick by one of the Harvard backs.

This, though apparently an accident, is really the result of thought quick as instinct.

He had noted the leather sphere going to one of the Harvard half-backs, celebrated for his long kicks, and therefore judged he would propel the ball with his foot; not run with it, and attempt to dodge the rushers waiting to tackle and down him. Consequently Everett had sprung for the territory where he thought a good drop kick would plant the ball, and guessing correctly, has made a fair catch of the sphere and so holds it, the Harvard goal-posts right in front of him, but many a long yard away.

He doesn't wait for the advice of the grand stand whether he shall kick the ball or run with it. To win this game he knows he must do both, for no human being can drive that ball over the Harvard goal at the distance he is from it.

As the crowd is yelling he is running swiftly forward, the crimson rushers and half-backs hurrying to tackle and down him.

Can he get near enough and kick sure enough and strong enough to send the sphere between those two distant goal-posts and over their cross-bar before he is overwhelmed?

It looks impossible!

On one side comes Blanchard, the Harvard half-back, to seize and throw him; on the other, Perry, the rusher, to tackle him round body or limb—low if he can, high if he must, but savage any way. Behind these, others of the crimson are hurrying ; while Wetherby, one of the Harvard backs (they had three in those days), is almost in front of him, well down by the goal, but charging like a locomotive ; for they mean to roll Phil Everett in the mud and pile half a dozen rushers on top of him, to slug him, crush the wind out of his body, and leave him battered and bruised, weak and windless, rather than he shall get a fair kick at Harvard goal on this last minute of a game that may be drawn.

There is only one Yale rusher to aid him. Lamb is on his right and will tackle Blanchard. Noting this, Everett runs more to the right, and so farther from Perry, and dodging him, speeds on with the Harvard rusher at his heels.

He has gained ten yards ; a herculean kick may now reach goal. Will he have time to make it ?

Even now he feels the breath of the Harvard rusher on the back of his neck and dare not stay, so speeds on.

But suddenly he hears a Yale yell—the Mercury of their rush line has come up with winged feet at a sprinting pace, and springing on Perry, has thrown an arm around his neck ; then jumping back, has thus jerked the crimson rusher to the earth with his head half wrung off his body.

Then Everett knows he has *just time* to kick before Wetherby, the Harvard back, will be upon him.

He drops the ball, and kicking rather high to give the favoring wind time to do its work, and also to avoid any chance of catch from Wetherby, smites the ball with his foot, giving it every pound of weight and ounce of power in his mighty body.

The sphere flies from the ground, the Harvard back makes a wild spring for it, but it is eight inches above his grasp and sailing over his head as it gradually rises in the air.

Then both teams and spectators gaze upon it, and there is silence.

The ball goes straight as an arrow for the goal-posts, but making its curve, seems to falter and have scarce strength enough to reach, the distance is so great ; then, caught, perhaps, by a stronger gust of wind, it gains new power and shoots over the cross-bar and between the goal-posts, while up to Heaven goes a Yale yell that might wake the seven sleepers, and the air becomes azure with banners, while the little girl waves her blue parasol and cries: "Didn't I tell you just to wait and see my big brother kick!"

But no one answered her taunts—the Harvard maidens are crushed lilies now.

The ball is put in play again, but before any effort of the crimsons can retrieve their fortunes, time is called, and Harvard stands beaten by a single goal.

So they all turn to leave the grounds, little Bessie Everett humming a Yale ditty and gazing contemptuously at the crushed young ladies who wear the crimson.

She has not made half a dozen steps from her seat on the grand stand when she cries out suddenly: "Why, Mr. Van Beekman, have you come to take me to my brother? Wasn't Phil's kick lovely?" and holds out her little hand to a Yale undergraduate who is pressing toward her in the crush.

"*Lovely?* It was real agitating—I actually clapped my hands!" cries this creature, who is very little, and is arrayed most strikingly in azure shirt, collar, and cuffs, with a blue scarf around his neck, a blue flower in his buttonhole, and exquisite blue gloves on his dainty hands. Curiously enough, he sports a single eyeglass and knickerbockers, for in the year 1878 American gentlemen still thought they might be considered gentlemen without affecting the fads of English costume or manner. "I'm so excited I think I shall go in for athletics myself!" he babbles on.

"Yes, they would improve you AWFULLY!" remarks Bessie, with the frankness of childhood, taking a sly but scornful glance at Van Beekman's diminutive calves, that are ludicrously exhibited by his knickerbockers.

"Awh, glad you agree with me. And what do you think of my *Yale* get-up? My tailor was excited over it. You see I'm blue all over."

"It would be simply perfect if you only had an eyeglass to match," cries Bessie.

"An eyeglass to match?"

"Yes, a *blue* one."

"A blue eyeglass! Oh! by Jove, that is a fetching idea. That will be an eye-opener. I'll order one for the Princeton affair next week. A blue eyeglass! By George, you're a genius, Miss Bessie!" he ejaculates, producing a diminutive pocket-book and jotting down the article under discussion.

He has scarcely time to finish this when Miss Everett, who is of an impetuous disposition, grabs his arm and shouts, for the hum of the grand stand is still very loud: "Why don't you take me to my brother, as you said you would, Mr. Augustus de Punster Van Beekman?"

A minute or two after this they are both gazing on the Yale half-back, who, having got into citizen's dress, is nursing a very black eye, for the slugging and scrimmaging, according to the custom of that day, had been something awful.

He is standing up, like a stag at bay, surrounded by a crowd of Yale undergraduates, who every now and again make frantic rushes at him and embrace and squeeze him as if they loved him—which they do, for Phil Everett has this day made one of those phenomenal plays that put a man's name high up in college annals, and are told of, around the campus, by students long after their hero has passed from university life, till they become as college household words.

Notwithstanding the boisterous attentions of his surrounders, the young man is looking very proud and happy, for the captain of his team, another giant like himself, has just given him an awful squeeze and whispered: "You've done a great thing for Yale foot-ball this day, old fellow!"

And so he has, for from that time to this, when the blue has met the crimson or the black and orange, and the scrimmage has been most savage, and the charging most furious, many a Yale rusher has tackled a *little* harder, and many a Yale back has kicked a *little* longer, as the memory of Everett's winning goal has come into his mind to fire his heart, amid the cries of foot-ball partisans and dust of foot-ball battle.

For Everett's kick was the first of those extraordinary exhibitions of strength and skill that, followed up by "Lamar's run" and the phenomenal playing of Camp and Moffat, and later on, Beecher and Bull, and Ames and Poe, have made college foot-ball what it now is, when beauty, wealth, and fashion by thousands crowd college fields and ovals to see Yale, Harvard, and Princeton fight like students and demons to carry the crimson or blue or black and orange to victory and glory.

There is no such crowd on this day of Everett's kick, though the Yale men about him make up for lack of numbers by abundance of enthusiasm. He puts them off, however, by saying : " Look out, fellows, here's a lady."

" A lady ! " they cry, all giving back.

Then one suddenly says, rather contemptuously : " Why, it's a child ! "

But another laughs : " By George ! she was the only Yale girl on the ground. I saw her wave that blue parasol every time we downed the magenta."

Then one of the team suddenly cries : " Why, she's Phil's sister ! " for the little lady has visited her brother at Yale the preceding term, and has been petted and made much of by most of the athletic set, having had the supreme honor and bliss of feeling the muscle of the stroke of the Yale boat, among the crew of which Everett pulled the bow oar.

So the crowd make way for her, and in a moment she is in her brother's arms, kissing him and telling him how proud she is of him, and how she has cried out for him and taunted the Harvard girls with him ; and that she loves him and is sure he can kick further than any man in the world.

This probably makes the giant happy, for he loves his little sister very dearly, and there is a smile on his face as he kisses her. But suddenly the look becomes a troubled one as she whispers in his ear : " If mother were only here for me to tell her all about it."

A moment after his face grows even more serious as she babbles on: " Phil, you must see father before you go back to Yale. He's awfully angry at you about something."

" About what ? " asks the young man, uneasily.

" I don't know exactly ; but he got a letter this morning—I think it was from England, because the butler said it was foreign—and when he read it he went on awful about you and forbid my coming to see you play."

" So you've disobeyed father and got yourself into trouble on my account ? " mutters Everett with a slight sigh.

" Oh ! I'd do it over again every time to see you kick," returns the little girl, giving her brother another hug.

But this interview is suddenly broken in upon. With a kind of simultaneous emotion, the crowd of Yale men, that has gradually been growing larger about Phil, make a rush at him, and though he struggles good-humoredly and cries out he won't have it, they pick him up, and singing a wild college glee, carry him in triumph out of the place and deposit him on the sidewalk.

Whereupon the Irish door-keeper of the base-ball grounds, becoming inspired by Yale sentiment and Yale victory, and getting his colors mixed, joins in with "The Green above the Red," and calls out : " Down with the Hairvards and the English, and all who float that bloody color ! "

This raises a laugh, and taking advantage of it Phil hurries his sister into her carriage, that has been waiting for the little lady ; then, stepping in himself, says to the coachman : " Home ! "

As he drives off, the crowd cheer him and give a Yale yell ; and even as he smiles back at them and calls out he's going to New Haven with them on the evening train his face becomes so gloomy and disturbed that his sister cries at him : " What are you so black about, Phil ? " then suddenly whispers : " Is it mother ? " and clings to him.

But he only answers her by a caress that is half a sigh, and goes into silent meditation till the brougham draws up in front of one of the handsomest residences on Beacon Street, both as regards house and location. It is a spacious brown-stone facing and overlooking the beautiful botanical gardens, from which, in the autumn, it receives the perfumes of myriad flowers and shrubs.

Telling his sister to run upstairs and he'll see her before he goes, he turns to the servant who has opened the door and says : " Father in, Thomas ? "

"Yes, sir," answers the man. "He's been asking for you ever since he heard you'd come from New Haven to-day."

"Very well, I'll see him now," mutters the young man, and steps into the library with a very solemn face to meet his father, Robert Everett, one of Boston's financial magnates.

This gentleman is as unlike his son as a nervous gray fox-terrier is to a mastiff ; his manner is quick, snappy, fidgety, save at sundry intervals, when he draws himself up and assumes the old-fashioned dignity of a past generation. He is evidently in a fearful humor, and greets his son with no more kindly words of welcome than a savage "So you've got a black eye, eh? Been fighting again, sir?"

To this Phil answers respectfully, though his other eye becomes red with passion and his lips tremble, showing a struggle for self-control: "I've not been fighting *again*, for I never fight. This black eye is a souvenir of the foot-ball match of to-day."

"And what's that but fighting—a mere excuse to punch each other's heads off in sections? The faculty think so also; they forbade this match, I'm told, and threatened suspension to all who played·!" cries the old man.

"Yes, sir."

"And yet you performed in it?"

"The faculty 'll come round all right."

"But *I* won't!" says the father, grimly. Then he suddenly cries out: "Who won?"

"Yale!"

"And you helped them?"

"I did my best, and, I think, my share."

"Ah! came here to disgrace your native town, Boston, by beating its college, Harvard, and holding it up to ridicule. For this you defy your own professors and risk expulsion and disgrace to my name—do you hear me, sir?—MY NAME!" And the old gentleman, working him-self up to a sexagenarian fury, goes into a long rigmarole of invective, pacing the floor with rapid footsteps, while the young man gazes at him with a little sneer of con-tempt, though he is nervously chewing the end of his brown mustache.

At last from want of breath the elder man gives the younger one a chance to speak. Then Phil Everett says quietly: "This attack on me and foot-ball and my college is not the reason of your anger. Suppose you give me the true cause, father."

"Then, if you will have it," cries the senior Everett, as if he had been anxious to save his son and is only forced to revelation by the young man's importunity, "here it is—from England." And opening a drawer in his desk, he produces a letter.

The document is from London, and signed by Messrs.

Shamerstein, Abrahamoff & Co., Bankers. It briefly asks for payment of a bill endorsed by Philip E. T. Everett, the paper having gone to protest ; and states that it has been placed in their correspondent's hands in Boston for collection.

"I took up that note to-day—look at it !" cries the father, producing from his pocket-book an I. O. U. for £400, dated some three months previous, signed by one John Colquhoun Heather, and endorsed by Philip E. T. Everett.

Then he remarks savagely : "What do you say to that ?"

" I say," cries Phil, "that I never received one farthing of that money. I had met Lord John Heather, and found him a perfect gentleman. I endorsed simply as a matter of accommodation. Heather has suddenly been called to India and must have forgotten the matter in the hurry of departure. He is an officer in the Scotch Fusileer Guards, and probably—like most men of his class— careless as regards business. I was notified of the protest and sent five hundred dollars on account. I have written to Heather, and know that paper will ultimately be paid by him."

" All right ; inform me when his lordship is ready to honor his signature and I'll be very happy to transfer the note," remarks the elder Everett grimly. " At present I have charged it to your account ; and this with other drafts gives you only five hundred dollars to go through your senior year."

" I'll get along with that," remarks Phil with a wince. Then he says hopefully : " But Heather will doubtless make it good before long ; I'm confident of his being an honorable gentleman."

" You're welcome to your belief in your lord," sneers the father. But here he comes to the true gist of the matter ; his face gets white with rage, and he cries out : " How did you come to be in London this summer ? and where did you pick up your aristocrat ? "

" Lord John Heather," says the young man rapidly, " is a friend of my moth—" Here he suddenly bites the word in two and swallows the latter part of it.

" A friend of your *mother's !* Don't try to dodge the word !" yells the old man, growing livid. " Then it is

2

as I guessed the instant I saw this cursed paper. When I thought you salmon-fishing in Labrador last summer you had gone over to England to see your mother."

"You guessed right," says the son, with a pale face but determined voice. "I went by the Allen line from Que-bec."

"Despite my orders not to visit that wo——"

"I'll trouble you not to say anything against my mother," whispers the young man. "If you do, I'll—" But he says no more, for his father cries out: "And you, Phil, my son, have turned your back on me! You—*you* —you!" and sinks down with tears of mixed rage and agony in his old eyes.

Looking at him, the son turns over in his mind the following facts: His father, an old man of sixty-five, made irritable by the strange combination of sensitive nerves and Puritanical nature ; his mother, still young at forty, who loves fashion, pleasure, and gayety, and, worst of all in her husband's eyes, does not hesitate to lavish his large fortune on the same. These two gradually drawing apart, until they have reached a practical sepa-ration. They have no grounds for divorce, save incom-patibility of temper and uncongenial dispositions.

The mother spending a great portion of her time in Europe, the father striving to make his two children take his part in the family quarrel—to alienate their affections from their mother.

It is this thought that makes the son gaze at his father sternly ; but as he looks, the tears in the old man's eyes soften him. He says quietly : "You can never turn my face from my mother's love. You know that, father! Best give it up ; let me honor you and her together. I shall do the best I can this year with my allowance. Good-by." And leaving the room, he goes upstairs to make some preparations for his return to New Haven.

The old gentleman looks after his departing son, and after a time sighs out : "Yes, I know that ; Phil 'll never give up his mother for me ; but he still honors me, loves me as his father. I'll—I'll—make up what money to him he loses by his boyish endorsement of that lordling's paper."

A softer and more paternal feeling comes into his heart, and all would be well did not at this moment

Bessie come running in, crying : "Where's Phil, papa ? " and then looking round, whimpers : " Oh, he can't have gone without bidding me good-by ! "

" You knew he was here ? " says the senior Everett, surprised.

. " Of course ; I came home with him from the match." Here remembering her father's command, she stops very suddenly and her pretty face gets red.

" So—you—went against my orders ! Are all my children to disobey me ? " cries the old man, looking in a way that would frighten Bessie had she not been petted and spoiled and is now about to show it.

" Oh," she says airily, thinking to carry off this situation as she has done a dozen similar ones, and not knowing her father's present nervous irritation, " I didn't suppose you *meant* what you said."

" And why not ? "

" Because that would have been *too* stupid."

" *Too* stupid, you—— ! "

" Yes, *too* stupid, papa, to keep me from having a good time because you were down on Phil. Besides, to see such a lovely game I'd go if you told me a hundred times not to, you dear old foolish papa, you—" Here she tries to pat her parent's head, and run her hand through his scanty white locks, and tickle his venerable ear ; a plan that has worked admirably up to this time, but now has a very bad effect, as it reminds him of some of her mother's former wiles to coax checks out of his bank-book.

" You impudent little minx ! " he cries. " How dare you call me old and foolish ? Unless you are respectful to me I shall punish you ! " And seizing her by one of her plump white arms he stands her in front of him.

Now this grip on her wrist hurts Miss Bessie, who is not accustomed to such treatment ; besides, her pride is wounded by his threat. She loses her temper and cries back at him : " Punish me ? I dare you to do it ! Punish *me ?* You can't bully me as you did my mother. Punish me ? I *dare you !*"

" SMACK ! "

She has been taken at her word, and is staring at her father, holding a little hand to her ear and cheek that have become pink under her father's discipline, upon whom she is gazing speechless and astounded, for until now she has never been boxed in her life.

The old gentleman is gazing upon his wayward offspring, astonished also, for he had never laid hand upon his pert little daughter before, though this time the pro vocation has been beyond his self-control.

He is about to be more astonished.

For now a great brown hand is inserted into the collar of his coat, upon which it takes a vice-like grip, and a kind of human derrick lifts him and skips him along on tip-toe, and with a wrench that tears the garment from neck to waist, gives him an awful yank that deposits him in an arm-chair with a scream of amazed terror, while Philip Everett hisses into his face: "You miserable brute! If you lay hands upon that child again I'll forget I am your son and—" He does not put the rest into words, but his look fills out the sentence.

"Don't you think you have forgotten *that* already?" whispers his father, giving a cool, steely, awful, unforgiving, unforgetting look at the young man, who, having made his preparations for departure, has been looking for his sister, and hearing her voice in the library, has entered just in time to see the box on the ear, but not what had provoked it.

"Perhaps; but I won't have you strike my sister."

"She was an impertinent child and deserved correction. And you dared in my own house to raise your hand against *me*—your father? It is the last time you shall ever enter it. Out of my home—FOREVER!" Then, with the same stony, uncompromising, unforgiving stare on his face, the old man rises to his feet and points sternly to the door.

But here Bessie, who has recovered her voice, throws herself between them and cries to her father to forgive Phil, who did it for love of her—that she deserved it— that he can punish her all he wants if he'll only forget what her darling brother has done.

But Robert Everett's hand still points to the door, and he says to his son: "*Out!* Let me see your face for the last time!"

"Not till you promise to keep your hands off Bessie."

"Certainly," says his father. "In a moment of provo-

cation I forgot myself. You may trust her with me
Out of that door!"

Then Phil, knowing Bessie is as certain of pardon as
he is of unforgiveness, seizes his sister, who is sobbing
at the work she has done, gives her a long, passionate
squeeze and kiss, and staggers from his father's house.

On the sidewalk he takes a long look at the home of
his childhood, and mutters: "An insult to his pride—
he'll never forgive that." Then he does something he
has not done before in his life—counts the money in his
pocket. A moment after he sneers: "I can't go through
Yale on nothing but a fifty-dollar note and two nickels.
By George, my best kick at foot-ball was my last!"

CHAPTER II.

PETE, THE COWBOY.

WITH a rather gloomy countenance, Phil takes his way
to the Parker House, where he imagines he will find
some college chums, who will doubtless give him something else than his own woes to think about.

But no young man is sad very long at the thought
of making his own living; it takes maturity to teach him
the terrors of the battle of life, its disappointments and
despairs.

By the time he turns down School Street he is whistling a popular air; and when he enters the Parker House
he is laughing to himself at the thought of how he'll
astonish his father by making a million or two in some
way; for the young Yale half-back has got to thinking he
can kick a goal as surely in the game of fortune as he did
in the day's foot-ball match.

No collegians chancing to be in the reading-room, he
picks up an evening edition of one of the day's papers,
and glancing over it has the pleasure of seeing his name
in big letters heading the account of the foot-ball game.

Immediately below he notes a letter from Silver City,
New Mexico, announcing wonderful discoveries of ore
in the Bully Boy mine, with a long account of its lucky
owners and the fortunes that the earth has yielded to

their persevering picks. One, whose credit wasn't good for a sack of flour has, according to this highly-colored article, just refused a million for his interest. In the fashion of all mining reports, this one runs along, mentioning rich discoveries *everywhere* in the district, and failures and disappointment *nowhere*.

This mass of exaggeration Philip, who has not yet learned the prospector's maxim that "Every mine is a good one until you look at it," believes, and when he rises from the perusal has made up his mind, with the prompt decision of youth, that Silver City, New Mexico, is the arena upon which he will run his first course to win for himself fortune. Fame, he fondly thinks, has already come to him this day.

This settled in his mind, he suddenly remembers he has had no dinner, and entering the dining-room, sees his foot-ball captain, with several members of the team, taking a severely Spartan meal ; for the Princeton game occurs the coming week, and in matters of training this dignitary is a strict disciplinarian to himself as well as the rest of the team.

If Phil is not to play, it is necessary that the captain be notified at once, so that a substitute may be ready. He hardly knows how to open a proposition that he feels sure will be combated as monstrous and horrible since this day's successful effort.

Thinking the matter over, he laughs grimly to himself: "I'll break the ice with ice-cream," and selecting a conspicuous table, whispers to his waiter directions for a generous meal. "By George, I'm out of training now; I'll enjoy it!" he mutters, and adds champagne to his order.

He hasn't got very far in his dinner when, looking about, he notes that his team companions are staring at his meal in horror, and his captain has a stern and terrible look upon his face, while Van Beekman, who is at an adjacent table, has turned white, for the poor little fellow has backed Yale heavily for the Princeton affair.

A moment after the captain rises, and striding over to Phil's table, whispers in an awful and severe voice : "Champagne ! My Heaven ! are you mad, Everett ? Champagne ! Stop drinking that poison *instantly !* " as Phil is just punishing another glass of the wine. A second

later, the martinet actually screams out : " Ice-cream ! "
for the waiter is putting a plate of that stomach destroyer
before his half-back. Then he gasps out: "You *are*
crazy !" for the captain, hardly believing his eyes, almost
thinks it an hallucination, and that either he or Everett
must be insane.

" Not at all," says Phil, quietly, finding his chance to
open the matter. "I've gone out of training and am
taking advantage of the fact to get the first square meal
I've had for two months."

"Out of training !" echoes the captain. Then he gives
a hideous laugh and cries out to the other Yale men who
have gathered about: " By the immortal Bob Cook ! he's
forgotten the Princeton match."

"Not at all," remarks Everett, calmly. " I shall not be
able to play in it."

" Not play in it !" cry several of his surrounders, who
look even more concerned than before ; for Phil Everett,
full of champagne and ice-cream, and fattened for days
on macaroons and syllabubs, will still be a harder man for
the Princeton rush line to tackle than any substitute that
they can put into his position at this late day.

After a moment's glum consideration, the captain mut·
ters: "You must have some weighty reason for this ? "

"I have," returns Phil, "and if you'll come with me
I'll tell it to you as a confidence that is your right."

So the two move off to a quiet corner of the café, where
Everett briefly states that family affairs compel him to
leave college at once.

And though the captain argues with him, nay, even begs
and implores him to remain till after the last game of the
season, neither reason nor entreaties have any effect ; for
this rapid young man, with the impatience of his age, has
jumped to the conclusion that every day away from his
Eldorado is the chance of a lost fortune, and if he does
not get to Silver City soon there will be no more mines
left upon which he can pounce to make him wealthy.

A few minutes after this interview Phil gives a sudden
start. It has just occurred to him that railroad tickets
cost money. Without funds, how shall he get to his distant Eldorado ?

This matter is made easier to him a moment after
ward. Van Beekman saunters up to him and says, for

the rumor has gone around : "Had a row with papa, eh ·
That don't amount to much. You should—awh—handle
your paternal as I do."

"How is that?" asks Everett, a little curiously.

"Why, kiss it out of him in public. My dad was once
going to row me at Delmonico's. I was only seventeen
and drinking B. & S., and he was going to pitch into me
for it. It would have been awfully embarrassing before
a lot of men, yer know. He had just shouted at me across
the café, in a fearfully savage voice : 'What's that you're
drinking, sir?' when I stopped him. I cried : 'Oh, is
that you, papa dear, you lovely old chap ; come down to
have fun with your little sonny? You look so pretty I
am going to kiss your dear old face !' And up I jumped
and seized him and embraced him and kissed him till I—
awh—actually kissed him out of the place, for he fled
from me in horror, my boy. But I tell you it took nerve
to do it. While the chaps were laughing and cheering
I took two more B. & S.'s to stiffen me. By the bye,
Burton paid his joint bet with us that he lost on this
game. Here's the bills. Tin is always handy when
daddy turns his back on you." And handing Everett
a wad of greenbacks, this juvenile philosopher saunters
away.

Phil gazes a moment at the money and sneers : "I
didn't know I was playing for my bread and butter when
I made that kick. Wonder if this would bar me out—for
professionalism?" A second after his face gets hopeful
as he counts the money, and mutters : "Two hundred
dollars ! That'll take me where I want to go." Then he
steps down to the Boston and Albany depot and takes the
train for New Haven.

The next week the Yale-Princeton game is played, and
without his services Yale loses to that plucky little New
Jersey college, whose backers may always feel sure that
the orange and black tiger stripes will never be lowered
so long as desperate fighting can hold them up.

Before this Philip Eaton Travers Everett had written
to his mother of his quarrel with his father, and his purpose to find fortune in the West, and was on his way to
New Mexico, with the most serviceable of his fine raiment
packed in a valise initialled "P. E. T. E.," and some three
hundred dollars in his pocket, the proceeds of a forced

sale of his college effects, less various claims upon him for local bills.

A few days after this he is standing in the bar-room of the "Pot-Luck" Hotel, Silver City, and has already found the road to fortune a hard one, having dropped one-half his cash in a poker game into which he had been beguiled by some professional gamblers, one of them a Mexican *monte* dealer disguised as a cattleman, another figuring as a Methodist parson, and the third as a drummer for a St. Louis dry-goods house.

Hotels in New Mexican mining towns at that time were made either of adobe or unseasoned lumber, their partitions always of the latter, and what was said aloud in one room was the property of the person in the next.

As Phil Everett is thinking of his loss rather in sorrow than in anger, grief changes to indignation, for he hears the voice of the supposed Mexican cattle-drover, in the office adjoining, laughingly telling in broken English how he scalped the Eastern jay.

Without thought of consequences, he steps into the room, and confronting the swindler, calls him a robber and slaps his face ; and is pulling off his coat to fight, and would be dead the next minute, for the gambler is drawing his pistol, when the cold muzzle of an old-fashioned Colt's revolver is clapped against the Mexican's forehead, and a quiet voice says in his ear : "Up with your hands, Three-Card Juan ! *Quick!* or I'll blow your brains into the spittoon ! I won't have no innocents without guns murdered round heah ! "

This address is very rapidly obeyed ; for it comes from Brick Garvey, the sheriff of the county, and one of the surest shots in the West.

"Now," says the old gentleman, who has white hair. and has been one of the pioneers of Texas, where he has learned the trade of slaying with Samson Potter, Sam Houston, Jack Hayes, and other celebrated frontiersmen —"now"—his voice is very kindly—"now, we'll investigate affairs a leetle." Then he suddenly whispers : "Hands up, Juan !—or ye won't know what's hurt ye," for he has caught a suspicious movement on the part of the *monte* dealer. "Perhaps it'll be safer for you if I remove your weepons," which he does with the expertness of long practice, confiscating a revolver from the man's hip-pocket, and bowie-knife from his boot.

"What kind of a show would you have had with these ag'in you, Tenderfoot?" he remarks, with a grin, to Phil, who is standing in his shirt sleeves. "What were you going to do with that sharper, anyways?"

"Hammer him!" cries Phil, and tells his story.

"Hammer him? What with?—a club?"

"No, with my fists!"

To this Garvey cries suddenly: "So you shall if you're able to. Stand up before him, Three-Card Juan! Stand up with nature's weepons and show if you're the best man; stand up or I'll perforate ye!"

Thus commanded, Three-Card Juan, who has had much experience in rough-and-tumble bar-room rows, draws himself together, and before Phil knows what is coming, launches himself like a wild-cat on the collegian.

As he does so Garvey cries warningly: "Lower yer head; don't let the Greaser git his fingers in your ha'r!" And some of the few spectators cry: "Look out for gouging!" for the *monte* man is an awful expert at this cruel Mexican trick, and would have Everett's eyes out of his head in a second had not the young man's hair been cropped short for foot-ball purposes, so Juan can get no finger purchase.

The next instant Phil has torn himself from his opponent's grasp, with his eyes even now inflamed and red, for the scoundrel has already done some work upon them. Then his big fist shoots out straight from his shoulder and Three-Card Juan goes into the corner in a bunch. But it is only to take another spring, and he is again upon Phil, biting, scratching, and kicking, though a minute after felled again; for his strength is as almost a boy's compared to the Yale rusher's trained muscles.

"Don't fight that cat scientific, you young fool! Use your feet; he does his. Your legs look good enough When he kicks, *you* kick!"

"So I will," mutters Phil, grimly, as his opponent, who has been circling round him, Indian fashion, thinking he sees an opening, springs for the collegian's face.

As the gambler rises to his leap, Everett, taking one step forward, swings his leg with the same weight and power he put into the mighty drop kick on the Boston grounds but two short weeks before ; his foot meets the little Mexican in mid-air, and sends him sailing through the open door on to the bar-room floor, where he lies writhing and would groan with agony and cry out only that he has no breath in him with which to do it.

A little gasp of surprise comes from the spectators, and Garvey cries in astonishment : " Good Lord, what a kick ! Darn me if you didn't hoist him as if he war a foot-ball. I'd bet on you ag'in a mule. Run, somebody, and get a tape-line and measure the distance the Greaser went."

And they do so—and to this day the marks are on that bar-room floor—it is called the " Tenderfoot's Kick," and measures twelve feet seven and one-half inches.

While this is going on Garvey suddenly asks : " What's your name, anyway ? "

And the hotel-clerk, who is anxious to have his say in the matter, answers promptly, " Pete ! " for he has read the initials, " P. E. T. E " on Phil's valise.

The collegian, who has not as yet registered, being perhaps rather ashamed of his part in what has just taken place, does not contradict him, and from that time on Phil Everett is known throughout New Mexico and Arizona by the humble but expressive cognomen spelt by his initials.

Shortly after, the Mexican showing signs of revival, Mr. Garvey remarks : " I'll jist put that Greaser in the lock-up ; the jidge 'll give him three months for card-sharping."

" Hasn't the scoundrel had punishment enough ? " remarks Phil, looking at the man, who can hardly move.

" Young man, I do this to save your life," returns Garvey, shortly. " If he stayed out, he'd perforate you sure By the time he's loose ag'in you must be heeled and able to take care of yourself. And before further trouble arises I'll give you a leetle advice : Shoot your man dead in this community *fust*, and call him a liar *afterward ;* otherwise, you'll be planted before you've got used to the climate. Let's liquor, boys ; and give that Greaser some whiskey, too. My under-sheriff runs a prohibition jail, and it'll be a long time for Juan between drinks." With this he drags the card-sharper off to jail, leaving the crowd shuddering at the horrible thought of a temperance prison.

Returning from this duty, he takes Everett aside and
asks him if he has got a gun yet.

Meeting with a negative reply, he leads his *protégé* to
a neighboring store, where, among other commodities,
they have arms for sale, and tells him to invest.

Which Phil, seeing the wisdom of his advice, does, and
is helped in the selection by the experience of his mentor,
who explains the " p'ints " of the weapon to him and how
it must be carried to be a quick draw ; that he doesn't
favor snap-shooting, even in a " gineral scrimmage," as
speed is important, but " fatality vital."

Having obtained the revolver for him, Mr. Garvey also
shows Pete how to use it, and in the course of a few days'
practice his steady nerves and good eye have done such
wonders that the sheriff is elated and remarks, " That
he thinks it's safe to let Three-Card Juan out of jail, as
Pete can take care of himself nights."

During these instructions Mr. Garvey works up quite
an affection for the young collegian, who tells him of his
reasons for coming to Silver City and his hopes of making a fortune in mines.

At this the old gentleman whistles sadly, and then remarks : " Thar's lots come with them ideas, but mighty
few goes away with them. Though, if one *does* hit it
rich, like the Bully Boy, it means sudden bullion ; but
cattle's the sure go, slower but more sartin, and jist as
big as mining in the long run."

Phil has, however, set his heart on mining, and Garvey
leaves him, promising to do what he can for him, and remarking, with a wink : " The sheriff sometimes hears of
things officially."

Some two weeks after these mysterious words, Garvey comes to Phil and brings with him the greatest
temptation that has yet come into the young man's
life.

" Pete," he says, " the Slap Jack mine has been in litigation. The litigation is ended, and so is the capital of
the owners. Now they offer a one-half interest for ten
thousand dollars, to be used in prospecting the claim.
It's been divided into four parts ; that's twenty-five hundred dollars for a share. I'm going in for one, and so

are Sam Hicks and Billy Benson, and I can git you the other share, that's one-eighth of the property. Of course, it ain't dead sure—you can't buy developed mines for twenty thousand dollars—but it's a fighting show for a big property. It's sartin on the same vein as the Bully Boy, and if they make a strike it will be a stem-winder; besides, Billy Benson's going into it, and he's the luckiest and sharpest operator about here. I'll lay my money alongside of his, and if you're a gambler, you'll put your chips on the same card."

The day before Phil would have told Garvey he didn't have the money; this morning he has received a letter forwarded to him from Lord John Heather; in it that nobleman has apologized for his carelessness in letting his paper go to protest, and enclosed a draft for the four hundred pounds with interest, which makes something over two thousand American dollars. This money Phil itches to invest in the Slap Jack. He turns the matter over in his mind. If he wins?—how easy it will be to take up the protested note and make his father think the Scottish lord a gentleman. If not?—he remembers his father's slur upon his friend, and that settles the affair. He endorses the draft to Robert Everett's order, and encloses it with a short note, asking his father to return the nobleman his note. Then he declines Garvey's offer, and loses his first and last chance of a fortune in mines!

Two months after, an eighth interest in the Slap Jack is worth fifty thousand dollars.

But if he can't have a *good* mine, Phil will get into a *bad* one; and together with a prospector named Follis he begins work upon "The Tillie," a location the latter has taken up and named after his daughter, a slip-shod girl of some eight or nine.

Follis's wife cooks for them while Phil and the whole Follis family live on the remnant of the young man's Eastern money, that by this time has been reënforced by a remittance of five hundred dollars from his mother. For weeks and months the two men work at the mine with pick and sledge and drill, and find no paying ore; until one day Phil's pile comes to an end, and Follis, who is as honest as he is unfortunate, tells him that their joint credit will not get another sack of flour, or pound of bacon; so the two dissolve partnership and leave "The Tillie" undeveloped, in which state it still remains.

In this desperate plight Phil, being too proud to apply to his mother for aid, asks his friend Garvey for work; and gets it on the latter's cattle range in the Valley of the Rio Grande, becoming a cowboy and gradually assuming some of the characteristics of the race, growing red in face, full in beard, expert with the lasso and rifle, and murderous in his rough-riding of the broncho ponies, over which he casts his lengthy legs, armed at the heels with long-rowelled Mexican spurs.

So it comes to pass that some two years after he had turned his back on the East, Pete, who has almost forgotten his real name, has a better offer and leaves the service of Brick Garvey for that of an English gentleman who has just bought out a Mexican stock-raiser in the valley of the San Francisco, whose deed purported to give title to a great many thousand acres of land that he claimed under one of those myths of New Mexican real estate, an old Spanish grant.

This gentleman, by name Thomas Willoughby, is of the best blood in England, and has been captain in a crack hussar regiment, before he fell in love with a portionless girl, and marrying, found himself not rich enough to keep his commission in a branch of Her Majesty's service where his pay did not liquidate one-half his mess bill. He has consequently resigned from the British army, and come over here alone to better his fortune, selecting, as most Englishmen do, a very poor place for his cattle enterprise.

He likes Pete's frank manner, though, the young man having grown rough, bronzed, and hairy, no idea of his cowboy's education or former position comes into his head; and the two live almost apart for several months with two Mexican stock herders and a half-breed named Pablo, who acts as cook.

This might have gone along indefinitely did not the cowboy one evening chance to astonish his employer. It had been a hard day on the range, and Pete, coming in covered with the dust of rounding up a hundred wild Texas steers, hears Willoughby remark that a little cream would improve their after-dinner coffee; for the rarest of articles upon a New Mexican cattle ranch is, strangely enough—*milk!*

The cows refuse to rob their calves, and every one is too busy or too lazy to coerce them.

Hearing this, Pete seizes a lariat, mounts his mustang again, and in half an hour returns with a bucket of the unattainable, having roped, thrown, and bound a long-horned Texas heifer, and forced her to rob her calf for Willoughby's benefit.

"By Jove! awfully obliged," returns the Englishman, and means it, though his voice has that tone of uninterest peculiar to his class. "I'm sorry you went to so much trouble after lassoing all those steers. It's about the hardest work I ever ran against; polo's nothing to it."

"No," remarks Pete, "but foot-ball is."

"Foot-ball?" laughs his employer. "What do you know of foot-ball, Pete?"

Then Pete surprises the captain, for he quietly says: "Two years ago I played on the Yale team."

"A YALE man—a *cowboy?*" gasps the astonished Brit-isher. "Left home and friends and ambition to be a cowboy? You must have had a thundering good reason?"

"Nothing that I'm ashamed of," answers Pete.

"I know you well enough to know that," says the Englishman, in a tone that wins the young man's heart. He seizes his employer's hand, wrings it, and mutters: "Don't ask my reason. Some day, perhaps—but not now." Then he strides out into the calm Western night and looks across the mesa at the great mountains that are growing soft and dreamy under the rising moon; and there are tears in his eyes, for he has received no letter from his mother for months, and feels that he is forgotten by the great world that had once been his world.

After this occurrence Willoughby always calls him Mr. Peter to his face, though he still thinks of him as Pete, being ten years older than his cowboy; but, gradu-ally drawn together by the solitude of these great plains and mountains, similar educations and tastes soon make the two men acquaintances, and after mutual service in saving each other from wild cattle and the various other casualties of a Western range, the two get to be com-rades and love each other with the love of the frontier, which is a greater and more enduring affection than civilization·is apt to nurture.

So things run along for about six months, when one night Captain Willoughby, whose absent loved ones are often in his mind, gets to talking about them, telling Pete something of his English life.

He has one half-brother, he says, a younger one, Arthur, the child of his father's second marriage with an Italian prima donna who took London by storm some twenty-five years before. "By George," he mutters, after a little sigh of thought, "I wish he were my elder brother; it would be safer for me." Then, seeing Pete's look of inquiry, he puts aside the subject as if it were an unpleasant one, and remarks: "I don't often exhibit these, but some day you may know them, Mr. Peter; they are my wife and child," and with this speech shows Pete two pictures—one of a beautiful woman of twenty-seven or so; the other a lovely little girl of perhaps eight or nine.

Pete's heart goes into his mouth as he looks on these specimens of feminine beauty, for the lady is of exquisite figure and face, with deep, true, earnest brown eyes, and the child, when she grows up, will be the counterpart of her mother, save that her expression, though very soft, has more determination.

As the cowboy gazes, the captain continues: "If anything should happen to me suddenly and unexpectedly I want you to forward this packet to them in England," and produces a packet and some letters tied with a blue ribbon.

A moment after he says: "I was so lonely without them I wrote to Agnes to bring my little Flossie to visit me a month ago; but since then news has come that may take me back to England. So I telegraphed for them to remain."

"I'm very glad of that, captain," returns Pete, in so serious a tone that his employer gazes at him astonished, and asks his reason.

"Because," says Pete in a very significant voice, "it's getting near Apache time."

"Why, we haven't heard of an outrage since I came here."

"No; it was winter; they were living on the reservations and letting their ponies get fat. Now it is spring, and we'll hear from the devils before long. I'm going to Lordsburgh ; keep a good look out, and at the first sign of danger get over to Clifton—AT ONCE ! Don't, in your unbelieving British way, believe—*too late !* Remember the Zulus annihilated your Twenty-fourth regiment in South Africa."

" Yes, and the Sioux destroyed your Seventh cavalry ! " cries the captain, not relishing this slur on English arms.

"So much the more reason for your fearing the Apaches," returns Pete, and goes to bed, as he must make an early start for his burning journey over the Gila plains.

The next morning, after another whispered warning, the cowboy, driving two half-breed horses kept for the purpose, sets out for Lordsburgh, some eighty miles to the southwest, a little town on the just completed Southern Pacific Railroad, to obtain supplies for Willoughby's ranch.

He will be due to return early on the fourth day, for he will stop over night at Yorks on the Gila and drive up the next morning, thus avoiding the midday heat of the sun that, at this season of the year, is almost unbearable upon these New Mexican mesas.

CHAPTER III.

THE LITTLE GIRL FROM ENGLAND.

" THE Apaches ! The Apaches are coming ! Nana has got a new lot of devils from the reservations ! Travel out for your lives ! The Apaches are coming !"

This cry, which is the herald of death, torture, outrage and mutilation to men and women on the hot plains, rocky mesas, and dry river-bottoms of Arizona and New Mexico, rings out twice into the light hazy air of a torrid, cloudless, lazy Western morning. Then Tom Willoughby, who has been comfortably smoking a brierwood pipe, and drowsily reading an old copy of the London *Times* on the fourth day after Pete's departure, springs up from the hide-seated chair upon which he has been lounging, and putting his bright English face, tanned by sun and weather, out of the half-open door of his ranch-house, sharply but doubtingly calls out, " Is that true, Bill Jones ? "

" True as I'm a living man, and you'll be a dead one if you stay here ! "

" Good heavens ! Where are they now ? "

" Just behind that red butte ! ' And Jones, reining in his half-breed pony, who scents danger and is as anxious to be gone as is his rider, points to a high sugar-loaf cone whose fire-burnt hematite sides are just becoming ruby under the morning sun rays.

" They'll be here in fifteen minutes ! "

" Yes, and a short fifteen minutes."

" The two herders must be warned! "

" The two herders are both dead.   They killed 'em a little farther up the river—that's what gave me time to warn you! "

" Don't you think we could stand them off in the *jacel ?* "

" Might in the winter ; can't now. They'd burn that thatched roof and you too in no time ; besides I must git on and start out the Comming's outfit. You ain't the only man that's got to travel out of this valley ! "

" All right, move on, Bill," says the young Englishman ; " there are plenty of horses in that paddock to keep Pablo and me safe from Mr. Indian."

" Don't you be too sure, Willoughby ! " cries Jones, turning in his saddle. " You're a tenderfoot ! You don't know the Apaches, and I do. Light out as if hell was behind you ! "

His last words are almost lost in the cloud of dust that the hoofs of his mustang raise, as he shoots away to warn other settlers, and save other lives that day in the valley of the San Francisco.

Left to himself the Englishman takes a long look up the valley and sees nothing that need cause fear ; the red butte shows perhaps a little more pigeon-blood in its ruby, for the sun is a little higher in the heavens. It is three miles away, but such is the wonderful clearness of the mountain atmosphere it looks as if you could walk to it in a short five minutes.

Away to the west the Sierra **de la** Petahaya looks very

blue, and would be bright as sapphire were it not for the heat haze that comes from the baked mesa in front of it ; to the south and east the Burro and Pinos Altos ranges loom up ; north of these the Black range, and behind them all a glimpse of the main chain of the Mimbres mountains have a similar tint as they melt away into the dividing range whose waters flow both east and west, some by the Rio Grande to the Gulf of Mexico, some by the Gila and the Colorado to the peaceful waves of the Pacific. For this valley of the San Francisco, where Tom Willoughby has located his cattle ranch, is just on the border line of New Mexico and Arizona, and almost between and altogether too near the San Carlos on the west and the Hot Springs and Mescalero on the east ; reservations where the American government nurtures the Apache all winter, when game is scarce, and strengthens his muscles on rations of Western flour and army bacon, and the accursed Indian trader makes his blood hot for slaughter and massacre on fire-brain whiskey, and sells him government repeating rifles and fixed ammunition with which to murder ambushed settlers and to shoot United States pursuing soldiers ; so that when the spring-time comes, and the ponies grow strong and fat, he is ready and equipped to out and massacre, which is the dominant instinct of his nature, and the pervading joy of his existence.

So, Nana having recruited and strengthened his band of renegados by some fifty new Indian devils, fat from reservation rations, is raiding the country, leaving only fire and blood behind him. A few skeleton troops of United States cavalry are following, scores of miles away, striving to overtake those who are never overtaken, for the Apache seizes new horses as he passes on, and as soon as he rides one pony to death mounts a fresh one, and so forward to new fields of massacre, outrage, torture, and joy.

These things are pretty well known to the young Englishman in the eight months he has lived here.

Until this time, however, the Indian scare that he has almost grown to regard as some fabulous bogey of the border has never been brought home to him, the valley of the San Francisco having been unusually peaceful since his location here; Nana and most of the renegade

Apaches having, since his arrival, been operating over the Mexican border.

Still he remembers having ridden past the grave of Patrick Cooney just twenty miles to the north in the Mogollon range, and seen upon it the inscription

"*Killed by Victoria's Apaches,*
THE PETS OF THE GOVERNMENT;*"*

and recollects that Cooney was slain but one year ago; and, as this comes home to him, Tom Willoughby wastes but little time in preparations for his departure.

He slips hastily into his *jacel*, and going to a little bedroom he uses as his own, throws open a trunk and takes a packet of documents and letters from it. These, after a hasty inspection to see that they are all right, he puts in the breast-pocket of his rough shooting-jacket. Next he takes out the photographs of his wife and child. Kissing them with warmest love as he places them in an inner pocket, he mutters, "Thank God, my darlings are not here!"

As he utters this, his actions become more rapid, and a determined look comes into his face as he takes down his Winchester and tests the working of its magazine and lock, buckles on his Colt's six-shooter, and fills his cartridge-belt with ammunition; for with the sight of the loved faces has come the thought, "I must keep my life very safe and sure to-day for the sake of wife and child."

The instant he is armed, Tom Willoughby buckles on a pair of Mexican spurs, slings over his shoulder the usual field-glass every travelling Britisher carries, and hurries to the corral that he has just before, in his uncompromising English way, called a paddock to the astonishment of Bill Jones. There he finds Pablo, the half-breed Mexican, saddling a pony in a way that shows he has heard of the Apaches also, and is more in a hurry to be off than his master.

Willoughby takes a quick look at what the man is doing and then says sharply: "Pablo, leave your saddle on Possum. Hitch up another pony for yourself!"

"No time. Apache too near. Possum do; he's the quickest!"

"Saddle up another pony, I tell you; Pete's due from Lordsburgh this morning. I'm going to take Possum with me; he may need it to escape with himself."

" No time.   Apache too near ! "

"Saddle up ano—— Get off that pony, I tell you !
QUICK !" And Tom Willoughby, leaving his own hunter,
which, with a Briton's love for his own island productions and contempt for the productions of the rest of the
world, he has brought with him from England, and which
he is even now saddling, covers the Mexican with his
six-shooter. " Do you suppose I'm going to leave Pete
unhorsed at such a time ? Get off, or by Heaven I'll
blow your cowardly brains out ! JUMP !"

Thus adjured, Pablo, after a nasty Mexican snarling
" Caramba ! " springs off Possum, who is by long odds
the smartest mustang in the corral, and with a brown face
that has become gray with pallor, and trembling lips that
mutter, " Apache too near ! " begins to saddle and equip
the next fleetest pony he can find.

All this time the Englishman has been hard at work,
with the exception of the moment he turned from his
horse to persuade Pablo to dismount, and in another
minute or so has his hunter ready to mount.

Then taking a hasty look at strap and buckle, for life
and death may hang upon the breaking of a girth, he
similarly inspects the accoutrements of Possum, and with
the halter of the cowboy's pony in his hand, Tom Willoughby rides out of the gate of his corral on his race for
life from the Apache.

Pablo, with that peculiar aptitude Mexicans always
have for handling horse furniture, is already in the saddle
and making a cloud of dust a hundred yards in advance
of him, on his way to safety.

Willoughby gives one look up the valley. The scene
is quiet as before, but just coming round the base of the
red butte that is now one ruby blaze under the sun's rays,
he can see half a dozen horsemen that make black silhou-
ettes upon its sides.

They are the advance bucks of Nana's band, joyously
coming from the murder of some miners near Mineral
Creek, on their track of blood and torture.

Noting these figures, the Englishman starts his hunter
into a sharp canter down the valley after Pablo, taking
care not to make the pace too fast a one, for he is altogether too experienced to let his horse pump himself out
at the start of what may be a long race. So, with the

Apaches but three miles behind him, Tom Willoughby lopes down the half-trail, half-road, with Clifton not more than twenty-five miles to the southwest of him, where he feels sure the men at the copper mines will be able to drive the Indians off.

Two hours after this, with his horse panting under him, he is where he should turn off to cross the San Francisco to Clifton—the Apaches but a mile and a half behind him.

But, even as he turns his horse's head to the west, the thought comes to him like lightning that Pete is due this morning with supplies from Lordsburgh, and must now be very near ; that in this almost unsettled country, with ranches twenty miles apart, he may be utterly unwarned and unaware of his danger.

As this idea comes home to him Tom Willoughby again turns his hunter's face down the valley and still keeps the Lordsburgh trail. The Apaches, who have seen him, have increased their pace, pulled up a little, and are now but a mile and a quarter away.

So the Englishman gallops on ; to his right hand, in its cañon, among its willows and cotton-woods, with cool and refreshing gurgle, the San Francisco runs nearly due south ; to his left is the sun-baked mesa, ornamented by a few sahuara cacti that look like gigantic candelabra. Among them here and there can be seen little dust clouds, each one circling in its own particular minia- ture whirlwind, while farther off and to the southeast rise abruptly from the mesa Steeple Rock and Half Dome, the advance guard of the Pinos Altos and Burro ranges, but cut off from them by the head waters of the Gila, which here becomes a river and starts for its long journey through the mountains of Arizona to join the Colorado, and with it redden the blue waters of the Gulf of California.

Over this scene is a bright blue sky, and atmosphere so clear that thirty miles would look as ten, did not the blazing sun make a heat mist that seems to mirage everything, for even as he rides Tom Willoughby thinks there is a cool, deep lake to the south of him, where he knows he can ride with burning, dusty hoofs for many a mile to the Gila ford.

The Englishman, however, is too well accustomed to

these freaks of Western nature to let them divert his mind for a moment from this life and death business upon which he is now engaged, and he rides on with short stirrup and bent knees, in British cavalry style, feeling all the time pretty easy about the matter. Yorks is not over twenty three or four miles away, and the stalwart widow and her daughter and her two big sons and their hired men will stand the Apaches off even without his and Pete's Winchesters to help them hold the big adobe.

By this time he can see the Indians are nearer to him, and as he notes this it requires some self-control to keep from urging his horse into a quicker gallop, though looking at his mount he can see that his hunter is travelling well within himself ; his breathing is unlabored, and his stride low and long, every bit of the beast's strength going toward what is most wanted now—speed.

Noting this Willoughby smilingly thinks : "Wait till 1 let you out, Major, and we'll show the gentry behind us something they haven't seen in this part of the world before—that is, how an English thoroughbred will run away from a Mexican pony."

Even as he thinks this, he remembers that the horse he is leading has given as yet no pull or jerk on his halter, and looking at Possum finds him loping contentedly alongside with an easier stride, and showing less wear and tear from dust and heat, than even his hunter.

This looking at Pete's horse gets him to thinking of Pete himself, and he remembers how a year has made him and a cowboy chums ; and rather laughs as he wonders what his fine friends in England would say to his comradeship with one of these Bedouins of the Western ranches, even though he has been a college man. But as he runs over the various adventures the American and he have had together his heart gets very tender to his absent chum, and he is glad he took the Lordsburgh road, even at the risk of his own life, to warn him.

From these reflections he is hurriedly aroused. Possum gives a sudden jerk at the halter, and tries to move off to the right, uttering a little whinny of joy. Turning his eyes from the road in front of him, down which he has been anxiously gazing in search of his coming cowboy, to the direction the mustang's head is pointed, Willoughby sees, with a start of surprise, a jerky mud-wagon drawn by two horses just coming out of some stunted cotton-wood which fringe the bed of the cañon of the San Francisco, that now flows upon his right, some two hundred yards distant. Though it has a little sun-top, apparently a very recent addition to it from the whiteness of its canvas, he instantly recognizes the wagon in which Pete had departed for Lordsburgh some few days before. The cowboy has evidently taken advantage of an arroyo going down into the cañon of the river to give his team a drink.

Turning his horse he leaves the trail, gallops at full speed toward the vehicle, the driver of which seeing him whips his hot and jaded mustangs into a lope.

As Willoughby gets within call, he shouts out: " Quick, Pete, the Apaches are only a mile behind! Leave the team ; jump on Possum and ride for your life."

At his cry, though still a hundred yards away, he sees a sudden commotion in the wagon. The cowboy says nothing, only lashes his horses, but there is a flutter of woman's garments on the seat beside him.

And the next moment the sun seems to grow red in the heavens and the earth to reel, to poor Tom Willoughby ; for as the jerky dashes alongside of him, a woman's voice is calling out : " Tom ! dear one ! husband ! " and a little girl is crying, " papa ! " and tossing kisses to him with dimpled hands, and he sees before him all that is most dear upon this earth, the wife of his bosom and the child of his heart, that he had thought safe from danger and death in far away old England.

For a moment he gazes at them in a horrified stupor, then reels in his saddle, and the sweat of dazed agony is on his brow, and he trembles and whispers with white lips, " The Apaches only a mile away." Next, he shrieks, " My God ! Pete, how could you bring these helpless ones HERE ?"

But Pete does not answer, he has already passed on to the road and is silently but savagely lashing his horses into a run that carries Willoughby's wife and child far in advance of him, though both of them wave their hands back to the frantic Englishman, who now spurs his horse wildly on to overtake the wagon.

This he does not do until long after Pete has reached

the trail and turned his team toward Lordsburgh and the south, in a long, slashing lope.

So they all race on, much closer together now, for this delay has told terribly, and the Apaches are but a very short three-quarters of a mile away.

After a few moments the Englishman ranges alongside.

Then the American for the first time speaks, yelling at him in disjointed phrases, broken up by the rattling and jolting of the wagon as it flies along. "I brought your wife and child at your wife's request—the wires said Indians a hundred miles away—your brother—ordered me to!"

"My brother? *Arthur?* HERE?" These are yells of amazement from Willoughby.

"Yes, Tom. He brought me to Lordsburgh. You don't think those men in the dust behind 'll hurt us?" cries his wife, hysterically, clutching their beautiful little girl, who can't understand the trouble, and waves her little hand to her father, and breaks his heart with tossing kisses as he rides on, dazed and desperate, in the dust beside them; for, from the moment he has heard his brother's name, Tom Willoughby has been stupefied.

But as he rides, the sweat of agony and anxiety on his brow, he mutters these curious words: "The infernal Italian villain, he has heard of the Indian raid, and sent me my loved ones to anchor me to death by their presence here. He wants us *all* to die—this time."

Thus they dash on, the Apaches gaining little by little, until after going a short mile, Pete slackens his pace and calls suddenly out: "We've but one chance!"

"What's that?"

"Make Comming's ranch, and fight 'em off!"

"Couldn't we get to those peaks?" says the Englishman, pointing to the left.

"Yes, to be trailed out of 'em and butchered to a certainty."

"Can't we make Yorks?"

"Not with your wife and child. We must stop at Comming's ranch."

"Can we get there with the wagon?"

"No, the team's too tired! We must go on horseback! You take your wife in front of you; your horse is strong and 'll carry more weight. I'll take the child with me on

Possum." And Pete indicates the mustang that Willoughby has led mechanically for the past ten minutes.

"All right!" mutters the Englishman, hoarsely.

"Then please take the reins, Mrs. Willoughby, and keep driving while I get my arms. Every minute counts," says the cowboy. And while the English lady, with pale face and compressed lips, but determined eyes, flogs the tired horses on, Mr. Peter straps his Winchester over his back, takes a look at his six-shooter belted to his side, and carefully examines his cartridge-belt.

This done, he seizes the reins again and pulls the horses sharply up; then jumping out, lifts both lady and child to the ground. Next, with one vigorous, athletic thrust, he has placed Agnes Willoughby in her husband's arms, and, calling Possum, in another moment he has swung himself into the saddle with the child in front of him. Then, ranging alongside of the Englishman, he says: "Give your little girl one kiss. She's been crying for it ever since she saw you!"

Then, perhaps Willoughby forgets his loved ones' danger in his loved ones' arms, and for a second is happy; the next he is pelting over the dusty road, followed by the cowboy, and making straight for Comming's ranch, on the lower San Francisco, just above its junction with the Gila—with a score or more of the foremost Apaches just about half a mile behind.

Two or three of these bronzed warriors smile a dusky smile under the vermilion of their war-paint as they see their game leave the wagon; they know they are hard-pressed, and one buck, a veteran in blood and torment, mutters: "Scalp sure!"

While another, a reservation pet, and who has been taken to the East by the Indian agent to acquire the vices of civilization, and has learned a little better English, says: "Why white man no leave squaws in wagon for Indian? Heap more squaws out there where sun rises!"

But talking or silent, in dust or sun, these tireless devils, who have already ridden fifty miles this burning day, still keep their staggering ponies to their unceasing lope, or as one horse falls exhausted mount another from the herd of captured stock they lead with or drive before them—and four long miles still lie between the fugitives and Comming's ranch. An awful distance now, for the dust and weight they carry are beginning to tell upon the English hunter and the piebald mustang, Possum.

The thoroughbred at first has the best of it, and moves away from the cowboy's pony ; but the former is made of muscle, and the latter of whalebone, and before two miles have passed the blooded horse is coming back to the little mustang ; the Indians, gaining foot by foot all the time, are now but a short third of a mile behind.

So they still race on, the hoofs of the horses crushing the dry gamma grass and small running cacti into the dusty plain. The Englishman with his arms about his wife, whispering words of love to her ; but she hardly answering, save by now and again a silent caress, keeps her mother's eyes turned backward in anxious glance upon her child, who is clasped to the cowboy's heart ; for Pete rides twenty paces to the rear, and a little to one side to avoid any chance of collision in case the thorough-bred has any accident from gopher or prairie dog holes.

All the time he is doing this, Pete is telling the little girl cute stories of frontier life, striving to keep the child's thoughts away from the present, as the burning heat has made her thirsty, and she is beginning to ask for water. In this he succeeds quite well, for the child has grown familiar with Mr. Peter, as she calls him, in their two days' journey from Lordsburgh, and laughs at what he says.

Suddenly, however, she cries out, " Fire-crackers be-hind us ! Mr. Peter, those men act as if it was Guy Fawkes's day. And what is that comes singing so sharp through the air, almost like birds ? "

" Those are flying grasshoppers, Flossie ; but sit more in front of me," says Pete, trying to shield his little charge from the bullets, and feeling rather nervous him-self, as it is the first time he has been under fire ; for the Apaches are now only five hundred yards away, and have opened a running fusillade as they gallop along, hoping by some chance to disable or kill horse or man. Of the two they would rather hit the horse, because then those it carries will surely be their prey, and perhaps the others standing by to assist may also fall into their hands *alive*, and that will mean the additional joy of torture.

But with his arms clasped lovingly about the girl, and

two great tears in his eyes, for Pete has got to thinking of the little sister he has in far away Massachusetts, he dashes on unhurt ; and now Willoughby gives a yell of triumph, Comming's adobe ranch house is in sight but five hundred yards ahead of them.

But as this happens, out flies old Comming himself, mounted on a mustang, and followed by a half-breed boy, and the two disappear in a cloud of dust down the road, riding like two streaks for Yorks on the Gila. For old Comming don't care to fight Apaches if horse-flesh'll keep him from it.

"My God, if we could make Yorks too!" mutters the Englishman ; but his wife is almost fainting in his arms, and he knows he must give that hope up.

Seeing this the Apaches drive their spurs into their ponies, and shoot, if not quicker, more accurately, for Pete wipes the blood from his forehead, that has been grazed by a passing bullet, and the Englishman's horse gives a sudden jump as his flank is seared by a United States carbine-ball, fired by a reservation Indian.

But this only makes the thoroughbred fly faster, though the mustang, more accustomed to the heat and dust, is now his leader. So Willoughby and Pete race up to Comming's lone ranch on the San Francisco, and dash into the open doorway of its adobe house ; Pete thoughtfully hurrying the horses also within its walls, though Indian bullets patter all about him as he barricades the entrance.

Here, gazing around, they find that all its occupants are fled, and they must look only to themselves this day to save from the clutches of the Apache, who spares neither sex nor age, this delicate woman and tender child that Providence has given to their keeping.

CHAPTER IV.

THE LONE RANCH BY THE SAN FRANCISCO.

THEY are no sooner all inside than Pete steps quickly to one of the little openings that serve for windows to the room, and carefully resting the muzzle of his Winchester upon the sill so that no protruding portion of his gun shall give warning, pumps three or four shots right into the advancing Apaches, who have carelessly come yelling on, hoping to carry the place with a rush before the fugitives are ready for them.

They are but two hundred yards away, and firing with a rest Mr. Peter's aim is pretty true. He says grimly, " That'll keep those beasts back for a minute!" Then he cries suddenly, " Look out for this side of the house!" and bolts into another room, that has a door and windows opening in the opposite direction, and is *just* in time.

A few Indians are coming as fast as ponies can bring them for the open door, when his Winchester cracks. The leader's horse is shot under him, the others turn back, while the dismounted man, who is a wary old warrior, makes a desperate effort to gain a little adobe storehouse some hundred yards to the west, under cover of which he will be a most unpleasantly near neighbor. But his Yankee blood growing cooler as the fight grows hotter, Mr. Peter, taking a rest and a careful aim, contrives to drop him just as he is on the threshold, where he falls, his head upon the floor inside, his legs, caught by the knees, drooping over the handle of an old plough which stands beside the door.

Checked in their first rush, the Apaches get out of short range. Then Pete barricades the door and steps back to the other room to find the captain using his gun at the front entrance.

To him the Englishman calls out, with a little savage laugh, " What luck on your side of the house ?"

" Pretty fair," returns Pete. " I've sent one of them to kingdom come. We'll have a little rest now."

" Not a long one, I'm afraid," mutters Willoughby, with a choked-down sigh, looking at his wife and child crouched up together in a corner.

But here in the confusion, for their shots have filled the room with smoke, and the two horses, frightened by the noise, are very restless, comes a quiet, woman's voice. The cowboy hears Agnes Willoughby say, " Let me bind up your wound, Mr. Peter," and looking down sees a little crimson stream running from below his knee down his leather leggings.

" It's only a scratch. I don't know when I got it !"

he says with a slight laugh; "but I'm very, very much obliged to you."

"Wounded!" cries Willoughby, following Pete's glance. "Thank God, there's no bone broken!"

"Just keep an eye on the back door, Captain. Those brutes may try to get in again; I'll be with you in a moment." And the Englishman doing so, the cowboy submits his wound to the ministering hands of the English lady.

As she lightly and quietly binds up the hurt, Mr. Peter feels himself tremble under her fingers. Agnes Willoughby is saying a mother's prayer to him, for she is whispering: "Whatever happens to me this woful day, try, try, and save my little Flossie. Promise, dear Mr. Peter, promise in the name of your own mother."

For answer Peter simply grips her delicate hand till she almost winces, and mutters: "For my mother's sake!"

Then he and Captain Willoughby take a short but careful survey of Comming's ranch house to determine its capabilities for offence and defence.

The first thing the cowboy looks at is the roof; this he is happy to find is made of Mexican tiles, roughly baked red and dry from Gila river clay. These are, of course, fire-proof; consequently they are safe from blazing arrows.

The house proper is divided into two rooms, each having a door opening on to opposite sides of the structure, the one by which they entered facing toward the trail; the other leading from an apartment that has been used as a kitchen, and giving access to a path that runs to the little adobe storehouse some hundred yards away, and, after passing it, is continued to the cañon of the San Francisco River, that flows peacefully among its willows and cotton-woods to meet the Gila, half a mile farther to the south.

As they make their examination of the ranch house there is one great advantage that strikes both Captain Willoughby and Pete at the same time; that is, the absence of all cover near it by which their enemies can approach unseen to make any sudden assault. With the exception of the storehouse just mentioned and an adobe corral some quarter of a mile away, the mesa is bare of everything for five hundred yards but gramma grasses, soap weed, and small cacti, that would hardly give hiaing to a jack-rabbit. A few century-plants, or mescals as the Mexicans call them, are scattered about, but none near enough to the house to give its defenders any uneasiness.

This fact seems also to have struck the Apaches, who are now holding counsel, sheltered by the adobe walls of the corral.

Though they pause to deliberate, they have no intention of abandoning the pursuit of these scalps they already consider theirs; for these dusky demons will conduct their raid perhaps even more remorselessly than in the days when they had only Mexican *haciendas* and farms to harry, and Mexican peons and herders to slay and torture; before the whistle of the locomotive showed them the happy days of burning ranches and scalping settlers were coming to an end.

Perhaps it is because they know this raid must be one of the last of their old-time pleasures, that they will be as cruel and relentless as of yore—to show they are true descendants of Magnus Colorado and Cochise, these dusky children of desert mountains and sun-dried plains, who can live and fatten on the baked leaves of the century plant, acorns, and tule roots; who can travel on horseback across the plain, or on foot over the precipice and mountain trail, a hundred miles in the twenty-four hours, and then perhaps, only tightening the belt to replace food that is unattainable, repeat the journey in pursuit of game or plunder; the only beings who could exist *as savages* in the land in which they have been nurtured and which they love even as they do murder and torture and blood.

On the trail and in sight of their prey, these blocd-hounds will never leave it till they worry it to death.

This is perfectly well known to Pete, and is even quite thoroughly believed in by Captain Willoughby. So the two make what preparations they can to meet the storm that will soon burst upon them.

 They immediately drive the two horses into the room that has been used as a kitchen, for the beasts are now so restive from fright and thirst that their frenzied movements endanger Mrs. Willougbby and the little girl.

 Then Pete suggests that the captain station himself in

the room with his wife and daughter, and by his fire keep
the Apaches back on the side that faces the trail and com-
mands the northern end of the house. He himself will
take care of the southern end of the house and the side
facing the river, for here he expects the chief efforts of
their foes will be made, as the only cover that can be
of service to them is on this side, viz., the little adobe
house used for the storage of farming implements and
mining tools; for old Comming, the fugitive owner of
the place, had been a ranchman, but becoming imbued
with the local mining mania that had been brought about
by the rich argentiferous discoveries at Silver City, he
had abandoned agriculture and taken to prospecting the
neighboring mountain ranges.

All this is easily apparent to Pete. He can see that
the irrigating ditches that run from the river almost to
the door of the house are dry and have not been lately
flooded; while piled against the old plough that stands
near the entrance to the storehouse are a number of
picks, drills, sledges, and other mining implements.

During the time Pete is making this inspection, both
he and the captain are nailing up at the windows slats
that they wrench from the deal table of the cabin, so
as to give but little room for the entry of bullets and yet
leave space enough to shoot through.

This closing up of the openings to the house stops
nearly all circulation of air and makes the place intoler-
ably close and hot under the blazing Arizona sun; and
now the little girl, who has hardly spoken aloud since
entering the cabin, but has looked on in a kind of dazed
infantile wonder, says in the confident, trusting tones of
childhood, " Mamma, can't I have a drink, I'm so very
thirsty ? "

" Of course you can, darling," answers Mrs. Willoughby
and turning to the American she says, " Mr. Peter, won't
you show me where to get it ?—I'm thirsty myself."

But Mr. Peter is already in the kitchen looking with a
serious face at the water cask, which is empty; Comming
and his man, before they had departed, apparently having
filled their canteens with the last liquid in it.

A moment after he returns and says quietly, " There's
not a drop of water in the house. This has been such a
pell-mell affair that I never thought of it before; anyway

I could not have got any, as old Comming has let his irrigation ditches run dry."

At this the captain, who has been at one of the windows watching the Apaches, who are apparently about to make a move of some kind, cries, " No water! What'll become of all of us without it on such a day as this ? "

" I don't think it will affect us vitally," answers Pete. " We'll have plenty of water in a few hours from now, or else we won't need any—these Apaches won't devote a great while to us. Hatch's cavalry can't be many miles behind, and the miners at Silver City must be moving soon.

" It doesn't make such difference to me," mutters the English lady, with a pale but determined face, " only "— here her lips begin to quiver, " only it will be so hard for my poor little Flossie."

Then with tears in her eyes she bends down and caresses the child, who looks at her mother and says, " Don't cry, mamma dear, I'll be brave like papa and you and Mr. Peter."

At this, Pete's throat, which was dry and parched before, gets a big lump in it, and he turns away into the kitchen to do what he can to keep the brave little girl and her mother safe from Apache hands this day.

But sentiment now gives way to action, and he calls out to Willoughby to look to his side of the adobe, for the Indians are beginning to move.

They divide into two parties, one band, much the more numerous, coming from the shelter of the corral out upon the open plain on Willoughby's side of the ranch house. These riding quickly about at long range give little opportunity to the Englishman for effective shooting, though they shower the house with bullets that knock out many a chunk of adobe.

The other party of some five veteran bucks ride into the cañon of the San Francisco and disappear under its bank among its willows.

Pretty well satisfied that the long-range attack upon the opposite side of the house is only a feint, Pete pays little attention to it, but keeps his eyes upon the willows and cotton-woods on the banks of the San Francisco.

He has looked and looked for nearly fifteen minutes,

when a sudden and unexpected bullet sings through the air and cuts from his head a lock of hair.

As he falls backward astonished, a yell of triumph comes to him from the little storehouse only a hundred yards away, and he knows that the Apaches have tricked him at the very opening of the fight, for by leaving their horses in the willows of the San Francisco, travelling down under its bank and then transferring themselves to Comming's largest irrigation ditch that runs behind the adobe storehouse, five or six of them have got possession of this point of vantage without the loss of a man; a part of the proceeding which pleases the Apache greatly, as he is a very careful calculator of the price he pays for anything—even scalps.

They have slipped round the adobe and inside its protecting walls so rapidly that they have not had time to remove the dead body of their comrade killed in their first charge, and he still lies in the same position in which Pete dropped him, his head inside the house and his legs over the handle of the old plough outside.

So they face each other, the Indians, whom Pete now counts and reckons to be five, not including the dead one of the former encounter, sheltered by the storehouse, and the cowboy behind the walls of the adobe.

Then the Apaches try to pick him off by close shooting, and the American strives to do the same to them, also keeping a sharp eye that they do not charge and force the door of the ranch house, which has no very secure fastening.

Elated by the success of their comrades on Pete's side of the cabin, this is exactly what the Apaches are now trying to do upon the front, defended by the Englishman Pete can hear the volleys poured in at close range, and the reports of Willoughby's Winchester as he turns loose its magazine upon them.

The rooms get full of smoke, and the house, close and hot before, becomes a kind of hades. The horses are panic-stricken and kicking things about in the kitchen, and over their noise the little girl's voice comes to him, crying to her mother for a drop of water, for now to the whole party comes the suffering of parched throats and burning thirst.

And so the fight goes on.

After having tested several times, by feints that draw the American's fire, whether he has been called away by the attack of the other side of the adobe, the Apaches in the storehouse, finding Pete always at his post, try another device.

They shoot very rapidly and closely at him ; in fact, so continuously that the cowboy suspects some new ruse, for by this time he has in him the same dogged spirit but quick mind that pulled the football game out of the mire at Boston, and sent the blue above the crimson only three short years before, though the work is much different and the stakes much higher in this game of the frontier.

Being suspicious, instead of shooting back Pete uses his eyes more sharply, and is not caught napping a second time. He sees that one of the Indians, apparently having gotten out of the back of the storehouse, has crawled into the irrigation ditch, and partly sheltered from his fire and concealed from his eye, is working his way toward the ranch house, hoping to get so close under its walls that he will be safe from any bullet from within.

Taking things quietly, the cowboy lets this buck crawl along his ditch until part of him is exposed to a slanting, downward fire, and then, mounting upon a cracker box that has done duty for the absent Comming as a chair, he contrives to put a bullet obliquely into the creeping savage that stops his advance.

With a little start of pain, his enemy wriggles quickly back behind the sheltering storehouse, getting there without being touched again, though Pete tries another snap shot at him. In his hurry, however, he has exposed himself a little, and when he jumps from his cracker box to the floor his cheek is torn open by a bullet from the covering savages.

This is all forgotten in another moment as the captain yells, " The brutes are running away, SURE ! Come in and look at them, Peter."

" No, thank you," returns the cowboy, " I've some here who haven't left yet," for he fears stratagem in this sudden stampede.

But even as he speaks he sees the warriors he is watching, in obedience to some signal, moving cautiously out of the back of the storehouse and taking such care to keep it between themselves and his rifle that he gets no chance for a fair shot, a difficult matter under the circum. stances, as the wounded Indian requires the support of two of his fellows. This apparently gives them so much trouble that they make no disposition of the body of the one killed in the first encounter, who remains, as when first he fell to the crack of Pete's rifle, his feet hanging over the old plough outside.

As his opponents crawl away Pete counts them, to be sure they have all gone, and makes their number five, the same as originally entered the storehouse ; then he watches carefully until he sees them reappear, mounted, among the willows and cotton-woods coming out of the cañon of the San Francisco, and still finding five, though the wounded one has to be held on his horse, he gives a sigh of relief, for he knows the Indians have left none of their number concealed by the trees or the river bank.

Then he goes into the next room and finds the captain in his shirt sleeves, the heat having caused him to throw off his shooting jacket. The Englishman is black with powder smoke, but very happy, as is the lady and the child.

The little one says, " We can get some water now, Mr. Peter, those bad men have gone away." And Mrs. Willoughby cries, " God bless you ! " With this they all get to shaking hands together, for this day's danger has made them like old friends.

After a moment the captain says to Pete, who has been using his big field-glass looking after their retreating enemies, " What made the brutes move off so suddenly ? "

" That ! " remarks the cowboy, pointing to three columns of bluish-white smoke rising into the clear air from the distant Mogollon Mountains.

" Ah, smoke signals from their scouts—Hatch's cavalry ! No chance of the scoundrels coming back now ! " cries Willoughby, and he proposes immediately to go down to the river for water.

" Don't take probability for fact," returns Pete. " We must not leave this place too soon."

" Anyway, your Yankee prudence won't object to this," laughs the Englishman, and he throws open the two doors of the house. " A little fresh air won't be fatal even if the Indians are."

This is a tremendous relief, for the place has been sti-fling, the heat of the day now being at its height, for it is nearly three o'clock in the afternoon.

As the smoke drifts out and the light comes in, Mrs. Willoughby cries out suddenly, "Why, you're wounded, Tom!" and examines her husband's arm with anxious eyes.

But he laughs. "What's a scratch to a man as happy as I? Half a yard of old shirt to tie it up will do as well as a dozen doctors!"

This doesn't suit his wife, who calls out for water with which to bathe it, and insists the member be placed in a sling, which she does with a woman's deftness, the captain kissing her and calling her his nurse sent by Heaven from across the sea, for this big English ranchman has been so racked with anxiety for his loved ones, that now the strain is over he hardly knows how to keep himself from blubbering like a boy, a performance which would do him good, and of which he need by no means be ashamed.

A moment after a sudden idea seems to come to him, for his face grows stern and his manner formal as he says: "What made you bring a woman and child into such danger, Mr. Peter? There is a telegraph office at Lordsburgh—the wires must have told of this Apache raid."

Before Pete can answer Mrs. Willoughby speaks for him.

"Tom," she says, "Mr. Peter is not to blame for any danger that has come to me to-day. You yourself wrote me to join you here."

"Yes, but afterward I telegraphed you to remain in England."

"I never received it; and hearing that I was coming, your brother Arthur——"

"Yes, Arthur, what of him?" breaks in the captain, suspiciously.

"Arthur said he would accompany Florence and me, as he had some mining interests near by—in Colorado, I think."

"Mining interests in Colorado? I never heard of them," cries Willoughby, suspiciously.

"Well, he came with us, and took good care of us as

far as Lordsburgh, where Mr. Peter was pointed out to us as being in your employ and about to return to your ranch ; and I asked him to bring me to you, and he refused, saying there was a rumor of an Indian outbreak— and then——"

"Then," Pete breaks in, "your brother instructed me to bring your wife to you, and I refused until there was further news of Nana's whereabouts—he had last been heard of in the San Mateo mountains—and we all went to the telegraph office for the latest news. Mr. Arthur went in ; your wife and child and I remained outside in the wagon. We had not been there five minutes when your brother came out and told me to drive off at once, everything was all right. A despatch had just arrived, stating that the Apaches had gone east, crossing the Rio Grande. And so I started out."

"You are sure a despatch came ?"

"Certain ! I heard the click of the instrument as I sat waiting."

"Why didn't Arthur come with you ? "

"Oh, how suspicious you are," chimes in Mrs. Willoughby. " There wasn't room in the wagon."

Then the captain startles both of them, for he cries. " I may be suspicious, but you don't know as I do that I have a brother who has a brain as bright as a Machiavelli, and a heart as black as one of those brutes out there," and he points to the retreating Apaches. "If I don't find that lying telegram at Lordsburgh, I'll——"

But any further threat is cut short by Mrs. Willoughby saying suddenly : " Where's Flossie ? "

Their conversation has been so exciting that the child has left the room unnoticed. The captain and his wife spring to the door opening on the trail.

Pete steps into the kitchen, and looking out sees the little maiden with a big tin pail in her hand, tripping across old Comming's neglected garden toward the storehouse on her way to the river. Looking over her shoulder she smiles back at him, and calls : " Going to get water for papa and mamma."

The cowboy is just running after her to help her, for by this time all thought of immediate danger has left him, when suddenly his heart gives a great jump. Chancing to glance at the storehouse. HE SEES THAT

THE BODY OF THE DEAD INDIAN HAS MYSTERIOUSLY DISAPPEARED.

Then forcing himself to calmness, for by this time Agnes Willoughby stands beside him, he calls out: " Flossie, play hide-and-seek. Drop in the old ditch, try if I can find you there ! " hoping the drain will be deep enough to shield the child from Apache bullets. At the same moment he draws the mother from the open door, for now he knows that the WOUNDED Indian assisted off by his fellows was the DEAD one, and a live demon, left in his place, is now concealed in the storehouse.

The little girl cries laughingly: "I'll play with you when I come back, Mr. Peter."

The mother says anxiously : " Why do you want Flossie to hide ? "

Then Pete makes a mistake, for which he never in his whole life forgives himself ; he forgets the self-sacrifice of mother's love that drives away all fear—even that of death.

As he mechanically handles his rifle, he whispers: " Quiet ! for your child's sake. There's a live Indian in that little adobe," and the tragedy comes upon them.

As he speaks, Agnes Willoughby, with a cry of anxious love, flies through the open door, and in a moment has reached her child and is dragging her back ; but even as she does so, a stream of smoke and crack of rifle come from the storehouse. And at this sound the gentle English lady, who had never suffered blow before, with eyes staring as if astonished, claps her hand to her heart and falls dead.

Pete has bounded after her, and would die beside her ; but now an insane man, one wounded arm in a sling, the other holding a revolver, and crying hoarse cries of despair, flies out of the open door of the ranch house straight for the ambushed Indian ; for Tom Willoughby has seen his wife die, and now only wishes to live long enough to avenge her.

Such rage defeats itself, and as his revolver discharges a harmless bullet, the repeating-rifle in the old store house speaks again, and, moaning out : " Save my baby, Pete ! " the Englishman falls dead over the body of his wife.

The next bullet will be for the cowboy, and as he drags the child back to the adobe, he expects it ; but it does not come, and somehow Pete gets his charge to shelter, saved by a jammed shell in the Indian's breech-loader.

Then for a second he stands, dazed and stupid—the horror has come about so quickly.

A minute ago they were all talking in that room ; now a dead man and woman lying there among old Comming's dried-up melon vines, and in his arms an orphan whom he has sworn, by the name of his own mother, to protect and save !

CHAPTER V.

THE BOX CAÑON OF THE GILA.

THIS thought puts the cowboy's senses into him again in a hurry. Anything to save the life of this little girl and his own must be done instantly. The Indians have heard the shots, and Pete can see by the aid of Willoughby's strong field-glass that some of them have turned their horses and are riding back.

He hurriedly tightens the girth of Possum's saddle as he stands in the kitchen, then hastily picks up the cartridge belt of the dead Englishman, for his own store of ammunition is nearly gone, and fortunately the two guns use the same shells.

As he does so he sees the packet of papers and letters in Willoughby's shooting jacket, and transfers them to his own pocket.

In all this business, which takes but a moment, he keeps one eye on the alert for the murderer, but this cunning savage, called " Mescal " by his fellows, from his love of Mexican fire-water, will take no chances and lies safely in the storehouse waiting to slay the American should he try to escape on the river side, for this gentleman is an old veteran in assassination and ambush, having served his apprenticeship in massacre ten years ago under Cochise.

He it is who originated the plan of replacing the dead Indian by his own living body, to shoot down the pale faces after safety had made them careless.

This ruse he had once before tried on a green United States trooper, calling to him faintly for water, after a fight in the mountains, and shooting his Samaritan through the body as he placed his canteen to his treacherous lips —an exploit Mescal was very proud of and tried to repeat in one form or another whenever opportunity offered. He is apparently greatly elated at his last success and chants a low monotone of hideous joy, though he will not take the risk of creeping out to scalp his prey, for his comrades will soon be here ; then he can do it in leisure and safety.

He understands English quite well and knew all that Pete said to the little girl, but spared her for the moment, hoping to bring her parents to destruction through their love for their child, as he, being a father himself, understands such sentiments, having at this moment two little brown vipers of his own, safe at the San Carlos agency, fattening upon government rations, and about to have the arts of civilization added to their savage vices at a boarding-school projected by the Indian agent, who has just written to the Interior Department that his innocent wards are even now being cruelly persecuted by the unprincipled whites.

Having the father and mother dead before him, old Mescal is now keeping a sharp eye out for the child and the cowboy, that he may send them to the happy hunting grounds also.

Mr. Peter has been pondering on the situation too. He is cut off from both Clifton and Yorks. On the east, north, and south of him the Apaches are drawing near in a circle he cannot hope to pass alive. If he were alone he might try it ; but burdened with the child it is impossible.

To the west is the storehouse and one savage's repeating rifle. He must risk that ! But even as he makes his preparations for this desperate venture, he discovers this slight chance is lost to him ; for as he leads Possum to the door to throw it open, he sees the storehouse has three more Indians in it, who have come back by way of the river-bottom and dry ditch.

He might escape with life from one rifle, but to brave four, fired by men who can strike a running antelope, is certain destruction.

With a sinking heart he seizes the Englishman's field-glass and sweeps the plain, north, south, and east, hoping the smoke signals may have meant approaching aid either from citizens or soldiers; but there are no signs of Hatch's troopers to the north, nor of Volunteers on the east or south from Silver City.

The only change in the landscape that he notes is a small but very black cloud that seems to hang in the air quite low down over the peaks of the Mogollon Mountains.   This is drifting slowly southward.

Then he scans the west, or river side, not that there is much chance of aid coming from this direction, but still he wants to be sure ; and finding no moving objects there save his enemies in the storehouse, he for the first time this day begins to despair, for *he cannot defend both sides of the house at the same time*, and the attack is about to begin.

The Indians on the mesa are rapidly approaching ; those in the storehouse are beginning to shoot to keep his attention to the river side.

Mr. Peter begins to think very hard, for he knows if he lives this day through he will owe it rather to his head than his hands.

While he is thinking he is mechanically transferring the residue of Willoughby's cartridges to his own belt. As he does so he gives a little start, and seizing the field-glass once more brings it to bear upon the storehouse, searching with its powerful lens the interior of the cabin. A volley from the Indians knocks the adobe about him, but he scarcely heeds them, he is too excited.

A moment after he gives a little cry of joy, for a ray of sunlight entering a window in the storehouse shows him the box in which he remembers old Comming kept his giant powder for his mining operations.   There it is, marked in big black letters, " DANGEROUS."

If the old prospector has not let his stock run out. perhaps he has found life and revenge together—for among Willoughby's cartridges he has just seen a few explosive shells, manufactured to order, with which to kill grizzlies, for Englishmen always have different sorts of ammunition for different kinds of game.

If he can blow up this den of his enemies, the road to the river will be open, and an explosive shell in a box of giant powder is just the combination to do the business.

He has little time for his experiment, for bullets are beginning to strike the opposite side of the house. He hastily cuts off the magazine of his Winchester, using it as a breech-loader, and rams in a cartridge with an explosive bullet. Then taking a steady aim from a rest, he puts a ball into the giant-powder box—with no result. Either the shell has been defective or the box has been empty.

Almost tremblingly he loads again, and aiming a little lower so as to be sure to strike the giant powder, if there is any in the box—fires !

Before he can get the gun from his shoulder he is thrown almost stunned and breathless back on the mud floor of the adobe, while the two horses rear and stamp in terror, and old Comming's storehouse, with its four occupying fiends, in a puff of rising smoke and cloud of flying débris, with the condensed roar of a dozen thunderstorms, has disappeared from the face of the earth.

The road to the river is open ; but there are plenty more Apaches coming from the mesa behind him.

He throws open the door, and lifting, very tenderly, to his saddle the little girl, who has appeared since her parents' death half-stupefied and is now moaning, though she says no word, he springs upon Possum and dashes in a straight line for the San Francisco.

As he rides past the bodies of the English lady and her husband, the little girl cries out, " Papa ! mamma ! wake up and speak to me ! " struggling so wildly to get to her lost ones that he can hardly hold her on the horse.

But Pete has no time for sentiment, though tears are in his eyes ; so, clasping his charge firmly but tenderly to his breast, he spurs on over old Comming's dried-up garden, and finding an arroyo rides down it into the willows that shade the bank of the San Francisco. The river, which at this beginning of the rainy season, is hardly a foot deep, he crosses more leisurely, letting Possum drink, and scooping up the water in his *sombrero* for the refreshment of the child and himself. Then dashing the cool liquid over the little girl's face she is greatly revived, and begins to cry out bitterly to be taken back to her father and mother, who can't be really *dead;* for the child has never before looked on the king of terrors, and it is hard even for the old to realize they are suddenly bereft.

This Pete answers only by soothing words as he spurs quickly on.

Coming out of the river cañon by a steep trail the cowboy reaches the mesa on the west of the San Francisco, looks back and sees the pursuing Indians nearly at the stream. For a moment he hesitates and is about to turn Possum's head toward Clifton, but gazing that way sees a few more Apaches crossing the San Francisco farther up to cut him off.

As this strikes his eye he also sees that the black cloud from the Mogollon Mountains has grown much larger, much blacker, and much nearer, and is now drifting rapidly toward him.

Then he suddenly turns his horse's head southwest and rides straight for the Gila, in the direction of San José, Solomonsville, and the Pueblo valley settlements.

Seeing this, a faint yell of triumph comes over the plain from the Apaches; for they know he has nearly thirty miles to travel, and they will run him down, weighted as he is by the little girl, long before he can make half the distance.

But Pete only glances at the dark cloud, even now nearer and bigger, smiles a grim smile and rides straight for the box cañon of the Gila.

He knows the country very well, and has made up his mind that he has just so many miles to travel, *and no more.* Giving Possum his head he lets him run at top speed, for he wants to have time to cross the river and prepare himself before the Apaches reach its northern bank.

So the mustang dashes on, the mesa hotter and dustier than before, for, though quite late in the afternoon, the sun seems to grow more torrid as the day advances. Pete, all the while, trying to make his charge as comfortable as possible, first carrying her on one arm and then on the other, and growing very tender to the little thing in her beauty and helplessness, for her long chestnut hair and deep, big brown eyes remind him of the sweet English lady lying dead on the prairie behind him, as the orphan whispers in his ear, " You'll keep me from those bad men back there, just like you were my own papa, won't you, Mr. Peter?"

To this he only answers with a tender clasp, and the little child, knowing she may have his life for her service, if it will do her good, for children are very wise in these matters of the heart, puts two dimpled arms round his neck and whispers, " Kiss me, dear Mr. Peter, kiss me ! "

This he does very reverently, and she, giving a little sigh of content, puts her curly head trustingly upon his shoulder.

A few minutes after Pete utters an exclamation of delight; he has struck the Gila, and the stream is as he remembers it. For the river soon after it is joined by the San Francisco flows through what is called in the West a box-cañon ; that is, it cuts down through the plateau, flowing in a channel of varying width, between banks that on each side are precipices, sometimes going straight as a plumb-line down to the water, and sometimes with varying inclines, but nearly always impossible of descent or ascent ; a phase of nature common to these Western rivers, making them often grand, tremendous, and gigantic.

The cañon Pete is gazing at is not a large one ; its banks are in no places very high, and its waters are in no places very deep: still it is inaccessible from the mesa for some distance up and down the stream—*save at one ford.*

To this the cowboy rides like a whirlwind, for it is necessary to get down one bank and up the other before his enemies arrive at the crossing, and he is exposed to their rifles as he struggles up the cliff.

Possum seems to divine this himself, and, urged by his master's spurs, bounds down a trail that at any other time he would descend with trembling limbs, sure-footed as these mustang ponies generally are. In a minute Pete has descended to the river's edge, and as he dashes across through waters that hardly reach his saddle girth, the cowboy again uses his *sombrero* and dips up a drink for Flossie and himself.

Then they rush up the trail on the other side.

Almost at the top the little girl, looking back over his shoulder, suddenly cries out : " Bad men behind us again ! " A rifle shot echoes up and down the cañon, and Pete, though shivering and groaning, contrives to drop his little charge safely behind a boulder on top of the plateau. The next moment he falls from his saddle desperately wounded, and writhes to the shelter of a neighboring ledge of rocks ; while little Flossie runs to him and caresses him, crying out with horror, for he makes an awful picture covered with dust and blood.

Taking a quick look at his hurt he finds that the bullet has gone through his thigh, but no artery being wounded, though the loss of blood is great, he may have strength to lie down and use his gun for an hour or more ; which, as Pete sees the great black cloud that is nearer, bigger, and blacker than before, and now covers half the heavens, he thinks will perchance be long enough.

But he has no time to think more ; he must fight now !

So, racked with pain, and trembling with weakness, Pete, charging little Flossie to keep where she is and not stand up nor expose herself, crawls to the edge of the mesa, and sheltered by some rocks, looks down into the river bed.

The Indians having seen him fall have come down the trail, and are now rapidly but incautiously crossing the stream. Once on the same side of the Gila with him, that black cloud that is now wildly whirling up to itself the dust of both foot-hills and plains, will do its work in vain.

He rapidly opens fire.

Aiming with care, weak as he is, his shooting is tolerably close, and a minute after his pursuers retreat from the water with one man slightly wounded.

Then dropping behind boulders in the river bed, they try, by a close and rapid fire, to force him to keep his cover, while one of them attempts to cross the stream, shielded by a ledge of rocks that rises in the midst of the running waters.

But Pete himself takes desperate chances now, and contrives to shoot so close at this fellow that he gives it up and returns to the other bank.

And this being over the cowboy lies groaning with pain and feverish with thirst, looking at the black cloud and praying it will come faster, for in this second *mêlée* he has been wounded again.

A moment after a little hand is laid on his shoulder

and a sweet voice whispers to his ear: "Dear Mr. Peter, I have brought you some water—you look so thirsty now," and turning feverish eyes upon the child, he sees Flossie with a drink in her straw hat she has gathered from a little rivulet that trickles over the brow of the mesa into the cañon below.

This draught gives him renewed strength and life to fight for his ministering angel. But as he turns to do so he gives a start and cries: "What's the matter with your arm?"

And she holding her little dimpled member to him, he finds it bleeding from a rifle-ball that has glanced cuttingly across it, half-way between the shoulder and the elbow, and just below a tiny mole. It will heal in a week, but the mark will be on the child's beautiful arm forever.

He would bind it up, but has no time; for now, after a slight consultation, the Apaches are doing the one thing he has feared.

Some hold his attention shooting from the opposite bank, while others go up and down the river-bed, striving to cross the water, which is not very deep at any place. This they do hurriedly, for they know they have little time, and the black heavens to the north have told them the cowboy's plan.

Which is, to prevent their crossing the river until the coming cloud-burst separates them from him by a rushing torrent that no leviathan can ford, nor mammoth stand against.

So they come on, firing as their swarthy bodies glide from rock to rock, or from willow to cotton-wood; a few trees at this spot studding the bed of the cañon.

And now the magazine of Pete's Winchester does its work, for he shoots one through the body; but this does not stop the others, and one is half way across and another is just springing to the rocks on the cowboy's side of the river, immediately below him.

Upon this enemy Pete fires, but cannot see him, for though the sun has not yet set, a sudden blackness comes upon the earth around them and descends upon the waters beneath them, making the cañon dark as night.

And even as this happens, Heaven, for the first time this long day, comes to the assistance of this wounded man and helpless child.

There is a noise overhead like that of the exploding storehouse, and in one mighty roar the deluge descends. Almost in a minute the river is a wild, whirling, reddish flood, that carries pebbles on its surface as if they were corks, and rolls big boulders down its bed.

Next into the blackness of the night comes one tremendous, vivid, electric flash, lighting up the depths of the cañon. By it Pete sees the Apaches have reached the path on the opposite bank, and half way up its ascent are now safe from the flood. All save one!

This wretch is still on the same side of the river as Pete and the little English girl. He has gained a ledge of rock that juts out from the cliff over the hell of waters rising to engulf him, and is trying to climb the almost perpendicular surface, now made slippery by the rain that pours down every inch of the cañon walls.

Then all is black again, and Pete, taking the revolver from his belt, nervously waits for another flash ; for this one savage upon *his* side of the river is certain death to him, made helpless by many wounds, and the little girl he has suffered so much to save—should he gain the top of the mesa.

The lightning comes again, and on hands and knees, peering over, the cowboy finds himself staring in the face of this bronze human cat, who has contrived to climb where a monkey would hardly find a hold. The two glare at each other—not five feet apart : the Indian reaching for a root growing down the edge of the cliff to swing himself to a foothold on the mesa, the white man raising his revolver ; the lightning illuminating the scene with the light of a Doré picture.

Then the savage, whose gun is slung over his shoulder, getting his feet into some crevice of the precipice, makes the spring of a panther for his enemy's throat, and the American's revolver gives out its fatal bullet.

There is a death-cry that goes up over the roar of waters, and the Indian, falling into the torrent beneath, is carried whirling down the cañon of the Gila, to be ground to pulp against its boulders and rocky walls.

At the same moment a scattering volley is fired from across the stream, and Mr. Pete giving a little sigh sinks down senseless by the side of the little girl, who strives with childish caresses and endearments to bring back to life and motion this man she knows has suffered for her safety.

After a time the coldness of the air and the descending rain revive him, and he wakes to find the last volley has broken his right arm and made him entirely helpless ; but he looks across the cañon, upon which the sinking sun is again shining, and sees the Apaches well on their way to the north, while separating them still rolls the Gila, flooded and impassable.

The smoke signals all up and down the range tell him the Indians will not dare to linger in the valley—that they are saved ; and he gives a faint cheer and goes to sleep again, watched over by the child, who has brought him water once more from the little creek.

Thus the sun goes down upon them, Flossie lying in her wounded protector's arms.

About the middle of the night he again begs for water, which his little Samaritan again supplies him, for the fever of his wounds is now upon him. Then he frightens the child, for he begins to rave and cries out : " Line up, boys. The Blue above the Crimson ! " and sings his college songs and gives out his college cries, and then the cries of all other colleges ; which is perhaps well for the safety of the little girl, as they keep at a respectful distance a band of roving coyotes that have scented death in the air, and have come down to get a meal.

These wary scavengers of the prairies are accustomed to the noises of the wilderness, but have never encountered such insane sounds as this raving college cowboy, who utters the war-notes peculiar to our institutions of learning, gives out. And when Pete in one wild moment gives them a deep sepulchral *Y! A! L! E!*—YALE ! succeeded by a series of Harvard Rah ! *Rah!* RAH's ! and followed up by a Princeton sky-rocket, with a terrific s-s-sis-BOOM !—A–A–AH ! the coyotes burst into a yelling chorus, and sticking their tails between their legs, fly from this creature who can make more horrid music than themselves.

So it comes to pass, early next morning, a band of volunteers from Silver City, headed by Brick Garvey, who have been following up the trail of the redskins, crossing the Gila, that has again fallen to its usual stream, and coming upon the mesa, are surprised to see a piebald pony grazing contentedly on gramma-grass, and to hear a brown-haired, hazel-eyed little girl calling out: "Wake up, Mr. Peter ; it's morning ! WAKE UP !" Then seeing the frontiersmen, she cries : "You're not bad men like the Indians ; help me wake up dear Mr. Peter, who is *very* cold ; so cold that sometimes I think he's like my dear papa and mamma—DEAD !"

CHAPTER VI.

BRICK GARVEY'S INQUEST.

"By the etarnal !" cries Garvey, "if it ain't Pete !"

In a moment they are all about the prostrate cowboy, who is just breathing. One of them, a local practitioner from Silver City, who has volunteered to come as doctor with the party, makes a hurried examination.

"Wal, Doc., what's the chances ?" asks the sheriff anxiously.

The young medical man shakes his head.

"Has he passed in his chips ?" queries the leader.

"Not yet—but he's going to."

"Not if I can help it, young sawbones," cries Garvey. "Put the divine fluid inside him. Whiskey's the best antidote for snake pizens, Injin bullets, and all other kinds of disease. Fill him with whiskey, bullet-holes and all."

The doctor does as he is told, and Pete after a time partially revives, though still delirious and incapable of giving any account of the affair.

Meantime others of the band, in their homely but kindly Western way, have attended to the little girl's wants ; and comforted by something to eat, Flossie gives them her childish version of what has taken place. How the bad dark men had made a bang noise, and her dear, dear mother had tumbled down and sighed and closed her eyes ; and her father had run to help and they had done the same to him ; and that Mr. Peter had taken her on a horse and ran with her to the place she now is, and had "fight-ted" the Indian men till the rain had filled the river, and had been very good to her and sang songs and called out all night, and frightened a whole herd of little doggies away.

Now, Mr. Garvey having followed the trail of the savages, all this is already known to his frontier senses as well as if he had seen it take place, though he does not yet understand the reason of the explosion of old Comming's storehouse, and questions Flossie on the subject, but can only make out from her tale that some way or other it was "Pete's doings that blew the Injuns up."

Adding their experience to the child's information, they all become impressed with the fight that Pete has made to save the little girl, and Garvey, who is proud of his Eastern protégé, remarks, gazing with eyes that are suspiciously moist at the form of the young man, who is writhing in delirium upon a pile of blankets hastily thrown on the ground, " Pete war the grittiest tenderfoot I ever seed. If he pulls through I'll make a man of him, even though he comes from Mass'chusitts, a place whar I'm told they breed philanthropodists."

" What are they ? " asks the young doctor, with a sneer on his face at Garvey's vocabulary.

" Philanthropodists, young man," remarks Mr. Garvey oracularly, "are cusses that love Injuns. And, by the soul of Sam Houston ! when I think of yesterday's divilments, I feel like scalping every philanthropodist in the country ! "

" There's a lot of them down at Lordsburgh now," says one of the party. " Raymond excursioners going to Californie. I heard 'em in their Pullman car talking about the outrage of sending troops after the poor Apaches."

" The *divil*, you say ! "

" Yes, they were expressing their ideas on the cruelty of murdering Injins."

" *Murdering* Injins ! " cried Garvey; "next thing we'll hear of assassinating rattlesnakes. Them philanthropodists are at Lordsburgh NOW ? "

" Yes ; they'll hardly git away from thar for another day or two—the track's been washed out by cloudbursts ahead of 'em."

At this news Mr. Garvey rolls his eyes in meditation, but a moment after astounds his followers by giving a 'remendous " Hoop ! Ki-Yi ! "

"What's struck you, Cap ?" says his lieutenant.

" Nothen but an idea," returns the sheriff.   Then he orders them to take the bodies to Lordsburgh to have them inquested there.

Some of his followers rather demur to this, saying that Comming's ranch is in Arizona, and it'll be against the law.

" Agin the law ? " cries Garvey. " True, we found them ar bodies in Arizona, but 'tain't far to the line, and what's to prove they weren't shot in our territory ? Besides, I'm Breckinridge Garvey, the sheriff of Grant County, New Mexico, and I'm going to have, in the town of Lordsburgh, in my jurisdiction, an inquest that will make philanthropodists shake in their boots, and be writ about in big type by the newspapers."

No one answers Mr. Garvey, for there is a very wild light in his steel gray eyes and a very earnest tone in his hearty Western voice.

His orders are obeyed, and some taking charge of Pete and the little girl, who clings to her erstwhile protector, and begs not to be taken from dear Mr. Peter, they retrace their way to Comming's ranch ; from which place they bring the bodies of Captain Willoughby and his wife, together with those of two unfortunate herders found killed farther up the valley. Then making a long night ride of it, for it is cooler travelling and Garvey seems in a great hurry, they pass Yorks and George Guthrie's ranches, and fording the Gila at Carroll's jin-mill, they come out on the great plains, and passing the ten-mile mounds, they get into Lordsburgh early in the morning, to find the Pullman car with its Raymond excursionists still waiting the train despatcher's orders.

Seeing this, the sheriff mutters sternly, " I've got 'em ! " Then turns and hurriedly asks, " Is Hank Johnston in town ?" and receiving an answer that that young frontier lawyer is even now in the Ormsby House, he bolts upstairs to find Mr. Johnston in the act of dressing.

In his bedroom they have an animated ten-minutes interview, and discuss one or two law points, Garvey leaving his legal adviser with this significant remark, " If you do this business right cute, Hank, it'll put you into Congress next election sartin as you're out of it now ! " A speech which places such a grin on Johnston's face that he narrowly escapes cutting his throat, being at the moment struggling with a dull razor and wiry beard.

Coming down-stairs on to the sidewalk from this conversation, Mr. Garvey is immediately addressed by a young man of English appearance and manner, who hastily introduces himself as Mr. Arthur Willoughby, of London, England.

He has very bright dark eyes that come from his Italian mother, and are in great contrast to the Saxon blue ones of the man who had been his elder brother, but is now dead.

He speaks hurriedly and with perhaps a little agitation. " You are the officer who headed the militia to march after the Indians ? "

" Yes, I'm your man," replies Garvey, shortly, for he has a good deal to do this morning.

" Then perhaps you can tell me if anything has happened to Captain Thomas Willoughby and his family. I'm his brother."

" My poor fellow," returns the sheriff in a low tone, " I'm not good at breaking bad news.   Your brother and his wife were murdered by the red brutes two days ago."

" Good Lord ! " gasps the young Englishman, and he appears deeply agitated.   Then he says slowly and very anxiously, " My little niece ? "

"Oh, Miss Flossie ? " says Garvey, glad to give some little comfort.   "She's getting her breakfast in the dining-room, and is as well and hearty as a child can be." Then he cries suddenly : " Great Gosh ! I broke this cursed news too sudden," for at his last words his listener's face grows very pale—he reels and supports himself against the wall of the hotel, in front of which they are speaking.

For the Ormsby House has only one stairway, and that is on its outside, and they are talking at the foot of this on the sidewalk.

After a moment or two, the young man by an effort pulls himself together again and whispers : " It can't be possible."

" Yes, it is, my poor boy ; your brother and his wife are in that house, being prepared for the inquest," mutters Garvey, pointing to a building south of the railroad track near the hotel.

" But it is not possible the Indians killed the parents and spared the child. I've heard too much about them to believe *that !* " returns Arthur, as if he would not admit the little girl had escaped.

" You're perfectly kirrict in your jidgment of Injins, young man," says the sheriff. " Your niece would have been dead with her daddy and mammy only she war saved by a brave man who risked his life, and perhaps lost it, for the kid's sake."

At this Arthur Willoughby's lips move, though no sound comes from them.

" As soon as you get through praying for him I'll take you to the child, and then we'll see what can be done for Pete. This ride on top of his wounds would kill any breathin' critter but a cowboy. He's a leetle out of his head now ; thar's two docs with him." With these words Mr. Garvey leads Arthur Willoughby, who seems too much overcome to have a will of his own, into the hotel dining-room, where they meet Miss Flossie, who has been under the motherly hands of some kind woman, and has just finished her breakfast.

At the sight of Arthur she bursts into weeping, and sobs out that her dear father and mother have been killed by Indians ; that she has only him and dear Mr. Peter to take care of her now.

"You'd like to see Pete, I suppose," remarks Mr. Garvey, after a moment.

"Yes, certainly ; he may have some papers," mutters the young man, and follows the sheriff, who leads Flossie by the hand, to a chamber that has been made as comfortable for the wounded man as loving hearts and kind hands could with only frontier conveniences, for Pete's exploit has got about Lordsburgh, and every one in it, including "Russian Bill," its pet desperado, is anxious to do something for the cowboy hero.

This room is immediately next the large one that will be used for the inquest ; both are entered directly from the ground alongside the railroad tracks, but there is a communicating door between.

On a bed in this apartment, the windows of which are all open to catch what little breeze there may be, for the heat of the Gila plains in summer is as scorching as that of a Libyan desert, the wounded cowboy lies. His head is done up in bandages, and he seems only semi-conscious. This is probably the result of morphine given during the doctors' work upon him, they having probed for and extracted the bullets that were in him, and set and bandaged his shattered arm. This has been put in a sling and lies over his breast as he rests upon his back, breathing deeply but quietly. His eyes, though dull and heavy, have a curious, wandering expression in them.

A hotel barkeeper is sitting and watching over him, a lemonade in his hand that he is administering to the sufferer with the tenderness of a woman. On seeing the sheriff, this man moves quietly back and lets him approach the bed.

" Pete, old fell '," whispers Garvey, bending over him, " I've brought you the little gal's uncle to thank you for saving her life."

Flossie, who has run to the other side of the cot, presses tenderly his uninjured left hand, and babbles: " Dear Mr. Peter, I'm so glad to see you comfortable. I hope the doctor will make you well soon, and so does Uncle Arthur." Then she points to the young Englishman, who is standing at the foot of the cowboy's bed looking at him in that unmeaning manner peculiar to a certain class of the English race, a stare that is too fathomless to be read by any play of feature or movement of eye or lip, for there is none, though Garvey, who is no physiognomist, thinks to himself " the Britisher's gratitude is hardly up to the requirements." He, however, says nothing, for at this moment Pete, following Flossie's hand, notices Arthur Willoughby.

As he does so, he half raises himself in bed, his eyes seem to light up with a feverish fire of anger and contempt, and he mutters, though the syllables come slowly: " The brain of a Machiavelli and the heart of one of those brutes—out there ! " And trying to point to the distant mesa with his wounded arm gives a groan of anguish, his eyes become dull again, and he falls back upon the pillow.

" Poor divil, raving ag'in ! " mutters Garvey. " Who ever heard in these parts of a Mach-o-vil ? Best come away and give him a chance to rest." Then he glances at the ministering barkeeper and says : " You'll stay with him, Jimmy, until relieved ? " And being answered with a nod from the mixer of drinks, Mr. Garvey, who is in a hurry about his inquest, leaves the room. He has already reached the plank used as a sidewalk when the young Englishman overtakes and stops him.

"He may have some papers belonging to my niece? Couldn't you get them for me, my good man ?" he remarks to the sheriff.

"Get 'em? Get 'em yourself! And look heah, people round these diggins don't call me 'my *good* man,' for they know I'm a tarnation *bad* one when I'm riled, sonny!" returns Garvey, his lips growing a little more set and slightly thinner, for he is not pleased at the patronizing tone or language of the remark.

"Oh, no offence, I assure you, Mr. Sheriff," answers Arthur. "But there may have been some papers given that—awh—wounded cowboy by my brother——"

"Thar war some papers."

"Ah !"

"And I've got 'em," continues Garvey. "But I ain't read 'em, and sha'n't till he's dead ; and if he don't die he'll settle what he does with them himself. So you come round when Pete's passed in his checks or got about, and we'll fix the documents."

At the word documents, Willoughby starts. He says excitedly : "But I'm going to England, you know. I carn't wait till the cowboy gets well or dies."

"All right ! leave your address with me, and if thar's any you ought to have they'll be forwarded by mail." Then leaving the Englishman gazing after him, the sheriff strides off to put his inquest in motion.

Standing by the railroad track with a bare head, the sun must daze Arthur Willoughby for a moment, for he hisses, though under his breath, these extraordinary words : "The fool would have been more civil if he'd known he was talking to an English peer." Then he stops suddenly, and looking at his little niece, who is in the open doorway, gazing at her defender who has grown restless and is tossing upon his cot, his eyes grow sly and cunning and cruel, and what Mr. Garvey would call "a Greazer expression" comes into them, as he mutters : "Not yet !" and looking at the cowboy, laughs the yellow laugh of disappointment, then sighs : "That infernal fool spoilt the most successful *coup* I ever invented."

A moment after, a smile comes over his face, and the Italian eyes grow sunny as he calls, "Come along, my sweet little Flossie—come with your uncle Arthur," and is leading the child back to the Ormsby House, when a deputy-sheriff steps up to him and says, "You won't mind bringing this little girl to the inquest? The coroner wants her deposition."

"Oh, ah, yes! the inquest, of course," returns Arthur. "They'll have it soon, I hope; we are going to leave by the next train for the East, you know." Here he pauses and remarks, after a moment's hesitation, "As soon as I have made arrangements for the funeral, and it has taken place." For the deputy is gazing at him in wonder that this foreigner seems to have forgotten the dead man and woman lying shrouded in the room in front of him, who have been his nearest relatives upon earth, and one of whom, a beautiful English lady, he has just accompanied from her pretty Sussex home to meet a cruel and violent death.

"You won't have long to wait for the inquest," remarks the man.

As he speaks, such masculine exclamations of surprise, indignation, and horror, mingled with one or two small screams from women, come from the Pullman car nearest to them that Arthur cries out, "Good heavens, what's that?"

"That," says the deputy-sheriff, with a curious look on his face, "IS MR. GARVEY SERVING HIS SUBPENIES ON THE PHILANTHROPISTS AND ROUNDING UP FOR HIS CORONER'S JURY THE RAYMOND EXCURSIONISTS!"

In this he is perfectly right. At present a great scene is taking place in the interior of the Pullman car.

There are two of these drawn up upon the track, awaiting telegraphic orders from the train-despatcher that will permit them to proceed. One of these, the more modern and luxurious of the two, has the car number 427, and is occupied solely by a very aristocratic and dignified woman of perhaps forty-five; she has evidently recently lost her husband, as she wears a widow's weeds. She is accompanied by a charming girl of fourteen or fifteen, also in full mourning, and is attended by a maid servant. She is in no way connected with the passengers in the other car, the magnificent Pullman she occupies having arrived only the night before attached to another train.

The other sleeper, which is rather shabby and road worn, is crowded by a lot of excursionists whom the energetic Raymond has lured by promise of a cheap trip to the Pacific slope from their native haunts in New England.

They have just got out of their narrow shell into the great West, and don't like its course on the Indian question. Imbued with true philanthropic ignorance, accepting that half-truth that the savage has all the wrongs on his side, and the settler and pioneer have none ; never having seen the noble red man on his native soil, they know not his debauchery, his worthlessness, his cruelty —they are not even aware that no man who has ever known the Indian as he really is, wild, wicked, and lazy, thinks there are any good Indians but dead Indians.

And now cooped up for three burning days in this little railroad station on the Gila plateau, they have struck the Indian question in full practical operation, and have been giving their views upon it to the rage of those who have suffered loss of fortune or friends or family from Apache raids.

This very morning, headed by one Rogers, an agriculturist, who has never been kept awake fearing savages on his New Hampshire farm, they have formed a meeting, and are about to send a protest to Washington on behalf of the persecuted red man.

As Garvey enters, the chairman has just begun reading the following address :

" To the President of the United States :
We, the undersigned, having witnessed, with horror in our hearts and tears in our eyes, the departure of armed bands of cow boys as well as United States troops from Lordsburgh to murder the peaceful, long-enduring Apaches of our reservations——"

At these words a baneful light springs into the sheriff's eyes, his hand goes to his revolver, and did Rogers know it, he would fall down and beg for mercy, being in greater peril of his life than has ever before come to him

in his sleepy bucolic existence. But controlling himself
with a mighty effort, Mr. Garvey simply says: "Stop,
stranger!—quit talking about things you are as ignorant
of as a nigger! I've got a supenee for ye, Ephram Doe
Rogers!"

"A subpœna," cries the New Englander. "For what?"

"A supenee to act on the coroner's jury."

"Pough! I'm not a citizen of the territory," cries Mr
Rogers airily. "Don't interrupt this meeting, sir!"

"No, I ain't going to interrupt this meeting. I'm
simply going to bag it for the coroner's jury. I got
supenees for every man of ye," says Garvey in a low but
determined voice, and he reads them out: "Asa Doe
Bullock, Hiram Roe Filkins, John Doe, Richard Roe,
etc., etc.," and forces a legal document into the trembling
hands of each one of the men; for he has a long, black
murderous revolver in the other that makes one of the
women shriek, "He's a road agent!" and fall on her
knees to him.

"My dear madam," says Mr. Garvey; he has learned
this form of address among the Creoles when a boy and
always uses it in cases of extreme politeness. "Ladies
and children are always safer for Brick Garvey's being
round; so is tenderfoots; but these men heah don't
know that the law permits a coroner to git his jury whar
he can find 'em, and they are going into that room to furnish a verdict on the men and woman murdered by their
Apache friends, and that ar verdict is going to be in
accord with the facts of the case, OR THE LORD HAVE
MARCY ON THE JURIES' SOULS!

"Ye'll march in ahead of me, gints," he says, "or there'll
be more inquests this morning." One or two of them
hesitate, but he calls out, "I war given this medal by the
Texas Legislature for killing Injuns, and I'd like a dupli-
cate of it from the New Mexican one for laying out
their sympathizers!"

Looking at him the men of the Raymond party see
death in his face, and without a word leave the car; and
followed by Garvey, who keeps his awful eyes on them,
they step into the room, where they are promptly sworn as
jurymen by an energetic young coroner.

The women of the party, filled partly with indignation,
partly with curiosity, and most of them wholly with sorrow,

for up to this time they had not heard of the death of any whites, and had, with a kind of moral atrophy, imagined that the Indians were the only sufferers, follow after.

The lady from the other Pullman car has just walked to the local post-office and inquired if the postmaster can give her the address of a gentleman living in the neighborhood named Philip Everett.

Not gaining the information she desires, and seeing the throng pass in to the coroner's investigation, she follows, and finds herself gazing upon a sight that holds her partly in horror, partly in sympathy.

Seated on one side of the room are the excursionists empanelled as jurors; beside them Mr. Garvey; in front of them the coroner; around the sides of the room, some of the men smoking, some chewing, some of the women fanning themselves, are the adult population of Lordsburgh, mixed with cowboys from the neighboring plains; miners from the adjacent mountains, some of Smyth & Babcock's teamsters, and a few railroad hands and colored porters from the cars now detained upon the tracks.

Most of them are in their shirt sleeves or dusters, the sun being scorching hot. Silence is upon them all. Their eyes are turned toward a little platform made with rough boards.

Upon this dais are six quiet forms, each covered with an ample white sheet; for to the victims Garvey's party have brought in have been added the bodies of some capitalists and mining experts, who, having come to this country to examine and buy a silver mine, have been ambushed by Nana's braves and shot down, as, unconscious of danger, they rode chatting and laughing along the trail.

So the murdered lie, similar and equal in death, save that a few wild flowers, gleaned from beside some irrigation ditch, and placed by tender hands upon the dead English lady, show that she is of the sex they honor and reverence in the Far West more highly and more tenderly than in any other land upon this earth.

A little to the side of these white forms are the witnesses, one a sunburnt cavalryman from Hatch's troopers, and among them sits Arthur Willoughby, holding on his knee his little orphan niece, who has tears in her eyes, for she knows she is in the presence of her dead mother.

In front of all this, his eyes flashing, his voice raised

in inspired oratory, is Hank Johnston; he knows the op portunity of his lifetime has come to him and he is going to use it. For this man, like poor Frank Tilford of California, was one of the few men in the West who still held that almost forgotten but magic art of oratory, the last exponents of the subtile power by which Webster and Clay, and Douglas and Prentice swayed men's souls.

No man who hears and sees Hank Johnston this day ever forgets the burning eloquence of his words or the vivid pathos of his gestures.

He addresses himself entirely to the excursionists; he knows no words can paint a picture to the New Mexican or Arizona pioneer equal to the horror of his own experiences. He tells these sight-seers from the East of the awful life of men who exist with the apprehension of sudden and cruel death always hanging over them as they pursue their daily vocations of peaceful industry—of the mother shuddering for her offspring who has been borne into captivity—of the husband reaching home at night from his cattle range or his mine to find the wife of his bosom murdered and his children slain and mutilated amid the smouldering ashes of his frontier home. "You who call yourselves philanthropists," he cries, "have grasped that mental 'will o' the wisp'—a *half* truth. You have sympathized with the Indians' *wrongs*. Now behold his VENGEANCE—on the innocent!" and he lifts up the covering from the dead.

At the awful sight a thrill of horror comes over the assemblage, and Arthur Willoughby turns his face away and buries it in his hands, and many others look down.

Then Garvey says in a quiet but deathly voice, "The jury will now inspect the bodies," and forces every man of them to gaze upon the work of the Apache.

And they do so with horror in their shuddering faces, while some of the women come and bend over the dead English lady and weep for her and pray for her. And to women's tears are now added those of men, for little Flossie suddenly cries out, "Let me pray, too, for my dear, dear mother who kissed me yesterday, but now is— in heaven!" and throws herself beside the dead face that seems to smile on her.

This gives the lawyer an inspiration. He says quietly

"What would my words be to the eloquence of this child.   She shall tell you of her own bereavement."

So they swear the little thing, Garvey in a choking voice speaking the solemn words to her, and holding a worn-out Bible for her rosy lips to kiss.

Standing up she gives her testimony in childish pathos and baby voice ; and tells how her darling mother, and her dear father she had come all the way from England to kiss, had been " shooted and killed," and how brave Mr. Peter had saved her from the bad dark men ; and she has only him to be kind to her now.

"But you have your uncle, Flossie, to protect and love you," mutters Arthur Willoughby, his dark eyes turned on the child as if he had a great and potent use for her.

"Bereft of parents the orphan turns to you, and may God do to you as you do to her ! " whispers the lawyer, and would put her in the young man's outstretched arms; ——but she is suddenly plucked away from his grasp, and an awful voice cries : " NOT TO HIM ! "

And they all see Pete the cowboy, who, some one having opened his door, the heat being so great, has staggered in with trembling limbs, and stands with band- aged head and arm, and glaring, rolling, fevered eyes, his one uninjured hand pointing at Arthur Willoughby who seems to cower from him.

Then he breaks out again in words that no one under- stands, for he mutters : " *Not till he explains that lying telegram that sent——*"

Then he suddenly pauses and reels, for the lady from the Pullman car is crying at him in a voice of love and horror : " MY SON ! PHILIP, MY SON ! "

Looking at her the cowboy screams : " MOTHER ! MY MOTHER ! AT LAST !" and springs toward her.   Then the blood bursts from a reopening wound, and he falls senseless and helpless upon the breast that nurtured him in childhood.

For a moment all is commotion ; next Garvey's voice is heard : " Pete's mother, boys.   Do what she wants ! " And they carry him out to the stateroom of Mrs. Ever- ett's Pullman car, where the doctor again examines him, and says that his life before hung on a thread, and is afraid the last excitement has snapped it.

A moment after they take up the inquest again and

make short work of it, for the Eastern excursionists bring in the strongest verdict ever brought against Apache murderers in the territory; and call for the prosecution of various Indian renegades, naming particularly Nana, their chief, together with other persons unknown to them.

" I reckoned that would be about your figure," says Garvey, shaking hands with the foreman. " No man ever seed Injin doings and didn't want 'em killed *quick!* The East only needs to know the West to cotton to it, and the North and South 'll agree better when their hands grip tighter! Let's liquor—all hands!'

This they do; and two hours after they all attend the burial of the victims; then, the road being in working order to the west, the train bears away the Raymond excursionists, waving their hands and shouting farewells to Hank Johnston and Mr. Garvey, who mutters, " Them philanthropodists are all right when you put the philanthropodie in the right place." Next he says suddenly to the lawyer, " Hank, what do you think Pete could have meant by that ' lying telegram ' he called out so queer about?"

" Oh, some hallucination of his fever. You're not going to take seriously the ravings of a delirious cowboy, are you, Garvey?" answers Johnston, who has been mightily annoyed at Pete's *coup de théâtre*, which has detracted from his own great effort.

" I reckon you must be right, Hank," returns Garvey. " I stepped down to the telegraph office and there war no despatches for any of them Willoughbys, dead or living. I'm going up to see if Pete's sinsible again, for if I allowed thar war anything underhanded in the taking off of that pretty lady as has just been planted, there'd be lynching round heah! I don't like that Britisher critter's black eyes; they've got too much Greaser in 'em to suit me.'

With these words the sheriff walks off to the Pullman, in which the wounded cowboy lies, and asks respectfu.ly for Pete's mother.

He is met at the door by the pretty girl of fifteen, who introduces herself as Miss Bessie Everett, Philip's sister, and requests the Westerner to come into the vestibule of the car, saying that she has heard of the celebrated Mr. Garvey in some of her brother's letters from Silver City

A moment after, they are joined by Mrs. Everett, who with outstretched hand and tearful eye, thanks him for the kindness he has done her son.

"That's nothin' to brag about, mam," returns Mr. Garvey. "I did my duty by him as I would by any immigrant whose feet war too tender for frontier boots. But if possible I'd like to have a little confab with Pete afore you take him East to nurse him up, as I hears you're going to."

"Certainly," replies the lady; "only my poor boy recognizes no one now, not even his mother." Then she leads the way to the stateroom of the car, where Philip Everett is in delirium, going over his fight with the Apaches.

Looking on this Mr. Garvey gives a little sigh, and remarks in a sympathetic voice: "'Tain't no use questioning him; but when he gits better, as I trust under your hands and God's marcy he will, jist ask him to write me what he meant by that 'lying telegram' he spoke of ; unless it was, as I reckon, only raving and crazy talk." Then producing from his pocket the package of letters the cowboy had taken from Captain Willoughby's shooting jacket, and handing the parcel to Mrs. Everett, he remarks: "I did 'em up in a big envelope cause they war a leetle—" He stops himself suddenly, it's hard to speak to a mother of a son's blood, and says: "Give 'em to Pete when he's better ; and if he dies, look over 'em yourself, and if any belongs to that young Willoughby, send 'em to this address."

Next he wrings the widow's outstretched hand and mutters: "When he gets all right let him come back to me and I'll make him. He war the toughest tender-foot I ever met. After his doings of t'other day we think a mighty sight of him round here, and some day, when his hoofs get tougher, we'll send him to Congress or do some other handsome thing by him. Give Pete this kiss from Brick Garvey;" and to the astonishment of the Eastern lady, he gives her a very hearty frontier embrace ; then patting Miss Bessie on the head, and bestowing upon her a similar favor, he strides out of the car.

A moment after, with a sigh, Mrs. Everett writes her son's name on the envelope.

While this has been going on, Arthur Willoughby has been engaged in preparation for his return to England. This has chiefly consisted in a rather curious interview with the coroner.

This young official he finds in a neighboring bar-room, throwing poker dice for drinks. Entering into conversation with him Arthur Willoughby, who has the Italian faculty of being very courteous when he wishes to be, soon becomes on friendly terms with the gentleman he is in pursuit of. Together they take a drink or two of fiery Valley Tam, that makes the young Englishman cough and splutter, and discuss the affair of the morning, the New Mexican official stating that it is the "he-est" inquest that has ever taken place in the territory.

This opens the way for Mr. Willoughby, who remarks that it will help him in settling up his brother's estate if he has an official copy of the verdict of the coroner's jury as to the death of his brother and his wife, asking to know the price of such a document.

" Five dollars to you," remarks the official addressed ; and, receiving the money, departs with Arthur for his office to make a copy of the same and attest it with his official seal.

This he makes up, filling in the names of all the Apache victims. As he is about to write the name of Captain Willoughby's wife, Arthur suddenly stops him, saying : " I believe you have made a mistake there. The name of my sister-in-law, murdered by the Apaches, was Florence, not Agnes."

" Why, the little girl's name is Florence," remarks the Westerner.

" Oh—ah—certainly, the child was named after her mother."

" Then I will soon fix that," returns the coroner, and promptly inserts Florence in the document, which now reads : " Captain Thomas Willoughby and his wife Florence ——"

There is a space of some three inches more upon the line, which the official leaves blank, beginning the next one with the names of the murdered capitalists.

With frontier haste he had already placed his official seal upon the document before filling in the names, and as he is making the correction the young Englishman,

looking out of the window, suddenly cries : " By Jove !
what's that row in the Pioneer saloon ? " pointing to a
rambling establishment opposite.

" Must be a fight between Russian Bill and Patsey
Marley ! If so, it means biz for me ! " cries the coroner,
and bolts hurriedly from the room, grasping his revolver
as he goes.

The young Englishman hurriedly adds two more words
to the document with the same pen and ink, in the blank
space after the name " Florence," and folding up the
paper places it in his pocket.

Then he saunters to the door to meet the returning
coroner. " Only a false alarm," mutters the official to
him ; " I'll finish up the inquest for you now."

" Never mind, I have saved you the trouble. It was
only the addition of a word," remarks Arthur. " Let's
liquor, as you express it in New Mexico."

With this the two return to the saloon, the young
Englishman bearing in his pocket an official record of
the inquest that would have astonished any one of those
who had been present at the same.

A few minutes after he finds the office of the notary
public and says to him : " You know the coroner's signature ! " " Certainly," replies that official. " Then please
certify to that signature under your seal." This is soon
done, for the coroner's handwriting is as familiar to the
notary as his own.

That evening the train leaves for the East bearing in
one car Philip Everett, in the delirium of surgical fever,
and tended by the loving hands of his mother and sister,
and in another Pullman, Arthur Willoughby carrying little
Flossie home to England.

As the train rolls out of Lordsburgh, it receives a
touching " send-off " from Mr. Garvey, who is on hand
with a number of his followers, cattlemen, and cowboys.
The sheriff says quietly, " Pete's mother, pards ! " and
they all respectfully and reverently take off their hats
and stand with uncovered heads, as the locomotive puffs
its way toward Eastern civilization.

Something like twenty-four hours after this they stop
at Pueblo, Colorado.

There Arthur Willoughby, though supposed to be *en
route* for England. leaves the train, taking with him his

little charge, giving as an excuse that he has mining interests in this state that claim his attention for a week or two.

Two months after this, amid the perfume blown into the windows of the Beacon street mansion from the flowers and shrubs of the beautiful Boston botanical gardens, Pete the cowboy awakes to a new life. The West has passed away from him, the East is around him. Hardship and poverty have been replaced by luxury and wealth, for his mother whispers in his ear, "Your father is dead, but he forgave you and remembered you in his will."

Yet his thoughts still turn to the frontier, and while lying in his mother's arms he asks curiously, perhaps doubting, "I saved little Flossie Willoughby from the Apaches, didn't I ?"

"Ah !" says Mrs. Everett, "don't think of that awful time ; it will bring the delirium back to you."

"Not if I'm satisfied on that point," says the young man, eagerly. "Tell me !"

"Then if you ask no more questions," replies his mother, "the pretty little English girl went home with her uncle eight weeks ago, alive and well ! "

"Thank God !" cries the invalid. A moment after he mutters, "I suppose Willoughby got the packet of papers all right ?"

To this his mother whispers, "Hush ! no more excitement at present ! " and turns away with a little troubled look, for she has just remembered that the documents Phil mentions have somehow or other been lost or mislaid by her on her journey to the East.

But, curiously enough, on the very day this conversation takes place, Arthur Willoughby is in the act of sailing from New York on the *Arizona* for England—ALONE !

BOOK II.

A DENVER BELLE.

CHAPTER VII.

DIARY OF A WESTERN DEBUTANTE.

NEW YORK, *January* 3, 1890.

A DIARY *à la Bashkirtseff* is now a fad in fashionable young-ladyhood in New York.

I've been dying to commence mine. Like Marie, I have unsatisfied longings—lots of them !—but, unlike Marie, I'm going to get mine. Matilde Tompkins Follis doesn't fall off or sulk on the homestretch. She's always got a little extra speed in her, and gets under the wire first, most every time.

This article, that I clip entire from the *Town Tattler*, will give my diary a piquant send-off :

"It is announced on the highest authority that the languid young club-man, Augustus de Punster Van Beekman, will very shortly lead to the hymeneal altar Miss Matilde Tompkins Follis, who lately made her *début* in society at the Patriarchs, under the wing of Mrs. Aurora Dabney Marvin, the widow who makes a business of introducing so many Western heiresses into the portals of the 'Four Hundred.' This marriage will shove La Follis *plump in.*

"The young lady's *silvery* voice is said to have attracted the impecunious Augustus.

"The bride will look lovely at the altar in a complete costume of woven 'Baby' silver. from her father's great mine, 'The Baby.'

"MEM.—Were it not for the 'Baby' silver we hardly imagine Augustus would come to time. as he is very exclusive ; the proud blood of the De Punsters and Van Beekmans abhorring plebeian streams, though their family estates have wofully dwindled, since in early Dutch days they swindled the Indians out of many fair acres up the Hudson and on Manhattan Island."

This article from the *Town Tattler* is so atrociously striking that I paste it into my diary, malice and all, as I sit in my luxurious boudoir, at No. 637 Fifth Avenue, the residence my dad—I mean father—has taken for the winter, having removed mother and me from Capitol Hill, Denver, to Murray Hill, New York, in order that Colorado's richest heiress may make her *début* in metropolitan society.

I am struck by the article—partly with joy, mostly with rage.

Were I not such an *ennuyée* from my exertions at Mr. Mac's ball at the Metropolitan Opera House last night that I haven't spunk for anything, and were it "good form" in the East, I should lay out that editor in true Colorado style.

Pshaw! I am going back to the wild Tillie Follis of Aspen mining camp, six years ago, before I was sent to receive a coat of British fads and French polish at Madame Lamere's Academy, No. 327½ Madison Avenue, at which my younger sister still resides.

Upon consideration, I shall take no notice of the paragraph. I sha'n't remember I have ever read it. I sha'n't know such a paper as the *Town Tattler* exists. The whole article is evidently filled with the malice that low-bred society reporters generally feel for the aristocracy, whose champagne they drink in ante-rooms, and whose dinners they report from butlers' pantries.

I'd have the writer, whoever he or she is (its malicious flavor indicates femininity), know that I, Matilde Tompkins Follis, am not at the portals, but *am plump in the middle of the swim.*

Has not Mrs. Rivington Van Schermerhorn and the Misses Van Damm called upon me? Are not the cards of those society magnates, Mrs. George Van Tassel Nailer, Miss Alice May Catskill, the Hon. Mrs. Ross Dumboyle, and Clara Jenks Remington, upon my hall-table? Don't such well-known club *boys* (I can't call them *men*) as Bertie Van Tassel, Georgie Remsen. and

Foxhunter Reach drop in to my afternoon teas and talk horse to me? At which I can beat them all, having spent a good deal of my early life on a mustang. And did I not clench my position by last night, when, between the pauses of a lanciers, and drowned by the romantic crash of Lander's music, I practically accepted little A. de P. Van B. ?

The De Punster and Van Beekman families are in the very Walhalla of the Four Hundred, and though Augustus—I call him Gussie now—is regarded as a little off color, as we express it in Colorado, by the heads of the family, he belonging to a collateral branch that has had, like most aristocratic houses, a scandal (some time during the Revolution, I believe); but chiefly because, with the wildness necessary to be a "thoroughbred" (Gussie's own expression), he has run through a pot of money. Still, with the millions father is sure to give me, I think the De Punsters and Van Beekmans will take him once more into the family fold, and the Colorado heiress along with him.

But as I gaze at the *Town Tattler* I give a shudder. What will dad—I mean my father—say? For little Gussie is the most dudish dude in New York ; and though a washed-out descendant of the old Dutch stock, a maniac of the most ultra Anglo tendencies.

My ! how dad does hate dudes ! When I think of how he'll treat my poor little Gussie, I—shudder.

But I don't care so much for father; I reckon ma'll fetch him round all O.K. in a little time. It's Bob ! the brave-eyed Bob; Bob, the hero who saved the Baby Mine from the jumpers for us—how sad Bob 'll look, and how he'll hate Gussie. But it won't be because he's a dude ; it'll be because——

Oh, pshaw ! what nonsense I'm writing. And then what'll SHE say when she hears I've gone back on Bob ; she who bosses the family ; my erratic younger sister, who has a will of her own, and such eyes !—Florence, to use a Western expression, being a "corker" !

I remember once, a few years ago, when ma for some childish cutting up was going to correct us (the Eastern term for a Western spanking) ; she looked at ma with big brown, flashing, blazing eyes till mother turned away and muttered something and dropped her hand—and my mother has faced a grizzly in her time. I may also remark that I caught it—I tried the look, but it didn't work in my case.

What'll SHE say?

When I think of dad and Bob and Florence, I cry out: "Oh, fashion and triumph and greatness, you are not all roses!"

Pshaw! yes, they are!

When I think of what Sallie Jackson and Lavie Martin and other Capitol Hill girls would have said if they had seen me last night dancing with a lord—no Italian barber count like the one who did all the West up last year, but a real English baron—when I think of the sensation that would have struck feminine Denver had they seen Lord Avonmere making up to me last night in Sir Roger de Coverley, which is the British expression for the American Virginia reel (shade of George Washington! how English we are now!), I can stand anything, any one!—dad!—Floss!—Bob!

Yes, even Bob, though I am a wretch to say it.

Mrs. Marvin introduced Lord Avonmere to me last night. Mrs. M. seemed to wish to impress me with him; so also did Avonmere; he hung on to me at supper until Gussie got so jealous that he spoke quite unmistakably the very next dance.

Lord Avonmere is very English in appearance, though rather continental in expression; a big, hulking fellow, with soft, naughty, black Italian eyes, and looks as if he had run the pace. I mean to ask Mrs. Marvin about him. She hates Gussie, and this paragraph in the *Town Tattler* will drive her crazy.

It's lucky she's out, as the servant has just brought in Gussie's card.

Mother, who has come in from Arnold & Constable's, has also announced him, for she has remarked: "That chit's ag'in in the parlor!"

I wish ma would say drawing-room. It's much better form.

I'll lock this up and 'll go down and see Gussie A-a-ah! the fatal moment——"

CHAPTER VIII.

MRS. MARVIN, OF NEW YORK.

THE young lady who has been writing the preceding drops her pen, gives a little dainty shiver, and after a settling shake to her imported afternoon gown and a hurried glance at her charming reflection in a cheval glass, leaves her boudoir, which is a creation in blue by Tiffany, and descends to meet the little " Gussie " of her diary.

As she passes down the oaken stairs of the great Fifth Avenue house, for the use of which during the New York winter season, furniture, bric-à-brac, pictures, and all, her father, Abraham Alcibiades Follis, the great Denver silver-miner and millionnaire, has paid a very pretty penny, Miss Matilde makes a delightful picture.

She is a Western girl, and fresh as the breezes of her own prairies, not yet having lost the roses from her cheeks nor the brightness from her eyes by the all-night balls of winter and the long round of watering-place dissipations, which so often destroy the freshness and impair the beauty of our more fashionable Eastern belles, making them look aged and feel old at twenty, about the time in life they would be emerging from a European schoolroom.

With the daintiest of hands and feet, that charm so common in American women, her figure, though beautifully rounded and curved, and only slightly above the medium height, has the graces that come from out-door exercise and the fresh air of the Rocky Mountains; of which she had had plenty, having lived a good portion of her early youth in a tent when her father was moving about prospecting for mines, and in a dug-out when he was at a stationary camp.

To this true health and beauty of person add a very piquant, bright, feminine American face, with the bluest of eyes, not of the indefinite kind of washed-out, worn-out womanhood, but filled with the peculiar fresh. deep color of the wood violet, that becomes almost a purple when lighted by the fire of passion ; a little mouth that can grow very firm, an inheritance from her mother, a frontier woman who had fought Indians with her own hands in the Sioux outbreak in Minnesota ; place in her shapely head that quick grasp of humor, wit, logic, and idea, common to the women of any country where they are encouraged and permitted to think and act for themselves ; clothe her with the dainty taste that characterizes an American woman with an unlimited pocket-book, when assisted by a French *artiste de la mode ;* permit a glimpse of one little foot in its light satin slipper peeping from under her lace *jupons ;* cast over the face, in the changing pictures of a magic lantern, a little shuddering blush—then a pout—next a very savage frown, that runs away into a laugh of mixed amusement and chagrin, and it is the picture of Miss Matilde Follis as she trips down to encounter so much of her fate as Mr. Augustus de Punster Van Beekman may have for her.

That she has a quick mind is evinced by her rapid change of expression as she has descended the stairs, for from the top step to the bottom she has dissected a thought that has suddenly struck her vivacious brain like a shock of electricity.

Evolved from the article in the *Town Tattler*, it is not a pleasant one, being this curiously humiliating idea : If Mrs. Marvin makes a business of introducing Western heiresses, where does the money come into the transaction ?   What's the merchandise ?

As the answer flashes, ME and MY FORTUNE, the shuddering blush has come upon her ;—with the thought of her beauty and her money bringing a commission to the pocket of Mrs. Marvin has come the savage frown ;—then the certainty that little Gussie can't be a paying customer, the widow being so down on him, brings the laugh.

She mutters : " I only thought Aurora Marvin a sponge. If she's a speculator, Matilda Follis won't be one of her securities ! " And opening the portière, steps into a reception-room to meet her expectant *fiancé.*

In this sudden idea this young Western girl has guessed the truth, but hardly the whole of it.

Mrs. Aurora Dabney Marvin is one of the anomalies and curiosities of our so-called " fashionable society."

Being left a widow at the close of the war, with no capital but what is in Western parlance termed " unadulterated gall " and " colossal cheek," she has stocked and capitalized this in social dollars, and has lived off it in luxury and plenty, and will so continue to do as long as American society is what it now is.

Beginning with no position whatever, Mrs. Marvin had made herself somewhat of a social power, by marvellous tact and unblushing assumption ; the first of which had given her the *entrée* into many of the houses of the more exclusive New York set, and the second of which had made her imagine she owned the family as soon as she had got inside their front door.

Most of her income had been produced by assuming to lecture for charity, with a check from the committee of the entertainment in her pocket. Her lectures on " The Kings I have met," " Intimate Princes," " Countesses I have visited," etc., etc., had raised her to high esteem in the cultured circles on whom she had deigned to bestow her literary pearls. She never discoursed upon " The Presidents I have seen," or " The Bankers I have dined with," though the last were numerous ; for Presidents and business men are American, and being a snob, she knew exactly how to flavor her dish with aristocratic seasoning to suit the palates of her audience, who saw her two hundred pounds of robust Yankee flesh surrounded by kings, princelings, and lordlings, and fell down and worshipped her as the intimate of royalty, with almost as much fervor as they would have done the kings and princelings and lordlings themselves could they have got a chance at them in person.

But this lecture business not being as profitable as formerly, the committees of ladies engaged in charitable entertainments making wry faces at her demands, which reduced the profits going to the deserving poor, Mrs. Marvin had, in the last few years, struck upon a new invention in speculation, for which, though she could not patent it, she enjoyed the exclusive right—*i.e.*, introducing to New York and European society the daughters of men who had made sudden and colossal fortunes.

These aggregations of wealth, just at this moment, are unusually numerous. They come mostly from railroads, mining, cattle, or manufacturing, fostered by that great iniquity of taxing the many for the benefit of the favored few, that has been practised in most barbarous aristocracies, but has been brought to its perfection by the tariff system of this so-called enlightened republic.

Fortunately for Mrs. Marvin's ingenious speculation, a good many of these sudden Crœsuses, surrendering to the insidious arguments of their wives and daughters, have made an advance and assault upon the society of New York and Boston, which has quite often yielded to their demands and admitted them to fellowship when their millions were numerous enough and their manners not too provincial.

Some others, defeated in their direct attacks, have with masterly strategy effected what has been called "The European Flank Movement."

They have left Newport, Lenox, New York, and Boston on one side, and, crossing the ocean, have married a daughter, by the power of a glorious *dot*, to some titled impecuniosity who has been willing to *honor* (?) a beautiful, young, cultivated American girl by taking her to his bed and board, if he received enough money to make the matrimonial pill a sugar-coated one to his high-bred self, to pay his gambling debts, and to gild his escutcheon so brightly that the democratic mud upon it is concealed by American gold.

Then, armed with a titled son-in-law, the old couple come back, attack our exclusive society, and conquer it.

Thus the social ambitions of women made Mrs. Marvin's American merchandise, and the necessities of impecunious aristocrats gave her the European customers necessary to complete her bargains.

It need hardly be stated that she always, under some understood or implied contract, received a handsome bonus or commission on the transaction, most generally from the bridegroom upon his fingering the money of his American bride.

The bargain, plainly stated in its naked horror, stood thus: On one side a young and sometimes beautiful American girl (without much knowledge of the world, mostly without very great self-respect or womanly pride), who gave her fresh youth and generous fortune to the possession of a man who usually had destroyed his own by a life of dissipated luxury, because he gave to her, by a desecration of all that is sacred in the marriage ceremony, some high-sounding title.

Her last operation in this peculiar line of trade had been a very great success ; she had married the daughter of a Western cattle man to a blue-blooded count of the German Empire—for Mrs. Marvin always warranted her goods. If she had an heiress on hand, one could be sure she was true plutocrat, and her *ducs*, and *comtes*, and *viscomtes* were all warranted of *sang azure* and mediæval manufacture.

This was of great assistance to her in her business, for lately some fearful mistakes had been made on the American side of the water. One Oil City heiress had married an Italian barber who had palmed himself off for a count on her parents. This wretch, after taking his miserable dupe home to his Italian hovel with a poetic name, *à la* Claude Melnotte, had, in contradistinction to Bulwer's poetic hero, given his unhappy victim the discipline a Roman peasant does his spouse—*i.e.*, beaten her daily with a vine stick because, forsooth, her drafts from America were not large enough nor numerous enough to suit his Italian taste. Another, a Harrisburg belle, had been taken to mate about the same time by a baron of one of the smaller German states, with much church ceremony, rejoicing, and flow of wine, and had to her horror and dismay found that she was regarded as little better than a morganatic connection by his blue-blooded relatives.

These disasters to the ladies of the Buck Tail State had produced for the time being a panic in the foreign title market that had taken all the glory of Mrs. Marvin's last successful *coup* to allay. No American mother doubted any nobleman she introduced ; no foreign aristocrat that didn't have faith in the fortune of any American girl she chaperoned.

Therefore Aurora Marvin's matrimonial business was in the full tide of success, and heeding the maxim, "Make hay when the sun shines," the widow, immediately after the celebration of the grand nuptial ceremony that made Malvina Shorthorns the Countess Von Hesse Kimmel, turned her business eyes about to find a nobleman, if pos-sible a little higher, a little nobbier, a little more *puissant* than her last, for her next speculation ; and had almost immediately found Lord Avonmere, of Avonmere Castle, Hants., Beachman Manor, Berks., and Oak Hall, Sussex, Baron in the Peerage of England ; or, rather, he had found her, for that nobleman had caused himself to be introduced to the American widow, to her glory and delight, for English titles are to foreign ones in the eyes of Americans very much as the flaming pigeon-blooded ruby of Burmah is to the humble Siberian garnet.

Of course Mrs. Marvin knew the gentleman very well by hearsay and reputation ; his escapades and adventures had been of a kind that almost caused his exclusion from London society. But a lord dies very hard—socially —and Avonmere was still received in some London houses, though in many of the best of them his card was not as welcome as it might have been.

Being perfectly aware that he had tied up the bulk of his income, as far as the law of entail permitted him, and having run through all his personal property and exhausted his credit, which also lasts much longer with a titled biped than with mortals of commoner clay, he was now living a by no means pleasant existence, pursued by duns and hounded by attorney's clerks, Mrs. Marvin, the moment she saw him, divined his desire in making her acquaintance, though both of them were much too well bred to mention the matter directly.

The time was the height of the London season, and in the course of two weeks, having contrived to meet the widow at a garden party, a reception or two, and a few dances and balls, the English lord and American widow became quite friendly, not to say intimate.

So matters ran along until Mrs. Marvin one day announced to Baron Avonmere her intended return to America, hinting that he might as well run over and visit the United States during the coming winter, and extolling the beauty and charm of American girls, as well she might. Concluding, she said : " You really should come over, Lord Avonmere ; who knows but perhaps one of my fair compatriots may induce you to settle down in New York. I'm told your own countrywomen have not been able to persuade you to give up bachelor joys and freedom."

" A-ah ! " returned the gentleman, attempting a little mock sigh, and putting on a saddish face. " Don't you know, Mrs. Marvin, that I'm too poor to marry ? "

" Nonsense ; you should do as the Frenchman does, demand a *dot* through your mother."

"But I have no mother," replied the young man.

"My poor boy," laughed Mrs. Marvin, "let me act as your mother; I'm almost old enough to." Here she gave a sigh that was a real one.

"And you will demand a *dot?*"

"I'll be more exacting than a French duchesse. I'll insist on the biggest portion ever given with even an American bride."

"By George!" he cried, for even British immobility could not resist an exclamation at this pleasing picture, and Avonmere had something of the Italian in him.

"She shall be beautiful also, and young. You may trust your adopted *mère* to pick and choose for you, as she would for her own first-born."

"Really!" muttered Avonmere, as he kissed the widow's plump hand. "You have—awh—quite converted me to the French method of betrothal, *belle maman.* You may expect me in New York in December."

With this he made his adieux, and strolled out from Mrs. Marvin's presence, knowing the matter was entirely understood between them, though after getting out of her sight he muttered to himself savagely : "Hang the old woman ! She daudled over that affair and played the delicate until I had about made up my mind to ask her point blank how big a present Von Hesse Kimmel had given her for his present financial ease."

Two days after this Mrs. Marvin sailed for America, with her mind pretty well settled as to the heiress she should next sacrifice upon the altar of aristocratic marriage ; for at this time the newspapers were full of the wonderful wealth of the Baby mine, and the number of millions Abe Follis had already salted down and put away out of it.

She had also incidentally heard from Miss Daisy Verplank, of New York, of Miss Matilda Follis's beauty and ambition, Miss Verplank having been for some time a room-mate with Miss Follis at Madame Lamere's select academy, Madison Avenue.

CHAPTER IX.

THE "BABY" MINE.

WITH this idea in her mind, Mrs. Marvin, very shortly after her arrival in the United States, arranged a little pleasure party to the Rocky Mountains, and visiting Denver in the late autumn, soon made the acquaintance of the female part of the Follis family, who were de lighted to know her, the widow's fashionable glory hav-ing been displayed in newspaper type from the Atlantic to the Pacific slope.

Filled with delight at this social windfall, Mrs. Follis and her daughter proceeded to break the hearts of Capi-tol Hill and Lincoln Avenue society by cramming Mrs. Marvin and the New York Four Hundred and foreign aristocracy into its envious ears until feminine Denver actually forgot to discuss artesian wells and the best filtrate for Platte River water to make it fit for human digestion, a topic that usurps the place of the weather in that Colorado town.

After taking up her residence for a month at the Follis mansion, her Denver hotel being so atrociously bad that she would have been tempted to forego her speculation had further residence in that building of magnificent architecture, poor beds, and vile cooking been necessary to its success, Mrs. Marvin felt herself intimate enough to propose that Miss Matilde should visit New York the coming winter, and, under her chaperonage, see a little of its society.

This offer was seized on with an avidity that made Mrs. Marvin jump ; and the matter was very shortly set-tled to their mutual satisfaction, Mrs. Follis proposing, as the plump Aurora's house was rented for the year, that Abe, her husband, should secure a furnished mansion on Murray Hill, and that Mrs. Marvin should be their guest until she departed in the annual spring exodus across the ocean.

" At which time I hope to take one of your daughters with me for a little European tour," suggests Mrs. Marvin, as she accepts the Follis offer, and thinks, with a sigh of relief, that she has escaped for a year all New York housekeeping bills, which are of a size and length to frighten a Crœsus and horrify a spendthrift.

"One of my darters?" ejaculates Rachel, Mrs. Follis, who is a lean, angular, masculine-looking woman; then she suddenly goes on in a way that makes La Marvin shudder, for Rachel has a backwoods manner of talking that indicates that the vacations of her youth have been long ones, and her school terms proportionally short. "Oh, it's Flossie you're driving at. Madame Lamher's fixing up her educash. She'll be hardly ready to take her po-sish in society till next fall. She's only seventeen, I reckon."

In her horror at Mrs. Follis's diction Mrs. Marvin does not notice the peculiarity of a parent's being doubtful of the age of her own offspring.

The arrangements are so satisfactory to her as regards the elder daughter that she puts the younger out of her mind, for Abe Follis, who loves his family with all his big, generous heart, gives Mrs. Marvin a *carte blanche* to make their house in New York equal to any one's.

The only difficulty in her matrimonial speculation bursts upon Mrs. Marvin's eyes the day before the departure of Matilde, her mother, and the widow from Denver.

It comes upon her with the suddenness of a Western cyclone, in the person of Robert Jackson, the owner of a fourth of the "Baby," and superintendent of the same, and considered one of the best practical as well as scientific miners in the West. To his bravery in fighting off jumpers, and executive management in the earlier history of the property, Abe Follis, who has been his partner nearly ten years, owes the immensity of his fortune.

At this time Bob Jackson, as he is generally known among the mining camps of Colorado, is a man of perhaps thirty two or three years of age, having the education and manner of a gentleman, though its polish has been somewhat worn off and its finesse partially blunted by his continuous life in "rough and tumble" mining camps, ever since he finished his Frieburgh studies and came to the West as mining engineer, to discover that German theory made very great and costly mistakes in the practical problems of American metallurgy and ore extraction.

His face, red from Colorado sun, his manner perhaps a little too abrupt, and his heart as big and as full of precious metal as the " Baby " bonanza, this gentleman strides into the Follis grounds, having come hurriedly down by the Midland Railroad from the mine, near Aspen District.

Half way from the front door he turns suddenly aside, for he sees Miss Matilde a few steps away plucking a late rosebud. The girl looks perhaps a little paler on meeting his glance, and pauses in her occupation, and were Bob not too much agitated himself, he would see that her hand is trembling slightly as she still grasps the rose-tree, unmindful of its thorns.

Mrs. Marvin, who is seated in the garden at the moment, the autumn day being a perfect one, as most Denver days are, notes this as she looks on, if the big, stalwart creature, who has eager eyes and agitated face, and is draped in a linen duster stained with hurried travel and plenty of alkali, does not.

Astonished and interested, Mrs. Marvin opens ears and eyes and looks on this hurried scene.

" Is it true, Tillie," he breaks out, for he has known her since she was a child, and addresses her in the easy manner of the West, " that to-morrow you are going East to live ? "

" Yes, *Mister* Jackson," says the young lady very slowly, though she has to steady herself by a strong grasp of the rose-bush.

And as the formal address comes to him and strikes his soul, for she had always called him " Bob " before, the brave eyes, that had faced the pistols of jumpers and the thousand horrors and perils of a great mine, droop before the beauty of this girl, as she stands with one white arm raised to pluck the rosebud that is no redder than her cheeks, one little foot advanced and trembling, two blue eyes, half haughty, half penitent, and a pair of coral lips that quiver as the breath comes panting from them.

Then Bob's great, big, honest eyes are raised to hers once more ; pleading and stricken he mutters : " Good-by —God bless you, Miss Follis." and staggers toward the gate.

7

A second more and Matilde is running after him and has laid a pleading hand upon his arm, and would offer him the rosebud and call him Bob, and probably never go to New York, for her eyes are all penitence now ; did not just at this moment Mrs. Marvin, who is an old society general, and has the cunning strategy and tactics of a social Cæsar, come hurriedly up, saying : " My dear, introduce him immediately, please. This must be the celebrated Bob, whose exploits the Follis family are never tired of praising."

This, of course, necessitates a presentation, and La Marvin, who has no idea of permitting Bob another *tête-à-tête*, goes into an elaborate description of the sensation she expects Miss Follis to make in New York society, until that young lady's eyes glow with triumph and again become haughty, and the dejected and enraged Bob, who is a child of nature in matters of the heart, bids them good-by, and doesn't come back again to catch his charmer alone, as he should.

As he reaches the gate his face is full of despair, and Mrs. Follis, who has been out for a walk, coming along the street, encounters and catches sight of him. She grows suddenly pale and cries out : " Bob, what's the matter with you ? Great Scott ! the mine hain't give out ? "

Rachel is quickly reassured, however, by Bob giving a melancholy laugh and saying : " You knew last month we had ore in sight to last five years ? "

" Yes," mutters Mrs. Follis, relieved.

" Well, the developments since that time on the eight and nine hundred foot levels have added two more years to the life of the mine. I was about to write this to Miss Flossie myself, as she likes to know about her property, but as you're going to New York you can tell her for me." Then he continues in rather a troubled tone : " Sometimes I almost wish it was not so infernal rich ! " and so goes away.

Does Mrs. Marvin, as she looks after Bob as he passes faltering down the street, feel sorry for the big heart she is going to break, so that she may dissipate on a foreign titled spendthrift the fortune he has risked his life so many times to protect and expand ?

It would seem not, for she regards his departing duster with a cynical smile ; then slips her arm in Miss Matilde's, and suggests, as they walk up the gravel path to the Follis's front door: "What a curious way Mr. Jackson has of talking of your sister's property; one would think it was segregated from your own."

"So it is," says Miss Follis. "You see, my dear Mrs. Marvin, Flossie is the heiress of the family."

"The *heiress*-of-the-family?" gasps the fat Aurora; then she grows pale, and whispering: "How hot it is!" sinks upon a garden bench with trembling limbs, for a horrible fear has come upon her.

"Though we brag of our Injun summer," says the masculine and lean Rachel, "the high air we have about here ginerally lays out people of your heft. I'll send you out a fan to aeriate yourself with." And going into the house on her errand of sympathy, followed by her daughter, she leaves Mrs. Marvin perspiring and agitated as well as indignant.

A moment after she is relieved and feels better, for Miss Matilde comes running back from the front door with a big palmetto for her; and gives the old lady a kindly fanning.

Mrs. Marvin gasps a little between breezes, but finally manages to get out: "You say your sister is the heiress of your family? Your father owns the 'Baby' mine, doesn't he?"

"Certainly—that is, the most of it."

This answer is reassuring, and the widow gives a sigh of relief.

"What I mean is this," continues Matilde; "if I want money I have none of my own, I must go to father for it—and I go pretty often! Flossie doesn't need to do this. She goes to her trustees. She owns in her own right one-fourth the Baby mine, Bob holds another fourth, and dad—I mean father—has the rest. You see, Flossie's adopted; she's not my *real* sister, though I love her as one, and she's as dear to father, I think, as I am myself. But we'd better come in, he's opening the front gate!" For Abe Follis is striding home to his midday meal.

Running to him, Miss Matilde gets a hearty embrace and sounding kiss, and they all go in to dinner, which, to the horror of Mrs. Marvin, the family take, after the primitive manner of the West, in the middle of the day.

During the meal the widow meditates as to how she shall learn more about the young lady they have been discussing. She knows most men are more communicative after dinner than before, and waiting till Mr. Follis has gone out on the back veranda to enjoy the cigar with which, as he expresses it, he "settles his meal," she follows him there, and after making herself very agreeable and charming, an art of which she has made a study, she brings the conversation round to his early struggles, and finds, to her astonishment, that the old gentleman is quite proud of his rise from poverty.

A moment after she suggests: "Won't you tell me something about the member of your family of whom I have heard so much, but never seen—the charming Miss Flossie ?"

At this, Abe Follis's red face glows with pleasure. He loves his adopted daughter, and every manifestation of affection for or interest in her goes to his great, big heart; for the old miner is one of those whole-souled Western anomalies who would divide his last slap-jack with you, but who would salt a mine on you, or skin you in a horse transaction, purely as a matter of business pride, in which each man is for himself and the Lord help the cutest.

"You're almighty kind to take a notion to my Flossie," remarks Abe, wiping his red face with a redder handkerchief that he takes out of his black slouch hat, and seating himself beside Mrs. Marvin. "And I'll tell you the story of the little gal and her coming into our camp and bringing the Baby mine and riches and wealth to as poor and starving an outfit as ever struggled for a grub stake in the Rocky Mountains."

"You rather astonish me," mutters the widow. "How could a child bring a mine to you ?"

"Oh, that war only a flower of speech, marm," returns Abe, with a whole-souled grin. "When I get excited I grow florid in my grammar. So I'll elucidate. We'd come up from New Mexico. I'd been there prospecting something nigh onto three years, with the worst kind of luck, part of the time with Pete, a young chap from the East, who didn't know nothin' about mining. He grub-staked us, and we used to work on the Tillie mine together, named after my darter, till we both were busted. Then the Leadville excitement still keeping up, I struck out for there. Leadville warn't no luckier than Silver City, but thar I fust come across Bob Jackson. He was knocking a living out of an assay office on Main Street, and one day he said to me : 'The Utes are most wiped out now, and if you'll take the chances of keeping your hair and'll go over towards Crested Butte, I think you'll get on paying mineral. You're an honest man and I'll grub-stake you.' And after a little we came to a dicker. He was to get one-third of all my locations, and I was to have two-thirds;, for a man took his life into his hands when he went into the Ute reservation in them days, jest after they'd killed Agent Meeker and Major Thornburg.

"So I took Rach and Tillie and lit out. Rach wouldn't have me go alone, and Tillie had to come, cause we didn't have nowhar to leave her.

"I had been travelling and prospecting for nigh onto three weeks, and hadn't got much more than seventy-five miles in a bee line from Leadville, for the trail war awful in them days. I was most worn out with hard work, hard grub, and no luck ; for I hadn't come upon a sign of paying mineral. We had turned up a little cañon to camp for the night, when on a sudden we heered a lot of screams and yells that come echoing along its walls, for it had purty steep sides, like most all gulches in the Colorado watershed, whar the scenery is powerful good for tourists, and awful tough on prospectors. 'It's a child,' said my wife. 'It's a mountain lion,' says I. ''Tain't possible a child could ever get up thar !'

"'It's a gal's cries !' repeated Rach, 'and if you're a man, Abe, you'll go and see what's the matter with her.'

"So I shouldered my Winchester, and, tired as I was, started up the gulch. Jist after I left the pack mules I heard the cry ag'in. I couldn't tell how far off it was, the echoes being so numerous, for the walls of them long, deep cañons act like speaking tubes in fust-class hotels and carry sound a tarnation long ways. I climbed over boulders and forced myself through chaparral for nigh onto quarter of a mile, and that took me most an hour, the country was so fearful rough. I'd have gone back twenty times, but every now and then the noise came to me ag'in, and each time it sounded more human. I'd travelled on for some five minutes without hearing any thing more, and had nearly made up my mind to about face, as it was gitting toward sundown, and it wa'n't a nice place to travel out of in the dark ; when of a sudden I came on a sight that made me feel powerful glad I'd come ; for on a ledge of rocks, sobbing softly now as if her heart would break, was a pretty little gal, her face pale from famine, her eyes most cried out of her head, her little arms and legs torn with briers and chaparral, unprotected and alone in that awful wilderness.

" Didn't take me long to get to her and speak to her. At the sound of my voice she shrieked out, 'Oh, a *man!* Alone !—ALONE !'—and rising half up moaned, ' Nothing to eat !   Poor Flossie ! ' then keeled over fainting like hit with a bullet, right on top of the ledge on which she stood.

" In a second I was down in a little creek of snow water, and dashing it over her with my *sombrero,* and the setting sun through a break in the cañon wall shining on her as she lay like a little marble statue.   As I throwed the water, drenching her to life, it ran from her limbs over the rock she war on and washed it clear of dirt : and as I threw more water the ledge got cleaner, and when the child awoke agin with a sigh and I lifted her up in my arms I gave such a yell of astonishment and joy that it brought my wife and daughter up the cañon to see if I war killed, for thar before my eyes glistening in the sun, was a mass of the richest carbon-ates and chlorides of lead and silver ever seen in Colo-rado.   I WAR LOOKING ON THE FLOAT ROCK OF THE BABY MINE.

" The next minute I got a drop of whiskey from my flask down her little throat, and began carrying her in my arms down the cañon ; for to this day I thank God that even in the excitement of the fust great stroke of financial luck that had struck me on this earth, I didn't for one minute forget the suffering child to gloat over the richness her cries had brought to me.

" Half way down the gulch I met my wife and darter on their way up. We put the little sufferer to bed in a bush shanty I knocked up, and for days and weeks my wife nursed her through delirium and mountain fever and pneumonie from her exposure ; for as near as I could reckon, Flossie must have been wandering alone for three or four days before I came on her and gathered her in.

"While this was going on I got a message through to Bob, and he came over like a streak from Leadville and we took up and located the Baby mine, naming it for the child as had drawn me to it. And Bob he argued that she was entitled to some of it, and said if I'd give up a little, he'd give up some, and together we fixed it so that Flossie had a fourth, Bob another fourth, and I had a half. And it seemed as if the little waif had brought luck with her, for the mine was a poor man's mine from the beginning, that is, it was very rich on the surface and didn't require a fortune to git into it, as so many of 'em do out here.

"So by the time Flossie had got her senses back to her, and could tell us something about herself, there was a thousand men in that little cañon ; and from that time on, mam, the history of the Baby mine is part of the silver question in the United States, and the financial history of America ! "

Coming to this point, Mr. Follis smiles blandly on Mrs. Marvin, and proceeds to relight his cigar, which has gone out during his oration.

"What did the little girl tell you about her being alone in that wild place ? " asks the widow with some interest.

"Well, nothin' very definite," returns Abe. "You see she must have been some days a wandering about, and the terror and excitement and the pneumonie knocked a good deal of recollection out of her—she couldn't have been more than nine or so when I found her. She didn't remember her own name at first, and if she hadn't called herself Flossie we wouldn't have known what to christen her. She said—this came to us by bits and driblets— that her daddy and mammie were killed by Injins, which was natural in that country at the time. But the astonishing pint of it war, she said they hadn't been killed *near* thar, and that she had been on a railroad and travelled a good deal with her uncle or some relation, after her parents was dead and buried, and that the man had gone off to shoot at an animal and never came back. That railroad travel must have been raving dead sure, cause the Utes were out on the war-path right round the place I come on her. The only name we ever got from her is Flossie ; and from her actions and style I'm pretty certain she's English and a high stepper. Why, half ·my

Tillie's culter comes from her pickin' up Flossie's man
ners."

"And you have never tried to find her relatives?"
queries Mrs. Marvin.

"What's the use?" answers the miner. "Ain't her
father and mother killed and her uncle probably chewed
up by a grizzly or some varmint?—and what does she
want relatives for? Don't Rachel and Tillie and I love
her better than any cousins she could pick up? Could
they give her any more money? Ain't her dividends
being invested by Bob and me, her trustees, till she owns
two new residence streets most entire, and has a pretty
lively smattering of business blocks on Fifteenth, Six-
teenth and Arapahoe streets, and Denver real estate is on
the boom now? Besides, don't she own half a Pueblo
smelter, and any quantity of C., B. & Q. stock, gilt edged
and silver lined, besides a lot of the water bonds of
Omaha and a Chicago hotel! WHAT MORE DOES SHE
WANT?"

"What more does she want?" echoes Mrs. Marvin,
rather overcome at his schedule of this juvenile Crœsus's
possessions.

The day after this conversation, Mrs. Follis, Matilde
and Mrs. Marvin depart for the more artificial East.

Arriving on the Limited about dusk at the Grand Central Depot, they are met by a young lady of exquisite
beauty and refined manner. A suspicion of hauteur in her
demeanor is contradicted by a pair of brown eyes, full
of trusting love, though her lips are wonderfully firm in
one so young, showing character and courage. She is
dressed richly, but plainly, in rather school-girl style,
though she is already over the medium height of woman.
She is attended by an insignificant little Swedish gover-
ness who speaks broken English, and who has been sent
from Madame Lamere's school to protect her.

This dignified young beauty is Miss Florence Follis.

On seeing her adopted mother and sister, dignity is
thrown to the winds, and in a moment she is in their
arms with tender kisses and cries of love and joy.

These being returned with interest, there is very little
conversation for a minute; then Mrs. Follis suddenly
says: "Excuse me, Mrs. Marvin, I have not presented
Flossie to you."

"I've heard of Mrs. Marvin," remarks the young lady, extending a perfectly gloved hand with a blasé dignity that makes the widow stare at this waif of the West, for she has seen this insouciant nonchalance before and knows it's genuine and comes from heredity, not affec- tation.

"Very happy to learn that," returns Aurora, pocketing her pride and giving the girl's pretty digits a friendly squeeze. "Where did you hear of me?"

"At school! Madame Lamere is giving a course of lectures to the first class, on the society leaders of America."

"A-ah!" This is a gratified purr from Mrs. Marvin.

"Yesterday she mentioned your name."

"Indeed! and what did Madame Lamere, whose estab- lishment I have so often said is just suited to our young aristocracy, say of me?" asks the widow, very much pleased at this educational compliment.

"Oh," returns the young lady struggling to disguise a *moue*. "She pointed you out to us as a shining example of what tact and tenacity would do when climbing the social ladder. She said with Mrs. Aurora Dabney Mar- vin before us, no girl, even though poor, and of no family influence, need despair."

"Humph!" This is a snort from La Marvin, who wonders if it is innocence or sarcasm she is gazing at, for the girl is looking into her eyes with that blank ex- pression peculiar to the English aristocracy.

A moment after Mrs. Marvin lisps, "So kind in Madame Lamere. Tell her I shall always feel grateful for her complimentary mention." Then she suddenly and effusively continues : "You must let me chaperone you in New York as soon as you come out, my dear, as I am going to do your sister."

For she has been looking at the noble creature before her, and remembering her fourth of the Baby mine, her bonds and stocks and Chicago hotel, and Denver real estate, she knows she has found another prize in the matrimonial market, one for whose beauty and fortune some ruined duc or marquise or comte will pay a large commission ; and reaching forward she would kiss her new and beautiful speculation on her velvet cheek. But the young lady drawing herself up, assumes a haughty stare and remarks : " I never kiss at first sight ; " and putting up a lorgnette in Madame Lamere's highest style of the art, she lisps out : " It's such awful bad form yet —awh—know."

A moment after she has turned from Mrs. Marvin, who is gazing at her in a dazed but admiring manner, for this old lady cringes at times to her social masters, and is squeezing Matilde's fairy waist and asking with eagerness of " Dad " and " Bob " and her Denver friends.

Then arm in arm the two young ladies walk out of the Grand Central Depot, making one of the prettiest pic-tures that ever left its portals, Mrs. Follis and La Marvin following after, the widow effusively descanting on the loveliness of these sisters ; the younger so statuesque, the elder so vivacious and both so beautiful.

On the sidewalk Miss Florence astonishes Mrs. Marvin again, for she becomes a school-girl once more, remark-ing significantly, but indefinitely, that she must be back at Lamere's by eight o'clock sharp or she'll catch it !

Then she leads her sister on one side and whispers suddenly : " Tillie, how are you off for change ? Can't you lend me a dollar or two ? "

" Great goodness, Flossie ! Haven't you got your own bank account at the Second National here ? " cries her sister.

" Hush ! Mademoiselle 'll hear you. I've got a ten thousand balance there, but Lamere won't let me draw but five dollars a week for pocket-money. I used to have what I wanted till I made the whole school sick on Maillard's chocolates and she came down on me. There —slide it into my hand when Mademoiselle ain't looking. Thank you, you darling." And she gives Miss Matilda another kiss, for her sister has slipped a roll of currency into this pauper school-girl's pocket

Then they separate, Miss Flossie going back to the tutelage of Madame Lamere, and the rest driving to the mansion in which Miss Matilde has been writing her memoirs and in which Gussie Van Beekman is now awaiting his promised one.

CHAPTER X.

A BURSTED SPECULATION.

As Miss Follis enters the reception-room she is greeted with a sudden and effusive drawl: "Awh! Delighted My dear Matilde! My—awh!—promised one. My——' and little Gussie, rising and seizing her outstretched hand, would have proceeded in a languid way to imprint the seal of their engagement upon the tempting lips of his *fiancée*, but as he gets nearer and nearer to her, her eyes grow haughtier and haughtier until their beautiful but chilly gleam protects the allurements over which they seem sentries.

Thus he stands like the ass bending over the thistle, longing to pluck the flower, but dreading the surrounding thorns.

Perhaps some memory of Bob has come to her to make her cold and formal to poor little Gussie on his first engagement-day, for the young lady's face, which has been a bright blush, suddenly grows white and pale. She turns away with a slight sigh.

"By George, how formal you are to me, Matilde!" cries Van Beekman. "One would think you did not love me, and I'll never believe *that*, yer know. Nevah! Nevah!"

"That—would—indeed—be difficult to conceive!" mutters the girl, a slight smile coming to her features to make them mobile and vivacious again. Then she suddenly says, for she has picked out her line of procedure, and with Western promptness immediately acts on it: "Sit down beside me!—Augustus, be a good boy, and I'll give you your *instructions*."

"My INSTRUCTIONS?" gasps Gussie, astounded. "Why, we're not married *yet!*"

"Certainly NOT!"

"Why, I never heard an engaged girl talk that way in my life—and I've been there before——" He cuts himself short here, thinking he may have been too frank. And so he has, for his *fiancée's* foot is patting the Axminster rather savagely.

"Oh, you have, have you?" remarks Miss Matilde,

icily. "Then *I* have not been there before, and——. Oh! what a lovely bouquet." In a moment she is at a side-table with a creation of Thorley's in her hand, and whispers: "For me?"

"Yes," replies Gussie; "I brought it for you—but you never give a fellah a chance—you drive along so. You ought to have some consideration for me. I'm not accustomed to be hurried—it's not our style at the Stuyvesant. I know a chap got blackballed there once—because he talked fast. There'll be one like that for you every day—Thorley has his instructions—and there'll be a ring this evening. It'll be sent up to you."

Which is perfectly true; for though Messrs. Gill & Patrick would not have trusted Mr. Gussie for a plated bangle, they were perfectly willing to send any engagement token he wished to Miss Follis, knowing they would be paid for it, if not before the marriage, certainly after the ceremony.

"You are **very good** to me," murmurs the girl; "but"—here a little gleam of mischief comes into her eyes—"I'm going to give you your instructions, just the same. There, sit down, that's a good boy, and listen to me, and—Oh, my laws! Ough! Don't squeeze my hand so, I wear rings!" With this she holds up to Gussie's repentant sight four little red fingers, crushed by golden bands that have been compressed with them, and blazing with jewels—for Abe tossed diamonds all over his women folks, in true Western millionaire fashion—and pouts: "See what you have done!"

A moment after she cries: "My hand is well—*stop!*" and stamps her foot. For Gussie, whose sluggish Flemish blood begins to simmer under the charms and graces of his alluring *fiancée* sitting close beside him, not having her coral lips at his mercy, has fallen upon and is devouring the little hand she has held up for his inspection.

Then she looks very sternly at him and again cries, "Stop!" in such a frontier voice, that he faintly mutters, "Cruel!" but heeds her. Though it is in an undecided sort of way, and every now and again, all through the interview, he makes little rushes and dashes for his sweetheart's alluring fingers, which she evades with the active wariness of a mustang dodging the lasso.

"Now, if you'll be quiet a moment, I'll explain to you what I mean by my instructions," remarks the young lady, with rather a mischievous smile on her face, as she gazes at Mr. Augustus de Punster Van Beekman, who is the same little gentleman who had appeared at the Harvard-Yale foot-ball game of a dozen years before, in a full blue costume, to the amusement of Miss Bessie Everett.

He has not altered much, only the passing years have made him more decidedly and aggressively English in manner and appearance. In fact, he is now what is in America derisively called an Anglomaniac. A species of imbecile who don't imitate the strong and noble points of the bulk of the Anglo-Saxon race that have made their little island the commercial power of the world, and carried the British flag in honor and glory to the extreme quarters of the earth ; but rather that unimportant moiety whose snobbish manners and affected caddishness have often brought reproach upon the British name. A class that assume to be part of the English aristocracy, of which they generally are but affected imitations—for the true representatives of the leading families of England are too certain of their high position to feel that it is necessary to be anything more or less than ladies and gentlemen to retain or maintain the respect generally given to their order.

Poor little Gussie, not being acquainted with English gentlemen, has imitated English cads, and is now generally a snob, though at times he has generous impulses. These do not last very long nor grow very strong. One ruling passion agitates his little frame ; that is, adoration of the British aristocracy, and if he can get hold of a *déclassé* Englishman who has wandered to New York because London is too hot to hold him—especially if he has a smirched title—the poor little man is happy.

This admiration of imported swells has been an expensive luxury to the little fellow, both in health and pocket. He has shown his idols New York in all its glory, paying their spreeing expenses when occasion offered ; losing his money to them at cards and paying it ; letting them owe similar debts to him, and not having the moral courage to demand his due for fear of losing their favor or acquaintance.

This loss of health is shown by various little lines about his eyes and face that should not exist in a man of thirty. This injury to his fortune is perceptible in some suggestive paragraphs in various newspapers, connecting his name with threatened legal proceedings in regard to overdue tailors' accounts and haberdashers' bills.

At present, though wofully pressed, he is putting up a bold front; liquidating only his club dues, so he cannot be dropped, and referring everything else to the indefinite future, that under his engagement to the great Western heiress has suddenly grown rosy with financial promise.

He is faultlessly arrayed in an afternoon suit, whose baggy appearance indicates London origin and trans-Atlantic importation, and has an absent look on his face which is the result of years of study.

Miss Follis gives this preoccupation a little start; she suddenly says: "You have seen the *Town Tattler?*"

"No-ah."

"Then you do not know that it contains a notice of your engagement to me?" mutters the girl, who, not appreciating the all-prying eyes of society reporters, imagines that he must have given out some hint of the matter.

His answer proves his truth, for he suddenly cries: "By George! That Dickson must have seen it, though! —that's why—I understand now!" and utters a little knowing chuckle.

"What's Dickson got to do with it? Who is Dickson anyway?" queries the young lady.

"Oh! Dickson's my tailor. He—he called on me to-day to ask when I would be measured for my spring—I mean my wedding-suit."

Which answer is entirely true, though Mr. Augustus does not mention that the aforesaid Dickson, his long-suffering tailor, had the day before threatened legal proceedings, and had broken in upon him this very morning with loud and threatening voice, to Gussie's horror. And when the poor little fellow had come out of his room, the savage Dickson, who while waiting his appearance had incidentally picked up from his table and been reading the *Town Tattler*, had risen with sudden apologies and humble demeanor, and begged the honor of supplying Mr. Augustus's spring raiment, also hinting at wedding garments, to the astonishment and joy of his delinquent debtor. This sudden knowledge of the ease that has come to him, even through the rumor of his engagement to the beautiful girl before him, makes him rather grateful to her—for the moment; for none of little Gussie's impulses last long, the better ones flitting quicker than the worst—as a rule.

"Very well," says the girl returning his smile. "Since it has got out, I wish you to make it public everywhere, and if I am questioned I shall not deny it. It will save trouble and set things right at once."

"Save trouble? Your father—is not here?" cries little Gussie uneasily rising and turning pale, for he has heard old man Follis described as a Western border ruffian.

"My father!" laughs Matilde; "he won't hurt any one." Then she bursts out merrily: "My poor little Gussie, I did not say *danger*, I said trouble. It is better every one knows this as soon as possible."

A moment after she turns away with an embarrassed blush, for she is thinking that it will be much better for "Bob" to see it announced as a certainty in the newspapers; then there will be no danger of his coming to New York to bring with him struggles between her ambition and her regard for him. She would not call it love, now, not for worlds.

Gussie, however, destroys lengthy meditation, by crying out suddenly: "I'll announce it everywhere; the clubs shall ring with my—happiness!" It has just struck him that more tradesmen in New York than his tailor should be very sure and certain of his good fortune.

"Now for the remainder of my instructions!" says the girl suddenly, for with this speech he has made an abortive attempt to capture her hand again; "We're going to run this engagement on the French system."

"The French system? What is that?" ejaculates Van Beekman surprised.

"Well," says his instructor consideringly, "the French system consists of extremely formal interviews between the contracting parties, always in the presence of the young lady's mother, until the fat—I mean happy, day. It's the proper European form—how does it strike you?"

" As rather hard lines on your mamma," murmurs Augustus, who doesn't seem to like the idea. " I shall drop in so often and unexpected, yer see. I shall come so early and stay so late, yer know, mamma will be rather done up next morning."

"Oh, no, she won't!" laughs Matilde; "you don't know mamma. At ten o'clock she will give you a hint—at least she always did in Denver."

"I nevah take hints!" remarks Gussie, who doesn't like the Denver allusion, with sententious sullenness.

"No? but you will take my mother's! Young men in Denver never refused them, they were so very pointed!"

"Were they?" laughs Van Beekman, then he cries with sudden vivacity: "As mamma is not present, I'll make good use of my time, Matilde."

"Excuse me, we will imagine my mother is here," remarks Miss Follis severely, becoming pale and red by turns, but haughty all the while, for this sudden use of her Christian name has given the girl a start, emphasizing as it does the familiarity that her engagement entitles little Gussie to assume to her.

A moment after she gives a faint little cry, partly of surprise, partly of rage ; for, inflamed by the tempting *morceau* before him that he considers sealed to him for time, Augustus, who has been working his nervous system up to the proper pitch, cries : " Matilde, how beautiful you are ! Your—awh—coldness kills me," and makes a sudden dive for her peachy cheek ; but being dodged adroitly contrives to lodge his engagement kiss upon the end of her pretty chin.

She would probably have been very angry with him for this attempt at amatory robbery, and perhaps would have ended their compact then and there, for the assaulted chin has grown very haughty and her cheeks are very red and her eyes very bright, when just at this moment she catches a silken rustle behind her, and turning suddenly sees Mrs. Marvin, who is a very dragon of routine formality and orthodox virtue, in the act of leaving the room with an expression upon her face as severe as that of an abbess condemning an eloping nun.

This is a case that will admit of no misunderstanding. In two antelope glides Matilde is beside the widow's re treating figure, speaking as she comes : " My dear Mrs. Marvin, as my chaperone in New York society, I owe you my confidence as well as I do my mother. Permit me to introduce to you Mr. Van Beekman, as the gentleman to whom I am engaged, and whose name I some day expect to bear—as my own."

Then the iron enters Aurora's soul—the expression of outraged virtue changes for one moment to that of rage, misery, and almost despair. That is when her back is towards Miss Follis ; then conquering her rage and choking down her misery, this wily old diplomat turns—. a sickly smile runs over her wrinkles, and by the time Matilde sees her face it is almost good-natured. She contrives to mutter : " My dear, you surprise me. Mr. Van Beekman, my—my congratulations. I—I know the *true* value of the prize you have won." Though as she thoroughly realizes this last, the words seem to falter and linger among her false teeth till they fill her mouth and nearly choke her.

" So glad you like the idea ! " murmurs Gussie. Then he says suddenly : " But I must bid you good-bye. I have to call upon Phil Everett and his sister—old college chum—one of Boston's heavy capitalists, and heavy swells now—Beacon-street family, Plymouth Rock— Puritan fathers—all that sort of thing, yer know. They're to spend a month or two heah. Have brought with them the catch of the season, Grousemoor, very rich, and a string of titles as long as his rent-roll. He has some investments with Phil on this side the pond, but before they let him loose among our New York belles, Bessie Everett, the little Boston girl, hooked him for herself. These demure Puritan maidens know a thing or two, I can tell you. You are acquainted with Grouse-moor, I believe, Mrs. Marvin ? "

" Oh, yes," returns Aurora, haughtily. " I knew him first as Lord John Heather ; next after the death of his elder brother, as Viscount Blackgame ; and now since the demise of his father, as the Marquis of Grousemoor. He has been very attentive to me on my annual visits to Eng-land. I spent a week at Heather Castle, one of his places in Scotland. You will see I make mention of him in my lecture on ' Titled Intimates.' "

" Awh, then I'll mention you to him." murmurs Gussie.

A second after he lisps: "*Au revoir* till to-morrow. Look out for the ring, don't yer know, Matilde," and taking a hurried kiss of his *fiancée's* outstretched hand, Mr. Augustus proceeds on his way in pursuit of the Everetts and Lord Grousemoor.

For a moment the two women gaze at each other ; then the elder impulsively says : "My dear, I hope you'll be happy !" and kisses the Western heiress.

"I'm very glad you're pleased, Mrs. Marvin," returns Matilde.

"Yes, yes," murmurs the widow. "But it's hardly the match I had imagined you would make with your attractions and social success this season. Why, Avonmere, who is also an English lord and great catch, told me confidentially to-day that you were the most beautiful woman he had met in America. There, don't blush —though it *is* very becoming."

And planting this idea in the young lady's ambitious brain, La Marvin leaves her and goes up-stairs to her room. Then locking the door, this poor old lady appears dazed, for she mutters to herself: "The girl fool ! The Colorado imbecile ! Who'd have thought an heiress would ever want to marry an *American?*" as if such an idea could never have entered a sane mind. Yet, all the time she is trying to think if there is any chance of her getting money from little Van Beekman for bringing his prize from the West for him. A moment's consideration drives away such hope from her mind. She knows the commercial Flemish blood that flows in his veins. He'll never pay for something he has already won.

Then, this idea bringing dismay to her, she begins to cry out, "That lazy lord !—lingering six weeks in England after the appointed time, till that little Dutch pauper sneaked in and got his paws on the prize. Has he ?— *Has he?*—HAS HE ? I'll circumvent him at the church door ! Oh, my heaven ! won't Avonmere be savage ! How shall I tell him ?—How ?—Oh my ! o-o-oh !" and she sobs and wrings her hands and stamps her feet till the tears run down her poor old cheeks in torrents, making fearful havoc among the powder that covers a too great natural redness of complexion.

For Mrs. Marvin had this very afternoon met Lord

Avonmere at a reception, and after hearing him drawl out that Tillie Follis is a captivating little minx—one that he wouldn't mind marrying if the treasure was enough and to spare—had whispered to him, "*She is the girl.*"

Then, riding up-town in her brougham, she had given him an inventory of Abe Follis's wealth and had descanted upon the immense settlement her listener might obtain with the heiress.

On this Avonmere had become enthusiastic, for the novelty of Matilde's vivacious beauty and piquant spirit had quite caught the Italian part of his nature, and, the day being cold, he had abstractedly marked with his finger upon the frosted window of the brougham before him, "Five per cent.," then looked inquiringly at La Marvin. A moment after, in a brown study, she had scraped with her fan in the dim moisture of the glass in front of her, " Ten per cent."

And they had carried this business on, till the pane the lord sat opposite was all " Five per cents.," and the glass facing the widow was a mass of " Ten per cents.," when suddenly he had grinned and marked, " Seven and a half per cent.," and she had smiled and inscribed, " Seven and a half per cent.," and they had both shaken hands, but neither said a word over this speculation in an American heiress, that has just been bursted by the despised little Augustus de Punster Van Beekman.

CHAPTER XI.

AN EVENING ON FIFTH AVENUE.

THAT evening Lord Avonmere calls; his card is brought to Mrs. Marvin, for whom he asks. She is in her room with a headache, produced by the revelation of the afternoon. But this old lady, who has something of the Napoleon in her disposition, ignoring her neuralgia and replacing her powder, comes down to meet her English customer; omitting, however, to bring her wares with her, though they are within call—Miss Follis not feeling in form for any evening entertainment after the long-drawn-out ball of the night before.

So, entering the same reception-room where Matilde had given little Gussie his instructions, she strides up to Avonmere and tells him the sudden obstacle that has come between him and the heiress.

This gentleman, in his conventional evening dress, would look a typical Englishman, were it not for his very dark hair, that has a romantic curl in it, and his black eyes, that never look one straight in the face and seem always seeking something that they never find. His speech and bearing are nonchalant and British, and never more so than when he hears this news, that is even more ominous to him than Mrs. Marvin imagines; for he knows perfectly well that he must marry some heiress, —and she must be an exceptional one, who brings him millions—and that very soon, if he would ever hope to go back and assume his station in the London world which is his delight and existence.

He listens to the widow calmly while she reproaches him for not having been in New York sooner—she had expected him in the middle of November, and he only came just before the New Year. Then she gives him an aphorism: "In matters of business punctuality is necessary to success."

"Quite true, my dear madam," he replies. "In matters of business money also is necessary to success, and I couldn't raise the funds for a proper appearance before. Egad! you wouldn't have cared for me to borrow from you on the *very* day of my arrival,—would you?"

To this potent question the widow gives an affrighted shiver and nervous but decided "No!"

"You need not fear any immediate appeal to your bank account!" he says, with a slight sneer and mocking laugh. "Before I left England I took care to provide myself for the New York campaign—I mortgaged my heiress in advance—I raised the money on *your* credit!"

At this Mrs. Marvin grows very pale and whispers: "What do you mean?"

"Nothing to frighten you," he laughs. "I was unable to borrow the necessary funds on my own promise to marry an heiress; Messrs. Pharisee and Sadducee doubted my success unaided, but when I told them that *you* were engaged in the transaction, they came up with ready promptness and alacrity—young Ikey Sadducee remarking that 'Your heiresses were as good as bullion.' They'd handled some of the Hesse Kimmel paper, and had received old Shorthorn's checks for same and interest."

"A—ah!" murmurs his listener, quite relieved and rather flattered; for she had horrible fears that he had slipped her signature across a bill or some other enormity of that kind.

After a moment's consideration, he continues quietly: "I don't apprehend much difficulty in getting rid of little Augustus—the young lady seems quite taken with my attentions—most American girls rather dote on lords. Couldn't you contrive for me to see Miss Follis this evening?—and from her we may judge how best to trim our sails."

"I think I can arrange that," remarks his coadjutor. And, asking him to excuse her, she goes off in quest of Matilde.

A few moments after she returns and, taking his arm, leads him to the library, where Miss Follis, with a frank smile and outstretched hand, awaits him.

The girl says: "I asked Mrs. Marvin to bring you here, Lord Avonmere; it's much more cosey than that dreary, big room. Mother is tired after last night, so I cannot have the pleasure of presenting you to her; and Mrs. Marvin——"

"Will be your chaperone this evening," remarks the widow very pleasantly, for Avonmere's calm reception of her bad news has restored her confidence.

So the three sit down and pass a very enjoyable hour, Aurora pretending to occupy herself looking at some new music lately sent home to Miss Follis, though she can't read a note, while the other two go into rather a *tête-à-tête*, Avonmere using all his powers of language and charm of manner to put himself on intimate and friendly terms with the young lady; and no man had greater resources of the kind when he chose to bring them to his aid. He has travelled a good deal; and when he wishes can assume a lighter and more fluent style of conversation than is usually given to Englishmen, this last being his inheritance from an Italian mother.

A very short time convinces him of the girl's social ambition, she confessing to him in excited Western slang that she is not accustomed to take a back seat, and has made up her mind to be at the top of the society heap in New York.

"At the top in New York, Miss Follis!" he lisps— "Is not that rather a poor ambition for *you* when there is a London and a Paris?" With this he goes into a description of the beauties and pleasures of European aristocratic life, mentioning lords and ladies, dukes and duchesses, with the easy freedom of one who has met them on an equal footing. On this the young lady's imagination, that has been properly prepared for the seed he is sowing, becomes excited; she begins to think an American triumph but a poor one, and New York and Newport by no means so fine as London or Trouville, a common mistake to un-travelled Americans.

Having got her to this feeling, Avonmere adroitly changes the subject to one upon which Matilde can do the talking, and from being a brilliant expounder becomes an attentive listener, simply mentioning that when he was quite a boy he visited New Mexico, Colorado, and the far West, as Miss Follis gives him a dissertation on her life in Denver.

This he finds very easy work, as the girl grows animated and much more beautiful; for Matilde is at her best when in action. So he sits in a lazy Italian way, looking at a very pretty picture.

Miss Follis is in a white evening gown, with just a dash of color knotted about her lithe waist; her bare, white arms, moving in graceful gestures to emphasize the tale she is telling; her snowy shoulders dimpled by each change of pose in head and body, while her blue eyes flash with vivacious fire, save once or twice when they meet his own. Then they droop, but grow darker and a slight blush comes over her cheeks.

A moment later Matilde says, " You say you were once in Colorado—see if you can recognize any of its scenery," and turns to a photographic portfolio near her. For Avonmere, looking at this beauty, has got something in his own Italian orbs that makes the girl restless under his gaze; and try how he will, he can't keep the passion out of them. He has even forgotten the Follis's millions in looking at the Follis's charms and graces.

He moves near her and assumes to examine the pict-ares. Mrs. Marvin gives an inward chuckle, and thinks to herself, " I could have got ten per cent. commission now," as she notes with her watchful old eyes that Avonmere, standing a little behind the girl, is giving his attention to Matilde's glowing beauty rather than to the stock photographs of Colorado scenery she has placed on exhibition.

But suddenly, the widow's wary glance catches sight of Avonmere's face, and it is as pale as if all the blood in his body had rushed to his heart. Miss Follis has in her pretty hands a photograph.

He takes this from her, and Aurora can see his own hands tremble a little as they hold it, and that his eyes have a curious troubled expression in them, as he asks rather faintly, " What place is this ? " and Matilde answers, " That—that is the celebrated cañon of the Baby mine. No one could look at those twin peaks at the head of it, covered with eternal snow, and ever forget it ! "

" No,—no one ever could ! " he mutters, and gives the picture hurriedly back to her as if anxious to get it out of his sight.

A moment or two after this, Avonmere remarks that he must say good-bye ; and Miss Follis bidding him adieu becomes quite cordial, telling him she has tea every Wednesday afternoon, and also remarking she will be happy, and she knows her mother will be pleased, if he will drop in whenever he finds no better amusement.

Bowing his acknowledgments and saying adieu to Mrs. Marvin, he passes into the hall.

When making some excuse of a forgotten message, the widow follows him, and the footman being busy with the front door, he whispers to her with British confidence, " Have no fear, I shall make myself intimate with young Van Beekman and find a way to his undoing "

" But if you don't ? " she asks anxiously.

" If I don't ? " he laughs, next suddenly mutters, Italian passion coming into his eyes, " But I will! I'd have that beauty were she no engaged girl, but had Van Beekman's wedding-ring upon her finger."

" Don't let me hear another such word from your lips!" cries Mrs. Marvin, growing very red. " Remember, sir

I am your mother in this affair—and an American with American principles!" For this lady, though she trades in heiresses, is of Boadicea-like but conventional virtue, and holds the wedding-ring very sacred, though it some-times covers a multitude of sins.

At this he gives a little laugh and says, " I thought it was understood this affair was to be conducted by you on the *French* system; why not carry into it Parisian ethics also, *belle maman?*" Then with a little laugh on his mobile features he gives the flunky at the hall door a liberal tip, believing it is always convenient to stand well with the servitors in any house he has an interest in, and strolls down the brown-stone steps on to Fifth Ave-nue; leaving Mrs. Marvin looking after him and thinking, "The horrid foreign wretch! if I'd known he would fall in love with the girl, I could have got *fifteen per cent.*

A moment after she says very haughtily to the footman who has been gazing at her Boadicea expression with open mouth, " What are you looking at, sir? Close the door at once. Do you want to freeze me?" and strides back to the library to find Miss Follis looking at a big diamond on her engagement finger in a rather contem-plative way.

" Isn't it a beautiful stone?" exclaims the girl, holding it up for inspection, and whispers, " I'm afraid it must have ruined poor Gussie."

" Yes, if he paid for it!" returns La Marvin, who has gone to turning over the photographs, searching for the picture of the Baby mine cañon. This she examines very carefully, striving to see what the picture contained to cause such extraordinary emotions to Lord Avonmere.

Though she racks her aged brains over this photo-graph, she can make nothing of it, and so follows Matilde up-stairs and to bed, where she again sets her mind upon the puzzle with no better success.

The subject of her anxious meditations lighting a cigar, strolls down Fifth Avenue, now bright with elec-tric light and made bustling with equipages bringing their occupants home from the theatres and the opera, and transferring them from dinners and receptions to the balls and dancing parties that generally begin about this time of the evening. These are less numerous than usual, a good portion of New York society having, like Miss

Follis, worn itself out at the great ball of the night before.

After wandering along a few blocks, he hails a passing "hansom" and says, "The Stuyvesant Club—Quick!" for he has made up his mind to become intimate with little Gussie, and knows the place where he will quite probably run upon him at this time of night.

He has in his pocket a visitors' card sent him for this rendezvous of the more Anglofied New York set, and strolls into the spacious hall of this establishment to hear the sounds of revelry coming from the smoking-room. Among the voices he recognizes that of little Van Beekman.

Then the flunky taking his hat suddenly begins to snicker, and a song is wafted to Avonmere's ears that makes him grit his teeth with rage as the hidden meaning of its refrain comes home to him, for it is an atrocious paraphrase of the popular ditty, "Baby Mine," and Gussie's friends end it with this significant chorus:

> I shall get it from papa, baby mine, baby mine,
> I shall spend it all, tra la ! baby mine, baby mine.
> It is coming quick to me, baby mine, baby mine.
> It'll all be brought by she, baby mine, baby mine.
> Then Beek 'll have a spree. baby mine, baby mine.

A moment after, controlling his features, he enters the room to find Augustus holding high carnival, surrounded by his particular cronies, to whom he has been imparting the news of his engagement, and who have been toasting him in champagne, which has gone to their heads and driven them to singing the doggerel Avonmere has just heard.

This has been the concoction of a stock-broking youth, one Grayson, who has just remarked, with brutal Wall Street wit, "We could spare the gals, don't yer know, but it's losing the money hurts us. We're shipping too much gold to Europe anyway. Gussie has saved the country this trip !"

Strolling up to this little savior of his country, who is slightly elated both by good fortune and champagne, Avonmere remarks : "I've just been calling at No. 637 Fifth Avenue and heard the news. My congratulations, old fellow !"

"Awh—thanks, my dear Lord Avonmere !" ejaculates Gussie with tremendous emphasis on the title.   "Please sit down with us," and introduces his friends to him.

On this Avonmere joins the party, and throwing himself into the conversation becomes so genial and pleasant that they all get to loving this hearty, jovial English aristocrat, and make a very jolly night of it ; little Augustus during the evening telling him he has just come from the Brevoort, where he has been to see Phil Everett and his pretty sister, Miss Bessie, who has captured the Marquis of Grousemoor.

"Is Grousemoor in town ?" asks Avonmere, a slight shade running over his countenance.

"Oh, trust him for that !" cries Van Beekman.   "Phil and his sister have come over from Boston to stay a month or two, and Grousemoor's so sweet on the charming Bessie, he could no more keep away from her than a fly could from fly-paper."   Then he goes on reflectively: 'I wonder how an English lord can marry in this country.   By George ! if I had an English title and an English estate, it would be an earl's daughter or nothing."

"Would it ?" mutters Avonmere under his mustache, and sits looking at the little fellow as he sips his wine with his caddish affectation and dudish ideas until on a sudden a smile of mixed amusement and triumph lights the nobleman's Italian eyes.

A few moments after, he bids little Gussie and his friends good evening and passes out ; but getting to the cloak-room of the club he goes into such a spasm of jeering laughter that the attendant handing him his hat drops that article in amazement on the floor.   But somehow the English lord has got into such a good humor that he doesn't chide the servant, though not as a rule polite to his inferiors.

Little Gussie is also happy, and issues from the smoking-room to be made more so.

Avonmere contrives to meet him in the hall, remarking : "You live up the avenue ? I am at the Saint Marc. Supposing we walk along together."

"Right you are, chappie !" cries the elated Van Beekman, whose elegance of diction has been somewhat destroyed by champagne.

The Englishman lighting a cigar, and the puny New

Yorker illuminating a cigarette, they leave the club, arm in arm, for Gussie is determined upon getting as close to the peer as he can, and in fact finds his support almost a physical necessity. As they stroll on their way, Avonmere deftly pumps his little companion as to his views on certain social questions, and just as they reach Gussie's door brings the subject round again to Lord Grousemoor's American *fiancée*.

He remarks : " American women are generally handsome. I hear Miss Everett is extremely beautiful. I don't wonder at Grousemoor's infatuation. I understand she'll have a very pretty portion, though of course no such a settlement as your Western heiress."

" Of course, little Bessie's good-looking and rich, but how any Englishman of *title* can wish to marry out of his own class is more than I can get through my head," babbles Augustus.

" Indeed !" murmurs Avonmere. " But I'm keeping you in the cold. Good night ! If you've nothing better to do, breakfast with me—to-morrow at eleven—will you ? "

" Delighted ! Won't I ! " giggles Gussie. " Saint Marc, you said," and passes into his doorway.

Gazing after him, the Englishman laughs a nasty little laugh again and then mutters : " His own caddishness shall be his ruin."

As for Augustus, he gets into his room and dances about and screams out significantly, " Skyrockets ! *Skyrockets !* SKYROCKETS !" then chuckles merrily, " Yesterday pursued by a beast of a tailor—to-day engaged to millions and chums with *two* Lords," and so goes to bed the happiest dude in New York.

CHAPTER XII

MADAME LAMERE'S ACADEMY FOR YOUNG LADIES.

IF the announcement of his engagement brings comfort, ease, and rest to little Gussie, it raises up a buzz of dissent, and even opposition, about the pretty ears of Miss Matilde.

She announces her happiness to her mother, and that lady cries out, astounded : "Going to marry that little sniff ? Tilly, don't joke on such a biz ! I should think you had too much ed-u-cash to fool about such a going on ! "

"But I mean it, mamma ! " mutters the young lady, with a charming, little surly pout, partly at Mrs. Follis's unbelief and partly at her diction.

"Don't you tell me fibs, Tillie ! " cries her mother. " I won't stand it from you now no more than I would if you was knee-high. No girl tells her mother she's keeping company with her fellah without a blush of maiden skittishness, and you ain't got the color of a chloride this morning ! "

"Blushes have nothing to do with facts," returns Miss Follis calmly. "It is not the fashion to blush now—in society ; and please don't ever use such an awful expression as 'keeping company with a fellow.' If any one else had heard it I should die of blushes, fashion or no fashion. Besides, you may know I'm not joking by *this !*" And she exhibits, perhaps a little defiantly, Mr. Gussie's diamond.

At this a mother's tears of tenderness come into Rachel's eyes, as she says, astonished : " You love that popinjay ? 'Tain't possible ! " Then suddenly cries : " Darter, I—I ask your pardon for calling your fellah that—if you're really sweet on him ! " And getting her arms about Matilde's fair neck, she sobs : " He's going to take you from me—I can see it in your face ;" this criticism of her choice having put a very determined look into the girl's eyes.

Softened by Rachel's tears, the young lady gets to crying also, and blurts out : " No man shall take me from you if you don't wish it." For she loves her mother very dearly.

And this settles the matter. After that speech Mrs Follis is as wax in her daughter's hands, and tells her with many caresses and some tears : " You shall do just as you like, my darter, and marry the man you cotton to ; and if father objects send him to me ; I'll take the ginger out of him in short order ! "

"It isn't dad—I mean father—that'll make the trouble, I think," mutters Miss Follis, forgetting the fashion and holding a blushing and tearful face upon her mother's bosom.

"No?" mutters Rachel.   Then with a sudden flash of thought, she cries : "It's Bob you're thinking of—you never promised him, did you, Tillie?" and goes on sternly : "If you gave your word, my darter, you shall live up to it!"

"Mother, as I'm your child, I never gave him hope!" answers Matilde.

"Then if he comes from Colorado to make a muss, you send him to me, and I'll teach him to raise his eyes to people that have moved out of his set—I'll—! You pass him on to me and I'll give Bob Jackson the settling down of his life!" And Rachel Follis looks her words. Her forefathers have fought Indians in Kentucky, and she has defended herself from them in Minnesota, and once faced a grizzly in the Rocky Mountains, and at this moment, though robed in silks and laces, she is the frontier woman of her earlier days.

This makes Matilde think she has got over the worst of her opposition, but in this she is mistaken, for the absent Bob has a very zealous and near-by champion.

Some three or four hours after Matilde's interview with her mother, Miss Flossie Follis, having obtained leave of absence from Madame Lamere, drives up from her school, and passing the attending footman in the hall, strides up the stairs to her sister's room, with a very determined look on her young face.

At the door of Matilde's boudoir—for Miss Follis has taken unto her own use a complete suit of apartments in this ample house—the girl raps sharply, and cries : "It's Flossie, home from school," and getting the answer : "Come in, you darling!" runs into Matilde's open arms, for the two girls love each other very dearly, having been inseparable companions and confidantes until the elder had left the younger at school and entered society.

"This is delightful!" cries Miss Follis, after their first caress. "Are you off for the day? How did you get out of Madame's clutches?"

"I—I had to go to the dentist," mutters the other, with an embarrassed blush.

"Oh, a little fib!" laughs Matilde.   "I am to be your

tooth-extractor to-day. Which tooth, Flossie ? " and seizing her sister she playfully forces her into an easy-chair, crying out : " Open your mouth ! I want a pretty pearl from your lips ! "

" Look out ! I always bite my dentist if he hurts," returns Flossie, and the two girls go into a laughing love-struggle, in which they make a picture that would have been very beautiful to masculine eyes, the one blonde and piquant, the other dark and noble. But finally, the patient conquering the dentist, the two sink down on a sofa, with arms around each other's waist, exhausted but still struggling.

A moment later Flossie asks : " How's mother ? Your dentist attack was so sudden, I couldn't ask before."

" Well, but at present out of the house," answers Matilde, lightly.

But here the conversation takes a sudden and awful turn. A severe and determined voice comes to her ears. " What is that awful *new* diamond doing on your en-gagement finger ? Oh, you needn't try to turn it round and hide it. *I've seen it !* Tillie, it isn't true ? That's what I came up about," and Miss Flossie, producing a copy of the *Town Tattler*, and holding the paper before her sister, says earnestly and reproachfully: " TELL ME IT ISN'T TRUE."

But she gets no answer to this. Matilde seeing her chance, carries the war into Africa. " You horrid, naughty child ! " she cries. " How dare you read that abominable paper ? That's nice reading for a boarding-school girl ! If Madame Lamere, or worse still, mother knew—WHEUGH ! " She emphasizes this with a piquant little gesture, and a miserable paraphrase of a laugh.

" That's nothing to do with it," answers Flossie, very seriously. " That paper was shoved before me by half a dozen girls. The school's full of it. I—I did not be-lieve it. Tell me it is not so. Tell me that awful ring is a lie ! "

Looking at her sister, Miss Follis thinks it is as well to have the matter out with her at once. She says slowly : " Florence, it is the truth ! "

To this the other answers with a great reproach in her voice, but one word—"*Bob !*"

" Don't talk of him ! " cries the older. " You shan't

ding his name into my ears. Sometimes I think it never leaves them, sleeping or waking."

"Ah! That proves that you have no right to wear another man's ring. That proves that Bob has *still* your heart."

"*Still* has my heart? He never had it. I never gave him hope. NEVER! How dare you reproach me?" answers Matilde, trying to unclasp her sister's arms.

But the other, unheeding her, goes on: "The awful vanity of this place has changed you. You are not the same little girl that used to stand by me waiting for the stage when it brought Bob in from Denver, loaded down with everything his generous heart could think of for our appetites and pleasures."

"They were for you as much as for me!" answers Matilde. Then attempting an affected laugh, she cries: "You seem interested in Bob yourself, why not give him the happiness I deny him?"

"And you dare sneer at his great love?" stammers Flossie, as she starts back from her sister, her face pale with astonishment and reproach.

"It was not a sneer—only a suggestion," murmurs Matilde, avoiding Flossie's eyes and appearing embarrassed and ashamed of herself, as in truth she is.

"You know that would be impossible," returns her sister gravely. "Bob *likes* me, he *loves* you. You've had his big heart, Tillie, since you were almost a child. Besides, why talk to me in this way? Haven't I often told you"—here the girl blushes and hesitates a little—"that I love another?"

"Oh!" screams Matilde, eager to change the subject; "haven't you got over that mythical cowboy you've always been dreaming about ever since I found a dear little sister who had forgotten who she ever was?"

But here Flossie gives Matilde an awful start: "Mythical?" she cries; "he is becoming more real to me every day. I recollect his name now!"

"His name?" gasps her sister in a half-frightened yet curious way. "What was it?"

"*Peter!*" answers Flossie very solemnly, and then says: "Sometimes I think the past would all come back to me now, if I could only get something to start with, I should remember my father and my mother——"

But before she can say another word, Tillie is round her neck crying : "If you find them, Flossie, if you find them, you won't desert us ? You'll break father's and mother's hearts. They are as true to you as if you were their flesh and blood, and you know I love you, or I'd never have taken this talking to you've given me to-day."

And Flossie, conquered by this outburst, cries: "Never ! Your father is my father, your mother is my mother, and you are my sister ! I could love no one more dearly ! "

Then the two girls get round each other and make love to each other and keep it up all the afternoon, not mentioning their quarrel by hint or allusion.

But Flossie, on going away, whispers solemnly : " Tillie, think of what I have said ; it would hurt you to have me leave you. Think how it will break that generous heart in far away Colorado, if he loses you. Don't let a social ambition destroy your happiness in life ! "

With this the school-girl passes down-stairs, and, Mrs. Follis not having returned, goes back to Madame Lamere's, and would perhaps have a hard time of it, for her absence has been too long a one, did not the signs of emotional misery on her face prove that she has visited the dentist and suffered greatly at his hands.

Some two days after this, Avonmere having made himself intimate with Mr. Augustus and his family history, including the revolutionary scandal, and fathomed every shallow of his puny and caddish mind, goes over his plan of action very carefully, and settles all preliminary details.

Then strolling up the avenue he rings the bell of the Follis mansion, and asks for Mrs. Marvin.

He has told her the evening before, at a ball given by Mrs. Bradford Morton, of his intended visit, and the widow is ready to receive him alone—the chief subject of their conversation, Miss Follis, being out of the house upon some feminine errand.

During these two days, however, Avonmere, though he has taken great care to show no attention to Miss Matilde that might make little Gussie jealous, knowing that small minds value most what they see others prize, has still contrived to keep himself pretty well in the young lady's view, dancing with her once or twice, and devoting five minutes to her at two afternoon teas. He has also contrived that she shall discover that he is considered of much more consequence in the social world than all the Van Beekmans and De Punsters put together, a fact he has not much difficulty in impressing upon her sharp Western intellect, New York society getting on its knees to a genuine English peer of the realm in a way that wears out feminine stockings and masculine trousers very quickly, as Mr. Grayson, the Wall Street wit, puts it.

After passing the compliments of the day, Avonmere comes rather bluntly to the business he has on hand, and says : " I do not think Miss Matilde will throw Van Beekman over."

" Indeed ! Why not ? " whispers the widow.

" Well, I think she has too much principle for it," he remarks. " I have sounded her, and she cut me off very short."

" Principle ?—It's stiff-necked obstinacy ! " cries Mrs. Marvin. " She was almost ready to toss over that wretch the day after her engagement. She would have hated and despised him by this time, if it had not been for her chit of a sister ! "

" Her sister ? " echoes Avonmere, somewhat astonished, for he has never heard of Miss Flossie.

" Yes, a boarding-school girl. She's at Madame Lamere's Academy now. What does she do, but having read in some copy of that immoral *Town Tattler* that she must have smuggled into the school, and for which, if I was Lamere, I'd——! " Her words fail to do justice to the idea, and she fills it out with expressive gesture. Then calming herself a little, she goes on. " Well, what does this minx do after reading a notice of her sister's engagement in the *Tattler* but rush up from her studies, and striding in to her sister, show her the article in the paper, and with the air of a Queen Elizabeth and the tact of an imbecile, demand if it is true. Then being rather curtly informed that it was a fact by Matilde, who has a very pretty spirit of her own, as you'll perhaps discover some day, the two sisters had an awful time, the younger giving the elder a regular oration, championing and espousing the cause of ' Bob,' a Colorado miner, who apparently has his eyes upon Miss Follis, with matrimonial views." To this Mrs. Marvin adds : " Of course the scene did not take place in my presence, for both

9

girls are far too lady-like to indulge in any such discussion in public ; but I learnt the facts from my maid, who
has a way of picking up news about the house in a
manner peculiar to herself and useful to me."

"A younger sister and a Colorado suitor, two new
complications ! " remarks Avonmere. "One will halve
Miss Follis's settlement, and the other may win girl, settlement and all."

"Matilde will have the portion I told you. That
should be enough even for you. As for Rocky Mountain Bob, he's far away at present," replies the widow
Then she goes on : "You indicated to me at Mrs. Morton's that you had something to suggest ; but at present
I hear nothing of it."   This last is in a disappointed tone.

"Precisely ! " murmurs the lord in his unconcerned
way. "I was about to hint that as we cannot induce the
young lady to jilt Mr. Gussie, we must induce little Gussie
to jilt HER."

"Induce a pauper to give up an heiress ? " jeers Mrs.
Marvin, whom this disappointment is making ill-tempered.
"You must be mad, Lord Avonmere ! "

"Perfectly sane, thank you ! " he replies.

Then, though all this conversation has been carried on
in an undertone, and their heads have not been five feet
away during the interview, he draws his chair close to the
sofa upon which the widow is sitting, and says imperi-
ously, "LISTEN ! "

With this, placing his lips quite close to one of the
lady's diamond ear-rings, he begins to whisper the plan he
has formulated in his subtile brain for making the pov-
erty-stricken Gussie de Punster Van Beekman discard and
disdain the reigning heiress of Colorado, Miss Matilde
Tompkins Follis.

At first, as his idea strikes her, she starts and gazes at
him as if not quite sure of his sanity and cries, "Impossible ! "   Then as he goes on, and the social invention of
this lord, with British doggedness and Italian cunning
comes thoroughly home to her in all its exquisite comedy, La Marvin throws herself back on the sofa, and
such shrieks and convulsions of laughter rush through
her fat frame that there is an ominous sound of breaking
lacings in the vicinity of her pinched-in waist.

Avonmere looks at her calmly as this goes on, but after

a time, fearing apoplexy, her face has grown so red, he lifts her up and says, " I thought you would enjoy the little comedy ! "

" Won't I ! " screams the widow, and goes off into another spasm, and with tears in her eyes mutters, " Poor little Gussie—O my ! I think I see him ! "

But Avonmere says pointedly : " Now to carry out my idea, I must have money, and a good deal of it. Can you get it for me ? "

At his mention of the pecuniary difficulties of his plan, Mrs. Marvin looks very serious. After a little consideration, however, she says : " I think I know how I can obtain the money you desire. I can answer you definitely in a few hours. How much do you want ? "

" It would not be safe to attempt the thing on less than a thousand ! " returns Avonmere.

" A thousand ? Oh, I can fix that surely. A thousand dollars is—— "

" A thousand *pounds*," he interrupts.

" Of course, I might have known that. The thousand pounds shall be at your disposal, if I can get them from the source I have in my mind. You shall hear from me this evening. Please ask Matilde to hold her brougham for me. I see she has just driven up," remarks Mrs. Marvin, glancing out of the window.

Encouraged by these words, he makes his adieu and passes out to meet Miss Follis, who is just alighting, with that grace of motion so common to American girls.

She gives him such a pretty bow and bright smile as he delivers his message, that Avonmere strides down the avenue, at one moment praying that Mrs. Marvin will get the money for his scheme, at the next cursing the little Augustus who has seized upon this beautiful prize, which his hands had reached out to grasp.

A few minutes after, the widow gets into the Follis brougham and says to the footman, as he closes the door : " Madame Lamere's."

This direction being very well known to the coachman, Mrs. Marvin soon finds herself in front of that fashionable young ladies' school and its door opening to her.

A moment after, she sends her name in to Madame Lamere, and is effusively received by that lady, who knows that her visitor can put her in the way of a good many scholars, if she only raises her voice and chants her praises a very little.

Madame Eulalie Euphrosyne Lamere is a *petite* bundle of foreign airs, French graces, British deportment, and broken English, complicated by an atrocious accent.

Cutting short her extremely vivacious and long-drawn-out nothings as soon as possible, Mrs. Marvin, who is American as regards business directness, requests to know if she can see Miss Florence Follis for a few moments.

"Ah! Zat Mees Fo-lees," cries the little school-teacher. "I do not like to—she es varie un-ruly; she is in disgrace, my dear Madame Marvin. She is an atrocity. She has a rebellion in her blood," and Lamere winds up with a French shrug indicative of horror and dismay.

"What has Florence done?" asks Mrs. Marvin, rather curtly.

"Ah! At ze opera class."

"The opera class?" cries the widow, astonished.

"Oui! Ven zey have a ver fine opera, I make up an opera class of my oldest pupils. I take a box, and zen under my instruction zey study ze music of ze grand maisters. Last night I took zem to—a Wagner."

"Yes, I saw you there," breaks in Mrs. Marvin, impatiently, she being anxious to see the young lady and get her business settled.

"Vel, I take zem there. I find myself in ze corridors of ze Metropolitan with five young ladies. Then zey grow wild wid ze lights, ze people and ze excitement. One gazes at ze dresses, another look at ze diamonds, all ze other at ze gentlemen. Zey are here!—zair!—every-whair! I am wild myself, like a hen with ducklins."

"I can sympathize with you," remarks Mrs. Marvin, giving a little sigh as she remembers some of her own troubles, chaperoning debutantes.

"Oh, zat is not ze worst!" continues Madame. "As soon as I get zem to my loge, Mademoiselle Florence sees a gentleman, tall, vith le bel air, and dark eyes come into ze box in which you and her sistar, Mees Matilde, sit. She say to me: 'I will go down and sit vid my sistar.' Mon Dieu! Tink of zat,—vith three or four gentlemans in ze box! If I had let hair, in one moment ze whole class would have demanded ze same privilege, and been scatared into the boxes of the Metropolitan. I say, 'You are mad, Mademoiselle.' She say: 'I am going down to zat box—I must see my sistar.' I say: 'It is not your sistar zat you want to see. It is zat gentleman vid ze black eyes.' Then she grows very haughty, and say vid zat grand air of hers: 'Madame, you are right!' At zis my young ladies all giggle out loud, and I nearly faint, but I whisper sternly to her: 'Mademoiselle, you shall not leave ze box, *nevair!* I will take you home first!' And she say: 'There is no need of zat; while I am under your authority I shall obey your instructions, Madame Lamere,' and growing sulky she goes to ze back of ze box. Zen after a few moment I see ze gentleman in ze next loge laugh a leetle, and I look round, and, Mon Dieu! Mademoiselle Florence is giving all my young ladies chocolate caramels, *witch zey are eating behind zair fans.*"

During this melancholy recitation, Mrs. Marvin has laughed a little. She now cuts off Lamere's pedagogic woes by saying: "Notwithstanding her disgrace, I wish to see Miss Florence immediately. It will be a very great favor to me. Mrs. Jameson was speaking about leaving her daughter at your school during her projected European tour——"

"I vill send Mademoiselle down *immediatement!*" cries the schoolmistress upon this hint of a new pupil, and she leaves the widow in the reception-room.

Waiting for the young lady's appearance, voices come to Mrs. Marvin's ears. They are from two school-girls who are passing through the hall to recitation.

One says in rather a loud tone: "Another swell caller. Miss Nobody of Nowhere'll be putting on airs."

The other says in a frightened tone: "Hush! If Madame heard you call her that you'd catch it!"

A moment after, Miss Flossie Follis enters the room; she is in a quiet tailor-made dress, very appropriate to a school-girl, but faultless as regards fit and style, for it simply displays the outlines of a figure that needs no other embellishment.

She has a bright smile on her face, and holds out her hand to Mrs. Marvin with easy grace.

"You look in very good spirits for a young lady who

is in disgrace, my dear," remarks the widow, accepting her salute.

"Oh, Madame Lamere says I'm rebellious, does she ! I should not be myself if I were not so—under the circumstances," laughs the girl.   Then she goes on suddenly, perhaps anxiously : "Who was that gentleman, rather tall, with dark eyes, in your box at the Metropolitan last night ? He sat behind my sister through an act."

"Lord Avonmere."

"Who ? " says the girl, apparently somewhat astonished at the answer.

"Lord Avonmere," repeats Mrs. Marvin.   Then, anxious to get to her subject, she laughs, "You did not think he was Mr. Van Beekman, did you ? "

"No ; I recognized Mr. Augustus without any trouble —the insignificant little blonde who whispered to Tillie the balance of the time."   Mr. Van Beekman's name has brought a sneer of contempt to Miss Flossie's pretty lip that pleases Mrs. Marvin mightily, for it prophesies that she will obtain the assistance for which she has come.

She sneers in return.   "Yes ; he is neither imposing nor popular.   I caught a remark in the crowd as we were waiting for our carriage last night, of ' Beauty and the Beast.' "

"Did you ? " cries the girl. "Oh, how can mother and you permit this horrible affair to go on ? You needn't explain to me ; I've heard all about it in the papers. I've given Tillie my opinion of the gentleman.   I've done what I could ! "   Then, perhaps ashamed at her outbreak, Miss Flossie pauses, blushing and embarrassed.

"Yes," assents Mrs. Marvin in a kindly tone of voice, "perhaps you have done too much, my child."

"Too much ! " cries the girl, getting excited again. "When I looked at his dissipated, worn-out face last night, and thought of—of a very noble gentleman who ——" She does not continue the remark, but a generous enthusiasm lights her noble features and makes her more beautiful than before.

Noting this, Mrs. Marvin comes immediately to her subject.   She says : "I called upon you on this very matter, my child.   I agree with you that Mr. Van Beekman is by no means a proper match for your lovely sister. She also would have thought so by this time——"

"You think, then, she does not love him?" interrupts Flossie eagerly.

"I am so certain of that," continues Mrs. Marvin, "that I am confident her engagement would have by this time been a thing of the past, had it not been for you, my dear."

"Not been for *me?*" cries her listener amazed.

"Yes; for YOU!" returns the widow. "Your enthusiastic heart made you lay aside your tact. You reproached your sister with her engagement. Her generous spirit makes her think it necessary to defend the man to whom she has given her rash promise. A mistaken idea of honor will compel her to abide by it, now she thinks him attacked—till, perhaps, the happiness of Matilde's young life may be wrecked upon a noble but quixotic sentiment."

"Then she will owe her unhappiness to my rash interference!" mutters the girl, and one perfect little foot that is liberally exposed by her short school dress begins to play a nervous tattoo upon the reception-room floor. A moment after she says : "I know Matilde's nature, she always stood up for the persecuted. She'll never give up that wretch. She is as good as Mrs. Van Beekman now."

"Not at all," murmurs Mrs. Marvin; "a little tact will save her. Shall we use it?"

"Save her? How?" asks the girl, so earnestly that the widow knows her point is gained.

"We will induce him to give *her* up."

"Give up Matilde with her beauty—with her for——? impossible!" replies Flossie, cutting 'fortune' short by a sudden contraction of her lips.

"That is what I said," murmurs Mrs. Marvin. "Will you aid me?"

"To the blood in my body!" cries Miss Enthusiast with a vehemence that makes the more conventional woman start from her chair.

"I shall not call upon you for that," she says with a little laugh, after settling herself in her seat. "All that is necessary is the money in your purse."

"How much?"

"Before I permit you to disburse your assets, I will first say that it is a sum beyond my individual command without great personal inconvenience, otherwise I should not have called on you."

"*How much ?*"

" My dear, you are too impatient ! " mutters the widow at this interruption. " I cannot explain the details of the affair—for that you must trust to me. The main point of the matter will be that Mr. Van Beekman will release your sister in a way that will produce no scandal and as little talk as possible under the circumstances. This is the probable outcome of the affair, though there is a bare possibility that he may still hold Matilde to her promise. That risk you must take."

" You give me your word of honor as a woman that it will in no way injure my sister, in name—honor—or good repute ? " says the girl very slowly and with a searching, anxious look in her eyes.

" As I am a mother myself, by the future of my own child, I give my word ! " answers Mrs. Marvin, growing pale and earnest herself, but meeting Miss Flossie's glance firmly. " The amount necessary will be six thousand dollars ! Can you furnish it ? "

" Is that *all ?* " says the younger Miss Follis. " Why, that's hardly more than four days' income ; I thought you wanted half a million ! "

" Four days' income ? " gasps the widow, rolling her eyes.

" Oh," smiles Flossie, " don't think me a Vanderbilt or an Astor. My income is mostly from a mine ; it is really part of my capital dug out and paid me, as a bank would honor my checks. If it came from real estate entirely, then I *should* be a capitalist."

" Who taught you all you know of finance ? " queries the widow.

" Bob, that is, Mr. Robert Jackson, one of my trustees. You may thank him for the power I have to give you the money at once. He deposited ten thousand dollars at the Second National here, and gave a bond to them so that I, being a minor, could check it out over my own signature. Bob's a very good friend of mine."

" I should think so ! " murmurs Mrs. Marvin, who recollects what Abe Follis in Denver had told her of " Bob's " getting the girl a fourth of the " Baby " mine.

" And I'm a good friend of his," continues Flossie. " But I'll run up-stairs and bring you down my check."

With this she leaves the widow, who meditates upon the four days' income and wonders if Miss Flossie would not, perchance, be willing to sacrifice herself in marriage to Avonmere, whose appearance seems to have interested her, and so save her sister for the " Bob " whose friend she has declared herself to be.

A moment after, the girl enters the room again, her pretty face black as a thunder-cloud, and cries : " You may thank Madame Lamere for not receiving the money this evening. Whenever I invest in too many *marrons glacés*, as a punishment she bankrupts me by locking up my check book."

" That can be easily arranged," suggests Mrs. Marvin. Then she sits down at a table upon which there are writing materials, and producing from her pocket-book a blank check fills it up.

The next instant Flossie has signed it and sneered, " Isn't it humiliating to be a school-girl capitalist. I'm going to try to get out of Madame's clutches."

" So I would, my dear. Then you can go to the opera like a young lady, not a school-girl ! " returns her visitor, folding up the check that she has made payable to " Cash " and placing it in her pocket-book.

" Oh ! another humiliation," pouts the girl. " You saw me there? An opera-class ! But it's very funny if you know the peculiarities of an opera-class."

With this her charming features relax and she goes laughingly on : " Whenever Madame Lamere wishes a free ticket to the opera, which is generally when the piece is popular and seats command a high premium, she makes up an opera-class ; that is, she orders four or five of her pupils to visit the performance with her, and so study its music. The price of the box is divided among the young ladies, she getting the best seat for nothing and making a few dollars besides, as she charges each girl the full cost of a carriage to and from the place, but jams the whole crowd into one hack without remorse. A fat girl sat on me all the way home last night. You say that handsome man who visited your box and talked to Tillie is Lord Avonmere ;—a British title, is it not ? "

" Yes, my love," answers the widow, getting effusive. " He has one of the oldest baronies in the English peerage." Then rising to go, she says, "I think you would enjoy New York society under my chaperonage. Why not let me persuade your mamma to permit you to leave school now and see a little of it this winter?"

"Will you?" cries the girl; "how happy you make me!" and gives the old lady such a genuine hug that she is astounded, for Miss Flossie has been rather formal in her intercourse with her up to the present moment.

As Mrs. Marvin leaves, she remembers the conversation of the school-girls and laughingly asks, "Who is Miss Nobody of Nowhere?"

"Ah, you heard them," cries the girl, growing suddenly red, but also laughing a little. "My school companions are not very grateful. I have made them all sick twice this week with caramels, and they call me THAT! It's a polite reference to the unknown pedigree and location of my direct ancestors."

"It does not seem to disturb you much," says the widow, biting her lip at her unfortunate question, being a woman of admirable tact and refined social instinct.

"No," answers the girl; and then astonishes La Marvin, for she continues, "because I know some day I'll be *Miss Somebody of Somewhere!*"

"How are you sure of that?" queries the widow, who has got to the front door-step.

"Oh," cries Miss Flossie, "it's all coming back to me. Soon I shall know everything about my former life; I've got the cowboy settled already!"

With this ambiguous reply she closes the door, and being in an apparently happy frame of mind, forgets where she is and goes about the school singing a noisy *chanson*, to the horror of two French governesses, a professor of music, an English servant-girl, and the pupils in general, and the vengeance of Madame Lamere, who has never heard such an outbreak in lesson-time before in her select establishment.

Getting into her carriage, Mrs. Marvin determines to have Miss Flossie and her fortune out of school at once, so that she may become another business property.

And in this she makes a woful error; for youthful beauty and enthusiastic truth sometimes win the battle of life against the diplomacy of old age and the machinations of speculators.

CHAPTER XIII.

AN AMERICAN LORD.

THAT very evening Miss Flossie's generous contribution for his rival's undoing is handed to Avonmere by Mrs. Marvin; that lady being very careful not to inform him of the source from which the sinews of war arise, and merely remarking that the money has cost her a great personal inconvenience, which she shall expect him to remember when he wins the matrimonial stakes.

With this money in his pocket, Mrs. Marvin having transformed Flossie's check into bills, Avonmere strolls to the Broadway Theatre, where a Gaiety Company direct from London are performing in an imported burlesque, and giving out English concert-hall jokes to an audience composed largely of that portion of young America who pattern their manners, wit, and general deportment after cockney snobocracy, thinking a London chorus-girl more fascinating than a New York one, especially if she makes bad work of her H's.

Approaching the stage door of this principal theatre of New York, his lordship elbows his way through a little throng of these gentry who are being kept at a very respectful distance by the doorkeeper, assisted by a special policeman; for the Broadway is run upon American business principles, and all entrance behind its scenes is strictly forbidden to those who aspire to social intercourse with the ladies and gentlemen of its stage.

In this crowd the English aristocrat gets an unexpected surprise. Gussie's well-known voice cries in his ear: "Avonmere! *Lord* Avonmere, old fellow, do you think they'll let you in? That beast of a doorkeeper has just refused to deliver a note for me to Rosalie Mountjoy, the most fetching little creature you ever saw. Her accent is perfectly adorable. Makes me think I'm in Lunon, yer know. I want her to take supper with me. Oh, dear! there's that horrid Frank Hicks; he's sweet on her too. I must get my note in ahead of his. What *shall* I do?"

"Do?" whispers Avonmere sternly, wishing to make Augustus's bonds as irksome to him as possible. "Re-

member that you're engaged, sir, and go home!" and
he passes on, leaving his interrogator crestfallen and
abashed.

Getting to the doorkeeper and pencilling on his card
a few words, he asks that Cerberus to hand it to Mr.
Chumpie, one of the comedians of the company. A few
moments after word is brought to him that that gentleman, with Mr. Machlin, another Thespian, will meet him
at supper at Delmonico's as he requests.

These gentlemen keep their promise, and, the performance being over, Lord Avonmere entertains his two theatrical friends in a little private room in that perfect
restaurant, with a magnificent menu and generous
wines.

In his younger and richer days the English nobleman
had been somewhat of a patron of the drama, and as such
had done Chumpie some favors when that comedian was
struggling to gain recognition on the London boards.
Mr. Machlin, the leading character actor of the company,
is also well known to his lordship, and both the players
are anxious to respond to any wish of their generous
host.

Over their wine and cigars, Avonmere proposes to the
two actors that they take part in a little practical joke at
the expense of young Van Beekman, whom they have
seen several times obstructing the stage door, and value
accordingly.

This joke is of such a peculiar character that they at
first look aghast, but as their noble entertainer goes into
details they burst into such shrieks of laughter that Avonmere fears they will disturb the ladies and gentlemen in
adjoining rooms.

When they are calm again, he goes on, explaining to
them that this hoax can hurt nobody, and is certainly
inside the law, and that when it comes out it will make
the two Thespians famous as did some of the jokes of
that inimitable *farceur*, both on and off the stage—the
elder Sothern—or that great American comedian, the late
John T. Raymond. "In fact, it will as good as double
your salary if you come over to New York next season,"
he persuasively suggests.

To this Chumpie, who is a large, unctuous man, gives
a grin and says : " Machlin and I get reputation from

this hoax; but your lordship, who I presume will pay us for our acting, and put up a pot of money to prove to our little American friend that he has a rent roll across the herring pond—what do you get ? "

"Oh," replies his host, "I get rid of a rival ; " and seeing that he must explain his position to obtain the aid of these gentlemen of the stage, who are pretty sharp men of the world also, he gives them the whole truth of his plot to induce Mr. Van Beekman to jilt the Western heiress.

" If he's such a cad as that," replies Machlin, " I'll help you down him with all the stage art I possess."

" And I'll play the New York solicitor to this little wretch's present glory and ultimate destruction! " laughs Chumpie.

" Very well," answers their host, " I'll engage your offices and notify you to-morrow morning. Dress rehearsal at two P. M. sharp, and a hundred dollars a performance."

With this the two English actors say good-night, leaving their host in a very affable humor, enjoying his cigar and inspecting his project from every point of view between smoke puffs.

Some two days after Lord Avonmere's theatrical supper party at Delmonico's, little Van Beekman, dallying with a late breakfast, for which he affects an appetite he does not possess, looks over his morning's mail.

Among his letters is one upon which he gazes with suspicion and aversion. It has a legal aspect, its envelope bearing the names of Stillman, Myth & Co., Attorneys and Counsellors at Law, No. 61 Wall Street, and lawyers' letters have not been pleasant reading to him in the past few months.

He greets this with a subdued imprecation and tosses it away from him, as if he imagined its outside predicted that its inside would be decidedly not to his taste nor liking.

He mutters : "I thought the news of my going to marry Miss Bullion would have quieted these fish. Here's a shark who does not read the papers ! " Then he moans : " My heavens ! what a head I have accumulated over night ! " and presses the afflicted member with his two white plump little hands, and groans, " I wonder if

Avonmere is used up likewise ?" for he and that nobleman, who has become his chum and intimate, have been making a very gay night of it, after having spent the earlier portion of the evening at a dance given by Mrs. Van Courtland Jones.

Almost at this moment Avonmere enters the room, for the chumship has become so close between them that this gentleman has taken apartments in the same house as Mr. Gussie, and the two breakfast together both for company and economy.

"A little seedy also, old boy !" cries Augustus.   "Try a B. and S."

"No, thank you, I haven't a headache," returns Avonmere.   "You'd better try another ; you need it !   If you don't mind, I'd like some of that omelet, though ; " and he proceeds to make a hearty breakfast, occasionally dipping into his letters, of which there are quite a pile beside his plate.

Little Gussie sits watching him, gazing at one or two of these epistles with envious eyes, their monograms and crests denoting they are from houses to which he has not the *entrée*, for New York society has not forgotten the past offences of its native-born offender, though perfectly willing to ignore the news of any indiscretions that have been wafted over the ocean to the discredit of an English peer of the realm.   Even the news of his engagement to the Western heiress has not altogether obliterated Mr. Gussie's shortcomings, and as yet the heads of the Van Beekman and De Punster families have taken no notice of his improved financial prospects, by word or deed.

Toward the end of his meal a curious little incident happens.   Lord Avonmere catches sight of the note his companion had tossed away from him nearly to his side of the table.   "Hello," he remarks, "another letter for me ! " and picks the missive up apparently to open it.

"Excuse me," interjects Gussie suddenly, "that is my letter, dear boy."

"So it is," returns Avonmere, glancing at the address. Then he hands the note to Van Beekman, saying : " It was quite a natural mistake, though.   Stillman, Myth & Co. are the American agents of my London solicitors. I've had one or two interviews with them since I've been here."

"Kind of lawyers to be hard upon a fellah?" asks little Gussie, nervously, as he inspects the letter.

"No, I should think not; rather conservative, old-fogy sort of firm. Safe and sure. Do a large English business," murmurs the lord, turning to his breakfast again, but seeming to make bad work of it, as his coffee goes the wrong way, causing him to splutter and gasp as if convulsed.

A moment after Van Beekman desperately opens the envelope, Avonmere glancing at him as he does so with a kind of mocking smile. This changes into a grin as little Gussie cries, "Well, I'm blessed! What can it mean?" and hurriedly and excitedly reads to his noble listener the following note written upon the office paper of the firm signing it:

NEW YORK, *January 7th*, 1890.

A. DE PUNSTER VAN BEEKMAN, ESQ.,}
    No. 33½ West 37th Street.   }

DEAR SIR :—

Our London advices bring us news of the utmost importance as well as good fortune to you.

The information is of such magnitude and detail that we beg of you to do us the honor to call at our office *immediately* upon the receipt of this.

One of our firm would have waited upon you in person, but the documents sent to us, which could never be replaced or reproduced, are of such financial as well as social value that we dare not trust them out of our safe ; and it is necessary for you to examine them in person.

Trusting you will honor and oblige us with an immediate call, we are,

    Your most obedient and humble servants,

        STILLMAN, MYTH & CO.

"A deuced polite note," murmurs Avonmere.

"*Too* deuced polite," echoes Gussie ; "I wonder if it can be a plant?"

At this his *vis-à-vis* gets very red in the face and looks uneasy ; but a second after, catching Van Beekman's meaning, laughs till the tears roll down his cheeks.

"I don't see anything amusing, if those chaps get

me down there on this letter and serve a summons or writ or some other cursed legal thumb-screw to twist the dollars out of my pocket!" cries Augustus, angrily. "Did you ever have an attachment clapped on you? How did it feel then?

"They'd never have got themselves so down in the dust to get service on you of that kind," answers Avonmere, getting his breath and voice again. "I never had such a humble letter from lawyers in my life. Oh, yes, I did once," he suddenly corrects himself; "the notification that I had become a peer of the realm, from my solicitors, was just about as cringing a communication as that is."

"You think it's safe to go?" queries Gussie, anxiously.

"I think if I had received such a letter as that from such a firm as Stillman, Myth & Co., I should expect at least a pot of money left me by will, or some other unexpected good fortune, and should be down there as fast as the elevated railway could take me to their office," returns Avonmere, very seriously.

"If that's your idea, I'm off at once." With these words Mr. Gussie rings for his valet and gets under way for Wall Street with a most cheerful alacrity.

A few minutes later Avonmere puts on his overcoat and saunters up Fifth Avenue. As he is passing the reservoir he meets Mrs. Marvin taking an early walk, either for shopping or exercise.

Her face is red, but as she catches sight of him it grows pale and anxious. Coming to him she says nervously, "Has he got the note?"

"Yes; he's flying down to Stillman, Myth & Co.'s," laughs his lordship.

"You are sure every precaution has been taken?" she goes on.

"Certainly," he replies. "Chumpie, Machlin, and I had another dress rehearsal yesterday, I playing the part of the embryo Bassington. Chumpie was so inimitable as the lawyer that I nearly laughed myself sick." Then his eyes become excited also as he asks, "How is my darl—?" He does not continue the sentence, but remarks casually, "Miss Follis is well, I suppose?"

"Very well," says the widow. "I've had exercise

enough and am about to turn back ; will you mind walking beside me ? "

" Not if you will take me into the house when I get to the door-step," laughs the Englishman.

" It's rather early," murmurs Mrs. Marvin, " but as you're quite a friend of the family now, you can come along."

Then the two stroll up the avenue, Avonmere's eyes glowing and flashing and becoming more Italian as he gets nearer to a morning view of Miss Follis's piquant beauty.

While this is going on up-town, Augustus Van Beekman is hurrying to Wall Street as fast as an elevated train can carry him.

Arrived at the address mentioned in Stillman, Myth & Co.'s note, he ascends by the elevator to find their offices upon the third floor of the building. Entering their place of business, which is rather small for a firm having a large legal connection, the general appearance of the offices pleases little Gussie, for it is intensely legal and very English. Files of the *London Times* and *Telegraph* are prominent, to the exclusion of New York journals ; piles of neatly tied-up and red-taped documents encumber the desk and office table, and a number of tin boxes are in racks prepared for them. The printed labels upon some of these impress his feeble mind as he notes : " THE MARQUIS OF NOTHINGHAM'S AMERICAN PROPERTY," " MORTON, BLISS & CO.," " LORD COMBERMOOR'S NEBRASKA INVESTMENTS," " ST. LOUIS BEER SYNDICATE," " LORD AVONMERE," " MICHIGAN SOUTHERN CONTRACTS," etc., etc. With such noble investors for clients and gigantic financial enterprises to manage, the little fellow feels this great legal firm would never trouble itself to collect a tailor's or haberdasher's bills, and feels more easy in his mind.

He has not time for much thought, however, being apparently expected. The moment he enters a white-headed old clerk bows to the ground before him and says : " Mr. Van Beekman, I believe ? Mr. Stillman, the head of the house, has waited, hoping you might do us the honor to call this morning. He will see you at once." Then with another bow and a kindly twinkle in his old eyes, this gentleman, who wears a blue swallow

10

tail coat with brass buttons, and who is in both action and get-up exactly the English solicitor's head clerk one sees upon the stage, ushers him into the private sanctum of Mr. Stillman.

Before Augustus is fairly in the room, that lawyer, who is of portly build and pompous yet deferential demeanor, is speaking to him.

He ejaculates, "My dear sir—my *very* dear sir," and bows and squirms and writhes before the astounded Gussie in a way that makes that young gentleman think, "No writ of attachment here—not if I know myself."

Thus reassured, the little fellow becomes thoroughly at his ease and remarks : "Awh !—how are yer ? "

To this Mr. Stillman returns : "Quite well, I thank you, my —— " but mumbles his last word with another obsequious bow.

"Jarvis, a chair for his ——."   He again checks himself, and the head clerk doing as he is bid, Mr. Van Beekman, who has looked at this in a nonchalant sort of way, is soon seated beside the lawyer's office table, upon which are various portentous documents, including an immense family pedigree, and Debrett's and Burke's Peerages.

"Jarvis, until this interview and —— revelation are over," remarks Mr. Stillman, pompously, "I am in to nobody."

"Not if Morton or Bliss call about closing that contract of the St. Louis Beer Syndicate with the English investors ? " asks the clerk, humbly.

"Not even Morton or Bliss. And just another word with you, Jarvis," answers the lawyer, going into the outer office after his departing clerk.

When there he closes the door behind him, and little Van Beekman, whose pride has been greatly tickled that his affairs should be given precedence to those of a great banking house, wonders what the deuce the revelation can be.

A moment after, Stillman reënters, blowing his nose, tears coming from his eyes—whether of joy or sorrow, it is difficult to tell.

Taking a seat behind his desk and turning to Mr. Gussie he says, consulting every now and then a document: "You are the only son of DeWitt Van Beekman and Margaret Schiedam de Punster?"

"Yes!"

"De Witt Van Beekman was the lawful issue of George Morris Schermerhorn Van Beekman and Lydia Mosely Bassington?"

"Y-e-s, I think so," mutters Augustus.

"And Lydia Mosely Bassington was the only daughter of Roderick de Vere de Ponsonby Bassington, a lieutenant in the Fourth Buffs, Howe's own Regiment of the British army, which was quartered here in New York during the Revolution. While stationed in America he married Martha Van Vlete Floyd Smith, of Jamaica, Long Island."

"That's the old Revolutionary scandal. I'm tired of that!" mutters Van Beekman, sulkily.

"You needn't be," returns the lawyer, impressively. "That scandal we've been working for months to clear away, and have done so. The Lord Chancellor of England has declared the union legal; that Roderic Bassington's marriage with Lady Clara Alice Vestris Follomby was bigamous—*bigamous, sir!*—and that you, his legal descendant, are heir to said Bassington by lineal descent in the female line; that is, to you comes all that his daughter Lydia Mosely Bassington should have inherited."

"Why, he's been dead a hundred years," returns Augustus.

"What's a hundred years to English law or the English peerage?" cries Stillman, looking at his visitor curiously and tapping with caressing hand Burke's volume that lies on the table in front of him.

At the word peerage, Gussie grows more interested; he says: "Why don't yer come to the point?"

"You will permit me to break the matter to you gently," replies the lawyer.

"Is it so very horrible?" gasps Gussie, with pale face.

"Just the reverse," murmurs Stillman, blandly. "But too sudden joy is sometimes injurious."

"Joy!" cries Augustus, "I can stand any amount of that! Get to business at once!" Then he says eagerly: "Is it money?"

"It is more than that," continues the lawyer, gravely.

"Brown, Studley & Wilberforce, the well-known solicit ors, our London correspondents, wrote us some time ago about this matter, which is of the greatest importance to you. We have been investigating the affair quietly and have every proof necessary. Mr. Myth, of our firm, has been in England on this business over a month. He cabled me yesterday that the British Crown had withdrawn its interference and had acknowledged your claim, and that Brown, Studley & Wilberforce were willing to place you in possession of the estates."

"ESTATES !" gasps little Gussie, who has been gazing at him with open mouth and rolling eyes, dropping his gloves in uncontrollable agitation.

"Certainly, estates ; *large* ESTATES! But more than that !" and the lawyer lifts up Burke's volume, sacred to the nobility of England.

At this little Gussie grows pale, some inkling of that gigantic bliss that afterward came to him getting into his feeble brain.

Turning to that part of the book treating on " Titles in Abeyance," Mr. Stillman reads : " Hugo de Malvoisen de Bassington came over with William the Conqueror, and fighting right valiantly at Hastings, received from his sovereign estates in the Kentish hills. His descendant, Ralph Beauclerc de Bassington, married Bertha, the heiress of the Saxon Thane of Harrowby, and her dower greatly added to the family power and wealth. Guy Vipont de Bassington, his son, being made Baron by writ of Richard the Second in 1387, George Wiltshire Baron Bassington was created Marquis of Harrowby by Charles II , retaining Baron Bassington as the second title of his family.

"In 1873 Thomas, Marquis of Harrowby and Baron Bassington, died without issue, consequently the Marquisate (*descending only to heirs male*) became extinct, but the Barony of Bassington, one of the oldest in the kingdom, was left in abeyance."

With this Mr. Stillman closes the book and addresses his listener, who, hardly breathing, looks wonderingly at him. "The title of Baron Bassington may descend through females. Going back to collateral branches of the family we come to your ancestor of the Revolution, Roderic de Vere de Ponsonby Bassington."

Mr. Van Beekman's cane falls to the floor with an awful crash.

"From him," cries the lawyer, unheeding the noise, " from him comes to you, through your female ancestor, Lydia Mosely Bassington, the estates of Harrowby Castle in Kent, Beaumanor in Lancaster, and O'Mara House in County Clare, Ireland, together with various personalty and the time-honored title of Baron Bassington of the English peerage. You are now, my lord '—Mr. Stillman is rising slowly ; so is Gussie, with a pale face, trembling limbs, and rolling eyes—"You are now, my lord, A PEER OF THE BRITISH REALM, and I am, my lord, your very obedient servant. Permit me to humbly kiss your lordship's hand."

Stooping to do obeisance, the lawyer gives a yell of terror ; for joy and bliss and ecstasy have been too much for little Gussie, and Augustus, Baron Bassington of the English peerage, has fallen faint and limp into his arms.

"Jarvis ! " calls Mr. Stillman, getting his client into a chair, "his lordship is rather overcome with the news. Some water for his lordship ! "

But just at this moment Gussie springs up, crying out wildly : "It can't be true ! Call me that again, Stillman, call me a lord again ! "

"What is your lordship's pleasure ? " asks the attorney, seeming quite merry and fighting down a laugh.

"That's right, I heard you ! You gave me my title ! I'm a lord, an English lord ! Am I really, or is it some cursed dream from which I shall awake to be only an American and kill myself in despair ? " screams the new-made peer.

His ravings, for now he is nearly delirious with joy and rapture, seem to affect the attorney and his clerk with a hysteria that is difficult for them to control, though they fight it down, even when Baron Bassington suddenly seizes Burke, turns to his title, and cries out : "Jove ! what a *lovely* coat-of-arms ! Two lions rampant supporting a baron's coronet."

After a time his excitement becomes somewhat less, and he pulls himself together a little and remarks, "This news rather takes the form out of a man, don't yer know ! " and suddenly gasps once more, "I can't believe it !" Then turning to his lawyer he says, looking at him very earnestly and imploringly, "You are certain that you have made no mistake, that I am an English lord?"

"I am as certain," returns that gentleman, with a gulp in his voice, "that you are Baron Bassington of the British peerage, and entitled to a seat in the House of Lords, as that I am Harold Stebbins Stillman, of the firm of Stillman, Myth & Co., Counsellors and Attorneys at Law and Proctors in Admiralty."

"That being the case," says Mr. Van Beekman, quietly reseating himself, "I'll take something on account."

"Something on account—oh, ah, yes ! Your lordship would like to touch a portion of your rent-roll?" replies Mr. Stillman, blandly. "That was anticipated by your London solicitors. Brown, Studley & Wilberforce cabled some money over for your account yesterday."

"Yaas ! Then you can—awh—give me a check for a thousand !" remarks Gussie.

"Jarvis, a check for a thousand dollars for his lordship, at once !" says the attorney.

"Dollars?" laughs Augustus. "My poor Stillman, don't you know the unit of the English aristocracy is *pounds?*"

"Certainly, if you put it on that basis, Lord Bassington," he says, and goes into the next room.

A moment later he returns, remarking : "I was compelled to make this out to the order of Mr. Augustus Van Beekman, as you are not yet known in the banking world under your true title," and hands that gentleman a check for five thousand dollars on the Park National. "Would your lordship please sign a receipt for this?" He passes a pen to Gussie, whose little heart beats with pride as he signs, for the first time in his life, after the fashion of the English nobility, "Bassington."

"You can open an account with this check, your lordship, under the name of Bassington, by which, after this, our firm will address its communications to you. We must, however, notify you that this amount is all that has been cabled over. If you wish further funds we will forward your draft on Brown, Studley & Wilberforce to London for collection, and the returns will be here in a little over two weeks."

"Yaas. Tell Jarvis to draw on my London solicitors for five thousand pounds," says Augustus, grandly Then with a sudden interest he asks, "What is my income from my English estates?"

"That I'm unable to state with absolute accuracy, but I believe it is between thirty and fifty thousand pounds a year, your lordship."

"Humph! Tell Jarvis to draw for *ten thousand,*" cries Gussie.

"Certainly, my lord," mutters Stillman, struggling with a grin; "but I deem it my duty to inform you tha. the tenants upon your Irish property are somewhat behind in their rents."

"The *devil* they are?" says his lordship, in a severe and awful voice. "Then evict the scoundrels *at once!* Advise Brown, Studley & Wilberforce that Lord Bassington's instructions are to evict AT ONCE!"

"Y-e-s, your lordship," gulps Stillman, who pops his head into a drawer of his desk and seems overcome at this order, for when he raises his eyes to his client his face is very red and there are tears on his cheeks.

"What's the matter with you, sir!" cries the new-made lord; "you seem amused."

"No, my lord, not amused, but—affected," returns the lawyer, very slowly. "Does your lordship know the cruelty of these sudden evictions—how the poor tenants are turned out into the road to starve?"

"I know the villains don't pay their rents," interrupts Gussie, "and that a lawyer's duty is to do what he is told!"

Crushed by this rebuke, Mr. Stillman mutters: "Certainly, my lord." And Jarvis having brought the draft for ten thousand pounds to him, their noble client signs it "Bassington," and says: "Deposit this to the—awh —account of Bassington at Second National Bank as soon as collected. You can send in your bill also at the same time."

With this he rises and begins to draw on his gloves.

"We will send in our bill, my lord, if you so desire," assents the attorney. "But, my lord, we had hoped to have the honor of doing your American business, as Brown, Studley & Wilberforce are anxious to manage your

European properties."   This last Stillman emphasizes by a bow that is low enough and humble enough for an obeisance.

His humility causes greater hauteur on the part of his client.   Little Gussie draws himself up and says: "Yaas, Avonmere recommended you to me over our breakfast this morning.   I shall take that into consideration.—Jarvis, a cab for me, my man."

To this the clerk answers, "Yes, your lordship," and bolts from the office ; but getting outside clinches his fists and mutters : "Curse his impertinence !" but does his errand.

Meantime Gussie chats condescendingly with the lawyer.

"Stillman, do you know you're rather like that infernal bad actor, Chumpie, of the Broadway ? Your manner and style are like his, but your face has not the humor in it !" he remarks superciliously.

"Your lordship has seen the gentleman act ?" asks the attorney, growing very red in the face.

"Oh, yaas !   I've seen him often, but I did not go there to see *him* ; little Rosalie Mountjoy was *my* attraction." And he gives him a sickening wink and leer.

Then he runs on, telling the lawyer that he guesses the reporters 'll be after him before night.   "I shall refer the beggars to you, Stillman," he adds.

"If you do that, my lord," says the attorney shortly, "we shall be compelled to throw up your business."

"Throw up *my* business ?"

"Certainly ! because the gentlemen of the newspapers will so crowd this office that we won't be able to do anybody else's business."

"Ah," remarks Gussie.   "I see. I'll refer to my London solicitors ; they're farther away."   Then he runs on, declaring that he shortly will go to England, and that he will give his personal attention to matters connected with his large landed property.   "By Jove ! it's a nobleman's duty !" cries Augustus.   "I'll down that low grovelling leveller Gladstone the first day I sit in the House of Lords."

"Certainly ; but to do that your lordship will be compelled to renounce your American citizenship," returns the lawyer.

" Lord Bassington's cab !" interrupts Jarvis, showing
his face at the door.

" OH, CURSE AMERICA !" says Mr. Gussie. " Don't forget that draft, Stillman !" And this little patriot departs,
leaving the lawyer and his clerk gazing at each other.

Then the first, with a jeer and a laugh, yells, " Oh,
Boycotts and Parnell ! He'll turn out all the tenants
on his Irish estates," and he imitates little Gussie, giving
his eviction sentiments with much affected haughtiness.

" The impudent little beggar !" cries the other. " It's
lucky he left or I should have kicked his lordship down-
stairs. ' Jarvis, a cab for me, my man.' "

" He said I was a bad actor," mutters the lawyer. " I
pray the Lord I'm good enough for his undoing ! "

With these ominous words Mr. Stillman looks at his
watch and ejaculates, " One o'clock, Machlin ; just time
to get to the theatre for rehearsal."

CHAPTER XIV.

PETE ENTERS SOCIETY.

" SECOND National Bank like a streak ! " screams the
new-made lord to the driver, as he jumps into the hack
at 61 Wall Street. Then he suddenly cries, " Drive
slow !—Be careful !—Five dollars if you get me home
without accident ! " for the fact has just entered his
head that he has suddenly become very precious.

This morning he recklessly came down-town on the elevated railroad ; this afternoon the cab must go very slowly
and gingerly on its way. So Augustus Baron Bassington is driven cautiously up-town in a very daze of rapture. The sun is brighter, the day is more pleasant,
though the people in the streets seem more lowly and of
poorer clay to this newly-manufactured nobleman.

As he passes his friends his bow is very haughty and
distant. He hardly returns the salute of Mr. Grayson,
who is on the sidewalk at the corner of Wall and Nassau
streets, and who calls after him, " Hello, Gussie, my boy!
After your Baby mine dividends ? "

" Disgusting, vulgar creature," muses this peer of recent manufacture. " You'll see what a dividend I've drawn. I shall cut you, my boy, very soon ; and I've other social scores to pay. Baby mine dividends ? " He gives a start as this comes into his mind, and mutters, " Wonder if they had any idea of this. Marvin has the peerage at her finger ends ; perhaps she gave Matilde a hint to trap me before I knew my rank. Perhaps she thinks I'll sully old Hugo de Bassington's Norman blood. Perhaps ? " And assuming a most virtuous and indignant look Mr. Gussie sinks back in the hack and tries to think how he can escape his promise to the Western heiress, and leave himself and his *sang azure* free to marry the daughter of a duke.

A moment after he raps with his cane on the cab window and calls, " Park National Bank—quick ! " for it has suddenly struck him he had just as well get his check certified. That will be an absolute *settler* to the slightest suspicion of a doubt ; that will down any sneering unbeliever in his social and financial windfall.

In a few moments he enters this great money exchange, and getting to the paying-teller's window pauses and trembles, fearing there may have been some mistake ; but a moment after, remembering the genteelly imposing business connection of Stillman, Myth & Co., he plucks up courage and says : " Certify this, please ! "

Then his little heart gives one great long jump of triumphant joy as that official puts the stamp of this great financial institution upon it, and initials it, and makes it good for its $5,000 face beyond peradventure ; for to Gussie he is also certifying that Augustus Van Beekman has estates in England and Ireland, and is Baron Bassington to boot.

There is no doubt of his wealth, there can be no doubt of his rank, both come from the same source. He is a Peer of the British Realm as surely as the Duke of Westminster. He astounds the teller by crying, " Money talks ! " and joy and ecstasy making his step light, springs into his cab once more to drive up-town to his haunts and clubs, to strike his cronies mad with envy, to make girls who had snubbed and matrons who had ignored little Gussie Van Beekman bow down and do homage before Augustus Baron Bassington of the Peerage of England —to be the sensation of the hour and talk of the town.

For into his little caddish, selfish mind, in all his good fortune, there never comes one thought of how he shall, in his happiness, make one other person on this earth, happier or more blessed by the great wealth and grand social position this day has brought to him.

At Brentano's he buys *Burke's Peerage* of the year, and turns down the leaf at Bassington. At Tiffany's he orders the following :

Baron Bassington.

besides unlimited stationery with his coronet, crest, coat-of-arms, and motto in full on both envelopes and paper. These he instructs them to have ready next day, if they work all night to do it. Speed is everything ; expense nothing !

Then he turns his face to the Second National Bank, and entering the portals of that establishment, he meets Phil Everett.

"I am going to open an account here. They don't know me. Would you mind introducing me, Phil?" he remarks to his old-time college companion.

"Certainly," says Everett, who looks but little older, though perhaps a little stouter, than Pete the cowboy, for a Boston capitalist generally has daintier fare and less exercise than come to the vaquero of a New Mexican cattle range. And taking him into the private office he presents him to the cashier of this institution as Mr. Augustus Van Beekman.

"That's all right as to cashing the check," says Gussie flippantly, "but as regards opening the account I'm Baron Bassington of the English peerage, yer know." Then he cries suddenly : "You needn't look at me as if I were a lunatic or embezzler !" For Phil is gazing at him in a suspicious way, and the cashier is examining his check with curious eyes.

With this he gives them a hurried synopsis of his interview with Stillman, Myth & Co., and remarks sententiously : "People don't plank down a thousand pounds
unless they know what they are doing."

"The check is certainly good," replies the cashier, to
whom the certification of the Park National is as well
known as his own signature. "You wish to open an
account with this?"

"Certainly!"

"Then place your signature here," and Mr. Gussie, for
a third time this day, proudly writes : "Bassington."

Passing out of the bank, Gussie suggests going to
the Brevoort with Everett, stating he would like to see
Lord Grousemoor and ask him a few questions as to his
new-found title. "Get a few pointers, yer know," he
adds.

To this Phil, who has never seen any great harm in the
little fellow's affectations, assents, and they drive down
Fifth Avenue to this most old-fashioned but aristocratic
hotel, where going up to the Everett apartments they
find Miss Bessie and the Scotch marquis, who have just
returned from one of the Philharmonic rehearsals and
are seated in the parlor.

To them Phil tells Gussie's wonderful story, and the
two heartily congratulate him, Miss Bessie playfully remarking that she had always believed little Gussie wore
his eye-glass like a true British aristocrat, whereas her
future *lord* and master never has sported any and she has
grave doubts of the genuineness of his title.

Whereat Grousemoor cries out,—that he dropped all
insignia of rank when he crossed the sea to win a Puritan maiden. He had supposed they would not find
favor in her eyes, but to-morrow he shall put on a regular Pall Mall appearance for his *fiancée's* benefit. For
these two are going to be wed in Trinity Church, Boston,
in about a month, and have no foolish affectation in talking about it. A moment after the Scotch nobleman
remarks : "A great responsibility has been placed upon
you, Lord Bassington."

At which Gussie gasps "Yaas," and colors with joy
and pride, it being the first time he has been given his
title from one who is, as he expresses it himself, a "top-
knoter" in his own rank.

"You have, I hope, some idea of the responsibility of your position, some notion of English politics?" Grousemoor goes on, for his ancestors had fought for bonny Prince Charley, and, like all Scotchmen, he believes in traditions, and is consequently a stanch old Tory.

"Yaas, pretty well up, thank you," lisps Gussie. "I've got an opinion of Gladdy and his Irish policy that'll make him dizzy when he hears it."

At this a little snicker comes from Phil and his sister, but Grousemoor, who is not averse to another conservative vote in the House of Lords, fights down his smile, and, biting his lip, says : "I agree with you in condemning the liberal Irish policy, which I and a good many other Englishmen believe means little less than the dismemberment of the British Empire. I'm glad your vote'll be for union, that makes the strength of any government." With this he turns the conversation to other topics, for he imagines that a discussion on English politics with this new-made peer will neither be edifying nor educational.

A moment after Gussie, who has come down more for this purpose than for anything else, blurts out : "Can you tell me, Lord Grousemoor, if I will take precedence of Avonmere? We're both barons, yer see, and I wouldn't like him to get the best of me at a dinner-party, if I can help it. I'm a stickler for my rights, yer know."

This produces a laugh from Miss Bessie, who cries: "Oh for a peerage ! Bring me a Burke, Lord Bassington ; I'll help you protect your ancestral rights."

"Will you?" says Gussie, gratefully. "I've got one here," and he produces the volume he has carried with him from Brentano's, into which the girl dives with a mischievous alacrity.

A moment after she petrifies Augustus, for she says very gravely : "Why, I—I can't find your name in the volume ! "

"Not find it in Burke? Why, I've seen it there fifty times myself to-day ! " cries the young man, an awful horror in his voice.

"It must be there, Bessie," says Grousemoor. "Bassington is one of the oldest of English baronies."

"Oh, Bassington !" cries the girl. "Of course. How foolish ! I was looking for Van Beekman !" and goes into such a spasm of mirth that the new creation glares at her, a malicious gleam in his watery eyes.

A moment after she says, consulting the book : " You go into dinner behind him. Unfortunately, Lord Avonmere is an Edward the Third and number 377, and you're a Richard the Second, number 401."

" Well, I won't be behind him long. I'm going over to England shortly, and I'll get Salisbury to revive the Marquisate of Harrowby ; it's mine anyway, by rights ! " mutters Gussie, petulantly.

At this Grousemoor opens his eyes and looks at the young man wonderingly. " Such a thing is sometimes done for a great political service," he remarks, " but not often."

" And ain't I going to give Salisbury one," returns the American lord. " Just you wait till I take my seat in the House of Peers, and I'll floor that low-down leveller Gladstone in a way that'll make little Churchill open his eyes.—You've heard me, Phil, at old Yale in the Skull and Bones ? "

Neither Everett nor his sister answers this effusion ; they think Gussie must have been celebrating his good fortune in champagne before his visit ; but Grousemoor with an ill-concealed sneer says, " You'll never win your marquisate by defeating Mr. Gladstone in debate."

" Well, I'll have a try at him, anyway," rejoins little Gussie. " And I've just given orders to evict his cronies, my Irish tenants. But I must be moving ; I'm going to razzle-dazzle the boys at the Stuyvesant with my great lightning change act from Gussie Van Beekman to Baron Bassington. Awfully pleased to have met you again, Lord Grousemoor. Men of our rank are so isolated in America." And he bows himself to the door, leaving them all astonished and somewhat horrified at the easy tone of his eviction remarks.

As the door closes after him, Grousemoor says a little sadly, " There's another cad for our order to shoulder. It's bad enough for such men as Avonmere to come over from London slums and concert-halls to disgrace our class ; but, by Jove ! to have the British peerage recruited by an American dude, seems hard indeed ! "

" Then you think there's no doubt about his title," asks Phil.

" Very little, I'm afraid," answers his lordship. " The

American firm Stillman, Myth & Co., I naturally know nothing of, but Brown, Studley & Wilberforce are my London solicitors ; and if they cabled him a thousand pounds as you say they did, and authorized him to draw on them for ten thousand as he says they did, he's just as good as in possession of Harrowby Castle."

" I presume this will please the Western heiress that rumor says he's going to marry," remarks Miss Bessie, coming, like most women, to the matrimonial aspect of the affair.

" Of what heiress are you speaking ? " asks Phil, who is a man of business rather than society.

" Why, haven't you heard of her ? Miss Matilde Follis—the beautiful Miss Tillie Follis of Colorado ? " says Bessie, opening her eyes.

" I have heard of Miss Tillie Follis of New Mexico," returns Phil with a grin. " I believe I've got blisters on my hands yet from pounding a drill in a mine named after her. But Miss Tillie Follis of New Mexico was not a beauty."

" Well, this Miss Tillie Follis of Colorado is—perfectly beautiful—she was the belle of Mrs. Bradford Morton's ball. But you never go anywhere in society ; you do not care for young ladies nor balls ; you only enjoy bank directors' company and stockholders' meetings. A misanthrope at thirty-two ! " cries Bessie, playfully shaking a warning head.

" I imagine you have made a mistake, Bessie," says Grousemoor. " The rumor I heard was that the Follis's millions were to reëstablish the credit of Arthur, Lord Avonmere."

" That's where you're wrong, Grousemoor. I had it from an authority in the disposal of American heiresses, Mrs. Marvin. Avonmere loves Matilde, but Van Beekman's charms were too potent. But if I am to have any dinner this evening, I must dress for it," and she rustles away, leaving the two gentlemen together.

" Well, bad as he is, I believe little Gussie is the better of the two. Avonmere's such a cold-blooded scoundrel," murmurs Bessie's lover.

" You're not very light upon the peccadillos of your brother peer," returns Phil who has only heard of Avonmere incidentally.

"Perhaps it is because he is one of my class that I am so severe on his peccadillos, as you call them, though Avonmere's have been sometimes what I term crimes," replies Grousemoor, who is a nobleman of the old school, and looks upon his title as a sacred thing, to be protected and upheld, pure and immaculate, not only from the outside world but from his own feeblenesses and passions, and regards a *faux pas* in one of his order as a greater sin than it would be in mortals of more common clay. "Avonmere drags his title in the dust. It's the blood of an Italian mother that does it!" he goes on, with true British prejudice. "He had an elder brother, Tom, who was all English—a captain in the Fourth Hussars. and as fine a gentleman as a man would want to meet."

"Then how is it Tom has not the title?" asks Phil.

"Tom Willoughby is dead!" returns Grousemoor. "He had a cattle ranch in New Mexico, somewhere neai the place to which my carelessness in not paying my note banished you. Captain Tom Willoughby and his lovely wife and daughter were killed by Indians——"

"Not the daughter!" interrupts Phil, suddenly.

"Certainly the daughter, or how could Avonmere get the title? It's a barony by writ, and descends to females. You see his brother Tom was Lord Avonmere for four days, though he didn't know it. As I understand, he was killed before his daughter; the poor little child was a peeress of England when the Apaches or Utes, or whatever the cursed Indians were, took her young life."

To this Phil says nothing, being in a very disturbed meditation.

"You look troubled, Everett," continues his lordship; 'nothing about those Atchison, Topeka and Santa Fé bonds?" for the two gentlemen have been caught to a slight extent in the financial misfortunes of that great railroad whose appetite was too big for its digestion. It is the reorganization of this company that has brought Phil to New York, he having a seat in the board of direct ors of the consolidated and rejuvenated properties of this great trunk line.

"No," mutters Everett, slowly. "It is not that, but I've been unfaithful to a dying man's trust."

"What do you mean?" asks his lordship, astonished

"*I mean to do my duty!*" says Phil, very solemnly.

" Can I help you, old fellow ? " suggests Grousemoor, noting from his companion's voice that the affair is serious.

" Not now ; but you are quite sure that Avonmere's surname is Arthur ? "

" Certainly ! "

" Then, in a few days you may help me very much."

" Call on me at any time," says his lordship ; and, noticing that his friend is greatly agitated, he goes off to his room, wondering what is the matter with Phil, who is pacing the floor in a nervous, excited, and tremulous manner.

As soon as he is alone the ex-cowboy mutters to himself, " Killed by Indians—little Flossie Willoughby? Not by these scars ! " and puts his hands to his face, that still bears the signs of Apache handiwork. A moment later, for he wishes to be very sure, he strides to his sister's room and knocks upon her portal.

" You can't come in, Phil, I'm dressing for dinner," cries that young lady from behind her door. " What do you want ? "

" You remember a little girl you met at Lordsburgh, when mother and you found me wounded and delirious ? "

" Of course ! Little Flossie Willoughby. Her father and mother had been killed. You saved her ! " comes Miss Bessie's voice firm and strong through the oak panels.

" Mother and you did not conceal her being killed from me because you feared the news might injure me on my recovery from the fever ? "

" Of course not ! How did that idea get into your head ? "

" The child was well when you saw her ? "

" Certainly, as well as I am now. She came into our car several times to look at you as you raved that day, between Lordsburgh and Pueblo, and kissed you and called you her dear Mr. Peter so many times that I got quite jealous. What's the matter, you're not ill, Phil ? " for a short quick gasp comes to her through the panel.

" No, I am quite well," he says, the words coming rather slowly. " Can you remember any particulars of the child during the journey? You know I was delirious for months after, and don't recollect half what happened."

11

" Yes," says the girl, " you don't remember your great scene at the inquest, when you grabbed the child out of her uncle's arms, and gave a melodramatic, ' Not to *him* ! Not to HIM !' What's got into your head to come and ask me such questions while I'm dressing. My maid is jabbering French maledictions at you in a whisper, and I'm a little cold—O–o–ough ! "

But the last of this is lost on Everett ; his mind has gone back to New Mexico. After he had recovered from his wounds his mother never mentioned to him what he had done at the inquest, fearing it might again unsettle him, and judging it to have been some delirious raving of the fever. So the matter had passed out of sight ; but now his sister's words bring back full recollection to his mind.

He mutters, " I saved her from the Apaches to give her up to a man with a brain of a Machiavelli and the heart of one of those brutes—out there ! " and quoting poor Tom Willoughby's words, imitates poor Tom Willoughby's gesture.

Then he walks up to his room and overhauls a package of papers.

The first of these is a letter which reads as follows :

PULLMAN, ILLINOIS, *December* 15, 1889.

PHILIP E. T. EVERETT, Esq.,
    Director
        Atchison, Topeka & Santa Fé }
           Railroad,
             Boston, Mass.

Dear Sir :

Some three months ago, in repairing car No. 427, which required radical alterations, a sealed packet with your name on it was found by one of the workmen employed.

From the dust with which it was covered, and the position in which it was discovered, it has probably been in the car for several years, having been forced under one of the heating pipes in the bottom of the stateroom.

This parcel was, as usual in such cases, delivered to the office for the return of lost articles ; but not being called for, and I noting your name upon the newly elected list of Atchison, Topeka & Santa Fé directors, I imagine it probably belongs to you, as car 427 ran over that line for several years ; consequently forward to you the packet.

Please acknowledge receipt of same in case it is your property, and oblige,

Yours most respectfully,

GEORGE LANGDON,
Assistant Foreman.

This letter, together with a package bearing his name in his mother's handwriting, had been forwarded to Everett from Boston some few days before ; but knowing that the contents of the envelope were the missing letters of Tom Willoughby, and the matter being of such distant date that it could hardly be of importance to any one now, Phil had neglected to open the package.

He does so no longer, and in a few moments the correspondence of the dead Englishman, slightly yellow from age and stained here and there with Phil's own blood, lies in front of him.

He looks hurriedly through the letters, which are not numerous, and are all from Mrs. Willoughby to her husband. They are chiefly on domestic matters, most of them being filled with descriptions, praise, and love of their little girl Flossie, who is just arriving at that age so interesting to mothers, when a child shows the first graces of budding maidenhod.

These throw no light whatsoever upon the subject he is investigating ; neither do the photographs of the child and her mother ; though with tears in his eyes he kisses that of the beautiful little girl, and sighs as he looks on Agnes Willoughby and thinks of her cruel death. But a closed envelope bearing these curiously prophetic words :

"TO MY EXECUTORS IN CASE I DIE BY APPARENT ACCIDENT,"

signed " Thomas Willoughby," seems more promising.

Under the circumstances any scruple that might make him hesitate to read this document would be childish. Phil tears open the envelope, and the following curious epistle meets his eye :

WILLOUGHBY'S RANCH, NEW MEXICO,
February 21, 1881.

News has just arrived from England that causes me to write this, for a new danger has come upon me.

By the death of my cousin in Cairo, Egypt, from cholera or some Eastern fever, I am the heir presumptive to the estates and title of the Barony of Avonmere.

And in case of my death by accident, additional danger might come upon my daughter Florence. It is as a warning and protection to her, and not from any wish of vengeance upon my brother Arthur, that I make this statement.

The belief that I will fall from some accident, in which the apparent hand of God can only be seen, but which shall really be directed by the hand of my brother, has been forced upon me by the following extraordinary incidents of my life :

FIRST.—In Colombo, Ceylon, when a portion of my regiment was stationed in barracks at that place, a Hindoo snake-charmer one day exhibited his art upon several cobras, permitting some of them to bite him. To one of these writhing brutes he did not allow that privilege, handling it with much more circumspection and care than he did the others.

During his exhibition that snake escaped, and he did not succeed in recapturing it—I think chiefly on account of his dread of the serpent's fangs, for these mountebanks have a habit of extracting the poisonous teeth of the reptiles they play with, dreading them as much as any of their spectators.

Two days after this, tiffin being over, some of the mess were enjoying their cheroots on the veranda facing the garden in which the cobra had disappeared.   Arthur, who was a government clerk in the East India service at that time, though only nineteen years of age, was seated among us.

He had been walking about the grounds smoking a cigar before he joined us. A little time after he turned the conversation upon various athletic feats, among others jumping.

There was a large stump of a tree at the bottom of the garden path.

In speaking of such feats, Arthur offered to wager that no one in the company could leap the tree ; something any one of us could easily accomplish.

I thought him a foolish fellow to lose his money in that way, but he offered to bet that none of us could do it, at a pound a head. This was immediately accepted by all.

In arranging the order of the jump, which was to be a running one, Arthur suggested that we go by seniority, all of us but himself being officers in the army.   This gave me the *first* leap.

Rather laughing at the idea of winning a pound so easily from my younger brother, I was in the act of beginning my run when poor young Majoribanks, crying, " Youth before beauty," ran ahead of me and sprang over the tree.

While in mid-air we heard him give an awful scream of terror, and as he descended on the other side another and more horrible cry came from his lips. He staggered back and sank down with exclamations of despair.

Running to him we found that he had jumped upon the cobra, which was lying on the other side of the tree, and had been bitten. He died in a little over an hour.

SECOND.—Arthur took passage for me in a ship infected by Asiatic cholera, bound from Ceylon to the Straits Settlements.

Before we arrived at Penang, two-thirds the passengers and half the crew had been thrown overboard. I luckily escaped, perhaps through having been acclimated by service in the jungles of Bengal and the Malay Peninsula.

I now have reason to believe my brother knew the vessel was infected when he engaged my passage.

THIRD.—On the yacht *Sylvie*, Arthur left us at nine P. M. to go on shore at Ryde. At ten only God's mercy saved us being run down by a Channel steamer. Our sailing lights had been reversed— Heaven knows by whom, but I suspect by my brother ; they were certainly right before he left us.

FOURTH.—At Shilton, a little station on the London and Northwestern Railway, while waiting to meet my wife and child, Arthur stood upon what looked like a shunt, and I beside him. After talking to me a moment he asked me to wait for him while he stepped into the station house to get a light for his cigar. Ten seconds afterward the guard ran out and pulled me off the track ; in five seconds more the Liverpool express rushed over the place I had stood—it was the main through line.

The station master incidentally mentioned to me that he wondered my brother had left me standing in such a spot, as he knew the station very well and had spent several hours there, off and on, watching the trains and noting their times of passage. "He saw the Liverpool express run over that line yesterday at that self-same minute," the man asserted.

This is what first forced me to suspect my brother, and further investigation compelled me at last to the conviction that he had deliberately placed me in the path of death in the other instances mentioned ; notwithstanding I gave him the benefit of every doubt, for it is hard to believe that one you love would be morally your murderer

I expect no danger from direct attack; but if I survive the present Lord Avonmere—what may I not fear? One who has made such efforts when he had only a pittance to gain, will be more inventive with a title and great wealth to help him design some new accident, some fatal mishap for the brother that signs this

THOMAS WILLOUGHBY.

P. S.—Inspect any accident that may happen to me, no matter how much it may appear the hand of God—for directing it will be the man I once loved, but now despise and dread, my half-brother Arthur Willoughby, whose mother's Italian blood must have had in it some stream from the Borgias.   T. W.

After he has read the last of this curious document, Everett does some of the hardest thinking of his life, sending the plea of business as an excuse for missing his dinner.

At dessert, however, he makes his appearance and rather startles his sister, for his eyes have a look in them she has not seen since the fever left him, nine years before.

His words astound Miss Bessie still more, but also relieve her mind. He says rather lightly, "I think a little society would do me good; what are your invitations for this evening?"

"None for you," she answers; "according to your orders I have refused every one for you this week; but if you want to make your *début* in the social world, there's a card for the coming Patriarchs, and an invitation to the great sensation Mrs. Warburton's Private Circus a fortnight afterward."

"A private circus!" he echoes, astonished.

"Yes—horses, amateur bareback riders. That would be the place for you," cries Miss Bessie, who is mightily glad her brother will cast away business cares and take to enjoying himself. "Pete and his lasso! The only original broncho act by a *real* cowboy! That would make a sensation," and she claps her hands; "I'll send your name in to the ring-master. We'll bring Possum down from the farm, and you shall appear on his back in your old costume of the prairie. I've got it up in the Beacon Street garret. It's lucky you've kept up your riding. Hurrah! you'll be the sensation of the show!"

After a moment, this proposition not being responded to enthusiastically, she quiets down and suggests : " As you're barred from private entertainments by your own act, why not come to a public one ? This evening, Grousemoor and I, chaperoned by Mrs. Livingston Willis, are going to the opera for an hour or two—join us There'll be plenty of people to look at and talk to if you don't care for Wagner."

" Thank you very much—I will," says her brother, and stalks away to his room to make his preparations, muttering with threatening tone : "*Perhaps I'll see him there !*"

CHAPTER XV.

LITTLE GUSSIE'S RAZZLE DAZZLE.

THE Metropolitan Opera House that evening presents its usual brilliant scene ; the boxes filled with the usual fashionable crowd, who come only for love of society ; the orchestra occupied by people who come for love of music and nothing else.   But no one of all the throng is attracted by a motive like unto that of Philip Everett.

He enters a little late and sits abstractedly behind Mrs. Willis's pretty white shoulders, giving out so little conversation that this fashionable young matron turns to him and remarks, with one of those charming *petite* pouts of which she makes a specialty : " Mr. Everett, she has not come yet ?"

" Whom do you mean ?" says Phil, with a start.

" Why, the lady you are looking for, of course. The people down there "—she points with her fan to the orchestra—" are listening ; the people up here "—she indicates the circle of boxes—" are talking ; you do neither: you simply look. Let me know when you see her."

" It's not a lady I'm seeking," remarks Phil, quietly. Then he suddenly says : " Who is that just coming into the box opposite to us ?"

" Oh, that's the beautiful Miss Follis of Colorado," answers Mrs. Willis. " If she's the lady you're in search of I'm sorry for you ; she's already spoken for by little

Gussie Van Beekman, who I hear has just been discovered to be an English lord, and I don't think an American gentleman would have much chance with a Western
heiress in comparison to a full-fledged peer of the British realm." Mrs. Willis's *loge* is a parterre one, almost
facing that which Mr. Follis has engaged for the use of
his family during the season.

Into this box Miss Matilde is coming, in all the glory
of a fresh new imported dress and flashing jewels. She
is accompanied by Mrs. Marvin, her mother not caring
for Wagner's music, which she says reminds her of
the wash-house strains of John Chinaman. Curiously
enough, no gentleman appears in their party. They
take their seats, and after distributing a few bows to near
by acquaintances in other boxes, elevate their opera-
glasses and proceed to take a survey of the house.

"There's the beautiful Miss Follis that I told you
about," whispers Bessie, leaning over to her brother and
calling his attention with her fan.

"Humph!" replies Phil; then he remarks suddenly:
"By George! she does look like Tillie Follis of New
Mexico, grown up, after all—lend me your glass!"
Through a powerful lorgnette he views the beauty of
Matilde. And this evening she is more beautiful than
ever, for the news of Van Beekman's elevation to the peerage has been brought to her this afternoon by Mrs. Marvin, and Gussie's good fortune the girl proudly considers
her own, and imagines she will be an English peeress
after all, and has said "*Lady Bassington*" to herself
almost as often as her *fiancé* has done himself a similar
honor this day.

There has been a great buzz all the evening, the boxes
having had something more exciting than the usual languid society news to gossip about, for the sudden elevation of Augustus Van Beekman, who has been on the
verge of ostracism by the more exclusive clique for the
past year or two, has given them an absorbing sensation ; and as they think the matter over they are very
glad they have not done it.

They had half forgiven him when he became engaged
to a great heiress; now they are wholly reconciled to his
eccentricities, and are hastily preparing themselves to
get upon their haughty knees and bow their aristocratic

heads to this little Manhattan Island dandy whom for·
tune has at last kicked into the English House of Lords.

Curiously enough there are few doubters as to the
truth of the news, though every one has heard it.

Little Gussie, on his arrival at the Stuyvesant, had not
waited long to tell his story and to impress it on his hear·
ers, stating that he had been cabled to draw at sight upon
Brown, Studley & Wilberforce for £20,000, and lavishing
his money to prove that his draft had been honored.

He has certainly got the estates, and, of course, the
title. A few minutes later, Avonmore lounges into the
club, and his manner confirms Gussie's news.

He strides up to the little aristocrat and says : "Bas·
sington, I've just heard of your being confirmed in your
title. I had a hint that you were the coming baron from
my London solicitors, Brown, Studley & Wilberforce, and
now the news is confirmed. My congratulations, old
man—Harrowby Castle's the prettiest place in Kent. I
hope you'll ask me down when you take possession."

"Won't I, old boy ?" cries Gussie, who thinks he'll die
with joy. "I've just come from Grousemoor ; he sent for
me to ask my vote for the Conservative party when I take
my seat."

" The devil he did ! " mutters Avonmere, rather aston·
ished ; though he is delighted that this proud Scottish
peer had furthered his plans.

So the two go off together to dinner, for Gussie says :
"You dine with me to-day—you must, Avonmere—by
Jove ! you wouldn't have me sit down with a com-
moner on such a day as this?"

Now, this occurrence being carried home by every
married club-man to his wife, soon got to the ears of
nearly all other ladies, and those who had not known
it before they arrived at the Metropolitan were very
shortly acquainted with the facts of the case by the
various visiting young men, who were delighted to have
something astounding to whisper into the ears of
beauty when they lounged into her box.

This news causes the appearance of Miss Follis to
make quite a sensation ; those who know her pointing
her out to those who do not as the young lady who
is engaged to marry the lucky little Gussie, the new-
made British peer, with fifty or sixty thousand pounds a

year ; for this Bassington fortune is growing as trans-
ferred from mouth to mouth.

Eyes that have been cold to her under this benign
influence grow warm, and Matilde Follis, as she sits in
her box, with the music of " Tristan and Isolde " floating
in the air about her, feels something more inspiring than
Wagner in the bright, congratulatory nods and wafted
salutations that concentrate upon her pretty face, though
Herr Seidl and his orchestra are fiddling their arms away
and blowing their lungs away quite stoutly, as all Wagnerian orchestras should do.

But if a buzz goes up on Matilde's arrival, a regular
hum invades the air to Mr. Gussie's grand entrance as
Lord Bassington.   The vocal accompaniment from the
boxes drowns the orchestra, and several German gentlemen in the body of the house, who have come this evening under the mistaken notion that they will hear an
opera, express their displeasure by a vigorous hissing
from the seats below ; but they might as well appeal to
the murmuring waves to stop murmuring as to expect
the wagging tongues of women to stop wagging when
this new star of rank and fashion first comes under their
eager opera-glasses.

" I see him ! He's there !—centre entrance to the
orchestra !—looking about for the box he'll first honor ! "
cries Miss Alice Morton Budd, the most innocent *ingénue*
of the season.

" By George ! " whispers the envious Grayson, who is
sitting behind this floweret of fashionable life, " you
women ought to call Bassington in front of the curtain
and cheer him as our Teuton friends used to do their pet
tenor Alvary ! "

" You forget Alvary often led his prima donna out
with him ; perhaps Bassington might bring his, and I
shouldn't applaud *her*. She looks as haughty as if she
had the coronet on her head already," returns Miss Budd,
gazing across at the Follis box, the *loge* she is occupying being next to that of Mrs. Willis and her party.

Miss Budd goes prattling on in this strain for a few
moments when Grayson suddenly whispers : " Hush !
he's coming in next door. See the fair Tillie looks
astonished and piqued because my lord didn't give her
his first greeting. His English lordship will get an

American talking to when he puts in an appearance over there. La Follis's eyes are blazing more than her diamonds," and Mr. Grayson turns his lorgnette upon Mrs. Marvin's *protégée*.

A moment after he says suddenly, and perhaps disappointedly, "George! did you hear that? Grousemoor has given him his title as if he'd already taken his seat in the House of Lords. It's a sure go! Excuse me a moment, Miss Alice," and bolts off to other boxes to tell them that Grousemoor has publicly recognized Gussie . Van Beekman as Lord Bassington.

This has come about in this way.

Avonmere and Augustus have taken dinner at an up-town restaurant in a private room, little Gussie clamoring for Delmonico's, where he can make a display of himself and his luck; Avonmere over-ruling this, fearing the all-seeing reporter, who he knows is even now tramping Fifth Avenue, looking in at all likely restaurants and clubs, and will shortly drop in to the opera in pursuit of Baron Bassington and his Aladdin tale for the morning papers. At dinner Avonmere has suggested the opera, wishing to force little Gussie close to Miss Follis, so that he may have every chance to slight his *fiancée*, shrewdly guessing the nearer they are brought together, the more the American lord will give the cold shoulder to the American heiress.

For Augustus has become very chatty over his wine, and has told Avonmere of his contemplated evictions on his Irish estates in a manner that makes his hearer writhe on his chair with suppressed laughter; and a moment after has asked Avonmere's advice on this very subject.

"It's rather a delicate matter, my boy," he has said; "but I know you'll give your opinion to a brother peer. What am I to do now in that unfortunate complication with little Follis?"

"I had supposed you were going to marry her," returns the Englishman with a smile.

Here Gussie astounds and actually overawes him. His little frame grows taller, his air grows more haughty, and his voice becomes very severe as he says, "I am surprised, Lord Avonmere, at such a suggestion. I have not forgotten my rank if Grousemoor has his. I had presumed that your opinion and mine coincided upon this question, which is at the basis of our rank. Blue blood for blue blood! Keep the *canaille* away! Curse 'em!" For vanity and champagne have by this time nearly made him crazy.

"That being the case," returns Avonmere, with a choked-down chuckle, "you should cut the young lady's hopes short *at once!* It's kinder. Perhaps even now she is dreaming of wearing your coronet."

"No doubt she is," interrupts Gussie with a grin. "She's been dreaming of this for weeks. Old Marvin, who has a nose for a peer like a pointer for a quail, scented me out long ago and put Matilde up to the game, and so she took me at advantage and literally trapped me, by Jove!"

"It does look a little curious," murmurs Avonmere.

"Curious? I should think so!" cries Gussie. "I shall cut the Follis affair in a way that'll make Miss Matilde open her eyes. Watch me do it at the opera to-night."

So the two take cab for the Metropolitan, Avonmere suggesting that as Grousemoor has recognized his title, it would be no more than polite for Gussie to drop into his box and pay his compliments to him, shrewdly imagining that if the great Scottish nobleman indorses the claim of Augustus to the Barony of Bassington, New York society will follow his lead in a way that will make the new young peer very haughty and snobbish to common clay and especially so to Miss Follis of Colorado.

He moreover remarks that he imagines Lord Bassington may be persecuted by reporters this evening and advises that he simply tell them his knowledge of his rank and draft for his money came direct from Brown, Studley & Wilberforce of London. "I wouldn't mention Stillman, Myth & Co. in the matter, or that firm won't be able to transact business to-morrow, the gentlemen of the press will persecute them so."

"That's what old Stillman said himself," returns Gussie, "and I've concluded to take pity on him and give him a rest." Which he does that evening, telling all inquiring reporters that if they want further particulars they can apply to his London solicitors, Brown, Studley & Wilberforce—a policy that insures him rank and title for a few short days; for had he set those lynxes of the press upon Stillman, Myth & Co., the peerage of Bassington would have passed from him within twenty-four hours.

Dodging such reporters as he can in the lobby of the Metropolitan, and promising interviews later in the evening to those that get their hands upon him, he leaves Avonmere and soon finds himself in Mrs. Willis's box, where there is a little throng of gentlemen.

For that lady is quite popular herself, and Miss Everett's face is fresh to New York and very pretty as well, besides, she is about to marry the great gun of the winter, and they wish to keep themselves in her memory, hoping for invitations to the Boston wedding, and social recognition from her as the Marchioness of Grousemoor upon their annual trips across the ocean to merry England.

Squeezing his way among these and getting three hearty grips in his passage, Mr. Gussie finds himself behind Miss Bessie's chair. That young lady holds out a welcoming hand to him, while the Scotch peer smiles and says, "How are you? Still booked to uphold our constitution against Gladstone?" For this nobleman has his party's welfare very much at heart, and is determined to enlist the new peer and give him the Conservative shilling at once.

"Yaas, count on me!" murmurs Augustus.

Then Mrs. Willis whispers a word to Grousemoor, and that gentleman says, "Excuse me, I did not know you were unacquainted—Mrs. Willis, Lord Rassington," and *—the trick is done!*

Three or four of the loungers in the box lounge out of it and into others, where they confirm Gussie's luck, stating that he has been introduced, under his title, to Mrs. Willis, by that strict upholder of social etiquette and class distinction, Grousemoor.

After this comes to its ears, New York society is very kind and cordial to little Gussie to-night.

This news finding its way to the De Punster Van Beekman box, old Van Twiler Van Beekman, who has hardly bowed to the scapegrace for years—he is only his first cousin—comes out into the *foyer* and pounces on Gussie as he leaves Mrs. Willis's party.

"You young rascal!" cries the old gentleman, slapping him on the back with playful cordiality, "what have you been doing with yourself ? We haven't seen you for months, and I don't believe you called this winter."

" Yaas, been rather busy with my Irish tenants lately," lisps Gussie, remembering that Van Twiler had hardly nodded to him as he passed him on the street but yesterday, and his last call at his old-fashioned mansion in Washington Square had met with such a chilly reception that he had never had the courage to ring his door-bell afterward.

" Come into our box ; Lydia is anxious to see you and give you your new title." And he drags Augustus to the ancient Lydia, who makes much of him in a cousinly familiar way which Gussie brings himself to endure, as the old couple have lots of real estate and no direct heir, and fifty thousand pounds a year is none too much for a dashing young nobleman to spend on his stable, steam yacht, and attentions to the fair sex, *monde* and *demimonde*.

After a little Gussie gets away from his old relations, being anxious for more juvenile adulation. He is followed, however, by the venerable Van Twiler, who, taking him aside in the lobby, whispers, " Cousin Bassington, we look to you to lift our family to the place it occupied in old Manhattan days, before its social supremacy was contested by more recent and perhaps larger fortunes. I've had you down in my will almost since you were born, and I hope you will make no mistake when you settle in life. I heard the other day with some concern that you had forgotten your blood in this modern craze. after wealth. I hope it is not so."

" Awh—you refer to that Follis gal," returns Gussie, airily. " With sixty thousand pounds a year I need seek no addition to my fortune. Lord Bassington will be very careful of himself matrimonially."

And he departs upon his triumphal tour, dropping in to all boxes to which he has the *entrée*, and being invited into some of the others ; saying a few words to old friends, and making a good many new ones. Thus to-night beauty, wealth, and fashion smile upon this new-made lord, for there is no place on earth where an English nobleman is so great a nobleman as in this city of New York, in the republic of these United States of America, among a certain clique.

But in all his peregrinations of the evening, he avoids approach to that *loge* where Mrs. Marvin sits accompanied by his sweetheart and *fiancée*, the young and charming Western heiress.

Other men whisper nothings into Miss Follis's pretty ears; other men sit behind her gleaming shoulders; other men lounge in and out of her box and catch the sweetness of her voice, that is gradually growing sad and subdued, or seek the brightness of her glance, which becomes pathetic as the evening wears away—but never the man whose betrothal ring she wears, Augustus, Baron Bassington.

Towards the end of the evening her eyes and voice take another change and become flashingly cool and stridently haughty, for by this time Matilde Follis knows she is under a hundred opera-glasses who are seaching every motion of her hands, every movement of her lips, every glance of her eyes, to pry into her heart and see how she bears the public desertion and neglect of the man who, on this evening if on no other, should have halved with her his social happiness and glory.

So this young girl, who has not been trained to concealing her heart, and who has been used to little but kindness, endures a crucial ordeal and social martyrdom that come to few women—thank Heaven !—in this life, and does it bravely and successfully; fighting down any tremor in her voice, subduing any nervous play of countenance that may betray the agony of an insulted self-esteem and crucified pride.

But the struggle ages her, and from the rise of the curtain on the third act to Isolde's dying song seems a lustrum in her life.

And on this spectacle the ladies and gentlemen of the parterre boxes gaze, criticising her motions and noting how she bears her humiliation. Some with little giggles —these are mostly unthinking girls ; others with smiles— they are women whose hearts have been destroyed in social battle ; and some—thank Heaven !—with just rage and righteous indignation.

"Miss Denver's coronet is growing pale," says Alice Budd, with a malicious smile.

"By George, he's just been in the boxes on each side of hers. After greeting the Laurisons, he is in the Rol ingstons. The general is shaking his hand off. Two unmarried daughters, you know. Isn't Gussie putting the Follis on a social gridiron?" replies Mr. Grayson.

"If he wishes to break his engagement he might have done it afterward, decently," remarks Mrs. Willis.

"How bravely she suffers," whispers Bessie to Grousemoor, and tears come into the girl's eyes, for an awful vision comes to her of her betrothed placing public scorn upon her.

"The cruel little snob!" mutters the true nobleman, with a smothered curse, for which his *fiancée* gives him an astonished but grateful look. "If you'll excuse me for a few minutes, I'll leave you to Phil's care and step over to Miss Follis's box," he adds. "I know her well enough to take the liberty."

"Certainly!" says Bessie. "But what do you mean to do?"

"I mean to uphold that insulted girl in the only way I can—by my presence at her side," he answers shortly. "I want Miss Follis to know that every nobleman is not what Bassington is—a cad!" and he departs on his errand, pursued by a pleased glance from his sweetheart.

While this has been going on, Phil, in a retired nook of Mrs. Willis's box, has been looking for the man he has come to see, in vain.

Taking pity on his loneliness, his hostess from time to time has leaned back and chatted with him on the past glories of opera in New York, telling him of the days when the Academy resounded with the plaudits of united Italy in its upper gallery, when Gerster and Patti and Campanini and Ravelli sang.

"Oh, you need not look at me as if I were old!" she interjects, with a little laugh. "It was only eight years ago, and I had just come out and was in love with music, Italian music, and thought Campanini the most enchanting of tenors. That house was prettier than this. Here we women in our evening toilets are like flowers in separate flower-pots in this wall of boxes. There in the open gallery *loges* we were all combined in one big glorious bouquet each night— But what's the matter?"

This last in rather a startled tone, for Phil has suddenly muttered: "By heavens, it is he!" and has hastily risen from B's chair.

"Nothing!" he replies, seating himself again.

"Nothing? Why, your eyes are blazing."

"Are they? Wagner's music must have got into them, then," says Phil, laughing slightly and forcing himself to calmness, though the sight of a gentleman in evening dress has made him see again the telegraph office at Lordsburgh, with Arthur Willoughby whispering in his ear the lying message that made him take a gentle English lady to her death just up the valley of the Gila. Then he goes on quite suddenly: "You know so many people in New York, Mrs. Willis, can you tell me the name of that gentleman who has replaced Grousemoor in Miss Follis's box—the one who is just taking her opera-glass?"

"Certainly!" replies the matron. "That is Lord Avonmere."

"Ah!" He rises from his seat and remarks: "Here's Grousemoor back and the curtain's coming down. You'll excuse me, I hope, from your supper party, Mrs. Willis, as I have some business that is imperative."

With this he leaves the lady, who thinks him rather an abrupt sort of a personage, and passes into the *foyer;* but after pacing the corridor toward the Follis box, Phil apparently changes his mind and goes hastily down the stairs and through the main entrance into the street. His first impulse had been to accost Avonmere and demand the particulars of Flossie Willoughby's death, for he believes this English lord has murdered the child who stood between him and wealth and title.

That would have been the way Pete, the cowboy, would have attacked the matter; but Philip Everett, the Boston business man, wants to be sure of his facts before he moves, and within an hour a long telegraphic message is speeding over the wires, addressed to Breckinridge Garvey, Sheriff of Grant County, Silver City, New Mexico.

Matilde Follis this night watches the falling curtain of the Opera House. Her mind is too dazed to be able to analyze her emotions during this performance, that has seemed to her like a Chinese play which lasts for years. The one predominating idea in her mind is—"It is over!—I've stayed to the end! Thank Heaven! None have seen me flinch upon the social rack!"

She has grown a little paler near the close; that is the

only outward sign of suffering she has given, for her eyes have become more haughty as the time has gone on. They have softened somewhat as Grousemoor has taken his seat behind her. Though he has only passed the compliments of the season, she has understood what his visit to her meant, and her glance has been slightly grateful. Avonmere, however, who is behind her now, she has received with cordiality as he took the seat the other gave up to him. She has turned, and affecting a little laugh that mocked itself as it issued from her lips, has whispered : " You can stay a little longer than usual this evening ; I've no other entertainment to go to, and shall remain to the end."

" Yes," chimed in Mrs. Marvin, " wait, and take us two lone women down to our carriage."

" That is what I am here for, with your permission," remarked Avonmere, looking at the girl for his answer.

But, thinking she sees compassion in his glance, her spirit grows haughty and she answers, indifferently : " You must please yourself, Lord Avonmere."

" Certainly, I always please myself when I am seated here," he whispers into the little ear conveniently near him.

She does not answer this, though he notes her look is more amiable than it has been in the last few minutes. So, after a significant glance that is returned by the wily Marvin, he remains quiet in his chair, and gazes at the white, glistening shoulders of the girl he thinks will some day belong to him; for he is now pretty sure, if he plays his cards right, pride will make Miss Follis give her hand to him, to humiliate the man who to-night has slighted her.

Thus he and Mrs. Marvin watch Matilde, whose face is very beautiful, though the pathos has all left it, and only pride and scorn remain upon it.

The sole evidence of emotion she gives is from a little foot that taps impatiently the cushion on which it rests ; this suddenly ceases, her hand clinches itself and her eyes have a cruel look—for it has suddenly occurred to her to tell her father of the public slight and leave her vengeance to him ; but she soon casts the whole idea from her, for she knows her father would kill her insulter, and Matilde Follis has too healthy a mind, with all its frivolity, to wish a blood atonement.

As she thinks this, the curtain falls, and passing into the vestibule of her box, she finds Avonmere ready with her opera wrap in his hand.

He cloaks her, and notes with sudden joy that some-how the girl's engagement ring has disappeared from her finger.

Mrs. Marvin also sees this, and her face becomes radiant.

Once or twice this wily old lady has tried to beckon the new-made lord to her box, but he has always looked away, and so made his slight of Miss Follis more marked.

So, quite pleased at her evening's work, the widow says pleasantly, "I'll move on before you, Matilde. Lord Avonmere will follow with you when you have your cloak arranged. Be careful of colds, my dear; the draughts in the lobbies of this house are simply Siberian."

Coming out into the *foyer* and descending to the lower lobby that leads to one of the *portes cochères* for the use of subscribers and box owners, Mrs. Marvin chances to run upon the derelict Gussie.

He makes an abortive attempt to dodge her, but she strides after him, cries, " Lord Bassington, you haven't let me congratulate you!" and placing a plump and pow-erful hand upon his arm, laughs, " From whom are you flying ?—Not from me, I hope?"

To this he listens, in an apologetic way, though he has neither the mind nor heart to appreciate what he has made Matilde suffer; still he has a feeble idea in his head, which tells him he ought to be ashamed.

" No—a, I'm dodging the reporters. They're after me —like flies!" he mutters ; and making a sudden dash to escape both Mrs. Marvin and the reporters, he comes right upon Matilde Follis, and so gives to her her one chance for vengeance in this long night—and she takes it !

The crush is very great around them—they are face to face, with no chance of dodging. He hesitates and is lost.

Raising his hat, he smiles his sweetest smile and says, " Good evening, Miss Matilde !" And she, looking straight in his face as if she had never known him, and talking quietly and easily, cuts him dead !—right under the eye of every one—for those about them are gazing at their meeting.

He blushes, grows red and stands abashed as she sweeps on under Avonmere's wing to the *porte cochère* and signals her footman for her carriage.

"By Jove!" says Mr. Mac, the great society leader, who is just behind her, to his friend Colonel Hicks Van Ransaleer. "Did you see that?—she cut the little cad like an archduchess. There's breeding in that girl, blood or no blood!" and following after Miss Follis, he cuts Lord Bassington also, though that new-made peer is holding out his hand, expecting an effusive greeting.

Then overtaking the girl, whose social training he has admired this evening, Mr. Mac says a few pleasant words to Miss Follis and asks her to be sure and come to the next Patriarchs', of which, like most other subscription entertainments, he is lord and master; and her carriage coming up, he and Lord Avonmere assist Mrs. Marvin and the young lady in.

As they drive away into the street, lined with equipages waiting to pick up their owners, Mrs. Marvin reaches over in the seclusion of the carriage and gives the girl a hearty kiss, saying, "You won at the last in a canter, you brave little girl!"

But she suddenly stops her chatter, for, the strain being over, Matilde Follis is crying as if heart would break.

BOOK III.

Miss Somebody of Somewhere.

CHAPTER XVI.

LORD AVONMERE'S GHOST.

THIS night Phil Everett has sent a telegram to New Mexico, but he desires information from England, and doesn't know exactly from whom to get it.

Waiting till Grousemoor's return from Mrs. Willis's supper party, he takes that gentleman aside, and knowing he can trust his secrecy and discretion, says to him : "You told me to ask your aid in a matter that you saw troubled me."

"Certainly."

"That aid I wish now."

"Very well, old man," returns Phil's listener. "It's serious, I see by your face. Out with it ! "

"I wish your aid to bring the murderer of Florence Beatrice Stella Willoughby, Lady Avonmere, to justice. That's her name, I read it in Burke at the Club coming from the Opera."

"What do you mean ?" gasps Grousemoor, half thinking Phil crazy.

"I mean that I have good reason to believe, Arthur, Lord Avonmere, murdered or in some way disposed of that child who stood between him and his present title."

"Good Heavens ! " mutters the Scotchman, his fresh and ruddy face growing slightly pale under this startling disclosure. " You must have good reasons for this ! "

"Lots!" says Phil; and, not believing in half confidences, he tells him all he knows, reading him the curious document that bears the dead Englishman's signature.

To this Grousemoor listens with occasional interjections of surprise and horror.

Concluding, Phil says: "Give me the name of some English solicitor to whom I can write for the proofs of little Flossie's death, that must have been given before Avonmere could get the title. I want to see how he said the Indians killed her."

The peer considers a moment, and then says: "Address George Ramsey, 4 Cornhill, London. He's the man you want."

"Thank you," replies Everett, "I'll write to him at once," and is about to go to his room.

"You're resolved to take up this matter, Phil?" says Grousemoor, striding after him. "Remember it's a very serious affair."

"I only remember that I loved the child he has wronged and injured," mutters Phil. "When I think of her, braving bullets to bring me water in her little hat, and I wounded and too weak to move, I—my God, if that cursed villain has killed her!" and tears come into the Boston business man's eyes.

The next day's outgoing mail steamer for England carries a letter, the reading of which would not have pleased Arthur, Lord Avonmere; though at present he is one of the happiest of men, for everything has gone to his wishes in the Follis affair.

Mrs. Marvin on the way home from the opera has played Avonmere's cards very well for him.

The first portion of the ride has been a journey of horror to the widow, for in an outbreak of sobs Matilde has talked wildly of giving up the struggle of society, and going back to Denver, and dad and Bob; where all are kind to her.

During this La Marvin has gazed upon her in speechless, panicky despair.

But as Matilde's sobs have grown fainter, Mrs. Marvin has plucked up hope again, and saying nothing about the treatment the girl has received from little Gussie, she has turned the conversation upon other topics, chiefly the attentions of Lord Avonmere and the compliment that Mr. Mac has paid her ; waiting for Miss Follis to bring up the subject that she knows is uppermost in her mind.

This has a soothing effect on the girl's nerves. After a little she says with a slight laugh : "It's lucky I never loved that wretch."

" Loved who ? "

" Lord Bassington—Augustus—*little* Gussie ! " sneers the young lady. " Then I might have succumbed under his neglect and have shown it to that grinning crowd. As it is, I believe I've rather the best of it, and shall have more the best of it before I've done with him." This last is said in a significantly vindictive voice.

" What do you mean to do ? "

" Crush him—crush him to the dust ! " cries Miss Tillie, and her ivory fan-sticks crash under her excited clutch.

" Yes, you might have a sweet revenge," murmurs the widow contemplatively. " There are older titles than that of little Gussie."

" Yes, and one of them—is at my feet," mutters the girl.

Then the cunning old diplomat puts in a deft master stroke. She whispers, " Of course—every one says that."

" Says what ? "

" Says that you have jilted Gussie for Lord Avonmere. They all thought this evening that Gussie, being dis-carded, did not *dare* to come to your box."

" Did they think THAT ? " cries the girl, with a triumphant laugh. " But we are at home, Mrs. Marvin." And running up her front stairs she says to the awaiting butler in the hall, " No supper this evening for me, thank you," and goes up to her room, a flash of triumph in her fresh young face ; leaving the widow gazing after her, with the smile of victory on her more mature and worldly coun tenance, at the heiress's significant words.

Before she goes to bed that night, Mrs. Marvin nar-rates this conversation in a note to Lord Avonmere, ending with the old adage, " Strike while the iron is hot ! "

This note sent by a messenger boy reaches Avonmere while he is at breakfast the next morning.

Another lingering Mercury of the District Telegraph

Company has brought to Mr. Gussie, whose apartments are on the same floor, a packet addressed "Baron Bassington," and demanded a receipt for the same.

As he gives this, Augustus notes the handwriting on the package, and turns pale.

He comes hurriedly into the breakfast room and addresses Avonmere. That gentleman is just finishing Mrs. Marvin's note, and looks up at him with a contented smile.

"I want to ask your advice—as a brother peer," says Gussie. "If there's any threat for damages for breach of promise—I presume the proper thing would be to refer her to my solicitors. It's the usual form in such cases when men of title are persecuted."

"Yes, I believe it's the usual form," mutters Avonmere, who has had one or two such matters on his hands with adventuresses in days gone by. Then he says suddenly and savagely, "You don't suppose that Miss Follis will bring suit against *you?*" and would break little Gussie's head and throw him down-stairs, did not his plans compel him to remain on good terms with Baron Bassington for a day or two longer.

"No, I hardly think so," mutters Gussie ; "but in case of any trouble I shall refer her to Stillman, Myth & Co."

"I should by no means go to them !" says Avonmere uneasily.

"No ! Why not ?"

"They'll charge you a pretty penny."

"Oh !" cries Gussie, "talent always comes high," and he opens the packet to find a little case containing his engagement ring and one or two other little knick-knacks he has presented—but no word from his *fiancée* of yesterday.

"By Jove ! not going to make a fuss after all. Poor little gal—feels too bad to say anything. I was much obliged to you, old boy, last night, softening the affair for her, palliating my ignoring her. The proper thing in a brother peer—do the same for you ! So that affair's over—now for others ! Oh, *what* a pile of notes !" he babbles on—hurriedly running through his mail. "Invites from everybody, and all addressed 'Lord Bassington.' Do you know, when I woke this morning, I thought the whole thing was a dream and I was Gussie Van Beekman

again—that awakening was worse than a nightmare—I
screamed. But I'm out of all little Gussie's trouble,
thank Heaven ! I've been having a levee this morning
—I've had all my tradespeople up and offered to pay
their bills, but they wouldn't take their money from Lord
Bassington, though Van Beekman's ducats would have
been reaped with alacrity,—so I ordered lots more to
please them. Bought a mail phaeton and a drag from
Brewster, and as for clothes, boots, gloves, and under-
wear, wait till you gaze on them. I must have spent a
cool ten thousand this morning."

" Pounds ? " ejaculates Avonmere.

" No, dollars ! And all I paid for were two teams,
one seal brown and the other cross matched. These
horse dealers are cash-on-the-nail chaps, so I gave 'em
my check. I think I'll go down to Gill & Patrick's and
look over their stock of jewelry," murmurs the new lord,
slipping Matilde's engagement ring on his little finger.
" Very glad Miss Follis didn't make a row."

" No," returns Avonmere who has listened to this effusion with a sneer of contempt. " Matilde Follis will
give you no trouble ; but you forget her father, who is, I
am informed, a very dangerous customer ; besides, the girl
has a half brother, or sweetheart, or some relative out
in the mines. He's a very sure shot, I'm told, and has
laid out his man in street fights more than once."

" Good Gad ! I'd forgotten the border-ruffian father,"
mutters Gussie. " What am I to do ? I'd better offer to
renew the engagement till I get across the pond."

At this Avonmere bursts out laughing, for the Crusa-
der blood of old Hugo de Bassington has fled from the
present lord's face, and his lips are trembling.

The Englishman remarks slowly, fighting down a tone
of sarcasm in his voice, " I think the safest way for you
to do, my dear Bassington, will be to say nothing about
jilting Miss Follis. She has a certain kind of plebeian
backwoods pride that will perhaps prevent her mentioning this matter to her cut-throat relatives, and they may
let you live."

" Yaas, that'll be the better way," lisps Gussie. " Mum's
the word ! " and he rises, leaving Avonmere looking over
the newspapers.

" Beastly jealous fellows those penny-a-liners," he says,

gazing back from the door. " The whole lot of them never gave me a head-line, when it's really a matter of national moment."

" My lord's carriage is in waiting," announces the servant with great *empressement,* and with a muttered " *Au revoir,*" Baron Bassington departs to new extravagances and social honors.

Avonmere is happy to note that the journals do not say as much about the recently discovered lord as he had expected ; most of their city editors being wary individuals and suspicious of sudden and unaccountable things. Though none of the papers express a direct doubt as to the new peer's title, most of them mention the affair as a rumor in articles of only moderate length.

" If little Gussie had mentioned Stillman, Myth & Co. to them," laughs Avonmere, " he'd probably had *longer* notices ; as it is, they'll make him celebrated in a day or two. If I know anything of the New York press they'll give him head-lines before they're done with him."

A moment after a new thought comes to him, he quotes from Mrs. Marvin's letter, " Strike while the iron is hot ! "

Then going to his room he arrays himself very carefully and faultlessly ; and with a face that is pale with anxiety at one moment and flushed with expectant passion at another, for in his earthly way he loves this Western beauty, Lord Avonmere walks out of his house and strolls up Fifth Avenue, rings the door-bell of the Follis mansion—TO STRIKE !

To his question, the footman says that Miss Follis is at home, and shows him into the reception room.

Here he sits down and meditates upon his plan of campaign.

But thought gives way to action under the rustle of approaching skirts. Looking up he sees Matilde standing in the open doorway, a slight blush on her fair face, a little tremble in her coral lips, and blue eyes that droop and languish as their glance meets his ; for the wily Marvin's well-planted seed has come to fruitful harvest and filled Miss Follis's mind with this one great idea— " Accept this man *to-day,* and the world will say that you, for his sake, *yesterday* jilted Augustus Baron Bassington —not he you ! "

Being brought up in Madame Lamere's best school of *aplomb*, though nervous and perhaps a little frightened, she says "Good morning" to him quite prettily, but doesn't hold out her hand, and mentions that her mother and Mrs. Marvin have just gone to Madame Lamere's to bring Miss Flossie home from school.

"Ah! your charming sister?" interjects her visitor.

"How did you know she was my *charming* sister? You have never seen her," remarks Matilde, archly.

"No," he replies, gallantly, "but I have seen *you !*"

"Oh, we're not at all alike," she laughs ; and then stammers out, "What conceit in me—taking a compliment I compelled you to make."

"Reject the compliment if you wish, but remember I've been holding out my hand for a minute," he suggests.

Thus compelled, she gives him a smiling blush and her hand also, which receives such tender treatment that the smile leaves her, and the blush grows deeper, as she explains to Avonmere that her sister is going to live at home, and come out in society right away ; Mrs. Marvin has suggested it, and Flossie has both implored and fought for it.

"And you ?" he questions.

"I fought for it also !—And when both her daughters take the war-path, the Indian fighter generally gives in," she rejoins with a slight laugh. "Flossie and I have always been together till this winter, and wish to be side by side again. Wait till you see her—but they'll all be here in a few minutes—and then you *will* say she is charming."

All this has been given him in rather an embarrassed, disconnected, jerky way, as if she wished to keep the conversation all to herself and permit her visitor to say very little. But Matilde's last remark brings upon her the *dénouement* she has half wished to postpone.

Avonmere knows his time will be short, and gets to business at once.

"You seem a little *distraite*," he answers, "after your social triumph last night," and moves his seat quite close to her, which makes her lose her head and give him an opening.

"*My* social triumph?" she echoes. "Why, I was so

overcome at my social triumph last night that I thought of taking this morning's 'Limited' to Denver!" Then, with a little hollow laugh she is about to place her chair in retreat, but is too late—for his hand is on her wrist.

He has his opportunity and uses it very quietly, very cunningly, but very quickly.

"You were going away—without a word to *me!*" he says, trying to keep the passion out of his voice and face, for he has a pretty shrewd idea that, if he does not frighten her by loving her *too much*, he will get her promise. The love business he thinks will come afterward.

She looks at him rather coolly, though she does not take her hand from his grasp.

He goes on, "If I had known THAT, I should have spoken last night—I would have spoken *before.*"

"Why, you've only known me a week!" she gasps in surprise, and her blue eyes opening very wide become gorgeously beautiful to him.

"True," he says, "I had forgotten that—it seems to me as if I had known you my lifetime," and the passion comes into his voice despite himself. "Do you know what I am going to tell you?"

"No," she gasps nervously. Then becoming cool, for she likes him less the more he loves her, and his eyes are beginning to tell their tale, she remarks : "How should I?"

"How should you?" he cries bitterly. "How should any woman know a man loves her? But since you will deceive *yourself*—I will unmask *myself!* I love you, and I ask you to be my wife—Lady Avonmere! You are the first woman who has ever heard those words from my lips." Which is the grim truth of the matter, for until dearth of money suggested it, his worst enemy could never have accused him of being a marrying man.

At this she grows very pale, and says very slowly, "I will be candid with you—I do not love you—I love no man! I'll have no more pretended affection on my conscience. Do you know, my greatest happiness last night as I smiled into that inconstant idiot's face was— that he had never kissed me!" She is red as a rose now, but manages to stammer out, "If you'll take me after this confession—if you think me worthy of your name now—my hand is yours," and she holds it out to him, trembling, and shaking, with both shame and fear —shame at what she has revealed, fear that he may despise her, and crush her pride by refusing the apology offered for her heart.

He looks at it a moment ; then takes the pretty member in his grasp and salutes it as his ancestor would have done in the time of the Second Charles. " I accept this," he says, lightly. " Agreed, we marry ; but neither of us love."

But here Mother Eve comes into Matilde ; she snatches her hand away and giving him a reproachful pout whispers, " You don't love me ? " and looking more beautiful than ever opens the flood-gates of his passion.

" Don't I ?" he cries. " By *this !* and THIS ! I do." And crushing her beautiful figure in his strong arms, he draws her blushing face to his, and after this Matilde Follis can never say of him as she did of little Gussie, " Thank God, this man never kissed me ! "

She struggles from him, throws herself upon a sofa with a faint affrighted cry and covers her face with her hands.

Though he cannot see the working of her mind, curiously enough he has done the very best thing he could to further his plans ; for now she thinks, " I can wed no other man ; shame, if naught else, will drive me to the altar with this one."

So he stands gazing at her, a smile of triumph on his clear-cut features and elated passion in his Italian eyes; her beauty as she pants and sobs is greater than it was before.

But this does not last long. Among the sounds of the great thoroughfare outside, is that of a halting carriage. She springs up, and whispering an affrighted " Don't speak of your victory, *yet*," flies from the room.

She is just in time ; a servant is opening the front door, and there are voices in the vestibule leading to the street.

These come to Avonmere in a confused manner.

Then Mrs. Follis enters and says cordially, " How are yer ? We've just brought my Floss home, she'll be down in a minute ; you wait and see her," and will take no denial, for she is very proud of her adopted child.

A moment after, Matilde comes back without a sign of the agitation of her recent scene. She has a pleasant little fib on her lips, having just run in to see that they had a good lunch for Flossie—servants are not to be trusted, and boarding-school girls are always hungry.

So he remains, and they go into a pleasant little chat, Mrs. Follis telling him, in her peculiar diction, of the way her daughter Floss has struggled to get out of Madame Lamere's clutches and take a " posish " in society.

Which Avonmere endures in a lazy, dreamy way, being quite anxious to get on good terms with the mother of his betrothed.

During this he occasionally steals a glance at the young lady, whose cheeks blush under his gaze, though her eyes have an appealing look in them when they meet his, which is not often, as she seems interested in everything but her *fiancé*.

Noting this, Avonmere wisely judges that his kisses have conquered this haughty young lady, and that he has only to play the master, to be it.

He is very happy in this idea, and when a moment after Mrs. Marvin comes in, he gives her a glance that telegraphs his triumph.

But even while answering it, that astute diplomatist sees his face change under her eyes and grow suddenly ashen. " The same as he showed when he saw the photograph of the ' Baby ' mine cañon," thinks the old lady, and looks round for the cause of this mental phe-romenon.

There is no change in the room, save that Miss Flossie, with sparkling happy eyes, at her freedom from school and *entrée* into the world, is standing in the doorway.

Mrs. Marvin takes another glance at Avonmere. Drops of perspiration are on his forehead, which is white as marble. He has even gripped the chair to save himself from falling—for he had risen to receive Mrs. Marvin.

" Can it be Flossie's voice ? " thinks his observer, for that young lady is crying out, " Oh ! what lovely rooms you've given me—the best in the house. Mother, you've robbed yourself."

" I got out of them not for your sake, but my own," says Mrs. Follis. " I don't like their posish. In that corner *suet* the racket from milkmen and hack drivers would have made your dad crazy, when he turns up from Denver."

" You always say something of that kind when you do anything particularly generous for me, mother," returns the girl, coming up to Mrs. Follis and getting hold of her hand.

The next instant Matilde has said : " Flossie, let me present Lord Avonmere," and turning round she for the first time sees the Englishman, and grows taller and more statuesque.

" Oh, Lord Avonmere," she lisps in the nonchalant way Mrs. Marvin had seen when she first met her. " I'm very happy," and holds out a welcoming hand.

" I've—I've heard of you from your sister," that gentleman contrives to get out, though the widow notes two little gasps in his voice, which has grown hoarser and more guttural than it usually is.

As the sound comes to Miss Flossie's ears, she looks disappointed for a second and then goes calmly on. " You've been very well known to me for some time."

" A—ah," he says in a kind of startled way.

" Yes, Madame Lamere's opera class have devoted their *lorgnettes* to you—I was one of them. I hope we'll be good friends. I'm going to my first dance to-night ; Mrs. Rivington's. Mrs. Marvin was so kind as to get me an invitation."

" But your clothes ? " gasps her mother.

" Oh, that's already arranged," laughs the girl. " Anticipating my nuptials, I ordered my *trousseau* a month ago. Behold White, Howard & Co. ! " and looking out of the window, she points to a wagon delivering a series of boxes and baskets with the brand of this well-known firm of caterers to woman's extravagance in dress.

" Nuptials ? Trousseau ? Great Scott ! Who are you going to marry?" screams Mrs. Follis, overcome and pale.

" Society, mother dear," lisps the girl.

" Oh, that's what you're driving at," gasps Rachel. " You gave me an awful turn with your enigmatical language." Then she says sternly : " I don't like double *entenders* from young girls."

At this there is a ripple of laughter, during which Avonmere contrives to take his leave, Miss Flossie saying to him as he bids her good-by, "Don't forget Mrs. Rivington's, I'm sure you have an invitation," in a tone that makes a very curious light come into Matilde's eyes.

A moment after, noticing that her sister has no engagement ring on her finger, the *débutante* gives Mrs. Marvin a grateful glance and remarks: "And now the society lady will take her lunch," assuming a grand air and striding off to the dining-room.   Here she is followed by Matilde, who talks to her as she feasts, for it is quite late in the day and the others have lunched long ago.

As for Avonmere, he gets down the street somehow for a block or two, then chancing to sight an empty cab, he hails the driver, gets in and is driven home, muttering to himself: "Impossible.   There was her mother and sister. What nonsense!   And yet—just how she would have grown up.   The image of Agnes Willoughby!   That trick of the eyes."   Then he suddenly gives a low but awful groaning laugh and cries: "By Jove!   I'm getting a conscience, like Macbeth—I'm seeing ghosts!"

CHAPTER XVII.

"DARN ME IF IT AIN'T PETE!"

"GOING to Mrs. Rivington's function to-night?" babbles Mr. Gussie, coming into Avonmere's apartments about nine o'clock in the evening of the day that gentleman has had his Macbeth soliloquy, and finding him rather out of sorts and in a very bad humor.

"I may and I may not," he says shortly and snappily.

"Then don't!"

"Why not?"

"Because I'm going to give a little supper to-night to some of the old crowd.   I want to show them how an English nobleman with a big income entertains," he says pompously.

At this declaration a peculiar grin comes over his listener's mobile features, and noting the returned engagement ring, which has sparkled upon Gussie's finger during the gesticulation of his last speech, Avonmere remarks : "You wish me to join your party?"

"Y—a—a—s. Thought you might like to give a brother peer your countenance."

"Anything but the supper?"

"Well, perhaps a little game afterward. The usual thing, yer know."

"All right!" says his lordship briskly. "I'll accept your invitation with pleasure, Lord Bassington," and he twists up a little perfumed note he has in his hand.

"Oh, by Jove! I know that handwriting," cries Gussie. "I've heard of you ; the populace say you cut me out with Miss Tillie. Rather absurd idea, isn't it!"

"Very!" answers Avonmere, who dares not say much for fear of letting his temper get the best of him. For this last insinuation has been made in such a self-confident tone that his listener wants to kick Augustus out of the room ; which he would do had it not occurred to him that it will be just as well if he gets back from Lord Bassington some of the money that had been paid to him by Messrs. Stillman, Myth & Co., to induce him to believe he was an English peer with a lordly rent-roll.

Besides, Avonmere has been considering his ways and means, and to give Miss Follis a betrothal token handsome enough to be a suitable present from a nobleman to a great heiress, will make a serious inroad on his available cash. Noting the gleam of the diamond on Gussie's finger, he thinks this may be arranged, and keeps his temper.

Therefore he says in his kindliest and most cordial tones : "My dear Bassington, I will be with you. At what hour?"

"Oh, about eleven! Delmonico's, room 11. I'm going to see my venerable relatives, old Van Twiler and Lydia. They've fallen in love with me since I became a peer. So has the rest of the world. Jeems, is my *broum* in waiting?"

"Yes, your lordship," answers the man, and little Gussie goes whistling off to pass a yawny hour at Washington Square.

Avonmere shortly after this writes to his *fiancée*, stating that business will prevent him seeing her this evening either at her own home or Mrs. Rivington's, and begging her to present his compliments to her sister and wish her a pleasant *début*.

This note he soon after despatches with a couple of magnificent bouquets from Klunders, one for Miss Follis and the other for Miss Florence; then feeling himself free from the chance of seeing the girl's face this evening, he gives a sigh of relief.

For in his soul of souls he is shrinking from the thought of meeting the flashing eyes of Flossie Follis.

"I'll have no more Macbeth soliloquies," he says to himself, with a shudder. "I'll not look on my pretty ghost till I've got my nerves in training."

With this he goes out to enjoy Mr. Gussie's hospitality, and meeting the young lord and several other of his intimate friends, they make a sportive night of it; and the cards being brought in, somehow luck favoring him, though he handles the pasteboards with rare skill, he wins quite a large amount of money, most of it from his host, who plays very badly.

Coming home together, Avonmere cautions Lord Bassington to be less reckless in his play; but is answered with this remark: "What are a few hundreds or a few thousands to a nobleman of *my* means?"

"Still, great as they are, you may find them exhausted," murmurs the Englishman. "Besides, you hardly played as well as the rest."

"Didn't I?" cries Gussie. "The luck was against me. The cards running fairly, I can play any man in New York—you for instance."

"I scarcely think so!"

"What?"

"You see I'm so very fortunate at games of chance," says Avonmere, confidently.

"Are you? Well, I'll back my skill against your luck," returns Augustus. "I owe you five hundred, I believe."

"Five hundred and forty-five," corrects his companion.

"Then come into my parlor, and I'll owe you nothing or more before we get up."

"It's too late—nearly four o'clock."

"Pough! that's about the right time for a thorough bred to wake up!" cries Gussie. "*Come!*"

"Very well, since you insist!" says Avonmere. "Though I warn you, I nearly always win!"

"Oh, rats!" remarks the new lord, who has too much champagne on board for caution, and will not be warned.

So the two sit down for a quiet game, and at eight o'clock in the morning Avonmere, rising up from it, has a check on the Second National for twenty-five hundred and odd dollars in his hand, and upon his finger sparkles the engagement ring that Matilde had returned to Mr. Gussie.

"You'll give—a fellah—his—hic—revenge?" stutters out the latter, who having added brandy to his champagne, is now in a fearful state.

"Certainly. I hope the loss does not inconvenience you?" returns Avonmere, very politely, and goes off to his breakfast, leaving Augustus to get to bed, muttering: "Inconvenience—a lord with sixty thousand a year? I'm afraid Avonmere's income can't be any great shakes. If so, I'll—I'll cut him, by the blood of old Hugo de Bas—Bassington! when I cross the—er—herrin' pond."

Strolling into Delmonico's, that he had left but five hours before, Avonmere makes a very comfortable break-fast, then walks down to Twenty-third Street, enters the Second National Bank, and as the clock strikes ten, presents Bassington's check, and gives a sigh of relief as it is paid. For he has been mortally afraid that there may not be funds enough to meet it, little Gussie's extravagance has been so great. Then strolling to Tiffany's, he twists the jewel out of the ring on his finger and orders it reset and properly initialled for his betrothal offering to Miss Follis.

Being promised that it will be ready by the afternoon, he goes home, and getting to bed sleeps the sleep of the wicked, which is sometimes as sound as that of the just —especially after the wicked has been spreeing, gaming, and tooting all night.

That afternoon, his man calling him about four o'clock, Avonmere rises from his slumbers, and feeling quite cer-tain he has driven the ghost from his imagination, for that is what he terms Miss Flossie, thinks he will stroll up the avenue and slip his engagement manacle upon Matilde's pretty finger.

This bauble has already arrived from Messrs. Tiffany, who usually keep their promises. So, with Gussie's diamond sparkling in his pocket, my lord is in a quietly pleasant state of mind when he rings the door-bell of Number 637 Fifth Avenue.

In answer to his inquiry, "Is Miss Follis at home?" the servant, with the carelessness of American menials, says: "Yes, my lord; she's in the reception room," and promptly shows him into that apartment, announcing him at the door.

The room has not yet been lighted, and, the season being mid-winter, is quite dark at half-past four in the afternoon; for in most New York houses the windows are very heavily curtained, partly to keep the apartments as warm as possible and partly to show off as much elaborate draperies and lace as can be exhibited.

As he enters, a young lady arises. Then, taking a sudden glance around the room to see there is no one else present, Avonmere, with the eagerness of that emotion he compliments by calling love, steps rapidly toward her. "My darling" is already formed and on his lips, when a voice comes to him and makes him tremble and grow pale once more.

But with an effort he controls himself and listens; for it is only the tones of Miss Flossie Follis, who is holding out her hand to him, and crying with the impulsive frankness of girlhood: "Thank you, *so* much, Lord Avonmere, for the beautiful bouquet you sent me last evening; I carried it to Mrs. Rivington's dance."

"I—am—glad you liked it," murmurs the gentleman addressed, with a tremor in his articulation that, fight how he may, will get into it; the voice is so like—that of the past.

"Oh, I did, thoroughly! I told Tillie it was much prettier than hers, though she would not admit it. But why don't you sit down? Mamma is out, so is Tillie and Mrs. Marvin, and I am arbiter of your comfort. It is too dark to see, but I know you are standing up and uneasy." Then ringing the bell, Miss Flossie says: 'Lights, Thomas!" in the easy tone of young ladyhood, that indicates she has already put Madame Lamere's boarding-school behind her, and instead of obeying, expects to command.

This being done, she turns to her guest, who has been gazing at her as if hypnotized, and asks : " Why were you not at Mrs. Rivington's ? " then pouts, " You might have come, to my *first* party."

" Impossible !—Business ! " murmurs Avonmere.

" Business ?—a lord has *business?* " she echoes in a suppressed laugh. " Why, I had supposed it one of the privileges of your rank to do nothing ? "

" Oh ! " returns the gentleman, " I work often."

" All last night, eh ? "

" What makes you think that ? "

" Why, you said so : your note told of midnight labors. Besides, I heard——"

" What ? "

" Well, Mr. Benson was at Mrs. Rivington's last evening. He came late—was introduced to me. He doesn't talk well to ladies. Seems to think it his glory to show how wicked he is : consequently, he is dangerous to the good name of the rest of you. In displaying his dissipations he discloses yours. He told me he had just left you and Lord Bassington. You had gone in for all-night poker."

" Did he mention no other names ? " asks Avonmere.

" No," returns the girl, lazily, playing with a bonbon holder she has in her hand. " The rest were Americans, I presume. Mr. Benson did not think their names would give importance to him, and so spared them."

" He didn't tell that story to Matilde, did he ? " questions the English lord with a start, his brain heaping mental curses upon the head of the babbling Benson ; for he has suddenly remembered that his note told his *fiancée* of important and unpostponable business.

" I—I believe he did," answers Miss Flossie, somewhat maliciously. " Mr. Benson is a curious young man. I asked him how he could leave such society as yours. Perhaps my vanity expected some of the stock-in-trade compliments of society men to society women, such as, ' I knew *you* were going to be here, Miss Florence,' or ' Mrs. Rivington always has such beautiful girls, though she's a little ahead of her usual form this evening.' But I was disappointed ; he's a Wall Street man and gave me a financial answer."

" And that was—— " says his lordship, who is anxious

to know the worst that Matilde may have heard of him.

"Well," laughs the girl with a mischievous glance, "he said, 'I never play with Lord Avonmere, it costs *too much money.*' But you mustn't be angry with him. Mr. Benson was only talking to amuse himself and me. Your family name is Willoughby, is it not?"

"Yes," returns the Englishman, for the girl's tone has been so easily conversational that for a moment he has lost all thought of the past. Then he suddenly asks, "How did you know?" in a voice that astounds her.

"Why," she says laughingly, "at Madame Lamere's we studied Debrett. Arthur, 23d Baron Avonmere—I remember—Thomas, 21st Baron—Florence Beatrice. Baroness Avonmere died aged nine—killed by Indians in America—country seats, Avonmere Castle, Hants—Beachman Manor, Berks. I looked you up again yesterday," and she laughs merrily at him, and plays with her bonbon box, while he sits gazing on her as if on a basilisk.

This glance is so peculiar that in a moment Miss Flossie would notice it, did not Matilde suddenly enter and take note of it for her own instruction.

She has just come in from some afternoon tea or reception ; and Mrs. Marvin, who is always pleased to chaperone the beautiful heiress, is just behind her.

They are both in carriage dresses, the widow looking dowager-like in satins and brocades that cover her two hundred pounds of ruby-tinted figure, while Matilde seems like a blonde winter-fairy in violet velvet trimmed with the fur of the silver fox ; though as she looks on Avonmere, apparently devouring Miss Flossie with his glance, the fairy's eyes become rather excited and annoyed and earth-born.

She says with a slight irritation in her voice, giving the gentleman, who has sprung hurriedly up to receive her, a rather haughty bow, "I am happy to see your midnight business, Lord Avonmere, is at length finished. I hope my sister has been able to keep you awake, after your prolonged exertions of last evening."

Thus compelled to compliment, Matilde's betrothed replies that Miss Florence has made his call a very pleasant one.

And Flossie murmurs, meekly, "I did my best to keep

him here till you arrived, and I am happy to say succeeded." Her eyes emphasize the last word in a way
that makes Matilde's orbs grow big with some new emotion—an expression of countenance that causes the
watchful Marvin great happiness.

Her enjoyment is not shared by the others, for the
conversation seems out of joint; Avonmere appears
unable to keep his eyes from the younger sister, which
causes the elder to be *distraite*, nervous and irritable.

Twice Matilde throws out hints as to Flossie's taking
time enough to dress for dinner, or suggests some errand
that will remove that young lady from the room.

But hints are thrown away on the younger sister, who
sits very calmly talking about the opera this evening, the
first one she shall go to as a young lady, and giving them
a dissertation on Madame Lamere's opera classes, till
at length Avonmere rises to go.

Matilde would follow him to the hall, for she is desperately anxious to have a two-word *tête-à-tête* with him ; but
in the exuberant spirits of young ladyhood her sister
comes out beside her and cries, "Don't forget our box
to-night, Lord Avonmere ! I wish to make a goodly
showing of young men on my first night as a *débutante*.
Madame Lamere's girls will be there, and I'm naughty
enough to wish the children to see that I am making
good running for the social stakes. You haven't shaken
hands with me coming or going."

" Oh, I've reserved you for the last," says his lordship
a little nervously, taking her offered palm.

At this there comes an expression in Matilde's eyes
that brings to Mrs. Marvin a chuckling joy.

" The dear little innocent, how she plays my game for
me !" thinks that female diplomat. "If Miss Flossie
keeps this up, Matilde'll be jealous enough to elope with
Avonmere."

That gentleman has just passed out—Miss Florence is
on her way up-stairs.

So, anxious to give this idea a good start and favoring
wind in Miss Follis's mind, the old lady rustles into the
hall and putting her arm round Matilde's waist, who is
standing pale and thoughtful, remarks laughingly, " Your
younger sister should have been kept at school,
eh ? "

"Nonsense!" cries the girl, growing very red. "Flossis can't take a hint—that's all."

"Then give her a fact that she must accept before—"

"Before what?" interjects Matilde.

"Well, young girls just from school are very suscepti. ble, and Avonmere is handsome.   A proof of your taste Tell her —*in time !*"

At her words, Matilde, who has grown red, cries, "Absurd!—She's only seen him twice," and trying a laugh she moves up the stairs, for she doesn't care to discuss such a matter with any one.

Mrs. Marvin looks at her *protégée* as she passes from her sight ; secure triumph on her ruddy face.   She knows she has planted, and there will be a reaping ; and so goes merrily to dress for dinner.

While this has been passing below, Miss Flossie is pacing her room above.   Striding about like a tragedy queen she mutters, "Am I right?   Can it be?—Heaven help me to play my *rôle* till I discover!" next cries, "Oh, for a little clew—something to start my awakening mind —some shock—some lightning flash—to save my Tillie in time !"

This is so wild, so disconnected, so illogical, that she seems almost a maniac, for she has thrown down her hair and tumbled off her dress, and her white arms are in such lovely but agitated gesticulation, they would denote the disorder of madness, did not a noble courage beam in her eyes when she cries out her sister's name.

Perhaps Heaven has heard her prayer, for shortly after this the Patriarchs' ball brings a very curious complication into this young lady's life, and also a sensation to Philip Everett.

That gentleman has devoted himself to business as far as he can since the time of seeing Lord Avonmere at the Metropolitan on the night of Mr. Gussie's "Razzle Dazzle."   He has not wished to see his suspect until he receives advices from New Mexico and England, fearing that he may let his temper betray him into some indiscretion ; therefore he has kept to Wall Street, knowing there was little chance of encountering this English lord on that arena of speculation.

On the day of this subscription ball he has, however, received a letter from New Mexico that has put him in such a fever that he has determined to seek an introduction to Avonmere and see if he can indirectly learn from him his version of his niece's death.

He accordingly proposes to accompany his sister, who is going under Mrs. Willis's chaperonage.

Arriving with his party at Delmonico's, he soon after leaves his sister, Grousemoor, and Mrs. Willis in the crush of the long red parlor, and stalks into the pretty ball-room. Grousemoor has promised to present him to Avonmere, both thinking it well that Everett should not recall himself to remembrance by introducing himself as Pete the cowboy of the Gila valley.

Here, dazzled by the electric lights that give its palmy and floral decorations a fairy green and supernatural color, he stands under the little balcony, from which dangle baskets of flowers and issues the crash of Lander's orchestra, gazing at the gorgeous robes of beautiful women and the dress suits of conventional men.

He has hardly been on his errand a minute when, standing by an embellishing palm tree in the corner of the room, Phil sees the man he thinks a murderer. A minute after, looking closer, he rubs his eyes in amazement and surprise, for seated under the green branches, laughing and talking to her supposed assassin, IS HIS NIECE AND VICTIM.

At least so Everett thinks.

At this moment, however, Mr. Benson strolls up to the young lady and addresses her as Miss Follis, at which the Bostonian stares again, this time perhaps more amazed than before.

Conquering any outward emotion, he asks a near-by acquaintance who the young lady is. " The one just rising up to dance."

"Oh," says his friend, "that is Miss Flossie Follis. Just come out. A great heiress and greater beauty. You'd better go in for her. Most of the men are. But you won't get a dance unless you catch a turn or two in the cotillion, and you'll have to play a pretty sharp game to capture even that."

Phil listens to this in a dazed way, his eyes following the girl, whose brunette beauty shines out of a pure white, drifting, fleecy, cloudy, lace, tulle, silvery, gauzy kind of a garment, which would be called by a modiste "a creation ; " by a poet "a poem ; " by a musician "a symphony ; " but is called by little Augustus, who is making his last night of it as Lord Bassington, though he doesn't know it, "a bang-up, knock-out kind of a gown."

Every movement of this graceful creature entrances his eyes ; he has not heard her voice, but knows it must be lovely.   She passes him so close that the perfume of her dress floats round him to intoxicate him more.   Her arm, white and beautiful as one of the lost ones of the Venus of Milo, is bare to the shoulder—her *right* arm ; and as his eyes rove over its beautiful curves he gets a shock that staggers him more than all the rest—so far.

On the pure white flesh of Miss Flossie Follis, the Colorado heiress's rounded limb, hardly noticeable now, is the scar of a wound, and above it, peeping out from surrounding snow, a tiny mole—the same marks that were on the arm of little Florence Willoughby, as she brought him water when wounded and fainting he fought the Apaches to save her childish life at the ford of the Gila.

Almost imagining the hot atmosphere of the ball-room has affected his mind, he staggers out into the cool air of the hall.   This, as usual, is filled with loungers and lookers-on, men who don't dance but who will be very ready and agile at the supper-table.

A moment after, thinking some stimulant may clear his brain, and such not being served at a Patriarchs' ball, he remembers it is not yet twelve o'clock, and the *café* will yet be open.   Not waiting for the elevator he descends by the stairs to the ground floor to go to that portion of the famous restaurant devoted to bachelor entertainment.

At the bottom of these he is greeted with this curious remark : "Are you fired also ? "

Staring at his interrogator, a tall, broad-shouldered, red-faced man, whose dress suit seems to be too large for even his immense frame, whose shirt-front is soft and flabby from lack of starch, and the weight of two immense diamond studs, Phil says in uncertainty :

"I beg your pardon?"   Then he ejaculates, "Abe Follis ! "

"Yes, and darn me if it ain't Pete !   How did you make your raise ?   Are you an excrescence like myself ! " cries that mining man, slapping Everett on the back

" Have you been ejected. too ? " Then he says in a melancholy tone : " I just warnted to see my Tillie dance once. She's a society hummer now. And blow me if I wan't invited down-stairs. If it hadn't been for making a row with ladies round, I'd have landed that committee chap out in the street thar. I ain't used to being sat down on by dudes ! "

CHAPTER XVIII.

AN EPISODE OF THE PATRIARCHS'.

" I'D never have recognized you, if it hadn't been for your voice and your catching on to me, Pete," continues old Follis. " You look like the real social article, you do,—but come on and liquor."

Everett here thinks he has some questions he would like to ask his former partner, and immediately assents. Then the two stroll into the *café*, Mr. Follis's enormous patent leathers creaking with newness at every step.

It is near midnight now ; the room is full, and under its electric lights sit stock-brokers discussing Wall Street, men-about-town gossiping of the latest *on dit*, the last social sensation, the new play, ballet, or opera—all of them drinking, most of them smoking ; a few, who have come down from the ball up-stairs on the same errand as Phil, discussing the ladies who are dancing above.

Pressing into the throng, Everett soon gets hold of Philip, the head waiter, and that official, with his kindly smile complicated this evening by neuralgia, of which he is a perennial victim, shortly finds a retired table in a corner of the room for the Bostonian and his companion.

Here they sit down, practically alone ; for the hum of conversation from surrounding tables confines their voices to their immediate vicinity.

A moment later Phil is about to speak, when Abe suddenly opens the conversation, springing the very topic that Everett has on his mind.

He says : " Did you see my two hummers up there ? " pointing with his big thumb toward the ceiling.

" Your *two* hummers ? "

"Yes, my darters—Tillie and Flossie, to be sure !" answers Follis, proudly. "What's the matter with you ?" for Phil is gazing at him, astonished.

"Only this," says Everett slowly and impressively. "In New Mexico you had but one child, Tillie ; now the intervening twelve years have brought you another, Flossie, and she, like a reversed Iolanthe, can only be eleven, but looks at least eighteen. I've heard the climate of Colorado developed female loveliness very rapidly, but your Flossie is a prodigy."

"Ain't she ?" murmurs Abe, with a guffaw. Then he says : "Pete, I'm going to let you into a family secret. In Colorado I didn't mind how many knew it ; but here, whar they talk of pedigree and blood and that stuff, they might kind of look down on my Flossie, and not think her as altitudinus as my Tillie, if they knowed that the Follis blood of Colorado didn't flow in her veins."

"She is not your child ?" says Phil, excitedly. "Then who's is she ?"

"Darn me if I know ! "

"Great Heavens ! I'm right, then ! " gasps Everett.

"What do *you* know ? " whispers Abe, in an anxious voice.

"What do you know ? " echoes Phil. "My knowledge is but conjecture till I have your story."

"Will my telling you do Flossie any harm ? " says the old gentleman, nervously. "Answer me, as you're a square man ! "

"No ; perhaps the reverse."

"Then, Pete, I'll tell *you !* " says Abe. And he gives him the story of the Baby mine in about the same words that he had related it to Mrs. Marvin when that lady was in Denver.

As he finishes, the young man says impulsively: "The date of the discovery of your mine ?"

"July 7th, 1881."

"You are sure ?"

"Sartin ! " answers Follis promptly. "I've given my evidence in court on that p'int over twenty-five times, and have affidavitted it about thirty more in fighting Baby jumpers."

"Baby *what ?* " cries Phil, for the expression is peculiar.
"Oh !—ah !—yes !—I understand ! "

"I don't mean sarvant-gal nurses," says Abe, with a grin. "I've heard that back-number joke afore." Then he grows very serious as he sees Phil making notes of what he has said, and goes on: "What do your questions mean, anyhow, Pete? Out with it! for anything about my leetle Flossie goes very near my heart."

"I can't tell you to-night. You shall know as soon as I discover anything definite!" answers Everett.

"Definite?" echoes Abe. Then his face grows scared, and he gasps: "My Lord! you don't think you'll find parents for Flossie—folks who'll take her away from Rach and me and break our hearts?" A moment after, his face grows calmer, and he mutters: "Floss wouldn't go, anyway. She ain't the gal to backslide on those who love her."

"Have no fear of that!" remarks Phil, who sees the old man's emotion and loves him for it. "If what I suspect is true, it will only add to Miss Flossie's wealth and honor, and there will be no one to take her from you until——" Here some sudden thought flies through his mind to make his face red and confuse his mind, and he mutters: "Till she chooses a husband."

"But can't ye tell me a leetle—something I can hint to the gal?" persists Abe, whose curiosity is on fire. "Some pointer that she can try and remember; something for my wife and I to work out; for no one on this earth would struggle for Flossie's interests harder than her adopted parents—not even Bob."

This resurrection of Bob, whom Mr. Follis had mentioned in his tale of the Baby mine as the child's friend, champion, and trustee, gives Phil a sudden though inexplicable pang.

Putting aside his own feelings, however, he says earnestly: "Follis, as you wish to aid Flossie, not a word of this conversation to any one! Promise me! You knew that I was square—in the West; trust me—in the East."

"I will, Pete, I will! My jaws are shut!" whispers Follis, giving him his great big hand.

"Very well," answers Everett, "here's my card," handing the miner a pasteboard that astonishes him, for he says: "You ain't Pete no longer?"

"That was my Western nickname," answers Phil. And he gives him, in a few words, the reason of his metamor

phosis from miner and cowboy to a director of the Atchison, Topeka and Santa Fé.   But closing this suddenly, he
mutters : " There's too much cigar smoke here—come
out into the air," and hurries Follis from his seat.   For
little Gussie and one or two of his friends have come
down from the ball, and sitting at the table next them,
are punishing B. and S.'s ; and Everett has just caught a
remark from Lord Bassington about Miss Tillie that
would not suit a father's ears.

Stepping on to Broadway, Phil again repeats : " No
mention of our conversation to any one ! "

" You've my word on that ! " says Abe ; " but come
and have a drink with the boys."   And he points to the
great hotel a little farther down Broadway that is the
headquarters of Western millionaires.

" No, thank you ; I've other business."

" Good-night, then.   I think I'll step over to the Hoffman : thar's so many mining men thar that I feel as
natural as on my own dump-pile."

As Follis walks across the street, Phil hurries back to
the ball-room, for what he has heard about Miss Flossie
makes him very eager to seek an immediate introduction.

It is now midnight, and the Patriarchs', generally a late
ball, is just in full swing and action.

He knows Mrs. Marvin is the chaperon for the Misses
Follis, and, having met her once or twice, hopes she will
remember him.   Contriving to get near her, he finds she
has not forgotten him.

Both her charges are dancing, so Phil and she have
a pleasant little *tête-à-tête*.

This lady is very gracious to the rich Bostonian, whose
sister is going to make the match of the year ; and a few
moments after, Miss Tillie making her appearance, Mr.
Everett has the pleasure of being presented to this young
lady.

Thinking perhaps it will not be pleasant for this New
York belle to be reminded of her New Mexican dug-out
childhood, Phil says nothing of having slept under the
same roof for almost a year with this piquant beauty who
smiles unconcernedly at him, and makes his acquaintance
over again.

As he speaks, a slight cloud of perplexity runs over the
girl's mobile features for a moment ; but her remem-

brance is very vague—she was a mere child at the time, and it is difficult to associate this self-contained man of the world, who is talking in the easy strain of polite society, with the brawny, unshaved, rough-and-tumble miner who swung a sledge over her father's drill twelve years ago.

In answer to the usual polite speeches of young manhood on such occasions, she says: " I have had the pleasure of meeting your sister, Mr. Everett."

" Does that help my chances with you for a dance this evening?" murmurs Phil, gallantly.

"It would," she returns, "were I not engaged for everything. I am sorry, but if gentlemen remain downstairs too long "—she gives her fan the direction of the *café* below their feet—"they should blame themselves, not us."

" Then there is no hope," remarks Everett, rather disappointedly, for Miss Tillie's bright eyes are very pleasant to look upon.

" Ah, you are not a ball-room man, I perceive," laughs the young lady.

"No? What makes you think that?" says her listener, with rather a shamed-faced look on his face, and not altogether pleased at having been diagnosed so quickly.

" Because then you would know," she replies lightly, " that there is always hope in the cotillon."

Before Phil can answer this with appropriate gratitude, Mrs. Marvin's fan taps him on the shoulder.

As he turns she says : " Mr. Everett, let me present you to Miss Florence Follis ; " and in ardent youth and radiant beauty, with the flush of the dance upon her fair cheeks, and the excited joy of her first big ball in her brown eyes, Flossie is speaking to him ; and her voice brings back to him the past of years ago.

He attempts to reply ; and the girl, giving him a laughing pout, cries : " You're not a good listener, Mr. Everett. I asked you if you were Miss Bessie's brother, and you answered me that you were a Bostonian. What has destroyed your ears ? "

" My eyes ! " ejaculates the inspired Phil, and gives a start at his own audacity.

" Your eyes ?" echoes Miss Flossie, wonderingly. Then she gives a big blush, and says rather haughtily, though

there is a smile on her face : "Yes, I noticed your eyes
had a far-away look in them.   Of what were you thinking ? "

"I was thinking that I would like a dance with you this
evening," returns Phil, who has made more lady-speeches
in the last two minutes than in the whole of his former
life.

"A dance with me ?   Then I don't wonder your expression was a *far-away* one," remarks Miss Flossie, rather
pointedly.   Next, noting his disappointed glance, she
whispers : "I'm engaged two or three deep this evening, but——"   And she looks demure and undecided.

"But what ?"

"You'll—you'll not censure a white prevarication ? "

"Certainly not ! "

"Of course, I forgot ! I've heard you're a Wall Street
man.   Quick ! here's Foxhunter Reach coming.   Your
arm at once ! "   And the next instant, as they move to
the rhythm of Lander's music, Phil feels her heart beat
against his as when, nine years before, his shielded hers
from Apache bullets.

In the next two minutes his life has changed.   Wall
Street, and Atchison and Santa Fé, stocks and bonds,
accumulated interest and net earnings, drift from him.
The Boston business man, with her lithe waist encircled
by his arm, the perfume of her breath upon his cheek,
and her inspiring eyes looking into his, becomes romantic as a Romeo.

A second after, the waltz being over, romance is
bowled out by his partner's practical whisper : "Mr.
Reach is looking for me ; see if I meet him with Wall
Street depravity ! "   And walking up to that gentleman,
she says severely : "You were not here during the dance
before this one ; " for she has noted Foxhunter's recent
return to the ball-room.

"No, but——"

"Then I hope you will remember the next time you're
engaged to dance with me ! " she returns in an awful
tone, her eyes very haughty.   Next she mutters in a
broken and wounded voice : "You may take me to Mrs.
Marvin, Mr. Everett," and trips away on Phil's arm,
leaving the robbed and browbeaten Reach astonished
and muttering explanations.

"I've never done such a thing before," she says to her partner, and looks ashamed ; then suddenly astounds him by continuing : "I wonder why I do it now ? " and grow· ing red as flame, cries : " Why don't you take me to my chaperon ? It's not good form to keep a *débutante* from protecting wings."

And Phil getting her to Mrs. Marvin, she astounds him more.

As he says to her, "I dare not ask you for another dance, I see conscience troubles you already about this one——"

" Pshaw ! " she answers impulsively. " I've no con· science in a ball-room—at least not to-night."

" What ? " cries Phil, " I can come again ? "

" Yes, the second from this ; its—its supper ! " she remarks impulsively and illogically ; then mutters : " What a minx you must think me ! *Au revoir*, Mr. Everett ! " and takes the arm of somebody, Phil doesn't care who, for he is dazed at the girl's actions.

Then vanity coming upon this man, who has received what many have asked for and not obtained, he thinks: " If Miss Flossie is a minx, she's the most charming, fas· cinating, and lovable minx in existence," and goes to watching her movements with some rather curious dis· coveries.

First, he notes that two or three times, as her eyes catch his, there seems to come into them a perplexed look, and once she passes her hand over her forehead as if struggling with some mental problem that worries her young brain.

Second, he perceives that whenever Avonmere is near her sister, which is quite often, Miss Flossie's eyes flame and blaze with some potent emotion—perhaps anger, cer· tainly not love ; though, curiously enough, she seems to like the nobleman's company, throwing herself in his way as much as possible, as if striving to draw his attentions from Miss Tillie to herself.

This peculiarity is apparently perceived by Miss Tillie also, who once or twice, catching her sister at this work, gives her some most unsisterly glances.

The lanciers particularly emphasizes Miss Flossie's peculiar feelings to Avonmere.

She is at the side of the set he at the head. While

he is going through the figure with the couple opposite,
she gazes at him with intensity, perhaps even with hate.
When he turns to dance with her, as she looks into his
face, her eyes grow soft, winning, even caressing.

"Perhaps it's the effect of family blood," thinks
Phil.

An idea that Avonmere himself has; for this wily gentleman, having been given a hint by his view of the cañon
of the Baby mine, has soon pumped out of the Follis
family the story of the girl's discovery and adoption, and
knows very well that the pretty white hands he holds in
his as he turns Miss Flossie in the lanciers are those of
his niece, who should, by every chance of nature, have
been devoured by wild beasts or starved to death long
years ago in the far-away Rocky Mountains.

As Phil looks on this, a very nasty expression comes
into his face, as he thinks of a letter he has just received
this day from " Brick " Garvey.

Brief, characteristic, and pointed, it states that the
only telegrams received in Lordsburgh the day Everett
had driven Mrs. Willoughby to her death had given the
true direction of the Indian raid. " That cuss was 'cuter
than an Apache !" concludes Mr. Garvey ; " he tied the
Britisher to destruction by his love for his wife and baby.
You lure your young lordling, with his Greaser grin,
here. Then the boys will lynch him sure, and the sheriff'll
be behind time, as usual ! "

Remembering what this man has done, which makes
it difficult to keep his hands off him, much less treat him
with the courtesy common to the chance acquaintanceship
of a ball-room, Phil suggests that, instead of remaining
with Mrs. Marvin and Miss Tillie and Avonmere, they
occupy a table with Mrs. Willis, his sister, and Grousemoor.

To this Miss Flossie assents; and finding Everett's
party, they all go down together to the big restaurant
upon the ground floor, that is now closed to general
custom, and in which there is plenty of room for every
one at the small tables.

Here the younger Miss Follis makes herself so agreeable, bright, and charming that both the ladies and Grousemoor fall in love with her—conquests which please Phil
greatly, though his watchful eyes can't help noticing that

at times the girl's gayety seems strained, not as if she were unhappy, but as if anxious and perplexed.

Perplexed when his voice comes to her ear, for at such times her big eyes seem to have caught the far-away look that was in his when first they met; anxious when she glances at the near-by table at which Avonmere and her sister are seated in earnest conversation, Mrs. Marvin, who sits with them, apparently devoting all her senses to the supper.

Toward the close of the meal Miss Bessie, with that air of proprietorship peculiar to approaching brides, whispers: "Grousemoor, take up Miss Florence with Mrs. Willis; I want to say a word to Phil."

"Delighted!" remarks that nobleman, and would do as he is bid, but Flossie suddenly says: "If you don't mind, I'll go over to Mrs. Marvin's table until they come up. I—I want to see Matilde a second."

"Shall I wait for you?" asks Phil.

"If you have the patience," returns the girl.

So Everett remains alone at his table, while she hurries off to the one at which Lord Avonmere and Miss Tillie are in full *tête-à-tête*, receiving a rather savage glance from her sister for this attention.

Paying no heed to this, Flossie seats herself beside Avonmere, and proceeds to make herself so agreeable that, finding she can't get rid of her, Maltilde rises and says: "I suppose it's about time for the cotillon. Let's go up-stairs, since Flossie is tired of her big Bostonian."

Now, the restaurant being nearly empty, and Miss Tillie's voice quite loud from anger or jealousy or some other unruly passion, this remark comes very clearly to Phil's ears, amid the pop of a champagne cork or two from distant quarters of the room.

His face grows red.

Glancing at him, Miss Flossie divines that he has heard and suddenly comes to his side.

"If you are ready, Mr. Everett," she says, with a rather quiet voice; "may I have your arm?"

"Certainly," answers Phil; and the two leave the supper-room just behind Avonmere, Miss Follis, and Mrs. Marvin.

As they walk very slowly, and the others quite fast, they are soon alone; and coming up the stairs. Miss

Flossie, growing red in the face, remarks: "What must you think of me? You have met me only this evening, and I first cheat Mr. Reach out of his dance, and next am equally rude to you—but—but——" She hesitates and seems so embarrassed that Everett assists her.

"But you have some reason for this last?" he ventures.

"Yes, and a very good one," says the girl; "though not the one my sister so kindly attributed to me."

"You are quite sure of that?"

"Come in to the german and I'll prove it to you," is her answer, as she is pounced upon by her partner for this dance.

Phil, however, has faith enough in her words to go into the ball-room, where, to his delight, Miss Flossie takes him out so continuously that he becomes the envy of half the men in the room, for the younger Miss Follis's beauty and fortune have made her quite a belle even in her first week of metropolitan society.

"It carn't be his darncing?" lisps Tommy Remson.

"It's because his sister's going to marry a lord. After my affair with her sister, Miss Flossie can't give me a favor, and so takes the—awh—next best article," suggests little Gussie.

"I think I've hit his point," says the more practical Benson. "It's his grip! Look how he squeezes her. Keep it to yourselves, or all the other girls in the room'll be after him also."

Whereupon these three young gentlemen, who have been looking at Everett's success with Miss Flossie, and do not like it, burst into a derisive giggle.

They are not entirely wrong, however. Phil does not waltz so well as these young gentlemen who make a practice of it night after night, but he holds Flossie Follis as he would hold no other woman in the dance or out of it. His arm circles her dainty waist as if he loved her; for the joy of adoring has got into his head, and the hope of reciprocity is in his eyes as his meet those of this girl floating with him to the music of Lander, which seems to Phil as that of the spheres. The melody stimulates his imagination; the ball-room becomes the hot mesa of Arizona; he is carrying a little girl who says: "Kiss me, dear Mr. Peter," as she rides in his arms; the thump of a big drum in the balcony is the stroke of Possum's hoofs on the trail.

From this he awakes with a start.

In his mad career, the thought of pursuing Apaches having made him dance very fast, he has nearly floored an unfortunate colliding couple.

"You waltz enthusiastically," says his inspiration, with a panting smile, for the pace has been a very hot one.

"Yes, like a cowboy!" is the smothered anathema of one of the run-against. At this a very extraordinary look comes into Miss Flossie's face, and she dances no more with Phil Everett.

But it is so near the close of the ball that he does not notice this, and goes home, very excited and very happy, and greatly in love; not with the calculating passion of a Wall Street man, but with the ardor of a cowboy, or a football rusher, or a Romeo.

In proof of this, he is no sooner at the Brevoort than he marches into Grousemoor's rooms. That gentleman, having left Delmonico's in advance of Phil, he finds already in bed.

"By Jove! what's the row?" mutters the lord, astonished at this intrusion.

"Do you know whom I've been dancing with to-night?" asks Everett.

"That's not hard guessing," replies the other, with a grin; "I only saw one, pretty little Miss Flossie Follis."

"Not Miss Flossie Follis," cries Phil, "but Florence Beatrice Stella Willoughby, Lady Avonmere, baroness by her own right in the peerage of England!"

This astounding announcement hardly produces the expected effect. Grousemoor cries out: "Go to bed, Phil. You are drunk!"

"Yes, drunk with astonishment—joy—love!—but not drunk with wine!" answers the American. "You know I thought Avonmere had murdered the child. He attempted it by one of his cursed 'hand of God' accidents, but she escaped, and I'll prove it to you!" Whereupon he sits down by his friend's bedside, and tells him all he has learned from Abe Follis of the finding of his adopted daughter. Concluding, he says: "The

child was found on July 7th, 1881. Arthur Willoughby
and his niece stopped at Pueblo, on their way from
New Mexico, on June 14th of the same year. In three
weeks he could have carried the child to the place he
deserted her. I recognize on her arm the wound of the
Apache. I am as sure that girl I danced with to-night
is Florence, Lady Avonmere, as that I was once Pete the
cowboy, who saved her life!"

"That being the case," says Grousemoor meditatively,
"do you think Arthur Willoughby, the man called Lord
Avonmere, knows it?"

"Why do you ask that?"

"Because, if he does," returns the Scotchman, with a
very serious face, "don't you think he may be trying
some of his 'hand of God' accidents upon his newly
discovered niece?"

"She's safe enough for the present," answers Phil.
"Don't you suppose I've considered that?"

"Why?"

"Because Avonmere, being a cunning scoundrel, will
attempt no injury to Miss Flossie Follis so long as she
doesn't know he has her fortune and her title."

"You are sure she does not guess?"

"Certainly!"

"But you propose to show her who she is?"

"As soon as I have the proofs—proofs that will destroy
any danger from him."

"How?"

"By making him an outcast and a criminal."

"When do you commence this business?"

"Now!"

"You are a rapid creature!"

"I'm an American business man, and time means success!" cries Phil.

And he sends a long cablegram to the London solicitor this very night, that makes that lawyer open his
eyes and cry: "My great case has come to me at last!"

CHAPTER XIX.

THE BOGUS BASSINGTON.

WHILE this has been going on, another interview, much more enthusiastic, theatrical, and savage, has been taking place between Miss Tillie and Miss Flossie.

The two girls had arrived at the Follis mansion on apparently good terms, though Mrs. Marvin and Avonmere, who had accompanied them home, had done most of the talking in the carriage. The few remarks of Miss Flossie to Avonmere, however, had been of a kind to put her sister upon her mettle, and had caused Mrs. Marvin to repeat her warning to Matilde to cut short any hope upon the *débutante's* part of getting their escort's coronet upon her brow. This she had whispered to Tillie after they had come into the hall and while Avonmere was making his *adieux* to her younger sister.

Therefore, after kissing Flossie good-night, Miss Tillie, some recollection of the girl's tender manner to Avonmere coming very vividly to her in the solitude of her own chamber as she disrobes, thinks she might as well at once define to her sister her status with Lord Avonmere. She mutters: "I'll stop Flossie's making a fool of herself right now!" and, throwing on a pretty *robe de chambre*, walks through the dimly-lighted corridor to her sister's suite of apartments, to find that young lady just dismissing her maid.

"I thought I would just run in, Floss, dear," says the girl, affecting an ambiguous smile, "and ask my little sister how she enjoyed her first big ball ? "

"Very well; sit down by the fire, darling, and I will give you my ideas on the Patriarchs'," remarks the young lady addressed, toasting five pretty little toes in front of the blaze. Then she says suddenly : "What did you think of Mr. Everett ? "

"Not much about him one way or the other." answers Miss Tillie, " though he reminded me of somebody I had seen somewhere else."

"Did he ? " cries Flossie; "he affected me in the same way!" And the far-away expression again comes into the girl's eyes.

"After that," remarks Miss Tillie, her face growing serious, "I saw my sister was interested in him; con sequently, did not interfere." Then she says suddenly, and perhaps bitterly : "Were *you* equally generous?"

"What do you mean?" answers Flossie, growing red.

"Oh, do not pretend that you don't understand!" cries Tillie. "Don't add deceit to your other transgressions against me to-night."

"Transgressions against *you* ?"

"Did *I* poach on your Boston business man with a big scar on his cheek? He got it at football, I presume, at which they say he was a mighty Yale kicker; his feet up-hold his reputation," remarks Matilde, severely, contemplating her own little slipper, that is extended to the warming blaze.

"Poach!" cries Flossie. "What do you mean? *My* Boston business man? Absurd!—I—!" and a pretty little blush contradicts her assertion.

"Perhaps I am wrong in my insinuation," sneers Tillie, "considering that you devoted at least one-half your smiles to Arthur."

"Arthur!"

"Yes, Arthur, the man I am about to marry," cries the other, who, having come to the gist of her remarks, has warmed up to her subject—" Arthur, Lord Avonmere."

"Impossible!" As this comes from Flossie's lips there is a look of horror in her eyes.

"Impossible! Why impossible? Has your beauty lured him from me?" gasps Matilde, growing pale at the thought, which is a very natural one, for as Florence Follis stands, her bright eyes flashing indignation, her noble figure posed under its white, clinging night-draperies, like that of a Greek goddess, she might cause any rival to fear the wondrous power of her loveliness.

"You are going to marry him?" says Flossie, in so broken a voice it gives her opponent courage.

"Yes," cries Matilde. And seeing on her sister's countenance what she thinks is jealousy and despair, her voice becomes bitter as she goes on: "By this ring I am!" And flaunts the diamond Avonmere has given her in Flossie's face, with a mocking laugh.

"Misery !" gasps the girl, astonishment and horror in her eyes—astonishment because she has never yet seen

this token upon Matilde's finger, Avonmere having suggested that it would be well she did not announce the
engagement to her family for a few days after the ter-
mination of the Van Beekman affair ; horror for some
unknown reason which Tillie mistakes.

" Misery ? " she echoes. " Yes, misery for you, and
you deserve it. How dare you ? "

" Dare—what ? "

" Dare to love the man I love ! "

" Love *him* ? " mutters Florence, with a shudder.

" Yes, love him ! " cries Matilde, who notes her sister's
appearance and thinks it is despair. And so it is—for
HER. " You can't pretend in this case it is Bob's cause
you are fighting, as you did when you attacked me for
little Gussie." Then, being very angry with other people
besides Flossie, this erratic young lady sneers : " If Bob
loved me—he'd—he'd come here and fight his own
battle." And rage or some other emotion brings tears to
Tillie's eyes.

To this her sister cries, " Hush! " in an awful tone.
" Don't dare to reproach him ! "

" And why not ? "

" Because "—here Flossie's cheeks grow pale and her
voice becomes low, and she whispers : " because he has
been fighting for your fortune."

" Fighting for my fortune ? Pough ! So was Gussie,"
echoes Matilde, with a nasty laugh.

" Fighting to *save* your fortune ! "

" Ah ! "

" Fighting the fire in the mine."

" Good heavens ! "

" For a week the Baby mine has been on fire. Father
don't know it, nor should I, but I wrote Bob to come here
as he valued his happiness, and he replied that the eight-
hundred-foot level was on fire, and he could not leave
his duty. He telegraphed me to-day he had it under
control. So he has saved your fortune. Has he lost
you, my sister, in doing it ? "

To this Matilde does not answer, though her lips
tremble ; there is a blush upon her face, her eyes have a
softer look in them, and perhaps Bob's battle might be
won now, did not his advocate make a fearful error.

Youth seldom knows when to stop, and Miss Eighteen

goes wildly on : "Can you hesitate—is Avonmere worthy of you ?"

"Why not ?" asks Matilde, in an undecided voice.

"Does not rumor say of him that he will marry no one save a rich woman for her fortune ?"

"Ah !" Matilde has risen, her cheeks flaming at the insinuation against her beauty and her charms.

"Does not that horrible old Marvin woman play his game for him ? Did she not come and get money from me to make that little Gussie think himself a lord, and, crazy with pride and caddishness, discard you, an heiress, that Avonmere might seize upon you and your fortune through your chagrin at being jilted and your fear of being the jeer of New York society ?"

"Stop ! you are crazy yourself," screams Tillie, who has listened with astonished, staring eyes to this address, which would astound any one who only saw the surface of the situation. But, true or false, every word is a torturing wound to her self-love, vanity, and pride, all of which are pretty well developed in this petted beauty and belle.

"I won't stop, and I'm not crazy !" returns Miss Flossie, who is growing very earnest in her work. "I've heard enough from Mrs. Marvin to join with one expression I caught from Avonmere's lips to-night to know I've guessed right. We were dancing together——"

"Yes, too often !"

"Bassington, or Van Beekman, or whatever you want to call him, bumped against us," continues the girl, unheeding the interruption. "Avonmere muttered under his breath, 'The miserable pauper!' He didn't think I heard it, but I did, and I know it means what I've told you. I know other things, also——"

"What other things ?"

"What I can't tell you ! But give him up before it is too late. Some day you'll bless me for this. Let me take his ring and throw it in his face. He marries you for your money. He is unworthy of you !" And with this impassioned though tactless speech, Flossie would pluck Avonmere's token from her sister's hand.

But that young lady, suffering from wounded vanity and pride, is in a most ungracious mood.

"Keep your touch off my engagement-ring !" she cries. "You wish it for your own finger. You want to be a peeress of England yourself, you plotter!" And she flashes the diamond in her sister's eyes.

At this a red spot comes on each of Florence's cheeks, and her eyes begin to glisten like the diamond held before them ; but forcing herself to humility, she mutters : " He is unworthy any woman's love ! "

" Except *yours !* " screams Matilde. " You, who malign him behind his back—to me, his sweetheart. You hear that? The girl he loves, the girl who loves him ! "

" A-ah ! " This is a moan of anguish, perhaps despair, which goads Matilde to madness.

She cries : " You coward, to slander in secret ! You—"

" Don't you dare to call me that ! " cries Flossie in a louder tone. " Don't make me forget I am your sister ! " And with glaring eyes the two white-robed beauties confront each other.

But now, to their dismay, another and a stronger voice dominates the apartment. It says : " Gals, ain't yer forgot that, both of ye ? " And striding between them comes another white-robed figure, more gaunt, not so lovely, but perchance much more potent as regards grip and fighting power in a scrimmage.

It is the sleepless Rach.

A door that connects Miss Flossie's bed room with her own has been left ajar, and the frontier mother, tossing sleeplessly on her bed awaiting the coming of the absent Abe, who comes not, has heard the sound of conflict.

" Floss, keep quiet ! Till, shut up ! Don't yer know your posish ? Bean't you ladies ? " she cries in a tone that makes both the girls pause and gaze upon her in awe and silence as she towers over them, the embodiment of angry justice.

She has been worrying over the absence of Abe, and would probably worry more did she know that gentleman was still in social confab at the Hoffman House, arranging with Hank Morris, of the " Bully Boy," Bill Chambers, of the " Boa Constrictor," and Charley Daily, of the " Last Blast," for a joint box at the coming *Cercle d'Harmonie* ball—a wild, hilarious, can-can revel which is much loved by the wicked Western mining man ; where those of them who are in New York in February can be counted on to make the wine flow and the ladies dance.

And to this annoyance is now added a dispute by her

daughters which is the last straw upon Rachel Follis's back.

" What are you twos fighting about ? " she says shortly. Getting no reply to this, she goes on : " Why ain't you in your own room, Tillie ? " then cries suddenly : " Did you come in here at three o'clock in the morning to raise a rumpus with Floss ? " and takes a step towards the young lady addressed with such a ' fightin' Injun ' look in her eyes that Tillie suddenly utters an affrighted " Don't ! " and takes refuge behind a chair.

But Florence, standing near, says quietly : " She did not, mother ; she came in to bid me good-night, and——"

" And you begun it ? " remarks Rach in an awful voice, while her long gaunt hand seizes Flossie's shapely arm.

" No, she didn't ; I did. Don't you touch Floss, ma ! " cries Tillie, desperately.

" Lord bless me if you ain't jist the same as if you were knee-high ag'in ! You were always trying to save one another in them days before we got so awful rich that there ain't no comfort in life," mutters Rachel, and having Flossie nearest to her hand, she suddenly falls to kissing and sobbing over this young lady, till Matilde, running to her, gets a second edition of the same.

Then, stifling down a sniff, Mrs. Follis says : " Now, darters, tell me plain and short what's the matter. I want to do justice between you."

" You can do what you like to me," says Flossie in a broken voice, "only don't let Tillie marry that—that Avonmere."

" Was that the row ? Are you cottoning to that gent ? " asks Rach.

" Yes," says Matilde shortly.

" Well, Floss, what have you got to say ag'in him ? " continues the matron.

" Nothing now—that I can tell you or any one," returns the younger girl in a troubled tone.

" Oh ! yer ain't got nothin' ag'in *him !* Well, I shouldn't think you hadn't," cries her mother, for Avon-mere, having made himself particularly pleasant in the last few days to Mrs. Follis, has quite won her open and trustful heart. Then she goes on, the fighting look coming into her eyes : " Seems to me you don't want Till to marry nobody. You came up here to raise a rumpus

about that other little sniff, Gussie.   Oh, don't ye attempt
to deny it ; I know mostly what happens in my house ! "
For at the mention of Van Beekman, Florence has appeared about to speak.   "You came and jumped on to
him, and now you're interfering with Tillie's new beau.
Don't you want her to get married to no one ? "

"None except *Bob*," sneers Matilde, who has become
indignant again at this recital of her wrongs.

"Oh, Bob's the caucus nominee, is he ? " shouts Mrs.
Follis in a more awful tone than ever.   "It's Bob she's
fightin' for !—Bob, who daren't come and stand up for
himself ! "   Then she turns on Flossie and whispers : " If
you let an envious spirit conquer you, and I hear of your
making a rumpus about Tillie's new young man, I'll
treat you as if you were knee-high, my darter—don't
forget that ! "

With this she stalks to the door, but hearing a little
giggle from Matilde at her sister's discomfiture, for at this
threat Flossie's cheeks have grown red with blushes and
her eyes suffused with tears, Rach turns round and says:
"And you, Till, if you come in here and rile Floss up
'cause you've got a fellah and she ain't got none, I'll do
jist the same to you, miss.   Don't you forget that,
neither ! "

And she leaves botb young ladies gazing at each other
in dismay.

They know that Rachel Follis is a woman of her word,
and have a great respect for her authority, which she has
enforced upon them as children, after the manner of King
Solomon, for she is a woman who reads the Scriptures,
and, believing them the living truth, acts upon their advice.

A moment after the culprits give a faint scream, there
being a sound of wild commotion down-stairs ; but Rach
puts her head into the room and says : " You stay quiet
here, pets—I think it's burglars; I'm going downito settle
'em."

"Ma, don't go ! " cry both young ladies in a tremor,
another crash and sound of breakage coming from below.

"Hush !   Obey me ! " says Rach.   "Don't be skeared,
no harm shall come to my precious ones ! "

And peeping out of their room, the two trembling
civilized creatures see the gaunt representative of the Far

West stride down-stairs with a murderous six-shooter in her hand as quietly as if she were going to her breakfast.

A moment after they hear her cry : " Why, Abe—if it ain't you ! "

" Yes," answers the head of the house ; "I stumbled over some of your break-bracks. The servants shift 'em about like Missouri River sand-bars. Ye never knows when you run ag'in 'em."

And then to the listening girls comes Rachel's voice saying : " Thank God, you're home safe. Abe, I was afeered you'd be captured by bunco men ! " followed by a shower of tender backwoods kisses upon the returned one.

For, like so many of us, this frontier matron most dreads the unfamiliar. She would trust her mate to the dangers of the wilderness with fortitude and equanimity, but trembles for the guileless Abraham amid the pitfalls of this great city.

Listening to this, Flossie whispers to her sister: " Isn't ma tender ? "

" Yes, and determined," mutters Tillie. And this bringing the remembrance of Rach's threat back to them, the two look very serious.

" I shall say no more about Avonmere," remarks the younger, " but, Tillie, as I love you and you love me, for heaven's sake don't marry him ! "

" And why not ? Give me a reason."

" I—I cannot."

" Yes, you can, you're jealous——"

But here their mother puts her head in the room and says : " What'll become of your beauty, my darlings, if you stand gossiping till morning ! " Then, catching something in the faces of her loved ones that she does not like, she cries : " Till, go to your own room ! Floss, to bed at once ! And if I hear another word out of either of your lips to-night, I'll settle ye like I did when ye tied fire-crackers to our Chinese cook's tail in Aspen ! "

A recollection that is so awful that Matilde flies to her chamber, and Florence to her couch without a syllable.

Now this conversation being partially reported the following morning by Tillie to Mrs. Marvin, it reaches the ears of Avonmere and sets that astute gentleman to thinking, which, in the course of time, produces some unpleasant results for the young lady both Mrs. Marvin and himself now regard as an enemy—*i.e.*, Miss Flossie Follis.

But the day after the Patriarchs also brings about a woful disaster to Augustus Lord Bassington, which, in its evolution, raises an insignificant but vindictive adversary to any and all of Avonmere's plans.

This *dénouement* has been approaching in the gradua' course of events, and is now about due.

In one of the morning papers issued after the Patri-archs appears the following squib :

"MYSTERIOUS DISAPPEARANCE ON WALL STREET.

" The suspicious occurrences connected with the opening of a so-called law office bearing the name and putting out the sign of ' Stillman, Myth & Co., Attorneys and Counsellors at Law,' has created some curiosity and excitement at No. 61 Wall Street.

" They engaged the office for a month, paying a somewhat extra rental on account of the shortness of their occupation ; but stated that if the location pleased them they would renew the lease for a longer period.

" This mysterious firm had only been in business two or three days when they suddenly disappeared, clerks, attorneys, and all ; since which time the office has been locked up.

" This morning the key was surreptitiously returned to the janitor, who entered the offices, to find them vacant. The furniture and be-longings, which had been quite elaborate, had all mysteriously dis-appeared.

" During their two or three days of active business, Stillman, Myth & Co. had but few callers and no mail.

" These facts were elicited by one of our ever-vigilant reporters from the janitor, who states that in his opinion Stillman, Myth & Co. were in the ' GREEN-GOODS ' business."

This article coming to the eyes of Lord Bassington as he partakes of his breakfast on the morning after the Patriarchs' function, produces great loss of appetite and vexation of spirit.

He bolts into Avonmere's apartments before that gentleman is ready to receive company, and cries out ·

" Look at that," shoving the paper under the nose of his brother peer.

As he reads, a curious expression ripples Avonmere's face, but a moment after he says : " Pough ! You know Stillman, Myth & Co. were not in the ' green-goods ' business, Bassington ! Did they take any money from you ? "

" No, but, by George, they've got my draft on London for ten thousand pounds," screams his lordship. " They may do me out of that. What would you advise ? By Jove, the beggars may rob me of ten thousand pounds. Even noblemen with sixty thousand a year can't afford to lose that, don't yer know."

On hearing this, Avonmere, who is in his dressing-gown, suddenly bolts into his bedroom, where Gussie can hear him gasping and struggling. A moment after he returns and mutters something about getting soap in his eyes, which look both red and watery ; then he sarcastic-ally remarks : " Why don't you cable and inquire about your ten thousand pounds ? "

" So I will ! " cries Gussie, and he orders his carriage, remarking : " I have been expecting that ten thousand, yer see. I have so many payments to make, there'd be weeping and wailing and gnashing of teeth if I didn't get it on time, don't yer know ? "

Which is perfectly true, for the little fellow has practically discounted a great portion of his expected money.

He has paid no bills, and has even borrowed from his cousin, the venerable Van Twiler, two thousand dol-lars to keep him running.

This has been cordially loaned by the old gentleman, who has said good-naturedly : " You young spendthrift ! But then, boys will be boys. Cousin Bassington, return it at your leisure."

Using this sum entirely for pocket-money, Augustus has succeeded in running himself in debt by orders for carriages, horses, *bric-à-brac*, works of art, and a thousand other accessories and appurtenances necessary to the maintenance of the rank of an English peer. Most of his spare *cash* has been bestowed upon the charming little Rosalie Mountjoy of the Gaiety troupe, who has fallen desperately in love with the little aristocrat since he be-

came a lord, and has summarily discharged from her affections the plebeian Hicks.

Consequently, as Mr. Gussie drives down to Wall Street
his bank-account is represented by a balance in two
figures, and his debts and liabilities, incurred since he
has received his title, by nearly twenty thousand dollars.
Therefore he is very anxious for his draft.

Arriving at Wall Street, he goes tremblingly up to the
office he had left in such high feather, joy, and glory but
a little over a fortnight before, to discover that the squib
in the newspaper is a horrible and undeniable fact.

But here, to his more rapid and sudden undoing, he
chances to encounter one of the reporters of a daily
paper.

This gentleman of the press, knowing his lordship by
sight, and noting his agitated and excited appearance,
introduces himself and begs to ask if Lord Bassington
has suffered any loss by the absconding firm.

" Loss ! " screams Gussie. " The beggars had my
draft on Messrs. Brown, Studley & Wilberforce, of London, for ten thousand pounds ! Two weeks ago they announced the discovery of my accession to the Barony of
Bassington and its estates, so I drew through them on
my London solicitors for ten thousand. That infernal
scoundrel Stillman was the man who first brought me the
information of my English title, and paid me a thousand
pounds that had been cabled to him to my credit ! "

At this extraordinary information " the knight of the
quill " opens his eyes and his ears also, and proceeding to
sympathize very greatly with Lord Bassington's evident
loss, becomes quite friendly with the unsuspecting Gussie, and finally draws from him the whole story of his
wondrous elevation to the peerage through Stillman,
Myth & Co.

After giving this information in an excited but somewhat irrelevant manner, Mr. Gussie bolts for a telegraph
office and immediately cables Brown, Studley & Wilberforce, stating that, as Lord Bassington, whose rents they
collect, he has drawn on them for ten thousand pounds
in favor of Messrs. Stillman, Myth & Co., and stopping
payment of the same.

Then he goes home and is miserably anxious all day
for his money. He tells the men at the club that " he

fears he's been robbed by those infernal scoundrels, Stillman, Myth & Co., of Wall Street, of a cool ten thousand pounds; they had his draft on his London agents for that amount," etc., etc.

But, wonderful to relate, no doubt of title or wealth ever enters his head.   He has enjoyed them for a little time, and they are to him as fixed and real as the streets he walks upon and the dinner he eats.

While this has been going on, however, the gentleman of the press has rushed for the office of his city editor, and after relating to him the extraordinary conversation he has had with the newly-made English peer, a cable is sent to the London representative of their paper, directing him to call on the well-known solicitors and cable at once the exact facts regarding Lord Bassington's title and estates; and next morning VAN BEEKMAN'S ARISTO-CRATIC BUBBLE BURSTS !

Arising to his breakfast, Gussie finds among his mail a telegram addressed to "Bassington," tears it open and reads, and as he does so the sweat of horror comes upon his brow, for these are its awful words :

"Bassington title still in abeyance.   No rents to collect for you. You have been imposed upon.

"BROWN STUDLEY & WILBERFORCE.

"Coll."

With a gasp of dismay he sinks, weak and unnerved, into a chair, muttering : "The idiots !—there must be a mistake.   I suppose they'll say they didn't cable a thousand pounds to me next ! "

Then a spasm of agony shoots through him, and with a shriek of horrified anguish he bounds from his chair and falls limp and groaning on the floor, for his rolling eyes have caught sight of an open newspaper upon the table, and in its largest type, and heading its most prominent column, he has read :

"THE BOGUS BASSINGTON !

"HA ! HA !! HA !!!"

CHAPTER XX.

"DEAR GAL—DO SOMETHING FOR HER SOME DAY."

"SHALL I let 'em hin?" asks his man with a grin, assisting him to rise.

"Who?"

"The creditors. They're in a body houtside, and are getting wery impatient, your lordship."

"Good heavens! So soon?"

"Yes, my lord, it's near eleven o'clock. They read the papers afore you was hup, and 'ave been 'anging about for two hours or more. They're getting hobstreperous now. There's a jeweller's young man talking about harrest, and the horseshoer has hinted he'll let you 'ave it from the shoulder."

"Great Lord! Yes, I hear them," whispers Gussie, with white lips. Then he suddenly cries: "It ain't possible. It must be a nightmare!" And rushing at the newspaper, gives a moan and drops it in despair. For its head-lines, such as "Gussie Now Regrets the Baby Mine," "Van Beekman's Masquerade," "Hicks's Chances Improving," "Naughty Little Mountjoy!" "The Hoax of the Season!" "Who Did It???" in startling type and sensational punctuation, appall and daze him.

But after a moment he forces himself to read the article, and learning in it more about himself than he had ever guessed before, utters such shrieks and groans of agony that his valet, though choking with laughter, sympathizes with his despair.

This fellow, a well-meaning youth of English birth, who has only been in Gussie's service a week, having been selected for his Cockney accent, now remarks again: "Your creditors! Will you see 'em, your lordship?"

"Don't call me that cursed name!" yells Gussie desperately; next whispers: "You let my creditors in, every one of them, and I'll go into Avonmere's rooms. While they're waiting for me here I'll get through the hall and dodge the beggars. Don't yer see?"

"Certainly, sir."

"Then wait till I'm in the bath-room." And Gussie disappears.

The floor is arranged after the following manner :

Van Beekman occupies a parlor and bedroom at the front of the house. Avonmere has the same accommodations at the rear. A bath-room for joint use is between. This has doors opening into both gentlemen's chambers, making it a passage between the two suites of apartments.

Into this Gussie slips, and panting like a hunted animal, locks the door to his bed-chamber behind him as he hears the rush of his creditors and their excited voices in his own parlor.

"His lordship his just dressing ; he'll see you hall, gents, in a few moments," remarks his valet.

Blessing his servitor for his ready lies, and moving along very cautiously for fear he may make a noise that will give his pursuers some suspicion of his whereabouts, the bath-room being rather dimly lighted from an air-shaft, the trembling Gussie perceives the door into Avonmere's bedroom is slightly open, and getting near to it, for the first time this day a ray of joy comes into his life.

He hears and recognizes a voice ! It is that of Stillman, the lawyer who first announced his title to him and paid him five thousand dollars on account of his rents.

For a moment he imagines this solicitor has come to see him and explain the horrible error the newspapers have made—that he must have got into Avonmere's rooms by mistake.

He is about to open the door and step in to him for hope and comfort when Avonmere's voice comes to him, bringing knowledge that petrifies him with despair, yet vivifies him with rage and fury.

"I brought you into my bedroom ; there's no danger of any one hearing from the hall. You did your work very well, Chumpie," remarks his lordship. "There's the money for you and Machlin. He jilted the heiress in short order. The young lady's got *my* ring on her finger now. The joke's all over town. You can tell your part in the hoax to the reporters and make what dramatic capital you can out of it, though I would prefer you omitted my name, if possible, in connection with the little cad's undoing."

"Thank you, my lord," answers the actor, and Gussie can hear the crinkle of the greenbacks as he folds them up and places them in his pocket-book. "You are sure the little brat's ruined?"

"What makes you so vindictive against him, Chumpie?" murmurs the peer with a smile.

"He called me a bad actor!" cries the Thespian.

Upon this Avonmere breaks into a laugh and says: "Well, you can be certain of your revenge. Little Gussie's ruined to all eternity in New York, socially and every other way. He owes twenty thousand dollars, run up on the strength of the coronet your dramatic hands placed upon his brow. His creditors are hunting for him now. Listen to them!"

At this moment a hum of rage from the front apartments comes to their ears, as the enraged duns discover Van Beekman's absence and start down-stairs to hunt up their debtor at his club-haunts or run him down on the street.

"They'll never forgive him; neither will society, of whom he has made a fool. The lower they have bowed to him the lower they will kick Baron Bassington of the British Peerage," laughs the peer.

"Yes, they'll evict him as he would his Irish tenants!" roars the actor; and he gives a jeering account of his interview with Augustus, in which he made him a lord of the realm, going over the affair with many chuckles and much glee.

When suddenly he stops in mid-laugh, and shrieking, "Good Lord, I'm murdered!" falls writhing on the bedroom floor, for little Gussie has sprung out of the bathroom with a howl of despairing rage, and has struck the comic Chumpie to the earth with an awful blow upon the back of the head with his trusty dude cane.

At first Avonmere starts back in horror and surprise, the attack on the comedian has been of such a jack-in-box order; next he bursts into such roars of laughter that the tears roll down his cheeks till he can't see; though he tries to pull himself together to go to Chumpie's aid, for the belligerent Gussie has fallen upon the Thespian again, and in a silent, vindictive, and fiendish way is thumping him into a mummy.

Seizing Van Beekman, his lordship pulls him off his writhing antagonist, and after a struggle in which Gussie fights fiercely, he tosses him into the corner of the room

"Curse you!" cries Avonmere. "Why can't you stay in your part of the house, you little impostor!"

"Who's made me an impostor? You and that play-acting liar," screams Gussie. And springing at Mr. Chumpie, who has half-risen to his feet, he gives him another vindictive thwack that brings him to the floor again.

"Keep your hands off him, hang you! Do you want to murder the man?" cries his lordship.

"Yes, and you too!" answers Gussie. "You made me a lord for me to jilt Tillie Follis—I heard you! For that you threw away five thousand dollars, you trickster!"

"Not *all* of it," sneers the Englishman in a nasty voice. "You forget our little game at poker. Quiet, or I'll send for the police!"

For at this Gussie has gone into a jibbering invective that makes Avonmere think the little wretch insane.

"To get that girl's money you've ruined me!" he yells. "They'll kick me out of society! Ha, ha! They'll bounce me from the club! Ho, ho! Yesterday a peer of England, now a social pariah! Ha, ha! Ho, ho! He, he! Up like a rocket, down like the stick! Look out for the stick, my Lord Avonmere! If it hits you in the eye—ha, ha! Ho, ho! He, he!—My God, I'm going crazy!"

And with a giggle of despair little Gussie bolts through his host's parlor into the hall, flies down the stairs, and shoots along the street toward Fifth Avenue, followed by one or two of his duns who have been lingering in the vicinity of his domicile.

"Egad! I think he *has* gone mad," says his lordship, looking after the departing Gussie.

"Mad!" groans Chumpie, cautiously getting to his feet, "I hope so. The little demon has bruised me till I shan't be able to do my comic dance for a week! A—a little brandy." And he staggers to a sofa.

From which, after being revived by stimulants, he is assisted to a cab by Avonmere and sent to his home.

Plastered and bandaged up, however, he contrives to get about later in the afternoon, and to impart his version of his wonderful hoax upon the aspiring Van Beekman to various inquiring reporters; also stating that the little cad being impertinent to him, he—Chumpie—had soundly

thrashed Augustus after the manner of the British P. R.
"The coward hit me with his brutal dude-club from
behind, twice," says the comedian, "but *after* that—after
THAT!" And he waves his hand and rolls up his eyes
in a manner that indicates if Gussie now lives he must
be blessed with a feline tenacity of life.

Then the evening papers giving whole columns to his
story, Chumpie, the great practical joker, the inimitable
farceur, appears that night at the Broadway Theatre to
a packed house, who give him a wild reception, mingled
with calls from the gallery of "How's his ludship?"

As for the butt of these gibes, after leaving his house
he has skipped down the avenue to his club. Within its
sacred portals he thinks he will be safe from pursuing
creditors.

He arrives there in a panting and despairing state.
He has passed two ladies that he had flirted and danced
with but two evenings ago at the Patriarchs.

The sight of him produces so much laughter in his
former partners that they forget to bow to him. They
roll past in their carriage as he mutters to himself despond-
ingly: "Cut the first dash! That's what they'll all do!
I know 'em! I'd better blow my brains out. No, no;
not till I've ruined that jeering devil Avonmere as he's
ruined me."

And this not very noble motive possibly keeps Augustus
Van Beekman from suicide this day, for he has the courage of a rat—an animal that, pursued and hunted, sometimes does very desperate things.

And on this day poor little Gussie is both pursued and
hunted. He has thought the club will be a place of
refuge. So it is, and so perhaps is the Hades of mythol-
ogy.

His creditors, outside fiends, cannot enter to torture
him; but there are enough energetic devils within to
keep the coals bright and red for the broiling and roast-
ing of Mr. Augustus.

In the hall, prominently posted up by a wag, under
new memberships, is a notice:

FOR ELECTION.

Gussie de P. Van Beekman, *vice* Baron Bassington,
of Harrowby Castle, England. ON ICE!

Proposed by Stillman, Myth & Co., Seconded by Baby Mine, and Sorrowing Members of the House of Lords.

Tearing this down with a gasp of rage, Augustus strides to the office and asks for his letters.

"What name?" asks the clerk, looking red in the face.

"Oh, curse it, White! all my names! Give me everything meant for me. Damn it, don't laugh!" he cries.

"I—I can't help it, my lord—I—," stammers the man, placing before him what he asks.

Seizing his mail, Gussie sneaks with it to the most retired spot in the house, a few jeering laughs following him from the smoking-room, though one man, whom he has scarcely known before, says: "Van Beekman I sympathize with you. It was a dastardly hoax of which you were a victim."

Then he looks over his letters in an aimless, dazed way.

All of them save one are addressed to him by his erstwhile title; they are mostly invitations to *fêtes* and functions. "By George! if poor Van Beekman went to one of these upon Lord Bassington's invite, I—I believe they'd kick Gussie out," he groans to himself. "They don't love me any more."

Of this he has immediate proof. A senile hand is laid on his shoulder, and a septuagenarian voice whispers in his ear: "My two thousand dollars, you infernal scoundrel!"

And springing up, Gussie is confronted by the venerable Van Twiler.

"That's not my name!" says the persecuted one, with an attempt at spirit.

"No—perhaps it's Lord Bassington? That's what you borrow money under!"

"Oh, cousin, why do you jump on me to-day?" says Gussie, piteously, breaking down. "Can't you see I'm so demned miserable I could blow out my brains?"

"The best thing for you to do, sir! You pay me my money or I'll have you in jail! False pretences, my Lord Bassington!—remember that!" And Van Twiler walks away, muttering to himself, "Confidence man!"

But the unhappy Augustus is too miserable to resent even this.

In a sort of hopeless, helpless semi-coma he sinks into a chair, lays his aching head upon the table among his letters, and the tears of little Gussie Van Beekman roll down upon and wet the invitations written to beg the presence of the haughty Lord Bassington to *fête* and revel.

A moment after his eye catches sight of a note directed to Augustus Van Beekman. With a snarl of rage, for he thinks it has been so addressed to remind him of his fallen greatness, he is about to tear it up unopened, but the handwriting is that of a 'woman, and unknown to him.

So, curiosity conquering anger, he tears it open, and gives out an astounded "By Jove!" after perusing the following:

"No. 637 Fifth Avenue,
"*Saturday, January* 25, 1890.

"Miss Florence Follis presents her compliments to Mr. Augustus Van Beekman, and begs him, in case he receives this communication in time, to call upon her, at the above address, at three o'clock this afternoon. She wishes to speak to him on a matter of some personal moment to himself.

"Should Mr. Van Beekman not be able to come as specified, will he oblige Miss Follis by informing her at what hour on Monday she may expect him?"

"What the deuce does she want me for?" he asks himself. Then a very wild idea entering his head, from which even this day's humiliation has not driven all conceit, he thinks: "Perhaps Matilde has hopes of me now I've lost my title, and has put her sister up to sounding me on the matter. I'll not balk her this time. By jingo, with those harpies outside, what fellah would?" Through the window he can see several of his duns loitering about to pounce upon him the moment he leaves the protecting portals of the club.

Looking at his watch, he finds he can just reach Miss Flossie's home at the time mentioned in that young lady's note.

"I'll give those infernal scoundrels out there a flying start!" he mutters, looking at his persecutors in the street with a sarcastic and unkindly grin.

Which he does after fortifying and strengthening himself with a sandwich and glass of wine.

He calls a hall-boy, and tipping him well, says: "Jimmy

go out and get that hansom with the smart horse and fly-looking driver, and tell him double fare if he does as I want him."

"Double fare 'll fix him sure," answers the urchin.

"Then give him these instructions." And Gussie whispering a few directions in his ear, the boy goes into the street on his errand.

A few moments after he comes in and hurriedly announces, "He's at the door!" but looking out, Augustus sees it's too late.

The cab is waiting opposite the portal, its door open and its driver ready to whip up the instant Gussie enters it ; but the people on watch for him outside, being wary and experienced in such matters, have come to the club portals also, making it almost impossible to elude them as he rushes to the hack.

After a moment's glum consideration, Van Beekman whispers a few words to Jimmy, accompanying his sentence with a dollar bill.

Then, in the course of a minute, that young gentleman hastily pursues, with cries and execrations, another hall-boy to the corner of Fifth Avenue, where, overtaking him, the two urchins go to fighting like fiends and roll about on the sidewalk with yells of pain and howls of anger. The waiting crowd rush after them.

As this happens, with pale face and flying feet Augustus springs from the portals of the Stuyvesant into the hack ; the driver gives his horse a vicious cut, and though Van Beekman's persecutors note the ruse and pursue him, he escapes. Then, after a wild rush of some squares, none of his followers being in sight, he orders the hansom to drive to 637 Fifth Avenue.

Here he is apparently expected ; the footman shows him into the reception room at once, and Miss Flossie, who has risen at his entrance, says to the servant: " At home to no one for the present."

Then the girl remarks quietly: " Mr. Van Beekman, I believe," motioning Gussie to a chair, though she seems somewhat agitated and walks about in a nervous way as if she did not know exactly how to begin the conversation.

Having nothing to say himself, Augustus does not attempt to assist Miss Flossie by opening his lips, save to chew the end of his cane, which he does, gazing at the young lady, whose embarrassment adds to her beauty, which is pale and red in alternate moments, though her eyes are very bright from excitement of some kind.

"Egad !" thinks Gussie, looking at the pretty tableau before him. "Flossie wouldn't do badly herself for yours truly."

He has a horrid familiar way of considering women in his weakly mind, and has been pondering upon the reason of this girl's note as he has been riding in the cab, with this astounding result : "Tillie is sure of Avonmere —a genuine lord—no chance of her. Flossie has seen *me !* Perhaps—no telling—these erratic Western gals —no telling !"

Before he has time for much thought, however, words strike Mr. Gussie's ear that make him start.

"I've been thinking over my conduct in regard to the deceit practised upon you, Mr. Van Beekman," the girl begins, "the miserable hoax I assisted in, the bogus title you were made to believe was yours."

"The hoax *you* assisted in ?" gasps her listener, astounded.

"Yes. Without me," says the young lady, struggling with a smile, "you would never have been Lord Bassing-ton of the English peerage."

"Don't laugh ! Hang it ! you didn't bring me here to have fun with me ?" yells Gussie, growing very angry.

"No," answers the girl slowly. "I brought you here to make some kind of an atonement. It was my money that was paid to you as if cabled from London by your solicitors."

"*Your* money cabled ?"

"Yes ; I've read about it in the morning papers. I know exactly the part I and my contribution played in the affair," continues Flossie. "It was my five thousand dollars that was given you by Stillman, Myth & Co. to prove you were a lord and had a rent-roll."

"Oh, it was you, was it ?" cries Gussie, savagely, the memory of his awful troubles coming very vividly to his mind and making him wild. "It was you ? Do you know what you've done ?"

"No," says the girl faintly, for the little wretch looks haggard, miserable, and pathetic, and she remembers him but two days before as the light-hearted, haughty, and supercilious Lord Bassington.

"Then, I'll tell you!" screams Augustus. "You've made me a bankrupt and an outcast. They say I'll go to jail for money obtained under false pretences. They hint I'll be kicked out of the clubs for conduct unbecoming a gentleman. Society 'll jump on me. For every kick Lord Bassington gave them, they give poor, unprotected Gussie a dozen. All the morning, duns have haunted my house till I fled from it. All the afternoon, people have pointed at me on the street and jeered at me. But five minutes ago on the avenue, a lady who had invited Baron Bassington to her dinner-party this evening cut Mr. Van Beekman dead. That's what I am, DEAD!—socially, financially—that's what I really will be corporally before night. There are two rivers——"

"Don't talk in that horrible way," interrupts the girl with a shudder.

"Won't I? Why not?" he goes on at her, for in little matters he is sometimes very shrewd, and a sudden thought has struck him that sympathy from the great heiress can do him no harm. "What else have I in life? An outcast with but the river to save me from prison and humiliation. I'll give the newspapers another item. Bogus Bassington shall have another head-line : Beekman's Bound to Beelzebub. That'll suit them. Don't shrink from me. I—I ain't crazy ; I'm only a poor society pariah. That's all, a PARIAH !—made so by a girl who has so much money she plays jokes that ruin men's lives ! That's all ! Ha ! ha ! ha !" And making a faint and abortive attempt to kiss her hand, he sinks writhing into a chair, while Flossie stands gazing at him, half in terror, half in sorrow and sympathy.

She falters : "It may not be so bad as you think. Couldn't I make atonement to you of some kind ?"

"Atonement ?—from *you* ?" he answers. "What atonement can you make for kicking a man out of his club and into prison ? That's what it means—jail—bread and water—convict's clothes—and no fashions."

"These matters may perhaps be arranged," remarks Flossie. "If you would only calm yourself—and think— not rave ! I am rich. I might——"

" Settle with my creditors ? " cries Gussie, springing up, and hope illuminating his countenance. Then he says desperately: " The governors 'll kick me out of my clubs, anyway."

" Couldn't your friends speak to them ? "

" I—I haven't got any friends," he gasps hopelessly.

" No friends ? " murmurs the girl, gazing at him in sympathetic horror.

" Yes, lots, till you robbed me of 'em," he mutters. " When you made me Lord Bassington, you put me so high they all hated me ; and now I'm down again, they'll show it."

" You have no friends—that would help you arrange your matters—if I would furnish the money ? " asks Flossie, coming to the subject in a hesitating, shame-faced sort of way.

" None I would trust," he replies. Then he cries joy-fully, " Oh, yes, there is. Phil Everett—you know him, the Boston chap you darnced with all night at the Patri-archs ! "

" Yes—I know him—slightly," returns Flossie, growing red.

" Well, you go to him and tell him—— "

" I go to him ? Nonsense ! "

" Yaas ! But you'll have to, if you want to fix my affairs. There's Gill & Patrick 'll have me in jail. It 'll take a man to negotiate with them. It was for the dia-mond ring I gave your sister—the one Avonmere won from me at poker. I saw it on Tillie's finger the other night. Kind of funny—one ring and two fellahs. Why, what's the matter ? "

For at this Flossie has given an exclamation of disgust, and covered her face with her hands.

" Yes, it's not nice, such social eccentricity, is it ? " he babbles on, the thought of getting rid of his creditors elevating his spirits. " Why the deuce did you help Avonmere against me ? He's worse than I am. You don't know Avonmere yet, nor the widow neither—they're a pair ; they're pulling in your sister nicely. They've—— "

But the girl cuts short any more of his gossip by rising suddenly and saying : " I made this appointment at three, because I did not presume it would be pleasant for Tillie to see you.   She will be returning home soon.   I must ask you to go before she comes.   I will pay the debts you have incurred, because you imagined as Lord Bassington you could afford to be extravagant.   I owe that to my conscience.   I shall do no more than that."

"Very well," returns Gussie, rising.   "I don't presume it would be pleasant to Matilde——"

"Miss Follis, sir !"

"Of course, Miss Follis.   I presume that is the more formal way.   Force of habit and all that, yer know. I'll go, as you suggest.   I'll send a friend to arrange with you the matter you spoke of.   Oh, Miss Flossie, you've saved me from suicide !   God bless you, dear girl, God bless you !"   And he seizes Flossie's hand, the beauty of which he has been admiring for the last minute, and smothers it in such kisses that she gives a startled scream, and pulls it away from him with flaming eyes.

Then he moves to the door, and turning, says with a little suggestive smile : "I—awh—think I know the reason you wished me to—awh—jilt Matilde.   *Au revoir.*"

"Farewell !" she cries very savagely, coming toward him.

"*Au revoir.*   By the bye, the name of the friend I shall ask to arrange my financial affairs with you——"

"Yes, let me know now, for I shall not speak to you again."

"No—a—you don't mean it.   Cruel !"

"The name of your friend, quick ! "

"Phil Everett.   Tell him to call at nine.   Must be fixed to-night, yer know.   You wouldn't have me a jailbird ?   Ta, ta !"

Then Mr. Gussie trips down to his cab, his mercurial temperament rising under the first ray of hope this day has brought to him, as he thinks to himself : "Dear little gal, going to pay my debts.   Do something for her some day !"

Flossie gazes after him, and mutters to herself : "The miserable coxcomb !   Shall I leave him to his fate ?   He'd never commit suicide.   Why not ?"   A moment more she thinks : "No, he has my promise.   His debts shall be paid to a cent.   Mr. Everett's coming at nine—on his business !"

Then her face grows a sudden vivid red, and her eyes

become brighter and more sparkling. She laughs : "How everything seems to force him near me. Pshaw ! what nonsense !" But runs up-stairs and gives such orders that her maid mutters : " Lawks, how particular she are ! One would think she was going to a ball—or is her best fellah coming to-night ?"

CHAPTER XXI.

" SHE SHALL REMEMBER !"

GOING direct to the Brevoort, Van Beekman sends up his card to Phil Everett, and this coming to Miss Bessie's pretty hands, that young lady runs to her brother's room, and knocking on his door, as soon as it is opened laughs, " His Lordship of Bassington wants to see you."

" Impossible ! I'm too busy !" answers her brother.

" Busy ! That's what you've been for the last two days, and you also, Grousemoor ; at least, I've seen very little of you !" says the young lady, giving her sweetheart, who is in consultation with Everett, a somewhat reproachful glance. " Is it Atchison & Santa Fé bonds, stocks or mortgages ?"

" Neither," replies Grousemoor in his sententious way. " It's cablegrams."

" You won't see Mr. Gussie, then ? His card says he has a message to deliver from Miss Flossie Follis."

" Florence Follis?" cries Phil. " Tell them to show him up at once."

" Ah, I thought he'd get audience !" laughs the girl " I'm glad Grousemoor did not shout out also ; but he's coming with me while you see Mr. Van Beekman."

" Certainly," answers the Scotch lord. Then turning to Phil, he remarks : " While he's here you might find out something of Avonmere from him ; he lives in the same house."

" Quite right !" answers the Bostonian. " I'll do it ; for if these telegrams are true, we'll be getting to business soon."

" What's the excitement ?" asks Miss Bessie suddenly

noting that the two men are looking at each other in an agitated, nervous way, after the manner of people who have some project out of the ordinary upon their minds

"Something you'll hear of soon," answers Grousemoor. "But here's the little cad I was so unfortunate as to vouch for as a Peer of the Realm."

Then he and his sweetheart stroll away, leaving Phil to meet Mr. Augustus, who is whistling an opera bouffe air and seems to be in extraordinary spirits for a man who, according to the evening papers, is being turned out of society and hunted by duns, and perhaps has committed suicide, for that is the rumor now published because no reporter has seen him for three hours.

"Stop whistling; come in and talk, quick!" says Everett. "I'm an awfully busy man. What's your message from Miss Follis?"

"Awh!—she's going to pay my debts!"

"Pay your debts?"

"Yes, Lord Bassington's debts—Flossie Follis put up the job on me. Did you ever hear anything like it? Flossie Follis—did you ever——"

"Stop screaming out that young lady's name! Do you want to have every bell-boy in the house hear you? Come in! Now, are you mad or crazy?" cries Phil, closing his door.

"Neither, dear boy, though if your great big business brain had stood one-half of what my poor, languid, society cerebrum has, you'd be in a padded cell and a strait-jacket! But as you seem curious, listen to a tale of woe!" And Augustus gives Phil a history of his adventures, including the episodes of his attack on Chumpie, and his interview with the younger Miss Follis.

At the first of these Everett roars with laughter, but at the second he looks very grave and mutters: "I must keep the child's name out of the newspapers."

"Will you call on her in my behalf?" asks Gussie.

"With pleasure," answers Phil, and means it.

"Then don't forget—nine o'clock!"

"Certainly. But if I do this for you, you must do something for me."

"Of course."

"Then from your story I judge you are not in love with Avonmere?"

"I—I hate him with my whole body !" answers Gussie.

"Very well.   You live in the same house with him. You keep your eyes open, and if he does anything out of the common, report it to me."

"You—you think—" gasps Gussie, excitedly.

"I think this," answers Phil : "if you want revenge, here's your chance for it.   If you wish to do a good turn to the generous girl who is perhaps going to keep you out of prison, here's your chance for it !   If you wish my aid in your troubles with creditors and with club men, here's your chance for it—if you keep your mouth very close, your eyes very open, and ask no questions.   Will you do it ?"

"Won't I !" answers Augustus, with a meaning wink.

"Very well, where's a list of your debts ?"

"In my pocket-book," says Gussie.   "Those marked with a star are private."   He passes the article to his questioner, and takes his leave with many remarks about gratitude as Everett joins his sister and Grousemoor at dinner.

At nine o'clock Phil rings the bell of 637 Fifth Avenue, asks for Miss Florence Follis, and a moment after is shaking that young lady's hand and looking into her eyes.

"You come on behalf of Mr. Van Beekman ?" says the girl, who is robed in delicate blue, with colored effects, and makes a brilliant picture, though she looks slightly ashamed as she wonders what Mr. Everett must think of her connection with the plot that made Van Beekman a lord.

This feeling makes her fascinatingly nervous and excited, taking from her big eyes any heaviness that earnest truth might give to them.   And Phil, gazing at her as he takes a seat, thinks she looks like a naughty fairy.

In regard to the naughtiness he is nearly right, for the girl is in a very haughty as well as touchy mood ; which is, perhaps, owing to one or two slights this young lady has suddenly and unaccountably received in society in the last two days, and also to a battle royal with Mrs. Marvin on account of that widow's general performance on the Van Beekman-Avonmere-Matilde engagement question.

This fairy effect is doubtless heightened by the dress she wears.

At the ball she looked as if in a cloud ; now she seems in a rainbow—from which her beautiful neck and arms spring out like those of a fay ; lace, tulle, and gauze, in the soft tints of the bow of heaven, floating about their gleaming whiteness, to make their loveliness rather that of the air than that of the earth.

"Don't you think you had better sit down ?" remarks Everett. "In that dress one fears you'll float away."

"Where to ?" she asks, a little astonished.

"To—to fairy-land," suggests Phil, who has forgotten all about business, looking at this girl he has been dreaming of and working for these last two days.

"Sometimes I almost wish I could fly anywhere !" answers Miss Flossie, and astounds him. "You'll find me earthy enough this evening, I'm afraid." Then she goes on : "You came to see me on business, I believe ? Perhaps what you will hear from me may make you think me like Iolanthe—a fairy whose sins should condemn her to the spring for life, to wash out her enormities. But I am talking to you as if I had known you all my life, and we only met two days ago. Doubtless you'll think me forward, also. Earthy and forward—to-night ; and at the Patriarchs rude, fibbing, and fickle. What do you think of me now ? Oh, no—not for *worlds !*" For Phil is about to open his mouth in rhapsody. "Nothing but business ; you came on Mr. Van Beekman's behalf."

"Yes," answers Everett ; "you've made him a very generous proposition, I believe ?"

"No, only an atonement," answers Flossie, slowly. Next she says suddenly : "When I wrote Mr. Van Beekman to-day I had no expectation of having to speak to any one else about the matter. I——"

"Neither need you do so now !" cries Phil. "Don't say a word—leave Van Beekman's troubles to me. Don't think of them again !" For the thought of explanation has brought a vivid blush of embarrassment over the girl's face, neck, and shoulders.

"Leave Mr. Van Beekman's troubles to you ?" says Flossie, slowly. "How will that help him out of them ? How will that pay his debts ?" Then she bursts out suddenly : "You mean to pay them *yourself !* To save me a few blushes—to save me a few embarrassed moments—you mean to rob yourself for my folly? No, no! I'll tell you everything. I insist! I couldn't sleep to-night! If you didn't know, you might think I had some selfish object in Van Beekman's downfall. You might think I was a really naughty fairy. Your generous offer proves that you deserve my confidence!" cries the girl, and makes Phil very happy.

Then, after the manner of women, she gives him an awful blow, for she says : "I feel I can tell you just as easily as I could Bob." And sitting down on the sofa beside him, in a mixture of blushes and embarrassment, mingled with a little laughter, she relates to Everett the story of Gussie's downfall, keeping Matilde's connection with the matter as much in the background as possible, though she doesn't hesitate to tell of Mrs. Marvin's perfidy to Bob.

This disclosure as to Flossie's trustee and champion puts her listener in a very good humor. He shrewdly reasons that if the young lady wishes the mining super-intendent to marry Tillie, she has no wish to be more than a very good friend to him herself.

But being anxious to have every detail regarding Avonmere for Flossie's eventful welfare, triumph, and right, Everett goes to cross-questioning the girl in a way that, under other circumstances, he might think ungen-erous. Thus forced to her own defence, she is compelled to let him into a good many family secrets, the revela-tion of which would not have pleased Avonmere nor Mrs. Marvin, nor, for that matter, Matilde nor her mother.

This idea also gradually comes to the young lady; she looks at him with reproachful eyes and mutters: "You act as if you were my father confessor. I—I don't know why I have answered your questions. I—I'm a traitor to Matilde! What would she think of me!—telling about the same engagement ring from two men?"

"That," remarks Everett, "is part of Mr. Van Beek-man's debts; the one it will be most difficult to settle. He bought the ring but did not pay for it—and then gambled it away." With this he turns the conversa-tion upon the affairs of the late Lord Bassington, telling her that his lordship owes twenty thousand dollars—for Phil can see the girl is reproaching herself for her revela-tions, and wishes to get her mind from this subject.

"So much?" she cries. "He threw all that away in a week? I'll—I'll have to telegraph Bob!"

"Not at all!" answers Everett. "All this can be arranged for something over five thousand."

"You can pay twenty thousand with five thousand? Oh, you must be tricking me ; you mean to liquidate the balance yourself."

"By no means. You shall pay every cent of Mr. Van Beekman's liabilities."

"With five thousand dollars?" cries the girl, astonishment in her eyes. "Oh, yes, I forgot you're a Wall Street man. Tell me how, you clever financier! I'd like to learn your methods; I'll try them on my milliner."

"Very well," remarks Phil. "First, you must lose everything you have in the world—you must become bankrupt."

"A—ah!"

"Then I'll compromise for you. Most of the articles Gussie owes for are things that can be returned—horses, carriages, furniture, jewelry, etc. These I shall send back, and the venders 'll be very happy to get them, plus a little cash for their wear and tear."

"Ah, I see."

"What he has made away with or used, and all money he has borrowed, I'll settle in full. I shall take this upon my hands. Your name will never be heard of in the transaction, and when you find it convenient, without even telling your trustees, you can repay me my expenditure."

"Oh, you're the fairy now!" cries Flossie ; then she sends a thrill of joy through her broker's heart, for she mutters, "My good fairy!" Next she puts him to the torture again, for she says : "Add your commission to your bill."

"How much?" asks Phil, glumly.

"Any price you please," she returns airily.

"And you'll pay it?"

"Of course!" indifferently.

"Very well. Remember your promise!" answers Everett, in so pointed a tone that, glancing up at him, Miss Flossie sees something in his eyes that makes her start and blush and grow very haughty.

Her English manner comes back to her ; she says in that indifferent way which, coming from a woman, always sends a chill to man : " Awh !—I forgot I was speaking to a business man. Perhaps it is better you state your commission first. The charge may be so high I shall have to employ another broker."

" My charges will be just the same as what Bob would make. I believe you placed us in the same category a few moments since, Miss Florence," answers Everett, getting red in the face.

" Oh, I'm perfectly willing to settle that way ! " remarks the girl. " I always pay Bob NOTHING ! " With this she gives him a little mocking laugh.

" Very well, we will consider the business settled ! " says Phil, making a move to depart, for he is greatly annoyed at his client's last words.

Then, noting that he is going away—probably angry, her visitor's face being flushed, though his manner is formal—a marvellous change takes place in this volatile young lady. She cries : " Business over, pleasure begins ! I was dreading a lonely evening ; the most of the family are at the theatre."

" But I've made a long call now—perhaps *too* long a one," answers the young man, but half mollified.

" Nonsense !   Mr. Everett, my man of affairs, was here *before* you on business.   Mr. Everett, my friend, has just walked in. I can call you my friend—of course I can ! You wish to be classed with Bob ! " cries the girl in a light, frivolous affectation of gayety that passes suddenly away as she mutters in a desperate voice : " And I've got so few friends ! "

" So few friends ? " gasps Phil, astounded.

" Yes, in New York," she cries, " where I want so many. Oh, my heavens ! if Bob would only leave the mine and come ! "   And wringing her hands, she sinks panting upon a sofa, while Everett gazes at her with wild eyes and throbbing pulses, for the beauty of this girl has been growing gradually greater all the evening. The concealed agitation of her mind has been breaking out in fits and starts, like flashes of electricity, here, there, everywhere, in her eyes, in her gestures, in her poses, and has made her loveliness almost celestial.

A second more and she would become hysterical, did

Phil give her time ; but he bends over her, forgetting that she is Miss Flossie Follis, the great heiress, and only remembering the little girl who had ridden all day in his arms and clung to his neck and kissed him on the Gila plains.

"Your cause shall be my cause ! " he mutters. Then, the splendor of her charms tearing the senses out of this man, he puts out an audacious hand, and, touching the girl's white shoulder, says : "Bob's not here, but Phil is ready to do you any service man can do a woman ! "

His touch electrifies the girl.

She rises up, grows pale, white, haughty, and whispers : " I must be mad, talking in this way before you. Forget what I've said, that's the only favor I can ask you. And yet I have so little time," she mutters; then breaks out again: " To think that that awful villain is growing closer, closer to my dear sister day by day; that when he marries her he will be safe from my vengeance ! "

"What do you know about him?" cries Phil, eagerly, for though she has not mentioned Avonmere's name, he guesses to whom she refers.

"What do I know about him? Only memories! *memories !* MEMORIES !—an unintelligible, flighty, will-o'-the-wisp horror ! That's all ! That's what makes me so desperate ! Oh, for some point to start from, something to be sure of, something I could *really* recollect ! "

" Something I might help you to remember ? " suggests Phil.

"You?" cries the girl, and she suddenly looks him in the face with searching eyes and whispers : " Your voice seems part of the past—the past that I must divine before that man and woman drive me out of society, where I can see him—talk to him—discover *his* past—expose him ! Oh, what nonsense ! You must think that I am mad to talk to you or any man in this way. If I stay here you will think me crazier than I appear to you even now ! Good-night, Mr. Everett, good-night ! " And she runs from the room, trying to gather up her hair that has fallen in disorder down her back, leaving Phil in a dazed state, during which he staggers from the house, muttering to himself: " BY HEAVENS, SHE SHALL REMEMBER ! '

CHAPTER XXII.

"NOT TILL I HAVE A NAME!"

BUT the element of time now comes into this affair with vital import. Meditating that the presence of Miss Flossie is a standing menace to his suit with her sister, Avonmere, during the next few days, makes plea to Matilde for early marriage, stating that urgent business will recall him almost immediately to England, and that he wishes to take his bride with him, as it will be almost impossible for him to return to America for a number of months.

This idea, which he presses persistently, is supported by Mrs. Marvin with her whole heart, and urged with every argument that her intellect can invent.

Curiously, this proposition also finds favor with Mrs. Follis, who, noting how abhorrent the affair is to her younger daughter, thinks the sooner she gets the matter over, the less chance there will be of its breaking her Flossie's heart; for she imagines the girl's opposition to Matilde's wedding comes not from hatred of Avonmere, but from love of him, and attributes her drooping spirits and sad eyes to jealousy and unrequited affection.

So, in the course of a few days, the rumor gets about the clubs and parlors of Fifth Avenue that Tillie Follis, the great Western heiress, is to be married to Arthur, Lord Avonmere, during the coming week. The ceremony will be quite private, and the bride will leave with her husband for England immediately after its completion.

And this reaching the ears of Grousemoor, he comes in to Phil one day, and in his blunt, sententious way says : " Are you ready to move yet ? "

" In the Follis matter ? " asks Phil.

" Certainly."

" No ; not for several days. The documents are not all here from England, and Garvey and the requisition papers from Colorado and New Mexico are not arrived."

" You must act sooner."

" Impossible ! I dare not ! I have too cunning a gentleman to deal with, and can give him no warning till I'm ready to strike him down and crush him in a moment ! "

"You must !"

"Why ? "

" Because in protecting one girl from this villain you are permitting another to fall into his clutches. Tillie Follis is going to marry Avonmere next week."

"So soon ? "

" When he's her husband, the other sister's hands will be tied.   To gain her position and name she will have to strike at that of her sister, and you know Flossie Follis well enough to know that she will never do that."

" The idea she gave me the other night," mutters Phil. A moment after he cries out suddenly : " There's but one way—we must send for Abe Follis and tell him every-thing ; he will promise secrecy, and stick to it.   And if he's the man he used to be, there won't be much chance of Avonmere putting the wedding-ring on his daughter's finger, even with the incomplete evidence we can show him to-day."

" That's about the proper form," answers Grousemoor. "Send for him at once."

Which they do ; and that evening to the astonishment of Tillie, rage of her mother, and dismay of Mrs. Mar-vin, Abraham Alcibiades Follis strides into his house and plays the Colorado father, and does it in such a way as to produce the very worst results both to Flossie and Tillie.

He comes home, and taking the latter young lady on one side, says: " Matilda, you know I've been a good, square, straight-up dad to you——"

"Yes, father," mutters the girl.   Then she cries out suddenly: " What's the matter ? "   For Abe's manner and appearance are of a kind that frighten her.

" I—I'm a going to break your heart, my child," says the old man in a pathetic, faltering tone.

" Break my heart ? "

" Yes ; bust it plum, wide open, as mine is from this day's developments.   The man you were to marry can't have you ! "

"Why not ? Is Arthur dead ?" gasps the girl.

" No; them kind of critters don't die ! You send that engagement ring back to him, and tell him that if Abe Follis finds him in this house after this, he'll kick him out of it !"

"Father! He—he has another wife?"

"Not that I knows of. I shouldn't have come to you if I'd heerd that about him. I should have gone to headquarters!" cries the frontiersman, the light of battle coming into his eye. "I wish that was the trouble; that I could have settled with him, and told about it afterward, when he was planted!"

"Then what is it?"

"Something I am not free to tell you about, darter. Something that's been proved to me, and I've given my word not to tell—for the sake of your sister."

"Your word not to tell me?—of the slanders about my affianced husband, made behind his back?—for the sake of my sister?" answers Matilde, a cruel ring in her voice on the last phrase. Then her head, which had been drooping, becomes erect and haughty, and fire springs into her eyes.

"'Tain't no good getting obstreperous, Tillie," continues her father. "You jist take that scoundrel's ring off your finger right now!"

"Your reasons?"

"I can't give 'em at present! Take off that ring! I'll get you another, bigger and prettier than that."

"Never, dad! never! I've given my word to the man you call a villain. Prove him one, and I'll take back my promise."

"Didn't I tell you I've given *my* promise? What makes you so sassy? That ring! Quick!"

Abe has risen with sorrow and indignation in his eyes —sorrow at having to destroy his daughter's happiness, indignation that she will not obey him, and destroy it herself. "Obey me!" he cries. "You know what I say is law in this house."

"Not with mother in it!" cries his daughter back at him, and flies to Rach's protecting arms with a laugh on her lips, but tears in her eyes.

Embraced by her mother, she sobs out that for Flossie's sake her father—her *own* father—has commanded her to give up the man she loves; for Avonmere persecuted she feels should be called that.

"'Tain't for Bob, Floss has set her father agin you now, my persecuted lamb," cries Rach.

Then she lifts up her voice and calls out: "Abe Follis!

A-bra-ham Al-ci-bi-a-des Fol-lis !" in a manner that echoes through the hallways of the great house, and makes its owner and potentate grow pale and sickly, and shiver in his boots.

He stands his ground, however, and the stalwart Rach finds the Colorado father is also a Roman one.

To her questions, arguments, and attacks, he simply says : " I've heard enough about that lordling to make me say that no darter of mine can marry him. I do it for Tillie's sake. You'll thank me for it afore long, Rach, so will my girl."

" What's your reasons ? What's Flossie been saying to you ? " cries his spouse. " Are you two in together to break poor Tillie's heart ? "

" No," says Abe shortly ; " Flossie has had nothing to do with this. She's all a good loving sister should be to Tillie, and a true, loving darter to both of us. Don't you trouble the child about this 'ere matter, or by the Kentucky Major ! you'll hear from Abraham Alcibiades Follis ! "

" If you've any good reasons for breaking your daughter's heart, you'll give 'em if you're a man, and not sneak away to your Hoffman House gang !" screams Rach in rage and anger.

For having said his say, her helpmeet has suddenly seized his hat, stepped out of his front door, and is now on his way down the avenue.

This he has done not from terror of his wife, but from fear that under her questions he may break his promise to Everett, and divulge secrets that may destroy Flossie's chance of gaining what he thinks are his adopted daughter's rights.

So, going to the Hoffman House, he writes a letter to Lord Avonmere, charging that young man, as he values his personal safety, never to enter his house again, or dare to speak to his daughter Matilda Thompkins Follis.

Then making a night of it with Hank Daily and other mining men, he does not appear at his home this evening, to the anger and solicitude of his spouse, who fears her Abe is going out of his head in this wicked city.

Now, this letter of Mr. Follis, being delivered to Avon-mere by a messenger boy, produces sudden consternation in that gentleman. He is not afraid of the mining man's threats of personal violence, but he is very much afraid Follis will withhold or curtail the gigantic marriage settlement he has expected with his daughter. He mutters to himself: "The widow must straighten this," and sends a note to Mrs. Marvin, begging her to be at the opera this evening.

And finding her alone in the Follis box, Miss Tillie not having the spirits to be present, and Miss Flossie having another engagement, he and the wily Mrs. Marvin have an awful discussion.

For this female social diplomat has worked upon Rach's rage against her husband, and Tillie's idea of her father's unreasonable interference in her love affair, until they have come to an understanding, in secret conclave, that, in a glow of triumph, she lays before Avonmere, and to her astonishment and rage he refuses the arrangement.

After a long consultation, over which they become so excited, that were it not for the roar of the Wagnerian orchestra, a great deal of Avonmere's and Miss Tillie's romance would become the property of the adjoining boxes; at the close of the first act the gentleman takes Mrs. Marvin down to her carriage.

As he assists her in, she whispers to him in a voice hoarse with rage: "You must marry her without a settlement!"

"Without a settlement I marry nobody!" is his reply; and he feels for a cigar.

"You needn't light that," she says, "I want to talk to you."

"We've discussed the affair pretty thoroughly already," he answers. "I see no need of going over the matter," and coolly lights his weed, to show her this interview is at an end.

"Throw that thing away and get in with me," she says with equal coolness, though there is a nasty ring in her voice.

"And why?"

"Because I wish to speak to you about—place your ear nearer mine."

Something in her manner induces him to do as she directs.

Then this old social general whispers a few words, and suddenly stops and says, "Hush! Remember whom you are talking to." For the English peer has uttered under his breath an awful oath. "Now, if you think it worth while to discuss the matter further, step in the carriage and drive home with me; there's something in the Follis house I want to show you."

And her whisper has been so potent that he obeys her without a word, and the two drive to 637 Fifth Avenue in silence, though each is thinking very deeply.

"You need not regard Abe Follis's letter, Avonmere," says the lady as the carriage draws up; "you are my guest, and enter this house at my invitation."

"Oh, I don't mind him!" answers the Englishman lightly, which is true, for there is no lack of personal courage in his composition. With this, he assists Mrs. Marvin out of the equipage, and silently follows her up the steps, into the room in which he has first been received by Tillie Follis. This is dimly lighted.

Without a word she turns up every gas-burner to brilliant illumination.

"For what did you do that?" he asks astonished.

"Because I want to see your face when I show you a picture." She throws open the portfolio of Colorado views, and exclaims: "The cañon of the Baby mine! You're as white as when you first saw it, and the recollection of it nearly gave your British nonchalance a fit! Do you want me to explain to you why you nearly fainted when you first beheld Flossie Follis? Ah, that hits you hard! You don't like the two mentioned together!" for at her insinuation Avonmere has sunk into a chair, with lips that tremble and cheeks that grow white.

"Do you want me for a friend or an enemy?" she goes on rapidly. "Will you marry Tillie without a settlement? and trust that her mother will see that she is as generously provided for as if you had her father's sign-manual to any document that lawyers can draw up? Don't you know he loves his daughter, and when you have his heart in your grasp you can bleed his pocket?"

"You put it quite strongly!" mutters Avonmere, still agitated.

"Besides, the girl is beautiful; you love her! Shall we be friends, or shall I——"

"No!" he says shortly. "You shall not! We are friends!"

"Then in proof of our friendship you will sign this," she goes on, growing commanding as he grows pliable, and places a document under his eyes.

"It is only a letter from you to secure me for my kindness to you," she remarks. "It proves that I believe thoroughly in Tillie's dower being as certain as if her father turned over his securities to you now. In proof of my faith I have raised the stipulated reward to ten per cent. of any money coming to you on account of your future wife. Sign!" she has already a pen in her hand and is holding it to him.

But he dashes it aside with a muttered curse, and says: "Never!"

"*Sign!* It is your last chance to wed Tillie Follis and her millions! SIGN! or I walk upstairs and tell her mother what I know of you, and she'll drive you out of her house! Besides, Miss Flossie, your enemy—the little girl you like so much—she'll be pleased to hear the news!"

And she would mock him and be merry with him ; but he seizes the pen, signs the letter, and says : " Now, your part of the agreement! "

"With pleasure. You shall see Mrs. Follis at once." And going into the hall on her way to the Western matron, this old female Machiavelli chuckles to herself : "That fool Avonmere—he was dodging bullets when I was firing blank cartridges. I wonder why Baby mine cañon and that waif of the wilderness frighten him so much? It's something awful. If I could only discover!" Then she mutters suddenly: "No! There are some things better left in the indefinite."

As for her customer, he thinks the matter over, and is rather pleased with the arrangement after all. He loves the girl as well as he can love any woman. With her heart in his grasp he has her father's purse also. Besides, if the younger sister loves the elder, his marriage will be an eternal barrier against her claim or her revenge.

"Egad!" thinks this easy-going scoundrel, "Marvin's medicine may be the best I can take under the circumstances."

With this he rises, and greets, in his polished way, the

stalwart Rachel, who has been awaiting Mrs. Marvin's report, and who now enters with her.

THEN THE THREE SIT DOWN AND MAP OUT THE VARI-OUS DETAILS OF AN ARRANGEMENT THAT, COULD HE HAVE KNOWN IT, WOULD HAVE SENT ABRAHAM ALCI-BIADES FOLLIS OF COLORADO ON THE WAR-PATH WITH GUN AND PISTOL.

Arising from this conference, Rachel remarks : " I'm sorry things couldn't have been done different and more in symmetery with our pos-sish; but Abe has been contrary ever since he got with that Hoffman House gang, and to-day he went on as if he'd gone plump out of his head. This stand of mine 'll put the senses into him agin."

" Yes," answers Avonmere, pleasantly, " I rather imag-ine this will be a surprise to Mr. Follis. Any more sur-prises for me, my dear Mrs. Marvin ?"

" But one," says the old diplomat. Then she laughs, "Go into the next room; she's there expecting you. That's what you get for being a good boy."

" Yes," says Rach ; " you can talk to her but ten min-utes. The child's worn out with her dad's cuttings up, and ought to have been in bed along ago."

" Agreed ! " cries Avonmere. And opening a neigh-boring door he finds himself face to face with his *fiancée*, whose beauty and loveliness make him forget that his heiress is still unportioned, for Matilde Follis to-night seems more alluring than ever to this man whose love for her money is half forgotten in his passion for herself.

Robed in some white clinging thing, her manner, tempered with the anxieties this afternoon has left upon her, and the hopes and fears this night has brought to her, her vivacious eyes drooping before the being she thinks she will soon call husband, her cheeks covered with the blushes of surrendering and conquered woman-hood, Matilde makes a picture that causes Avonmere's dark eyes to flash, and his Italian pulses to bound. *He really thinks he loves his sweetheart.*

Shortly after this, being compelled to go by the im-placable Rachel, who makes him stand to his contract, the gentleman comes into the hall, and finds Mrs. Marvin waiting for him ; she has a smile of contentment on her matronly face, being pretty certain Matilde's beauty has destroyed any regret her customer may have had at the goods she is delivering to him not being exactly as invoiced.

She murmurs : "Is she not beautiful? Are you not glad you threw away your cigar and came with me this evening, young man?"

"Very," answers Avonmere. "But with your permission I'll light another to help me on my walk home." As he does so he remarks casually : "You've done what you promised in regard to our pretty little opponent?"

"Certainly," whispers Mrs. Marvin. "It's in the clubs; it's in the air; the women are all talking. Miss Flossie Follis will soon be longing for the genial climate of Denver."

"Yes," he sneers; "your sex are not generally kind to an heiress and a beauty when she can't tell who papa and mamma are. I've given our gossips another and stronger rumor in regard to Flossie's origin."

"What is that?" asks Mrs. Marvin, eagerly.

He whispers a few words in the lady's ear that make her gasp with astonished horror. "How do you like that, Madame Machiavelli?" he laughs, and goes whistling merrily on his way.

Suddenly he pauses, looks across the street, and mutters : "By George!" for on the opposite sidewalk, too much engrossed to notice him, Miss Florence Follis, in a pretty walking dress, is coming up the avenue on the arm of Philip Everett.

Though Avonmere does not know it, the very matter he and Miss Marvin have been sneering about has produced their *tête-à-tête*.

For the last few days the Bostonian has been perfecting his plans. The affidavits from England have just arrived, having been hurried by cable without thought of expense. They are exactly what he wishes, and he only waits the coming of Garvey and a deputy sheriff from Colorado with certain requisitions from the governor of that State, and similar documents from the head executive officer of New Mexico, to open his batteries.

Very much engaged, he still has found time to drop in at various society functions where he has thought it probable the young lady whose cause he has espoused may be found ; and in this, as in most other matters he has attempted lately, has met with a fair amount of success.

And though he has seen the object of his anxiety and devotion, the results of his interviews have hardly been of a nature to cause him extraordinary delight or self-confidence.

In fact, from the time of her peculiar interview with him, Miss Flossie has seemed to dread any approach to a *tête-à-tête*, and by various feminine devices has held Mr. Everett at arm's length. Once, driven to it by Phil's persistence, she has almost snubbed her devoted follower, though she has done it in a shame-faced way and with eyes that begged his pardon as she check-mated the gentleman's move which would have compelled her to sit out a dance with him in Mrs. Van Courtland's conservatory during a *fête* at that lady's hospitable house.

During this time, whenever Phil has seen the girl, he has noticed that some new feeling seems to dominate her.

Her appearance is that of a woman struggling with something so illusive and intangible that she cannot do battle with it, though she feels its malign influence ; and as time goes on, this contest apparently becomes harder.

On Monday she has been haughty and erect; on Tuesday, angrily defiant ; on Wednesday, for he sees her this evening at a fashionable fair given for some charity or other at Sherry's, she seems haughtier than ever ; though at times, her guard on herself relaxing, her beautiful eyes have an appeal in them.

Phil at first proudly thinks to himself alone. But watching the young lady, to his astonishment he finds the girl's pathetic glances are turned most generally to women, and have, he thinks, been met quite often by ill-concealed sneers.

"What the devil's the matter with her ?" asks her observer to himself. A moment after, this is answered by Mr. Gussie, who comes beside him.

" I've been trying to see you, old man," says the little gentleman. " It's been awfully kind the way you managed my settlement with my creditors, and put in a word for me with the governing committee at the Stuyvesant. I can hardly thank you enough."

" Thank that young lady there," answers Phil, glancing at Miss Flossie.

" Yaas, but she won't let me, yer know ; appears not to remember my face ; looks at me as if she'd never seen me before ; cuts me dead ! I should think a fellow feeling would make her kinder this evening."

" What do you mean ? " whispers Everett, eagerly.

" Why, haven't you heard the rumors ? They've been about the clubs and everywhere for the last few days ; they're getting more pronounced, I can tell you. Poor little devil ! did you see her wince then ? Mrs. Farnam Van Cott cut her dead, and I saw that woman try to kiss her the night of the Patriarchs. Both Miss Flossie's and my social booms have busted since that night."

" What do they say about her," cries Phil, " that makes that old harridan dare to insult my—" he suddenly checks himself, and mutters : " Tell me the rumors."

" But you mightn't like 'em."

" Tell me every one of them ! "

" Yaas ; but you look as if you'd hold me responsible for them if I did ! "

" I shall hold you responsible for them if you *don't*," says Everett, forcing a smile.

" Well, then, first it was reported that the girl is an adopted daughter with no known parents at all. Now it is rumored—mind you, only rumored—don't be angry—that she is old Abe Follis's child ; but her mother—well, her mother is Dutch Kate of Aspen. That's the reason they say old Abe has put so much property in Miss Flossie's name ; that's the reason he has such rows with his wife that he don't dare go home and bunks at the Hoffman. There's another chap mixed up in it somehow, called Bob. Nobody seems exactly to know how he comes in ; it's all rumor, don't yer see. But Sammy Tomkins, who's been over the Denver and Rio Grande twice, says he's seen Dutch Kate, and Flossie Follis is her living image, only thinner of course ; Dutch Kate's fatter than old woman Marvin, and weighs three hundred. Now don't go running against windmills, old Chappie. Keep cool ! " For Phil's face appalls him at this moment.

' I will keep cool," he answers ; a second's thought
17

telling him with what crafty deftness the facts have been made to support the lies in what has been told him. "You'd better tell Sammy Tomkins not to let Abe Follis hear his description of Dutch Kate of Aspen, or he'll need a tombstone," he shoots out at Gussie.

Then he strides up to the persecuted one, who, on seeing him, grows haughty, and says nonchalantly, "Good evening, Mr. Everett, you don't seem to be charitably disposed to-night."

"Why?" asks Phil.

"Oh, I've been looking at you," answers the girl, making an attempt at a smile, "and you've kept persistently where there's lots of talking, but no business."

"Come and direct my business efforts. I thought you were to be in the flower booth."

"So I was—but—" here Flossie's voice falters despite herself, her head droops, her eyes look ashamed, and she mutters: "There was some misunderstanding about the matter, and I—I—" A moment after, some sudden resolution seems to come to the girl. She says: "Will you do me a great favor?"

"Certainly—anything!"

"Then take me home. The night is fine, the distance not far. I want to ask you a question, and Mrs. Shelton won't be sorry to get rid of me." Her voice is a little bitter as she speaks of the lady under whose wing she has come.

For answer Phil silently offers his arm, and taking her to her chaperon, Miss Flossie states her errand, and finds that lady, who invited her a week ago in the height of her social success, is very happy to do without her company, now a cloud has come upon the glory of the *débutante*.

So they pass out of the place, Phil catching a remark or two in the crowd, that makes the young lady on his arm shiver.

"The beautiful Miss Nobody of Nowhere!" he hears in a man's voice; and shortly afterwards: "They say she's the image of her mother, Dutch Kate of Aspen," in a woman's tones, with a cruel little giggle behind it.

But there is only a moment of this, and Everett thanks Heaven as he gets the girl to the sidewalk.

Then she turns, lets the breeze play about her head a moment, and taking a long breath of relief says quietly

"I suppose you know what they are saying about me in there?"

"The miserable cowards!" bursts forth Phil. "I recognized the man who made one of the remarks," and he turns as if to go back.

But she puts a detaining hand on his arm, and whispers: "Hush! From ladies and gentlemen to-day I have received more punctilious kindness than ever; from the rest—what matters it? Besides," they are walking along the street now, "no man can protect a woman without compromising her unless he is her husband—or——"

She pauses suddenly, for Everett interjects: "Or her affianced. Let me act for you as that?"

As he speaks, the girl's hand is suddenly withdrawn from his arm, and she moves a little away from him.

For a moment she walks by his side in silence; then suddenly turns to him, looks him in the face, and mocks both herself and him by sneering: "Ah, the third offer I've had to-day!"

"What do you mean?" asks Phil, astonished.

"This," she says lightly, but sarcastically: "two men before you offered me their names because I had none of my own—creatures who would not have dared to raise their eyes to me but for rumors that malign the memory of my mother, and throw a slur upon as true a man as ever breathed, Abe Follis, who took me to his generous heart when I was orphaned and deserted! These things offered me marriage, hoping despair would make me throw self and fortune into their arms. Now you, whom I respect, make me the same offer from pity. Is that not equally humiliating?"

"From pity? from *love!*" whispers Everett, trying to get her little hand in his.

But she draws away, and asks herself almost savagely, "Would you have said this to me to-night did not these rumors float about me?"

"No!"

"A-ah!" This is a faint sigh, hardly audible to Phil, though it makes his heart beat very fast.

"But I should have asked it soon! Love would have opened my lips before long. Your answer, darling, to my question?" he cries.

But the girl cries back: "Pough! You are **mad!**

Who'd marry a girl without a name, who should, by the custom of the world, be an OUTCAST!   And if you would, I've too much pride to accept such sacrifice.   No man shall talk to me of marrying or giving in marriage till I HAVE A NAME!   I had intended to ask you something, but your question has stopped mine. I shall fight my battle as best I can, till he gets my darling Tillie, or— Pshaw! I'm beginning to rave again! It's lucky we are at my doorstep."

"And you'll give me no more answer than this?" asks Phil, chewing his mustache savagely, partly at his own *faux pas*, and partly at his charmer's *hauteur*.

"Neither to you nor to any man, while I'm Miss Nobody of Nowhere!—Forgive me!" whispers the girl.   Then she flies up the stairs and into her house, as if afraid to let him press her further.

But he runs after her, and catching a little hand as it is hurriedly closing the door, whispers: "What did you mean by 'forgive me'?"

"Please let go!"

"Not till you answer!"

"What I meant," says the girl, excitedly, and still struggling, "was an apology from Miss Flossie Follis because Miss Nobody of Nowhere was so haughty to you. O—o—oh!"

For Phil has suddenly imprinted a long, lingering, fervent kiss on the one hand of both the young ladies mentioned, and has gone down the steps whistling as merrily as Avonmere did but a quarter of an hour before.

CHAPTER XXIII.

MRS. WARBURTON'S CIRCUS.

GETTING to the Brevoort, he meets Grousemoor, who is by this time nearly as interested as Everett in Miss Flossie's affairs, and comes in from the club with a frown upon his face.

"What's the matter, old man?" says Phil lightly, in confident good humor.

"This," returns the peer sententiously: "that Italian

scoundrel has gone to circulating rumors about the girl that'll perhaps drive her to suicide if she hears them, which she's bound to soon, for the women have got to talking about her and snubbing her, I understand."

"She's already heard them," answers Everett, his face growing black. "But there's no danger of suicide ; Miss Flossie's made of sterner stuff."

And he gives his companion an account of his interview with the young lady ; then says with a sigh : "I wish I could make things easier for her."

"*You* can't," replies Grousemoor, "but your sister and Mrs. Willis can. Under their wing, society would treat her differently than when protected by that widow Marvin, who only half likes the girl anyway, I imagine. —Mrs. Willis and your sister are up-stairs now."

"Then let's broach the matter to them at once," suggests Everett.

So they go up to that young lady's pretty parlor, where Phil blurts out : "Bessie, I've a favor to ask you and Mrs. Willis. Will you not ask Miss Flossie Follis to go with you to a few entertainments this week ?"

At this question, the maid and the matron look at each other in a peculiar way. Then his sister says : "I'd like to accommodate you if possible, Philip, but—" here she blushes a little, glances at Grousemoor, and continues : "You know I've so much to do to get ready for —for Boston."

"The idea of asking a young lady agitated by her *trousseau* to think of anything else !" chimes in Mrs. Willis. "I'd take the duty off her hands if I were going out myself much."

Then Everett, who has a point-blank way with him, bursts out suddenly and gloomily : "That means you have heard the infernal lies about that persecuted girl, and *believe* them ! "

At this, Mrs. Willis gives a little startled "Oh ! " and his sister says quickly : "How do *you* know they are false ?—and you, too, Grousemoor ? " looking inquiringly at both the men ; for her *fiancé* has just backed up Phil's speech by " It's a thundering shame ! "

A moment after, Miss Bessie goes on : "You two seem the champions of this young lady."

"Certainly," answers the nobleman.

At this his sweetheart gives out a little affrighted "Ah !" and looks somewhat horrified, slightly jealous, and *very* curious.

"It's no use, Phil. To have their aid, we'll have to trust them with our mystery," mutters Grousemoor.

"A mystery !" cry both the ladies in one voice.

Then Miss Bessie says : "Oh, that's been the cause of your private conferences, secret cables, and numerous telegrams for the last ten days! That's the reason I've so little of either brother or lover !" and she gives her nobleman such reproachful glances that he laughingly cries: "Out with it, Phil ! *Quick,* for your sister's peace of mind ! "

"Very well," answers her brother. "Now listen, and remember, as you are women, this is a *secret.*"

"A SECRET ! " and both ladies become greatly excited.

"A secret that you must keep—one I have half a mind not to tell you."

"Rather than that," cries Mrs. Willis, "I'll promise anything ! "

"Amputate my tongue if you like, only leave my ears !" gasps Bessie eagerly.

"All right," says Phil, "prepare to use them ! "

And sitting down, he tells the whole affair as far as it has progressed, together with his plans for the confounding of Avonmere and the righting of Miss Flossie Follis.

To his wondrous tale Mrs. Willis listens almost in unbelief.

But as he goes on, his sister breaks out into little cries of astonishment and interest.

Finally, on his producing affidavits received from England, stating that the proof of Florence Beatrice Stella Willoughby, Lady Avonmere's death had been chiefly made by an official record given under the coroner's seal, with an account of the inquest on her body, together with those of her father and mother, which took place at the town of Lordsburgh, in Grant County, New Mexico, in the month of June, 1881 ; and that the verdict of the coroner's jury had been that the said Florence Willoughby had received her death at the hands of one Nana and his band of renegade Apaches and other persons unknown :

she suddenly cries : "That is false. I can swear myself ! I saw that child, as well and strong as I am now,
leave the railroad train at Pueblo, Colorado ! "

"You believe this waif of the West is a peeress of
England ? " gasps Mrs. Willis.

"Pretty nearly," answers Miss Bessie. "Phil can
swear to the marks upon her arm ; and now I think of
it, all my chat with the young lady at the Patriarchs I
was trying to recollect where I had seen her face. From
nine to eighteen makes a great change in a girl, but I
almost think——"

"Then prepare to be certain," says Phil ; and he
shoves under her eyes a photograph, and asks : " Who's
that ? "

"That," answers Miss Bessie, confidently, "is the
likeness of Flossie Willoughby, or rather Lady Avonmere, the little girl I saw at Lordsburgh in eighty-one."

"Right ! " says her brother. "It is the picture poor
Willoughby had in New Mexico, the one returned to me
among his letters, and his curious statement I've just
read to you. Now, whose likeness is that ? " and he
places another before his sister's excited eyes.

"That," cries Bessie, "is Flossie Willoughby—I mean
Lady Avonmere—also."

"WRONG ! " cries Phil. "That is the picture of Miss
Flossie Follis, one year after she was found and adopted.
I obtained it from her present father."

"Then the two are one ! I can swear it ! " says Bessie
Everett very solemnly. Next she suddenly astounds
them all by breaking out, "And now for the punishment
of that cruel villain who could leave a helpless child to
starve and die in that awful wilderness ! "

"You are certain she's Baroness Avonmere ? " gasps
the society matron.

"As sure as I am that you are Mrs. Livingston
Willis ! "

"Then I'll do all I can to help you ! " ejaculates that
lady.

"We can count on you both ? " asks Grousemoor, who
has been watching this scene in quiet interest.

"Body and soul ! " answers Bessie.

"Yes—like—like detectives ! " chimes in Mrs. Willis
with a little shudder, for she is rather timid about burglars

and detectives and such people, classing them all in the same category.

"So you *will* take up the cause of this persecuted girl?" remarks Phil.

"Won't we!" cries Miss Bessie with enthusiastic eagerness. "Mrs. Willis will drive up to the Follises to-morrow, and invite her to stop with her; then we two'll take her into society, and if any one dares to slight her, we'll say: 'Take care! This is not an unknown waif you're snubbing, but Florence Beatrice Stella Willoughby, Lady Avonmere, and peeress in her own right in the Kingdom of England!'"

"Yes, and give Avonmere the hint! Then we'll have him and every money-lender in Britain who's got a lien on that spendthrift's rents to fight along with him before we are ready," cuts in Grousemoor.

"Pough! Don't you suppose he knows who Flossie Follis is already? Who's spread all these rumors to break the girl's heart?" answers Miss Bessie airily.

"Doubtless he knows it; but he is also perfectly sure Florence doesn't know it, and has no idea that we have any knowledge of the fact or are taking any steps in the matter. His ideas are concentrated on Miss Tillie Follis and her fortune. When I come upon him it will be like a thunder-clap!" answers Everett.

"Then we're to say *nothing* of our *protégée's* rank?" murmurs Mrs. Willis in a disappointed tone.

"Not for the present; but you can be kind to her, and invite her to your house, and use your great social influence for her protection from the rumors that float about to annoy her and to put her to shame," answers Mr. Everett.

His diplomatic allusion to Mrs. Willis's great social influence quite reconciles that matron to a few days' secrecy, and she readily consents to chaperon the coming Lady Avonmere.

Then they all go to discussing Phil's plans for the un-doing of the villain uncle; when suddenly his sister, who has occupied her time in thinking, not talking, cries out: "Do you want more proof—*good* proof?"

"Of course!" answers her sweetheart; "all we can get."

"Then make Flossie Follis remember Flossie Willoughby!" pants the girl, all excitement at her idea. "Give her memory a starting point, a fulcrum upon which the mind of Miss Nobody of Nowhere will swing into that of the child peeress of England! If we can swear we saw this wonderful mental evolution, that will be good evidence to the world and to the law."

"But how?" answers Everett. "That's the thing I've been trying to do for a week."

"How? By letting her see that Phil Everett the Boston capitalist was Pete the New Mexican cowboy?"

"Pshaw! I can't take her to the Gila plains!" cries Phil.

"Pough!" answers his sister enthusiastically. "Take her to Mrs. Warburton's circus! Show Florence Follis how you saved Florence Willoughby that day in New Mexico! Do your great cowboy act, with child and Indian accompaniments!"

"Impossible!" says Grousemoor.

"Not at all!" answers the girl, who has become enthusiastic over her plan. "This is Wednesday; the circus is Friday night."

"But the Indians?"

"Get 'em from Buffalo Bill's 'Wild West.'"

"And the child?"

"Borrow a Fauntleroy from one of the theatres. Telegraph to-night for Possum from our Massachusetts farm. I'll see your old cowboy dress gets here from home in time. And then—oh, Phil, if you succeed you'll have an awful responsibility!"

"Responsibility? Why so?"

"Because," answers Miss Bessie solemnly, "the moment you give Miss Nobody of Nowhere a name, an English peeress will give you a heart!—Ou-gh! take care! I'm not Miss Flossie Follis!"

For upon this view of the situation Everett has given his adviser a salute of extraordinary fervor, coming from a brother's lips.

"Why, he's in love with her!" cries Mrs. Willis with amazed eyes.

"Of course he is!" laughs Grousemoor. "I saw it at the Patriarchs."

"And I saw it when he was a cowboy—a delirious cowboy! Why, where are you going?" says Miss Bessie.

"To be a cowboy again," answers her brother. "I'm going to telegraph for Possum." And he leaves the room, followed by the laughter of Grousemoor and the two ladies.

Then they all go into the plan with the enthusiasm of a great excitement.

Next morning Mrs. Willis invites Flossie to spend a few days with her. This invitation is eagerly accepted by the girl, who is very grateful for social kindness about this time, and is readily acceded to by Mrs. Follis, who has a project on hand that she greatly fears will fall under her adopted daughter's brilliant eyes.

The other arrangements are made with the speed that money gives and the facility social influence permits.

Phil finds Mr. Foxhunter Reach, the amateur ring-master, is very willing to put his grand cowboy act on his programme, in the place of honor before the " Mechanique."

Mrs. Willis obtains from Mrs. Warburton an invitation for her *protegée*.

Possum and Pete's frontier equipments are all on hand; so are the child star and Indians.

Phil is about to go down early on the day of the performance for a dress rehearsal, when into his room at the Brevoort comes a figure that causes him to spring hurriedly up, and a voice speaks to him that makes the last nine years of his life seem but a day.

He cries: " Garvey, by heavens ! " and seems to see the Gila plains again.

For this wiry old frontier sheriff has scarcely changed since last he saw him on the mesas of New Mexico ; and though his hair is somewhat thinner, his eyes have still that wonderful brightness and gleam of perennial youth that kindly nature gives to some very old men —patriarchs whom dissipation has not robbed of vitality nor enthusiasm.

" I come up quiet, Pete," says the old man, " for fear that chap we're after might hear of my being in town, and skip afore we got the drop on him ; likewise Burroughs, the Colorado deputy—he's more up to this extrading business than I am, and he helped me out up at Albany, and we've got the papers all right if you've got the man to fit 'em."

"We can put our hands on him at any time," says
Phil. "We'll do it to-morrow afternoon!"

Then he explains to the sheriff his peculiar plan to
right Miss Flossie Follis and undo Avonmere, showing
him the documents from England, remarking on Arthur
Willoughby's shrewdness in getting the report of a coroner's jury in New Mexico made acceptable evidence in
English courts. "You see," explains Everett, "he first
got a New Mexican notary to certify to the coroner's seal
and signature; then a United States commissioner for New
Mexico to certify to the notary's seal and signature ; and
then the British consul to accredit the commissioner's
seal and certification, which was all he knew about the
matter."

"And so our drunken young coroner's seal became
English evidence? That chap you're after's pretty
peert. You'd better nail him to-day," remarks Garvey.

"Impossible!" answers Everett.

Then after making all arrangements for the next day,
he goes down to Mrs. Warburton's beautiful country
place near Cedarhurst, where her roomy, old-fashioned
barn has been turned into a beautiful temple to the honor
of the horse—an animal that a certain set of New York
society worship with the same fervor that another portion bow down to the golden calf.

At this time of the year, the weather not being pro-
pitious for the glorification of said beast either by horse-
racing, polo-playing, or fox-hunting—that is, chasing the
anise-seed bag—they have concluded to give their four-
footed deity an ovation in the way of a circus; Mrs.
Warburton, one of the high-priestesses of the order,
kindly spending her money and throwing open her house
and grounds for the Bucephalerian mysteries.

After being hospitably welcomed by his hostess, he
finds his child star, a pretty little precocity of about
eleven, awaiting him with her mother ; also four or five
Indians, these last being borrowed from a section of the
"Wild West" *en route* for Europe.

Then, followed by his motley crew, he takes his way
to the barn.

This edifice, built in the lavish luxury common to
New York princes of finance, is a palace in wood, of noble
size and dimensions, and large enough to stable the horses

of a battery of artillery, with a troop or two of cavalry thrown in.   It is still in the hands of a crowd of busy workmen; but the master of ceremonies has kept the arena open for Everett's rehearsal, and most of the details having been prepared before in New York, he goes through his act for three or four hours, and is kindly informed by Mr. Reach, the amateur ring-master, that he thinks his performance will be a " go."

Then he has a consultation with the electrician in charge, who starts at his suggestion, but finally accedes to his request.

And so evening falls upon Mrs. Warburton's beautiful house and grounds, which now become brilliant with sparkling electric lights.   These are strung down the avenue and placed here and there through the gardens, and also illuminate the barn, with its brilliant decorations and arena filled with perfumed sawdust, its over-hanging trapezes and swinging bars, and stable outside filled with neighing horses and grinning grooms.

By this time the performers are nearly all present, in various stages of preparation for the coming *fête*, and the guests by special train will arrive from New York in a few minutes.

The brilliant audience are pretty well seated, when Mrs. Willis, Miss Bessie Everett, and Flossie Follis, accompanied by Grousemoor, having made their bows to their hostess, enter the building.   The orchestra is playing ; the peanut and candy girls, in full cry, are tossing their wares about with as much activity, vim, and attention to business as circus lemonade men ply their vocations for their daily bread at " Barnum's Greatest Show on Earth."

The performance has not begun, and the buzz of expectation floats up through the air to the electric lamps burning above.

The three ladies fortunately find seats near the front row, Miss Flossie sitting in the middle, Mrs. Willis on one side of her and Miss Bessie Everett on the other, both ladies all expectation, interest, and eyes to see how a certain portion of the performance will affect their *protégée.*

Grousemoor takes a position immediately behind the young lady, even his matter-of-fact Scotch heart beating a trifle quicker as he wonders whether to-night will bring back the memory of her earlier days into the beautiful head that is poised in front of him.

They have been seated only a few moments, Miss Flossie contentedly munching some peanuts, obtained from one of the peanut maidens, dreamily listening to the orchestra, and rather indifferently looking over her programme, when she suddenly attracts the attention of the two ladies and gentleman who are watching her, by a little subdued " O-oh ! " and a start of interest.

Looking carefully at her, they see she is inspecting the latter end of the athletic bill of fare, which contains the following announcement :

ACT XII.—THE COWBOY.   An adventure in New Mexico.
    Pete.   By an original cowboy.
    Apaches.   By genuine Indians of the " Wild West,"
      by permission of Buffalo Bill.
    The Little Girl from England.   By *la petite* Fauntleroy.

SYNOPSIS.

PART I.   *The Sports of the Plains.*   By Broncho Pete.
PART II.   *The Rescue of the Little Girl from England.*   The ride from the lone ranch on the San Francisco, where her father and mother have been killed, Pete bearing in his arms the child, and followed by Nana and a band of Apache braves.   The crossing of the San Francisco— the hurried drink—the child crying for its mother and father lying dead among the melon vines of Comming's ranch.   The chase across the mesa.   The box cañon of the Gila—crossing the cañon.   The wounded cow- boy.   The fight at the ford.   The little Samaritan. " Dear Mr. Peter."   The rain-storm and cloud-burst —*what the lightning showed !*

She reads this portion of the programme several times, each time more attentively ; a startled, wild expression comes into her face ; and though the band is playing the opening quadrille, and four of the prettiest horsewomen in New York and four of the most graceful horsemen of the various hunting clubs are prancing through the opening quadrille on polo ponies who vivaciously dance to the music, she hardly looks at them ; and her eyes have a far-away expression that not all the applause of that enthusiastic audience can take from them.

Once or twice in the evening she seems to rouse herself by an effort. She laughs slightly at the clowns when they are at their funniest ; the trained dogs get little attention from her, though she dotes on canines ; the bareback riding of the famed Mlle. Sylphonia, which is done to immense applause by a graceful gentleman in low neck, short sleeves, tulle skirts, and the same general get-up of the dashing lady rider of the circus, attracts her eyes, but does not gain the attention of her mind.

Whatever thoughts she has seem to be far away from this brilliant scene, this crowded auditorium. Once or twice her lips tremble ; several times tears are in her eyes, and Grousemoor, looking at her, thinks to himself : " If the announcement on the programme affects her so, what will the performance do to her ? "

Turning from her, he sees on the opposite side of the arena Arthur, Lord Avonmere. This gentleman has run down to this performance alone ; Mrs. Marvin, Mrs. Follis, and Miss Tillie, having great preparations before them for the coming day, remaining in New York.

" By Jove ! " thinks the Scotch nobleman, " he'll recognize the thing also, perhaps take a hint and give us no end of trouble."

But nothing can be done to remedy this matter now, for " PETE, THE COWBOY," is the next act on the programme.

The orchestra breaks into a wild flourish, and he comes dashing in—just the same dirty, bronzed, rough-and-tumble bedouin of the prairies that Broncho Pete was nine long years ago, his face made up from a photograph of that time, his dress the one in which he fought and bled on the banks of the Gila—the same bullet-holes in it, the same blood-stains still dark upon its cloth and leather. The saddle is the same ; and Possum, kept well and strong, and living easily on Phil's farm in Massachusetts, is the same wiry brute that raced over the hot mesas with Everett on his back, when he saved the little Flossie Willoughby's life.

" By George ! he's the genuine article ! " whispers Mr. Benson to Miss Budd.

" His dirt seems genuine enough," replies that young lady with a giggle.

But words are drowned in a wild yell of applause. Accident has permitted Pete the cowboy to make a hit on his *entrée*.

Little Gussie, who has officiated as a dude clown, and been nearly beaten and slapped to death several times in the evening by his *confrères*, two stalwart, burly, brutal, and funny creatures, has just thrown a lighted pack of fire-crackers under Possum's hoofs.

With a snort of terror, the mustang is bucking wildly; but Phil has not forgotten his old tricks either, and his strong knees grip the broncho's sides as they did in other days.

Then he pursues little Gussie, who, flying from the pony's mad rush, takes refuge upon the railing of the ring, and thinks himself safe, and chuckles in the glee of the dude mixed with the mirth of the clown.

But even as he does so a lariat whirls from Pete the cowboy's once practised hand, and the dude clown caught in its rawhide noose is yanked down from his perch of safety, and rolled over and tumbled about in the sawdust of the arena, uttering hideous cries of real terror, that the crowd greet with a howl of hilarious joy.

This general enthusiasm and excitement veils the greater agitations of Arthur, Lord Avonmere, and Flossie, his niece.

As Pete rides in, Miss Flossie is leaning forward; her eyes rest on the piebald mustang ; she gives a short, sharp sigh, and presses her hand to her heart, that Grousemoor can see by the throbbing silk and velvet above it is beating wildly.

But if the effect is great on the niece, it is tremendous on the uncle ; and glancing at him the Scotchman sees him pale as death, with drooping jaw, and lips that mutter in stupefied surprise.

While this is going on, Pete gives his exhibition of cowboy riding in the reckless, devil-may-care way common to the real article, and dashes off in a volley of applause ; for he has done some tricks of horsemanship that have astonished the fox-hunting, polo-playing contingent present, and his episode with the dude clown had already made him a favorite.

And so part first of "The Cowboy" ends.

There is a slight interval ; the musicians change from the wild galop they have been playing to a heart-touching Spanish air that stimulates the imagination, and brings the tears a little nearer the eyelids ; and as this is taking place the Scotchman notes that the girl sees Avonmere, and a wonderful change takes place in her.

From now on he notes she is fighting with herself—fighting to restrain some immense emotion that is dominating her mind ; fighting to control something that she fears will conquer her ; and her manner is so repressed that she astounds Grousemoor and disappoints Bessie Everett and Mrs. Willis, who are eagerly looking for some wild outburst of returning memory and melodramatic passion.

A moment after, part second begins.

The rattle of firearms is heard off, and Pete dashes in on Possum, carrying in his arms a little girl who makes Bessie Everett scream with astonishment, for the child-actress has been made the likeness of Florence Beatrice Stella Willoughby, Lady Avonmere, whom Phil carried in his arms from the Apaches. As he comes in he slightly checks his horse, walks him along as if fording a river, and stooping down simulates taking up the water in his *sombrero*, giving the child a drink, and pets and caresses her, telling her not to grieve. Then tossing the liquid over her face, the little girl, who has been sobbing silently, suddenly cries : " Take me back ! I will go back to my dear father and mother ! They were alive five minutes since, when the dark bad men made the bang noise, and mamma fell down, and papa—the dear papa I came all the way from England to see—cried : ' Save the baby, Pete !' and fell down beside her. No, No ! They can't be *really* dead ! "

And she struggles to get from his arms and to run back ; but he, clasping her tight upon his breast, whispers to her and soothes her, then shouts : " For the box cañon of the Gila !" and putting spurs to Possum dashes along.

A moment after, with whoop and war-cry, the Indians spurring their ponies come on the scene, and race wildly after him. Till running the course some two or three times, Pete suddenly checks Possum, apparently rides into another river, gives the child another drink, and coming to a part of the arena where some painted rocks have been placed, the little girl says, " Bad men behind us again ! "

A shot comes from the pursuing Indians, and dropping the child in safety behind one of the rocks, Pete claps his hand to his thigh, and tumbles writhing, wounded and groaning, from the mustang.

Seeing this, the child takes to caressing and soothing him ; but he cries : " I must keep them from crossing the Gila till the cloud-burst ! " and crawls with his gun to the top of the rock and looks over.

During this, the Indians at the opposite side of the arena have been gesticulating and pointing to the heavens, and one says : " Heap big rain ! Cross the river and scalp ! "

Then they dismount, and leaving their horses in care of one, come across what they pretend is a river-bed, shooting at Phil, who returns their fire and drives them back.

They retreat, and he lies groaning and wounded ; but at his side is the little girl, who has caught some running water in her little straw hat, and placing it to his lips says in sympathetic voice : " Dear Mr. Peter, I've brought you some water ! You look so thirsty now ! "

And he replies : " What's the matter with your arm ? " then cries : " Curse the Apaches, they've shot you just below that little mole ; the mark 'll never leave you ! "

And she whispers back : " It's going to rain and fill the river, isn't it, Mr. Peter, so you can save me ? "

Even while she is speaking the audience start, for the electric lights are growing dim. But one among them does not note the darkness, for the world is growing bright with hope to her, and she is muttering to herself : " Dear Mr. Peter—the cowboy of my dream ! "

Then the Indians come on, hurriedly firing, and of a sudden every light on the place goes out and it is dark, and the child is calling : " The river's rising to keep them from us ! "

Then there are crashes of thunder and flashes of lightning, and by its fitful lights the Indians are seen flying— all save one who is on the rocks with the cowboy and the child—and darkness comes again.

A moment after, another and more vivid flash illuminates the arena, and the Indian is climbing up the rock while Pete is glaring into his painted face, and as the Apache springs for his adversary's throat the cowboy's revolver speaks. There is a mighty clap of thunder, and over it comes the death-shriek of the brave and all is dark once more.

While in the gloom Flossie Follis is whispering : "I remember how my poor mother and father died. Dear Mrs. Willis, take me from here !" and Grousemoor supporting her to the open air finds that she has fainted in his arms.

A moment after, the place becomes bright with electric lights once more, and the audience are gazing at each other in surprise, for the arena is empty of rocks, horses, Indians, child, and cowboy, and the three clowns are doing a harum-scarum tumbling act.

But during the darkness Avonmere has also gone out. He walks about the grounds with a dazed expression, and goes to muttering : "Everett—the name of the woman who claimed him as son ; Bessie—the name of the girl who nursed him as sister ; both saw me and the child leave the train at Pueblo. Phil !—Pete !—By heavens ! the delirious cowboy of the inquest! He's shown strange interest in her. *This conglomeration to-night was to make her remember.* By Jove ! it's lucky all's fixed for to-morrow ! Whatever they do will be TOO LATE ! "

This last reflection has such a soothing effect upon his lordship's mind that he walks to the house, and finding some congenial spirits in the supper-room, which is now crowded, the performance being finished, he makes a very hilarious night of it, till the special train carries him back to New York.

When Phil emerges from his dressing-room, once more the man of the world, he finds the arena deserted, and the guests at the big country-house enjoying supper and preparing for the dance.

He looks about for his party, and to his astonishment none of them are there ; but while engaged in his search a servant hands him a note. This has been hurriedly written on a card and reads :

"You've succeeded too well for her nervous system. Have taken her to Mrs. Willis's. Follow us soon as possible.

"GROUSEMOOR."

Getting to his hostess to bid her good-by, that lady

informs him that, Miss Follis becoming suddenly ill, Mrs. Willis had taken advantage of a train that left immediately after the performance to convey her party back to New York.

Five minutes after this, Everett, having obtained Mr. Gussie's company for the trip, drives from Mrs. Warburton's. Reaching the main Long Island Railroad, they fortunately catch a delayed accommodation train at Valley Stream, and get to New York but an hour later than Mrs. Willis's party.

Chartering a night hack, Phil drives Mr. Van Beekman to Thirty-seventh Street, leaving him there with these significant words: " You've watched Avonmere for a week and discovered nothing! Watch him from now on, and if he doesn't make a move soon, he never will ! "

" Won't I, old chappie ? Wouldn't I like to down him as he downed me ?" is the answer of Augustus as he limps into his house with sundry groans and sighs, the results of his clowning in the early evening.

Then Everett rushes his hack up Madison Avenue to Mrs. Willis's. Here, finding the house lighted, he rings the bell, and a moment after is the centre of an excited trio.

"She remembers everything," says Grousemoor.

" Lady Avonmere won't go to bed till she sees you," ejaculates Mrs. Willis.

" Go in and win her," whispers Bessie. She leads her brother into a cosy little parlor at the rear of the house, and a moment after Phil is standing before the girl, who has risen in beautiful agitation to receive him.

There are tears in her eyes as she murmurs, "God bless you, dear Mr. Peter, you have given me a name ! "

" Yes," he says, a perhaps mistaken generosity prompting him to claim nothing from one who owes him so much. " And to-morrow I propose to make the world recognize what you remember ! "

Then he informs her of certain arrangements he has made for the coming day, charging her to be ready when Mr. Follis comes for her.

"Of course I—I shall do as you desire," says Flossie, with a slight sigh in her voice, and perchance a little reproach in her eyes.

"Very well, then you'd better get all the sleep you can; to-morrow's ordeal will probably be more trying than to-night's."

And he would leave her.

But the girl steps after him, lays a hand that is trembling, perhaps from weakness, perchance from some emotion, on his arm and stammers: "You—you—don't let me thank you for—for saving my life as a child, and giving me memory as a—a woman. You're—you're very unkind to me, dear Mr. Peter."

"I—what have I done?" gasps Phil.

Then a blush of mingled shame and pride flies over her beautiful face; she mutters: "Nothing! You have done NOTHING!" next says very haughtily and very coolly, "Good night, Mr. Everett," and so leaves him.

"Is she yours?" asks Bessie, excitedly, catching Phil in the hall.

"No; she seems a little annoyed," answers the Bostonian in a perplexed tone. Then he describes his interview to his sister.

As he finishes, she sneers at him one word: "IDIOT!" in a tone of jeering contempt; then steps to Grousemoor and says: "Let us take this cowboy away from the heiress to whom he once gave life, and now gives a grand name and another great fortune. Let us get him away before the dolt makes the girl whose heart he's won, hate him—*hate* him! and HAVE JUST CAUSE FOR DOING IT! His forte is catching cattle and clowns, NOT WOMEN!"

CHAPTER XXIV.

AN INTERNATIONAL BRIDE.

THE morning brings an unexpected complication. Everett, dressing leisurely for breakfast, is disturbed by a loud knocking upon his door, and little Gussie's voice comes to him through the panel, saying in excited tones: "Let me in, old chappie! I have got a corker in the news line for you. Too much hurry to bother a bell-boy with card; this is an eye-opener!"

As the last words leave his lips, the door opens, and Mr. Van Beekman, who is panting with haste and excitement, finds himself pulled into the room, and Phil saying to him in a very serious voice : "What is it ? "

"My dear boy, what time are you going to slap down on Avonmere ? "

"Two P.M.," says Everett. "All arrangements are made for that time."

"Then you won't get him ! "

"By Heaven, I will ! What do you mean ? "

" I mean if you don't jump on him this morning pretty early—dear boy—there will be nobody to jump on this afternoon. You know you asked me to keep my eye open on anything that Avonmere might do. So I enlarged the key-hole in my bath-room door for my little eye, and piped him after the manner of detectives. What do you think he is going to do ? "

"How can I guess ? Tell me !"

" Well, all last night after he came home from Mrs. Warburton's circus, he and his valet were packing like madmen."

"Ah ! Going away ? " cries Everett.

" To Europe, my boy."

" To Europe ? " echoes Phil, astonished.

" Yes. This morning to my astonishment—I don't think he had been in bed all night—I heard him dressing at eight o'clock—most unusual hour for him—so up I gets—equally unusual hour for me. He didn't stop to take breakfast, neither did I. There was a coupé at the door, and my man, who was loafing about the hall by my instructions, heard him tell the driver : ' No. 4 Bowling Green.' "

" Ah ! the office of the Cunard Line ! "

" Certainly. I know that as well as you ; so he had no sooner driven away than I got a hack myself and drove down there, and what do you think I found ? By George ! a stateroom taken on the *Aurania*, that sails at 1 P.M. to-day—he's going it extravagant this time—and extra berths for—what do you think ?—a valet and maid ! "

" Maid ? " cries Everett. "You must be mistaken ! "

" No, I don't think so. However, *he's* going anyway. If you want to put your hand on him, you'll have to be moving."

"So I will ! " cries Phil, and he makes his arrangements rapidly, not even stopping to breakfast.

Assisted by Gussie, who has worked himself up into a grand state of excitement, and by aid of numerous well-tipped district telegraph boys and special messengers, he gets together, about half-past ten o'clock, most of the people that he wants.

Then Van Beekman speeds back to his own apartments, with instructions, in case Avonmere leaves his rooms, to follow him wherever he goes.

But after doing this, Everett, as an extra precaution, despatches two deputy sheriffs to wait at the Cunard pier and hold Avonmere there, in case he should make his appearance, at all hazards.

While this has been going on, he has held a rapid consultation with Grousemoor.

"You must never let that man get across the water," says that nobleman, who is endowed with a good deal of solid Scotch hard sense. "You must fight him here."

"You think it would be much more difficult to win across the water ? " asks Phil.

"Almost impossible. *Here* you find this man, Arthur Willoughby, commonly called Lord Avonmere, alone and unaided; *there* you would not fight him, but every money-changer who has advanced him money, and receives in payment the rents of the estates he occupies as Baron Avonmere. By George ! You would have half the money-changers of England against you; they always make a pretty long and hard battle for their shekels," says his lordship.

"Then I'll nail him here !" cries Phil; and with that goes to Garvey, who has made his appearance, and is sitting waiting, with the same quiet smile upon his face with which he would have tackled a horse-thief or served warrants on cowboys or Mexican *banditti*.

"If you're ready, we'll start agin the enemy," remarks the frontier sheriff. "But fust let me be sure," and he examines his revolver carefully.

"For God's sake, Garvey," says Phil, noting this, "remember that you're in New York, not in New Mexico; the man you arrest will be unarmed."

"Well, ef he turns up his hands quick enough, there ain't no danger from me nur Bobbie Burroughs," remarks tl-e New Mexican official, with a grin, pointing to the Colorado deputy. "Burroughs has the fust chance at him fur murder, and I takes my second for felonious forgery. It seems to me, Pete, ef you're in a hurry, we'd better ketch your game before he leaves his den."

So in two hacks Phil, accompanied by Grousemoor, Garvey, the deputy sheriff from Colorado, a New York policeman to make the arrests in the name of the State, Phil's lawyer, a notary public, and a deputy from the British consular office, make their advance on the unconscious Avonmere.

"With this crowd," remarks the frontier sheriff, "we ought to be able to get away with the hull British peerage."

They arrive at Thirty-seventh Street, and Phil gives a sigh of relief as they find a carriage in front of the house in which Avonmere lives; he knows his enemy is still in his grasp.

Little Mr. Gussie is waiting at the door, and comes to Everett quite excitedly, saying: "Just in time! That hack is to take him away. Old Abe Follis and Miss Flossie are in my parlor up-stairs; they arrived on the Q. T. five minutes ago."

"Much obliged," says Phil, who has been very anxious on this point, and, followed by his posse, he also comes up to Van Beekman's parlor.

"You can make your arrangements here," says his host. "Meantime, I'll pop my eye on the keyhole in my bath-room door, and report Avonmere's movements."

For Phil has gone into a hurried consultation with the object of his solicitude and Mr. Follis.

That gentleman seems to be much the more excited of the two, and wrings Phil's hand, who has hurriedly explained the situation to him, and says with tears in his voice: "I'm skeered, Everett, in making my little Flossie such a social hummer, you'll be tracing me out of a darter."

But the girl whispers to him, the ring of truth in her voice: "Never, father! Never! You have loved me as a father, and you are as much my father as if I were your own flesh and your own blood!"

Then Phil leads Garvey to her, and, recognizing the frontier sheriff, she seizes his hand and thanks him for

what he did for her as a child.   And all this time Phil
stands in misery, for she never says a word more about
gratitude to him.

But, before he can despair greatly, Gussie hurriedly
comes from his bedroom, and says : " You must nip him
now !   He's getting his baggage out ! " and there is a
great noise of moving *impedimenta* from the hallway.

" Very well," remarks Phil to the policeman.   " Make
the arrests as I have explained them to you ; do exactly
as I have bid you, and it will be the best day's work you
have ever done ! "

" All right," replies the officer, " I understand ! " and,
preceded by the policeman, Mr. Everett's legal army
advance on their opponent.

As they reach the hall, the door of Avonmere's parlor
opens, and that gentleman issues therefrom, leisurely
drawing on a glove, robed in his finest raiment, a new
glossy silk tile on his head, the breast of his coat of faultless cut ornamented by a white and fragrant flower, and
with a smile of triumph upon his lips.

He says to his valet : " Jones, remember my instructions ! " and is about to pass down to his hack, his hand
in his vest pocket feeling to be certain that a little trinket
is there ready for the finger of the woman he loves.

He is strolling past Phil's minions with a look of
wonder in his eyes, for he thinks such a crowd curious
in the halls of this quiet apartment-house, when the
policeman, tapping him on the shoulder, says : " You are
Lord Avonmere ? "

" Certainly ! " he replies.

" Can I have a word with you ? "

" Yes ; but only a word," he answers, looking at his
watch.   " I haven't time for an extended conversation."

" Will you please step back in your room ? "

" No !   Say what you want here."

" Then, Arthur Willoughby, commonly known as Lord
Avonmere," says the policeman, "I have a warrant of
arrest for you, issued by the proper authorities of the
State of New York, on requisition from the governor of
Colorado, to answer the crime of MURDER ! "

" From the governor of Colorado ! " cries his lordship,
thunderstruck ; then he begins to laugh nervously and
says : " You must be crazy !   This is some practical joke

to prevent my getting—" Next he looks quickly at his watch, and gasps, "I can't remain!"

"You must!"

"Of whose murder am I accused?" he asks, his lips trembling a little, as he sees the affair is serious.

"For the murder of your niece, known at the time of her death as Florence Willoughby, but in reality, according to English law and usage, Florence Beatrice Stella Willoughby, Baroness Avonmere, a peeress in her own right in the kingdom of England." This the policeman reads from the document.

"I am arrested for the murder of Florence Willoughby in Colorado! Why, it has always been understood that the child was killed in New Mexico."

"Then it has been falsely understood!" cries Phil, who has remained a little in the background, coming forward. "I can prove by my sister's and mother's evidence that you left the train with Flossie Willoughby at Pueblo, Colorado. If she died in that State, you are the one man who knows the particulars of her death! Show us *how* she died."

At these words, Avonmere, growing very pale, and shivering a little as if a chill had come upon him, cries: "Ah, this is a move of yours! I expected something of this kind since last night. Come this way, Mr. Everett; come into my room with these gentlemen! But for God's sake, BE QUICK!"

So they all walk into his parlor, which they find denuded of his ornaments and personal belongings; but the furniture, being the property of the house, is undisturbed, and they make themselves comfortable on the chairs about the room.

While they are doing this, Avonmere has passed his hand once or twice through his hair, as if in very serious but very rapid reflection.

Apparently having made up his mind to act, he suddenly says to his valet: "Go down-stairs, Jones, get the balance of my trunks that are in the hall out of it, take them down to the steamer, and wait for me there."

Next, turning to Phil, he says: "You see I have very little time. I have an idea of your business with me; get through with it as rapidly as possible—that's all I ask," and looking uneasily at the clock on the mantel, which shows the hour of eleven, he mutters : " I can only give you five minutes ; " then cries : " You know as well as I that I am not the murderer of the young lady described in these papers ; you know SHE IS ALIVE ! "

" Certainly ! " replies Phil. " I know she is alive."

" You have taken this extraordinary action," continues Avonmere, "not to prove that I murdered my niece, but to prove that the young lady for whose benefit you did your cowboy act last night at Mrs. Warburton's circus is not Flossie Follis, but Florence, Lady Avonmere."

" Precisely ! " says Everett.

" Then if I prove to you the lady mentioned in this warrant is alive, and Mr. Everett admits its truth," says Avonmere, sharply, turning to the officer, " I presume you will let me go at once ? "

" That ain't my business," replies the policeman. " That's the say of the deputy from Colorado."

" Then, if you won't let me go in five minutes, by Heaven, you'll get no proof from me ! " cries Avonmere, sinking into a chair and simulating nonchalance, though his eyes begin to look very wild. " You can have the pleasure and the expense of taking me to your confounded State and trying me there," he goes on, suddenly. " I will prove she lives to the Colorado jury, and have a nice bill of damages for false accusation against" —he looks meaningly at Everett and sneers—" the gentleman who is doing all this because he is in love with my pretended victim."

Now, to try Avonmere for the murder of a living woman is not at all what Phil wishes. The very declaration that his opponent has made is what he is working for ; and noting the tone of despair in the man's voice, he sees Avonmere will probably be very willing to give proof of Flossie Follis's identity, providing he is promised immunity from arrest.

" I think," says Everett, shortly, " the deputy from Colorado, who knows my wealth, will be willing to accept my bond for one hundred thousand dollars to hold him harmless in case you prove the person you are accused of murdering is alive, if he does not press the execution of the warrant against you, Avonmere ? "

" That's as you say, Mr. Everett," remarks Burroughs " Let him prove the girl lives, and it would be absurd to arrest him for her murder, and I will take the security you offer to withhold the warrant."

"Are you willing to make the proof under this agreement?" asks Everett, rapidly turning to Avonmere.

"Instantly!" agrees that gentleman, with a sigh of relief. "You have some person with you who can administer an oath?"

"Certainly!" says Phil. "That was already provided for."

"Ah!" returns the Englishman, a cynical smile lighting his Italian eyes, "you have understood your work, and done it very thoroughly."

Then, with another hurried glance at the clock, he sits down at the table in the centre of the room, and writes very rapidly while the party gaze on him in silence.

After four or five minutes hurried composition, Avonmere says: "Will this suit you?" and reads the following lucid, didactic, but clear statement:

"I, Arthur Willoughby, who have for nine years thought myself Baron Avonmere, of the peerage of England, do hereby, in justice to the person now known as Miss Florence Follis, of Colorado, but in reality my niece, Florence Beatrice Stella Willoughby, Baroness Avonmere, of the peerage of England, make under oath, and of my own free will and volition, the following declaration:

"After my brother, Arthur Willoughby, and his wife's demise in New Mexico, I took my niece with me to return to England. Being compelled to look after mining interests in Colorado, I left the Atchison, Topeka & Santa Fé Railroad at Pueblo, and journeyed to the town of Leadville. The prospects I had interest in were much further toward the Utah line, a portion of the State at that period made very dangerous by the outbreak of the Ute Indians, so I could obtain no men to go with me to make an examination of my properties. Therefore I started alone. I was compelled to take my niece with me, from inability to find any one to take charge of her, and my expectation that I might be compelled to make my way out of the basin of the Colorado River by the Mormon settlements in Utah. So I took the child on horseback with me, carrying her most of the way upon my own saddle, as it was impossible to travel rapidly. I had journeyed in this manner for six days, when, in a gulch I have since recognized by photographs as that now known as the cañon of the 'Baby' mine, I left my little niece alone, tempted by the sight of some big-horns half way up the mountain side

"In stalking these I was led a much greater distance than I had expected. When about to return I found myself cut off from my niece by a number of the Ute Indians, at that time in warfare against the whites. Not daring to go directly to the child, I made a *détour* to get to her, and lost my bearings. Then, unaccustomed to travel in those great mountains, I missed the cañon entirely, and though I attempted for one week to find the child, was never able to do so. Next, my provisions being exhausted, and thinking she had been either captured or killed by the Indians, I made my way to the Mormon settlements, and reached Salt Lake, and from there, by rail and steam, came to England, believing, as Heaven is looking on me now, the child to be dead through no fault of mine, but merely an accident of God.

"Therefore, I did not hesitate to accept the title and estates that should come to me through the death of Florence, Lady Avonmere, whom I by this document declare living, and to be now known as Florence Follis, of Colorado. I relinquish all my rights in the estates and all titles that have come to me through my mistake. The girl's adoptive father, Abraham Alcibiades Follis, can, by his statement, prove that he found the child where I left her."

"Will my oath to this be sufficient?" he asks, with curious anxiety and eagerness.

"Yes," answers Phil shortly, "if you recognize the young lady in the presence of witnesses."

He steps out of the room, and a moment after leads Flossie into it, followed by Abe.

"Is this the girl mentioned in your statement?" he asks.

"Yes," answers Avonmere, "I swear it."

"Very well. Take his deposition," says Everett. And to the astonishment of Avonmere, his affidavit is recorded, not only by an American notary public, but also by a British deputy consul.

"Ah!" he says. "You want my evidence good in England. Now, I presume I can go. Good morning, gentlemen!" Then, with another glance at the clock, that shows ten minutes after eleven, he is hurrying to the door.

But Garvey, who has said nothing, and quietly remained in the background until this moment, taps the policeman on the shoulder, and that official says: "Not yet!"

"What do you mean?" cries Avonmere. "Have I

not satisfied you that the girl is alive ?   I can't stay longer.
You don't know from what you are keeping me ! "   As
he utters this, he looks curiously at Abe Follis.

"There is another warrant to be served on you, Arthur
Willoughby ! " remarks Garvey sententiously, and the
policeman, with his hand on the former nobleman's
shoulder, again says : "You are my prisoner ! "

"What's the charge ? " cries Avonmere, with a smile
so forced that it is hideous, for he is growing desperate.

"This," says the officer : "you are my prisoner on a
warrant issued by the Governor of New York, on requisition of the Governor of New Mexico, for feloniously
altering and forging a so-called report of a coroner's inquest in New Mexico, stating that the jury found Florence Willoughby had come to her death by hands of
Nana, his band of Apaches, and various other persons
unknown ; which document you have used to prove the
child dead in the courts of England, as attested by the
oaths and affidavits of various officials of the English
courts."

"You can't git out of that charge, like you did the
former ! " cries Mr. Garvey.   "The very affidavey thar
that proves that you didn't commit murder, proves that
you committed forgery ag'in the laws of New Mexico,
and for which I'll take you back thar sure as my name's
Brick Garvey !—ah, you recollect me now, Arthur Willoughby ! "

For at this speech, the man whom he has addressed has
uttered a startled moan and turned very pale, and is
lifting his hand in an excited way, and looking at the
clock in despairing agony.

Then he bursts out, pleading as for life itself : "My
God ! Everett, let me go *now !* I can't stay ! I have
given the girl all you want ! She's got my titles—my
estates—my wealth ! Let me go NOW ! "

And the scene from this time on becomes one of awful
intensity, made hideous by, every now and again, little
jeering laughs from Gussie.

"Never ! " cries Phil. "NEVER ! I might have spared
you for your crimes against this child, whose death I
believe you planned by starvation or the beasts of the
wilderness, but I'll never forgive you your lie when you
came to me outside that little telegraph-office in Lords

burgh, and, as I heard the click of the instrument, you gave me the false despatch that said Nana and his band had crossed the Rio Grande, when the wires were crying that they were hurrying to the valley of the San Francisco, and so sent Agnes Willoughby, that gentle lady, to her death by the hands of the cruel Apaches. DO YOU THINK I'LL FORGIVE THAT? There are some wretches men do not forgive nor women pity." And he stands glaring at the man who now grovels before him.

But at this moment the girl is in front of him.

"Did he do that?" she cries. "In the uncertainty and gloom—the lurid remembrance of the past, I thought he had merely deserted me, a little child, in the wilderness—that's all! I did not know that he had sent my mother and me to my dear father who loved us, to chain him to death. I remember now! I REMEMBER NOW! Rather than spare you, Arthur Willoughby, I would give up all my titles—everything this day has given me—to know that you are punished for your crime against my dead mother—my dead father, that I remember now lying among the melon vines and the smoke—crying: 'Pete, save the baby! Save the baby, Pete!'" And putting up her hands to her face in her horror of the wretch she is looking at, and who now fawns upon her and calls her niece, she staggers back to the arms of Follis, who, like all else in the room, is scowling at this creature who had given, to the cruel Apache, innocent womanhood and helpless childhood.

"You need not fear," cries Garvey, "though I, as sheriff, am bound to protect him ; if you come to Grant County and make that speech to the boys, they'll give you your fill of justice and vengeance too, and thar won't be no need of jidge or jury ;—though, of course, I will have to try and do my duty and protect him."

To this Avonmere cries : "I know what you mean! They'll murder me! My God! I will not go back." And, springing to the door, half opens it trying to escape ; but in a moment the policeman and the deputy sheriff are upon him, and he is manacled.

THEN HIS PUNISHMENT BEGINS!

For at this moment there is a rustle of women's dresses in the hallway, and Tillie Follis, followed by her mother and Mrs. Marvin, stand at the door.

The girl is in some light lavender-colored bride's dress, with bridal blushes on her fair cheeks, and eyes that are expectant but indignant.

As he sees her, Avonmere gives a low, quick moan, and, starting backward, hides his manacles behind the table; his head droops with the agony of despairing shame, and silence comes over the room.

But Rachel, her eyes only on him, cries suddenly: "Avonmere, we waited at the church for you—Tillie, the minister, and I—until we thought something must have happened. Send these men away, and come right off. There is just time for the wedding now!"

And, striding into the middle of the room, she seizes Avonmere by the arm.

Then she starts back and utters an astonished cry; she has seen his handcuffs. But now she gives an affrighted gasp, for Abe Follis, with the roar of a grizzly, has sprung out from the shadowed corner in which he has been supporting Flossie, and has seized the bride by her delicate wrist and is glaring at her and whispering, in a hoarse voice: "You, my darter, dared to marry without my consent and blessing!"

But Rachel, with backwoods grit, is between them and calls out: "Abe, it was my fault—all mine!"

Then he cries, in awful reproach: "You, the wife of my heart, were going to marry our Tillie to that scoundrel unknown to me, her daddy and your husband? The moral murderer of a man and woman! The attempted assassin of our adopted child, that he's kept out of her rights and glory for nine years! This bogus lord!"

"Great heavens! Abe, how was I to know?" stammers Rach, with eyes that for the first time can't look her husband in the face. "Forgive me. I—I thought you were out of your head!"

Next she cries, wildly: "Where's the critter who intro- duced this villain into my house, and would have palmed him off as genuine on my innocent Tillie? Whar's that Marvin woman?" And, with a "fighting Injun" look, she would pursue and fall upon and rend to pieces the matri- monial broker, did not Mrs. Marvin, with affrighted screams, fly from the room.

And now a more horrid scene than all takes place.

The two sisters are fronting each other.

"Forgive me," cries Flossie. "I could not let you marry—even though you loved him—this villain who has stolen my title."

"He is not a lord?" gasps Tillie.

"No more than that creature, jeering in his face was," and she points to Gussie, late Baron Bassington.

"Not a lord!" screams the girl; "*not a lord!* THEN WHY SHOULD I WANT TO MARRY HIM?" But, as she says this thing, shamed and dazed, she sinks into her sister's arms, her bridal robes floating about and partly covering both.

And, looking on this beauty that should have been his this day, with all her wealth and all her charms, the man once called Lord Avonmere begins to laugh the laugh of despair, and cries : "Take her away! Take away the bride who loves me! THE TYPICAL BRIDE OF THE INTERNATIONAL WEDDING !" And jeers them with cynic laugh, then screams, "Take her away—her beauty makes me mad!" and flies at Tillie Follis as she lies before him, in all her loveliness of face and pose and figure, and would fondle her with manacled hands, and caress her with felon's kisses.

But the frontier Rach has him by the throat, and Garvey and the policeman are upon him.

And so they leave him to law and to justice.

And he sits with bowed head and rolling eyes—the same weird, blood-shot eyes as those of poor Tom Willoughby when he saw his loved wife and child delivered to the cruel death of Indian massacre.

CHAPTER XXV.

HAPPY COWBOY !

FROM this hideous interview they all would go away in a hurry ; but Mrs. Marvin, in her anxiety to escape from the stalwart Rach, has taken the Follis equipage and driven off with it, so the family are compelled to wait in Gussie's parlor for another carriage.

Here both Grousemoor and the lawyer assure Flossie

that the affidavit so deftly drawn by Arthur Willoughby together with the evidence at their hands, will give her both title and estates ; and they all go to congratulating Lady Avonmere.

But as the world gives her honor, the girl grows curiously humble. Her manner seems to say : " My battle with society is over ; I am on guard no more."

Most of her attention she gives to Matilde, as if by silent caresses to beg forgiveness for saving her from a villain ; though she finds time to even beam on Mr. Van Beekman as he lisps : " Awh—delighted to have restored you, Lady Avonmere. to identity and estates."

But when Abe and Rach talk about her going to England and living with dukes and potentates, she is in their arms, crying she is their daughter, and will do whatever they tell her, to show them how much she loves them.

But now Mr. Gussie's man comes in and announces that he has carriages at the door, and the party all go hurriedly down-stairs ; except Flossie, who lingers and says to her father : " Just one word to Mr. Everett before I leave."

" Oh, about that scoundrel in there ! " remarks Abe, pointing his thumb toward Avonmere's apartments : where Phil is now having a few parting words with Garvey ; for, fearing an appeal from Willoughby to the English consul that may delay matters, the frontier sheriff is preparing to start his prisoner for the West at once.

So coming out from this interview, Everett finds a young lady who says to him, " One moment ! " and waves him with a somewhat haughty gesture to Mr. Gussie's parlor, from which all the others have gone down to the street ; then whispers with trembling lips, anxious manner, and reproachful eyes, " Why do you, of all, to-day keep from me ? " next gives him a little piteous pout, and affecting lightness says : " You have not even congratulated me. Why, Mr. Van Beekman was kind enough to do that, and to insinuate that he was happy to have restored me my memory and my name."

" Did he dare claim that ? " says Phil, savagely, " that which has been *my* work, anxiety, heart, soul !—ever since I gazed in your eyes and knew you lived and had become a woman ? "

"And you were working to give me a name *before* that night?" mutters Flossie, disappointment on her face.

"What night?"

The—the night I told you when I had a name I'd answer—" stammers the girl. Then looking angry, she cries out: "Are all cowboys as stupid as you, Mr. Peter?" and is going away.

But the cowboy has caught her, not with his lariat, though just as strongly, and is whispering: "You have a name *now!* Is *this* your answer? You expected me to speak last night; that's why you were haughty. You darling—you——"

"Be careful!" cries his victim in blushing laugh. "Perhaps I'm a ward in chancery, besides a peeress of England."

"What do cowboys care for chancery or titles—cow-boys who love—" says Phil, who is handling the possible ward in chancery and certain peeress just as if she were a plain, ordinary, every-day betrothed kind of girl.

"I—I see they don't!" murmurs the young lady. Then she springs away with a startled cry, for Abe is gazing upon them astonished, and remarking: "Hello, Pete, what are you doing to my darter?"

"Kissing her," says Phil.

"Yes; isn't it wonderful, papa?" cries Flossie. "Phil, you remember what I said to you that awful day in Ari-zona—'Kiss me, dear Mr. Peter!'—I—I've loved you ever since then—since you saved my life."

"And now you're going to marry me?" answers Everett.

"Ask papa," says the young lady, with a demure courtesy, pointing to Mr. Follis.

After about two questions, Abe, putting Flossie's hand into Phil's, remarks: "Well, blow me if you ain't the darndest, luckiest cowboy I ever heerd on!"

"Yes, and the happiest," cries Phil.

Then there is a little more emotion, and Abe takes Florence down to the carriage, muttering: "No dukes or princes need apply; the Follis peeress is already staked out and located," and other allusions his wife thinks insane as they drive up the avenue.

As for Phil, getting to the Brevoort in a state of bliss.

glee, and rapture, he finds his sister waiting, anxious for his news.

"Success!" cries Miss Bessie; "I see it in your face. I'm going up this afternoon to ask Lady Avonmere to be one of my bridesmaids."

"Impossible!" says Phil, "she's in search of bridesmaids herself; besides I can't be Grousemoor's best man."

"No! What do you mean?"

"I mean," remarks Everett, pompously, "I'm going to get married on the same day, by the same minister, in the same church." Then he suddenly cries: "Bessie, you kiss me as if I were Grousemoor."

"Ah, speaking of me?" remarks that nobleman, who has come in with a serious face.

"Yes," cries his sweetheart, and tells him of the double wedding.

"Just the idea!" returns her *fiancé*. "Economical! and if that Atchison, Topeka and Santa Fé keeps going down——"

"Oh, don't mix up finance with love," cries Miss Bessie. "I'd marry you if you hadn't a cent for your fortune, or a title to your name.—Our marriages, Phil, are of flesh and blood and heart and soul, not of stocks and bonds and securities and titles. They are not what is now called INTERNATIONAL."

Some few evenings after this, Everett, coming from the presence of his betrothed, with whom he has been arranging a few hurried bridal details—for the wedding-bells are not far away now—is met in the hall by Mr. Follis.

"Hello, Pete!" he remarks, with a genial grin, "how do I look now?"

"About the same as usual."

"Well, I'm different. You are gazing at a man who's boss! When you laid out that so-called Lord Avonmere, you made me a happy potentate in my home. That Marvin widow skipped in a hurry—didn't dare face my Rach; but, bless you, a pappoose could down my wife now, she's so humble—so's Tillie. They've been holding out the olive-branch to me ever since they nearly broke my heart by deceiving me. But you can do me a favor."

"Anything in my power."

"Then ask Bob to stand up with you."

"Bob!" says Phil, in surprise. Then, in sudden understanding, he goes on : "Oh, Mr. Jackson, the superintendent of the Baby."

"Yes ; Bob's just arrived from Colorado," continues Abe. "He was fighting fire in the mine for weeks, and when he got that under he was snowed in for two weeks more and couldn't get anywhere. It makes a man powerful huffy and cranky to be snowed up, and since he's got here he seems all-fired put out and riled up about something. You know Tillie's to be Flossie's bridesmaid, and I thought if you asked Bob to stand up with you—it might kinder make things easier for my Tillie. Kinder—don't you see ?" Abe finishes up nervously with a wave of his hand.

"Yes, I see ; and I shall do as you ask with pleasure. Bob Jackson has Flossie's confidence and love and must be a noble fellow," returns Everett.

"Then I'll make you two acquainted," says Follis. And going into the dining-room, where they meet Bob Jackson, the young men soon get to be very good friends.

A few moments after, Abe leaves them together, and Phil making his request, is answered in the affirmative. But before they rise, Bob gives Everett some information that astonishes him. He says : "I know pretty well what has happened in this house in the last few months. That —that scoundrel, who nearly ruined both you and "—he checks himself suddenly and goes on—"that scoundrel will never trouble your sweetheart again ! "

"Arthur Willoughby ?" cries Phil.

"Is dead !" answers Jackson. "Killed trying to escape ! "

"Shot ? "

"No ; run over by a railroad train at a little station in Kansas. As he got nearer the West his fears increased, and he took a desperate chance to get away, and lost it. I haven't said anything to the family here about it. The newspapers will tell them to-morrow."

As Phil is going out from this interview, Miss Tillie meets him in the hall ; she is walking about with her father. "My poor crushed rose," murmurs Abe, patting her pretty cheek.

"Poor crushed rose !" laughs Matilde, whose vivacity seems to have come back to her about the time of Bob's arrival. "You should have seen the poor crushed rose to-day at Mrs. Rivington's. The poor crushed rose crushed her sister Lady Avonmere into New York society. She just walked all over them with Baroness Avonmere in the peerage of England. Yes, and you should have seen that Marvin woman fly from me. That old lady is just now the most unhappy marriage broker-ess in New York. She was going to get a commission for me from Avonmere—ten per cent. of my marriage settlement. She ran away from the house so fast she left the document behind her." With this she exhibits Willoughby's letter to the wondering eyes of her father and Everett.

As to Mrs. Marvin's misery Matilde is right ; the widow's punishment is almost greater than she can bear. She cannot kiss the beautiful Lady Avonmere, who has become the very sun of New York society, when she meets her at *fête* or revel.

Once, overcome by longing and desire, Aurora ap-proaches the peeress and diffidently opens her fat arms, and in one second supreme bliss will be hers ; when of a sudden so contemptuous a stare is launched upon her that she recoils from Flossie's haughty gaze, and creeps away, murmuring sadly : "Misunderstood ! Misunderstood ! "

But Lady Avonmere and her family soon leave New York for Boston. The bells of Trinity ring out their wedding chimes. And, gazing on the pretty ceremony through his eyeglass, Mr. Van Beekman, arrayed in pur-ple and fine linen, sighingly remarks : "Poor gals ! If they had waited ! They didn't know I'd beat old Van Twiler by about—five minutes ! "

This remark applies to his venerable cousin, who, in almost the act of changing his will, had suddenly ex-pired, and the unaltered document made during the brief period of Gussie's lordship had left to " his beloved cousin Augustus Van Beekman, commonly known as Lord Bassington," enough of this world's goods to permit him to be a club man forever.

A destiny he will probably fulfil, and become in time one of the venerables of the Stuyvesant. And some two or three decades from now, when our clubs have gone up beyond Central Park, or to the west side, or wherever else fashionable New York moves to, he will sit looking out at the maidens tripping the Boulevard as his predecessors do now at those on the avenue, and say, altered to the style of the coming epoch : " By Jove ! New York is not what it used to be in the days of dear old Fifth Avenue, when I downed that English adventurer— that Willoughby, who tried to foist himself on our set as a. lord ; when I made the beautiful Miss Nobody of Nowhere what she is.   I'm going to Lady Avonmere's ball to-night ; she's got a daughter now, don't yer know, dear boys."

And irreverent youth of the twentieth century will sneer in the slang of their day : " That old chump Van Beekman's got at his Miss Nobody of Nowhere story again."

FINIS.

The SPY COMPANY

A Tale of The Mexican War
By Archibald Clavering Gunter

"A stirring tale of love and fighting, quite in Mr. Gunter's old-time manner."—*New York American*, January 31, 1903.

"A worthy successor to 'Mr. Barnes of New York,' and 'Mr. Potter of Texas.'"—*The North American*, Phila., Pa., February 15, 1903.

"A tale of stirring incidents and ingenious plot . . . . . A novel in which there is not one dull moment."—*The Literary News*," New York, March, 1903.

" No chapter in the history of these United States is more picturesque and romantic than that which relates to the acquisition of Texas.   In the 'forties,' when Texas was in a transition state, held by Mexico, claiming to be an independent nation and drifting into the possession of the United States, all at the same time, the local situation was as complicated as the most imaginative novelist could desire, and this involved state of affairs was cleared up by the Mexican War, just in the right way to afford a strong climax.   Full advantage of these attractive elements has been taken by Archibald Clavering Gunter, author of 'Mr. Barnes of New York,' in his latest work, 'The Spy Company."
—*Evening Telegraph*, Philadelphia, January 31, 1903.

Very handsomely illustrated.   Frontispiece in colors
Cloth, $1.50   Paper, 50 Cents

At all booksellers or sent prepaid on receipt of price by

Hurst and Company,
PUBLISHERS,   NEW YORK.

A Lost American

AN EXCITING TALE OF CUBA

BY

ARCHIBALD CLAVERING GUNTER

AUTHOR OF

"Mr. Barnes of New York," "The King's Stock-
broker," etc., etc.

"The plot of Mr. Gunter's latest novel is laid in Cuba, during the ten years' war. The scenes and incidents of the story gives additional interest in view of the late conflict, and much capital is made out of our instinctive horror of Spanish methods of warfare. The hero of the story is an American, imprisoned without trial, in a Cuban dungeon and sentenced to be shot. . . . Once started we find no breathing space until Howard has happily married his lady love."—*The Amherst Literary Monthly.*

Cloth, $1.50   Paper, 50 Cents

For sale by all booksellers, or sent prepaid, on receipt of price, by

Hurst and Company,

PUBLISHERS,   **NEW YORK.**